ENDLESS BEAUTY

BOOK ONE

LISA HELEN GRAY

Copyright © Lisa Helen Gray
Copyrights reserved
Edited by Stephanie Farrant at Farrant Editing
Cover Design by Dark City Designs
No part of this publication may be reproduced or transmitted in any form or by any means, electronic or mechanical, including photocopy, recording, or any information storage and retrieval system without the prior written consent from the publisher, except in the instance of quotes for reviews. No part of this book may be scanned, uploaded, or distributed via the Internet without the publisher's permission and is a violation of the international copyright law, which subjects the violator to severe fines and imprisonment.

This book is licensed for your enjoyment. E-book copies may not be resold or given away to other people. If you would like to share with a friend, please buy an extra copy. Thank you for respecting the author's work.

This is a work of fiction. Names, characters, places and events are all products of the author's imagination. Any resemblance to actual persons, living or dead, businesses or establishments is purely coincidental.

PROLOGUE

HARRIETT

Thick fog billows from the DJ booth. It floods the ground and thins as it rises. Bodies, bumping and grinding around me, disappear into the smoke.

Beer and sweat mingle in the air, but it all falls away as I close my eyes and let the music flow through me.

Dancing is what I love.

And at one point in my life—before I lost my mother to cancer—it had been my dream. It was all I ever wanted to do.

Now, I get paid to dance.

Choreographed, timed and seductive, it takes a toll just like any recital or leading role would. It requires practice, time, and strength.

But this…

This is when I feel free. There are no expectations, no muscle memory to theorise, and no one to yell if I miss a step.

This is me dancing for me.

I glide my fingertips up the sides of my silk dress and into my hair, as my hips sway seductively, moving to the beat of the music.

It feels good to forget school, to forget work, and just be. If only for a night.

And with Gabby, one of my best friends, at my side, I'm having the time of my life.

But then, all spontaneous nights out are the best ones.

Gabby and I had been settled in for the night round mine, when I received a message from Woods. He's a doorman at Tease—the stripper club I work at—and was working security at the Fight for Charity event. Charlotte Carter was there too, surprisingly, and Woods was worried about her. She's one of the most kind and nurturing people I know, so I didn't think it was her scene.

It's a night where the rich—and sometimes the famous—come together in support of a 'charity organisation'. Mostly, it's a bunch of people who want to see men fight. I bet the fact it's for a good cause passes their notice.

Charlotte is our friend from the club. She started coming in every Friday to do research for a book she was writing, and her quirky, bubbly, blunt personality pulled everyone in. When she got up on stage to experience the life of a stripper for herself, and accidentally knocked out our boss, we became best friends.

When we learned she was here with her new guy, Drew, we came to support her—or at the very least, keep her safe. Woods scored us some tickets, and we didn't waste any time changing out of our PJ's.

The last guy she was with, hurt her, and although I like this new guy, I wanted to be here to protect her, just in case.

We needn't have worried. Everyone had already fallen in love with her by the time we arrived. If anything had kicked off, one of them would have stepped in and helped her if needed—that, I am confident about.

Charlotte left a while ago with her giant of a guy, but the after-party is still in full swing and most likely will be until the early hours of the morning.

Gabby, not only my best friend but another dancer from Tease, takes my hand, so I give her all my attention. Her lips move, but I don't hear what she's saying, so I lean into her.

"You need another drink?" I yell over the music.

"No," she replies, raising her filled glass. "I'm going to head back soon, but I thought you should know that hot, lethal and tattooed is staring right at you and has been for a while."

As soon as she warns me, the hairs on the back of my neck stand on end.

He's watching.

And like his gaze is a touch, I feel it all over.

Rampage.

That's his fighter's name. I'm not sure what his real name is, but with Rampage as his nickname, it doesn't matter. He's the event headliner, the person men and women came here to see tonight, and he's drop-dead fucking gorgeous. And not in a pretty way. He's a guy you drop your knickers for; a guy you'd let take you any way he wanted; a guy you want to taste, devour, and lick. He's the guy women would cheat on their husbands for.

He's *that* guy.

When I met the fighter earlier on in the night, my entire body coiled at the sight of him. There was something alluring about him, and I couldn't keep my gaze away.

As first impressions go, he definitely made a mark.

There was such a strong intensity between us that it knocked any coherent words out of my mouth. He watched me like he had never seen anyone like me before—which is stupid, thinking back on it. I'm not the only gorgeous girl here tonight. There are many. Albeit, not as cool as me, but still... Half of them did everything they could to get his attention, and I reckon with a crook of his finger, they'd have gone willingly.

But when he looked at me... I couldn't describe it. I still can't. But it felt good—so fucking good it knocked me off my axis. And anything that makes me feel good, I'm all for.

When a few girls went up to him, touching and flirting with him, I coiled up tight for another reason. I didn't like them touching him. I didn't like them flirting with him. And when Eloise—a stuck-up cow somehow connected to Drew—began to run her hands all over him, I wanted to claw the bitch.

I'm not used to having that kind of reaction to anyone, so I escaped him and his looming presence the first chance I got. I went to the bar and downed some shots. The desire left as quickly as the shots went down my throat. Yet as hard as I tried, it didn't stop me from thinking about him. As the hours passed, the more I began to believe the desire and need I saw in him were a figment of my imagination.

Slowly, I turn, and through the haze of the fog, I spot him standing at the edge of the dancefloor, his gaze solely on me. Desire rolls over me. He's just as hot as I remember, if not more.

His lips tug up a little at the corners like he's having inappropriate thoughts. I lift the glass Gabby hands me to my lips, whilst helplessly checking him out.

He's all man.

Everything about him screams man, and I can't believe a guy like him does anything by half.

With dark hair, dark eyes, and cheekbones that look as strong as his jaw, he's a man I *like* watching me.

He has a few bruises, but he doesn't look anywhere near as badly beaten as the other guys he went in the ring with. I'm pretty sure one left in an ambulance.

And a part of me wants to know if he fucks as well as he fights.

When his smirk turns into a full-fledged grin, like he can read my mind, his dimples pop out, and I get a mini orgasm right there in the middle of the dance floor.

"Yeah, you aren't going home alone tonight," Gabby teases as she leans in to take the drink from my hand.

Pulled back to the present, I turn to her and give her a pointed look. "We never leave anyone behind, remember? If you want to go, I'm going too."

Her gaze flicks over my shoulder, and her eyes widen in surprise. "If you don't want to stay and see if he's as good as the rumours say he is, tell me now and I'll *totally* get you out of here. But if you want to stay, Woods is flagging me down and I can catch a ride home with him."

A warm hand runs over my hip and over to my lower stomach with a surprisingly soft yet seductive touch, and my blood simmers.

"Text me when you are home," I warn her, and with a nod and a grin, she leaves.

I turn and stare at his white T-shirt clinging to his chest, before tilting my head up to his gorgeous face. "Can I help you?" I call out.

He leans down, and the move is smooth, classy even, as his hand goes around to the small of my back. He tugs me closer, his breath at my ear. "What's your name?"

I pull back a little and run the tip of my finger down his chest. "It's not my name you really want."

There's a glimmer of amusement in his gaze, but also something else. Something warm. Inviting. "And what is it you think I want?"

I stare at him, dead in the eye. "Me!" I'm not one to beat around the bush. If I want something, I go for it.

His hand clenches at the small of back, and I arch my eyebrow, daring him to argue. "Then you thought wrong," he rasps.

He leans down, his gaze never wandering as he stares right back at me. My heart beats wildly as his lips brush against mine.

I need more.

Just a taste. Just a glimpse of what it could be like between us. The spark is electric, and my stomach coils in preparation.

He bumps his nose with mine, and with the close proximity, I'm able to smell the mint on his breath.

I want him.

I want him so goddamn bad, and it's been a long time since I've had the desire to fuck someone. Relationships never work out for me. Once they find out I'm a stripper, they either end it or think they can fuck me any way they want, and I'll take it. I like it dirty, but I have my limits, just like anyone else. And I won't stand for anyone treating me like I'm less than.

My breath catches when he moves, and then his lips are at my ear. "I want to buy you a drink, dance with you, and yeah, I'm not gonna lie, I want to fuck you. I've imagined being inside you since I first laid eyes on you. I want to peel this dress and whatever you have on underneath off your body, and fuck you until you can't remember your own name. I want…"

I sway into him, entranced and horny as fuck, when suddenly, he pulls back. I immediately miss his touch and the promise of pleasure he offered. And as I stand there, wanting and needy, I begin to debate whether or not it's a good idea to pull him into the closest bathroom.

He's still close, close enough to tower over me, but not in an intimidating way where I naturally recoil. It's intimate, sexual, and I wish he didn't pull back. He's been in my thoughts, off and on, all night.

He lifts his hand to straighten the dress strap on my shoulder. When he hooks his finger under the thin strap of silk and gently runs it down to where it meets my dress, the back of his knuckle touches my flesh, almost burning. My nape tingles, causing the tension in my shoulders to relax.

"I have to go," he tells me regretfully.

He suddenly drops his hand to his side. I tilt my head to meet his gaze once more, finally pulling myself out of the lust-filled haze he's cast me in. He's no longer watching me. He's staring at something behind me.

I glance over my shoulder, seeing a man in a suit watching him. It's a guy I recognise from the team that surrounded his corner in the fight tonight. The same guy I accidently spilt a drink on in an attempt to get a closer seat to the fight. I had been trying to find a table, when I heard Charlotte screaming from above. I lost track of where I was going and bumped into the guy now glowering at us. My drink went all down his white, crisp shirt, and as I stare at the orange stain, I feel no remorse for it. I might have if he had been politer about the whole thing, but he was a dick.

A little embarrassed by the subtle let down, I try to shrug it off. "Shame. Things were just getting good."

"Yeah," he murmurs, and his jaw clenches at the man behind me.

I lean up on the tips of my toes and kiss the corner of his mouth, hoping to ease his annoyance. "Bye, handsome."

"Wait, what's your name?" he calls, and a few people stop to watch us.

I wink in his direction as the corners of my lips stretch into a smirk. "Wouldn't you like to know."

With that, I turn and sashay my way off the dancefloor, making a beeline for the exit. I don't need to stick around any longer. The guy who pulled Rampage's attention away and dampened his mood, happens to be in my path, and his glower follows me the entire way.

I can feel Rampage's gaze on me too, but I don't turn back, content in the fact it will be another night using my favourite dildo to get off. Which is a shame, because it's been a long time since I had a bed partner. But at least I'll have a new fantasy to play out in my mind while I bring myself to orgasm.

As I move past the suit, a hand grips my wrist to the point of pain. If I wasn't used to wearing high heels, then the tug he then gives me would make me lose my footing.

"Get the fuck off me," I growl, and try to shrug his hand off. He tightens his grip and leans in.

The coldness seeping from him doesn't even give me pause. I've dealt with worse men than him.

"Go home and stay away from Rampage! I know exactly who the fuck you are, you little slut, and you won't be getting a penny from him."

He lets me go as quickly as he grabbed me, but not one to take shit, I thrust the palm of my hand up and strike his nose. He cries out and falls to the floor as blood spurts from his nostrils. Satisfied he's got what he deserves, I spin on my heel and leave, ignoring those watching with their cameras out. I don't bother to give him a response. It would mean caring about what he thinks, and I just don't. I don't know him. This man is nothing to me. And although I'm shocked by his abruptness, his issues are his own. Not mine.

I carry on like he didn't accost me and I didn't break his nose, and walk out with my head held high. It's not the first time someone has figured out who I am, but it is the first time someone has ever gotten physical with me.

I wave to the last of security remaining, familiar with them since this isn't the first time Woods scored us tickets to an event such as this.

Rain begins to fall as I step outside, and like luck is on my side, a few taxis are parked just out front. I head to the closest one and pull open the door. As I put one leg inside, a hand comes out of nowhere, jolting the door.

I glance up, surprised to find Rampage and not the dickhead I just hit.

"Are you okay?" he asks, almost in a panic. "What did he do?"

"Something he won't do again," I reply, and go to get in the taxi.

He places his warm hand over mind, stopping me. "Let me have your number."

My smile slowly creeps up. "And why would I do that, handsome?"

He leans in to tuck a strand of hair behind my ear, then places his hand on my jaw. "Why wouldn't you?"

"You tell me. Your friend didn't seem to like that we were talking."

"Forget him. He'll be nursing that broken nose and black eye for a while," he tells me, his voice rough. "I want to take you out, at the very least to apologise for Colin's behaviour. I've not been able to keep my eyes off you all night. I want to get to know you, and I think you want to get to know me."

The mood is gone, thanks to his friend, but it doesn't mean I can't give him a chance.

I gently remove his hand from my jaw. "I tell you what, handsome, if we bump into each other again, I'll take you up on that offer."

I slide into the car, and as I go to shut the door, he holds it open and leans in. "At least tell me your name."

I reach over, running my hand over his strong neck, and rise off the seat until my mouth reaches his.

The second I get a taste, I know I'm going to regret not taking him home. Warmth blossoms in my chest, and sparks ignite between us.

He deepens the kiss, and our tongues clash together in a frenzy. My fingers grip his T-shirt, and I almost pull him into the taxi with me. There's a bite of liquor on his tongue, and it heightens the desire building inside of me, making it hard for me to keep my thoughts together.

By the time he pulls back, I'm breathless and out of sorts.

I press the tips of my fingers to my lips, aware of him watching me. I've never been kissed like that. The spark, the need, it had already been there, but when he kissed me, it's like the world fell around us. It was just us. The kiss is only the beginning, a taste of what it will be like between us.

And yet, all good things must come to an end, and the night is truly over.

For me anyway.

"Goodbye, Rampage," I call out, and as I reach for the door, he steps back, as stunned as I am.

That kiss was something.

My lips buzz as I close the door, leaving him standing on the kerb. I rattle off my address to the taxi driver before sagging back against the seat.

I should have pulled him into the taxi.

1

HARRIETT

The aroma of coffee beans hits me the second I walk through the door of my favourite café. I'm here regularly since it's not far from the university or my home and the owners are my kind of people.

The coffee calls to me like a siren, and just like anyone in a trance, I don't notice anything around me—no one but Neil, the coffee god who has been serving me since I first started this university five years ago.

It isn't like I'm an addict. I don't have a problem with caffeine.

I only have a problem without it.

And with no free time to spare after working until six this morning, then sleeping in and rushing to get to class, I never got a chance to stop and get my morning fix.

With a dramatic sigh, I slap my hands down on the counter. "Please, for the safety of everyone around me, bring me coffee. And make it strong."

He grimaces, used to my theatrics. "I did start to wonder how long it would be before you came in here when you didn't show this morning."

"I won!" Milly calls out, and the million bangles around her wrist jangle when she gives a victory fist pump. "I told him you'd be able to last until classes were over."

"And you?" I ask Neil, who ducks his head to hide his smirk.

"Lunchtime. And when you didn't show—"

"He got scared and started clearing tables to the side so you wouldn't trip over any like last time," Milly teases, dropping a large, disposable cup in front of me.

I take my first sip, and it is pure heaven. "I would give my pink-glittered, purple dildo away if it meant getting this every day."

"TMI," Neil remarks on a chuckle, and moves on to serve the next customer. I remain at the counter, which is also a norm for me.

"You look tired," Milly comments, brushing her frazzled curls behind her ears.

"I feel it. And not just because I need sleep. I'm tired to the bone. They didn't lie when they said the last year was going to be the hardest and most gruelling."

"You are still at the hospital, right?"

"I am. I'll be getting my Masters once I'm done with this term—which is only a few weeks away—and then fingers crossed, I survive the next five years doing the specialist training programme."

"Just think of it like this, once you're done, you're done. You've worked hard to get here. And after, you'll have a high-paying job and will be able to put all of this behind you," she praises. "Just don't forget to keep coming here for your coffee."

"I won't. I'd hate to go to prison before I have a chance to use my degree."

"I still think it's weird you want to work with dead bodies," she comments on a shiver. "And that's coming from me, who *is* weird."

"I don't just work with dead bodies," I fire back, but get distracted by the news headline running across the bottom of the television. "Another body has been found."

Milly glances up at the television as the screen changes to a news anchor standing outside a crime scene. Milly drops the towel on the counter, pulling my attention away from the screen.

She shudders. "We've been following the story. The first couple who were murdered lived near Neil's old childhood home. I can't believe he or she has managed to kill four people now and not get caught."

"There's no pattern other than the fact they were all tortured the same way. None that I've read about anyway. So, unless there is forensic evidence, a witness, or a pattern, they have nothing to go on. The first two victims were a retired couple; used to be foster parents. They had been dead two days when they were found. The second was a recently retired police officer, and there's nothing to connect him to the couple. He was due back from his fishing trip nearly a week before he was found. When he didn't return, his daughter went looking. She found him dead in his fishing cabin. The reports said he was dead three days. And from the looks of it, this woman was last seen two days ago, but unlike the others, her body was found in the Bountford Nature reserve, which isn't far from here."

"Your attention to detail scares me."

"I can't help it. When they mapped the murders, I noticed they were getting close to here."

Neil taps his knuckles on the counter. "Isn't Blue Lagoon a stripper's club?"

I glance back at the screen, and sure enough, the young woman works at Blue Lagoon, a stripper's club that used to be Tease before our boss found a more suitable area.

"The place is a shit hole. Anyone could have done her in," a young lad replies after grabbing his fruity drink.

I arch an eyebrow at the comment. "Why would it have been anyone?"

"We went there for my brother's stag party a few weeks back, and the girls were skanks. I'm not surprised one of them got killed."

I stand a little straighter and turn until I'm fully facing him. "Because she's a stripper?"

He laughs, thinking I agree with him. "Yeah. I mean, they've all got daddy issues. They probably didn't get enough money and robbed the wrong person. She's a stripper, for God's sake."

Neil clucks his tongue. "It's not a dirty word," he mutters.

I point a finger in the lad's direction. "So, let me get this straight.

You went to a stripper's club, paid to get in, but it's the stripper who's problematic? She's doing her job. You're the one who is paying for the service so you can *feel manly* for at least a night. These women are confident in their own skin; they wouldn't be stripping if they weren't. And each night men openly ogle them, and maybe shell out for a lap dance or two, but it's the woman with the daddy issues," I fire back, remaining calm.

His gaze warily goes to those who have stopped to watch our conversation, before turning back. He runs the palm of his hand down his crumpled T-shirt as he clears his throat. "You don't know what the fuck you're talking about."

"Oh, but I do. You're sour, which can only mean one thing. An erotic dancer's job is to flirt with you. It's to make you feel good about yourself, which is why men go there. Not all, I'll admit. But you thought you would get something for free, so I'm guessing she moved on to someone who would make taking her clothes off for strange men worthwhile, and you didn't like it. But even if that's not the case, being a stripper doesn't warrant your comment. She's making a living. It doesn't make it okay for someone to kill her."

His face reddens as he jabs his pointy finger at me. "Fuck you! That isn't what happened at all. I don't need to go to a strip club to get a chick. I can get them whenever I want."

I arch an eyebrow. "It was your brother's stag-do, right? Which means you're probably the best man, or at the very least, involved in the planning of this stag-do. *You* chose to go there. If the women are skanks, as you called them, then why would you celebrate *the last night of freedom* there? Have a word with yourself, little man. And the next time you go to insult an innocent woman, take a look in the mirror, because we all have flaws. Yours are just disgusting," I spit out. "And word of advice: boys who loudly proclaim they can get any chick they want are the boys who can't admit they don't. And I don't blame women for keeping clear."

"Stupid bitch," he hisses.

I see his hand jerk and his arm cock-back. He raises his fruity drink that's topped with cream, and I move, smacking the bottom of the cup. The red liquid flies out of the cup, and the cream splatters all over his face. The drink soaks into his T-shirt. He jerks back with a hiss.

I point in his face when he straightens and glowers at me. "Make one more move towards me and you won't like what I'll do. I've not finished my coffee, so I won't be able to control my actions," I warn, my tone dropping. "Once I'm finished, you'll be trending on TikTok, and the world will see your downfall. There's no coming back from that, so I suggest you leave whilst you can." He flinches at the crack of my knuckles. "Leave!"

He blows out an angry breath, his gaze following the crowd, who have their phones held up, most likely recording. Neil has his phone out too, a big grin on his face. "Keep going. I need the followers; I only have twenty-six right now."

The guy storms out, and the crowd begins to clap, laughing and hollering. By the time he gets to the door, he's running.

I keep my eyes on him through the glass door whilst downing the rest of my coffee. Once it's empty, I turn to the applauding crowd and take a bow. "I take tips in the form of coffee." I spin around and drop the cup down on the counter. "One more please."

Milly grins and hands her husband the cup without glancing in his direction. "Girl, this one is on the house. That was awesome."

I shrug. "He had it coming."

"I'll buy the next one," a young girl with bright red hair announces. "My sister worked at a strip club for a little while. I know you weren't standing up for her personally, but it meant a lot to hear it."

"You're welcome, babe," I tell her, as a guy in his late forties hands a fiver over to Milly.

"That's for her next one."

Milly laughs when Neil hands her a mug. On the front, he's written 'Girl boss'. My phone begins to ring, and after excusing myself, I answer the call.

"Dave, you know I only work weekends," I answer before he can say hello.

"I'm calling a staff meeting. Can you get here in the next thirty minutes?"

My brows pinch together. "Sure, but can I ask why? Because if it's about the black eye Trixie has, it wasn't my fault. I swear. Charlotte came to rehearsals, and we've been teaching her some moves. Trixie barged in as she was doing the leg out—"

"I don't want to know. That girl should come with a warning."

"I thought you liked Trixie?"

"I'm talking about Charlotte," he retorts. "So, are you coming in? I don't have all day."

"Sure. I'll be there soon."

"And make sure you've had fucking coffee 'cause I can't be dealing with your shit. Not today."

I snigger when the line goes dead. Before I can place it back in my bag, a new message pops up from a group chat I have with my friends.

> Gabby: Did someone tell Dave about Charlotte? He's called a meeting.
>
> Emily: I didn't. It might have something to do with the breast fillet incident.
>
> Gabby: Shit, I forgot about that one.
>
> Olivia: I reckon he's mad about the dildo thing. In my defence, I didn't mean to let go and I didn't know he was behind me.
>
> Harriet: He knows about Charlotte. Or some of it.
>
> Harriet: Em, he doesn't even know. I got it off the chair before he came in, but you really need to stop gluing them to your outfits.
>
> Harriet: And Liv, he'll get over it. I'm sure.
>
> Harriet: I'm on way now. Meet you all there. Xoxo

I pocket the phone and head back to the counter. "Thank you," I tell them as Neil hands me another drink.

"You have enough tips here to buy you drinks for at least a week."

My eyes widen at the announcement. "No way."

He shakes the money pot, and my eyes bug out. It was only a plastic cup before. "Believe it."

"That is so awesome," I reply. "I really need to head out, but I'll back in the morning."

He winks, tucking the cup under the counter. "See you tomorrow."

"Thanks for the tips, everyone," I call out.

"Bye," they call back, like we are old friends.

I leave the café with a wide smile on my face. Once I'm outside, I put in my headphones and begin to make my way to work.

STEPPING into Tease when it's closed is always eerie. There's no life or music and the normal lighting is switched off. In its place, dim, warm light fills the space.

As I walk past what we call the red section, I begin to hear voices. The red section is one of my favourite stages to be on. It's more seductive, and on that stage, taking your clothes off isn't required. It's where Dave, our boss, puts the most confident of girls because they don't need to use bare flesh to seduce the punters. We have to allure them with sex appeal, and on that stage, under the red light, you do.

My other favourite stage is the dance room. It's the main part of Tease and where most women and men sit to have fun. There're stages in the centre and to the side, but working in here feels more like a night out. You get the most interaction in here. The VIP area is where we get the most tips. For some reason, Dave doesn't like me and my girls up there. Apparently, we can be too gobby, but whatever. Most of the men who go up there are arseholes anyway.

There are other rooms, more private behind closed curtains. I've only ever worked a few times in those since being here.

I spot two of my friends sitting in our booth. It's where we sit to chat before the doors open, and wind down after a shift. And like today, where we sit during a staff meeting.

I slide in next to Emily. "What's going on then?"

"No idea," she whispers. "I had to leave Poppy with my neighbour."

Poppy is her daughter; a beautiful little girl who loves *Trolls* and *My Little Pony*.

Gabby slides in next to Olivia and drops her bag on the table. It lands with a thud. "You are never going to guess what I just got told."

"That you should be sectioned?" Olivia retorts.

Gabby rolls her eyes. "Yes, they promised me the room next to yours. Isn't that great?"

I slap my hand on the table, getting her attention. When those two argue, it never ends. "What did you get told?"

She makes sure none of the other dancers are listening in. "The boss, *boss* is coming," she whispers loudly.

"No fucking way," I reply, and bounce in my seat.

The last time he was here, I was off sick and never got a chance to meet him. That was two years ago. Gabby started not long after his visit.

At that time, Emily had only been with us a few months and was still in training. After his visit, she got put behind the main and VIP bar, which was lucky since she found out she was pregnant three months later. Olivia and I have been here the longest. Three and a half years.

But our bond feels like a lifetime.

I can't picture my life before them, and I don't want to imagine it without them. We've gotten each other through every high and low.

"I don't think I've ever met him," Gabby replies.

Olivia leans in, squinting at Emily. "Em, you okay? You look a little pale."

She does look pale, and her hands are trembling in her lap under the table, where only I can see. "You okay?"

She shakes herself out of it before lifting her head. "Do you think we are getting shut down? Do you think they're firing people?"

Gabby shrugs. "The club is the best in the country. They'd be stupid to shut us down."

"What's really going on?" I ask, since I don't believe that's what has got her unsettled.

She drops her hands on the table, and everyone notices the subtle shake to them. "There's something I need to tell you. I was scared before and didn't want to admit it, but—"

Dave shoves through the door leading to the office and claps his hands twice to get our attention. "Look alive. The manager is making changes involving your safety here at the club."

"What?" I murmur, sitting up straighter.

Trixie, our nemesis, steps closer to our booth with another dancer, Leonie. "I hope he's staying this time. We had great chemistry the last time he was here, and I swear, if we weren't interrupted, we definitely would have fucked."

"Really?" Leonie replies. "Is he as good looking as the others say he is?"

"Drop dead gorgeous. Hopefully, with this visit, he'll promote me. Dave is being unfair. I've been here the longest and deserve a better position."

"You mean other than on your back," Olivia fires back.

Trixie's lips twist into a snarl. "Listen, you little—"

"Trixie, pay attention," Dave barks, but my focus is pulled to the office door.

Stepping out is a man I've never seen before. He's tall, built, and my god, he oozes sex. He has on black slacks, shoes that look like they have just been polished, and a white, crisp shirt rolled up at the sleeves.

He is sex on legs, and from the bulge in his trousers, he clearly has something to back up all that sex appeal.

"Oh my god, that's him," Trixie whispers. She's as enthralled as the rest of us. When she lowers her tank top to show the lace of the red bra she's wearing, I almost roll my eyes.

"Oh fuck!" Emily whispers, and I'm shocked when she takes my hand.

"What?" I whisper. "What's wrong? Do you know him?"

The others shuffle closer and lean in, but she doesn't reply, too busy watching the new arrival.

I watch as he scans the room, his gaze briefly pausing on Emily. There's something in his expression, something I can't put my finger on, before he masks it.

"For those who don't know me, I'm Cole Conner, the owner of Tease," he greets. "I won't take up too much of your time."

"He can take up all my time," Trixie purrs under her breath.

"As I'm sure you are all aware by now, there have been murders that are—for my liking—too close to home. The police are warning people to be vigilant, and with the new victim being an exotic dancer, I'd be stupid to ignore them," Cole reveals, shocking everyone but Dave. This is the last thing I expected to be brought up. "I'm going to use this time to improve on the safety in and out of the club. From now on, no one will leave work from the front of the building. If you can, drive in pairs or carpool. You'll be escorted to your vehicles by security. If you don't have a ride home, we'll arrange something for you. I know this is difficult for some of you as you have to get back home before the club closes, but for those who leave at five-six, we will work with you and come to an arrangement. If anyone has any questions, now is the time to ask."

I'm not the only one to put my hand up. "Why are you worried about the murders? It was only released today that the new victim is a stripper. Do you know something we don't?" I ask.

Dave shakes his head at me. "Does there have to be a reason?"

"Well, no, but I've been asking for changes for years."

"Men don't come here to watch you dance on a bar," Dave points out, and that harassed look is back.

Olivia pipes in. "But it would be so cool. You'd bring in more people with a bar like that."

"And I'd get to live out my *Coyote Ugly* fantasy," Gabby announces.

"I know, right," I agree, having loved that film as a teen.

"We could totally pull it off. Emily can sing, since she's the only one of us who can hold a note," Olivia adds.

"I could—"

"Enough," Dave interrupts.

Cole shoves his hands into his pockets. "We'll be in the office if anyone has any questions or concerns," he explains.

"Emily, I know you've got to get back to your daughter, but if you could spare another five minutes, I'd really appreciate your opinion on the menu for the cocktail bar."

Emily pales, and her gaze goes from Dave to Cole. There's a slight shake to her hands as she crosses them over her chest. She nods in reply, but soon enough, ducks her head.

My gaze sweeps over Cole, wondering why his presence is affecting her so much. They've never met, and although he's extremely hot, Emily has never been one to shy away.

He cocks his head to the side, his eyes boring into Emily. His brows knit together, and when she doesn't pay him attention, his lips thin.

Luckily, Dave diverts his attention and the two leave for the office. As soon as they're gone, we shuffle out of the booth. The three of us turn to her and cross our arms over our chest.

"What's going on? Do you know him?" I ask.

"He couldn't keep his eyes off you," Olivia agrees.

She slowly lifts her head, and although her eyes are watery, there's something else. Guilt. "H-he's…"

I run a comforting hand down her arm. "It's okay. You can tell us anything."

"Alibis for life," Olivia agrees.

"I didn't know he was the owner at first. I was new and I thought he was friends with Dave. He got a handsy customer off me my first week on the main floor and took me out back."

"I remember, you got hurt," Gabby adds.

"Dave knew him, so I thought he was an okay guy, not some sleaze. I swear, I'm not a slag. I'm not like Trixie, who sleeps with punters. But he was different. It felt different. I've never done anything like that before or since."

"Slow down and tell us what's going on," Gabby demands softly.

She assesses the room to make sure no one can overhear. "He's Poppy's dad. He's the guy I slept with. I swear, it wasn't until the day after when Dave told me, that I knew. And I didn't think I'd see him again. Dave said he mostly runs the London club. And then when I found out I was pregnant, I feared what he would do. I didn't want an abortion, and I grew scared that he'd take her from me because I work here."

"He fucking won't take her anywhere," I bite out.

"I was going to tell him, but he never came back. And I felt uncomfortable asking Dave. But she'll be two in a few months and—"

"Emily, hurry up. I don't have all day," Dave yells.

She grimaces and wipes under her eyes. "I have to go."

"It's fine. We'll message you and arrange a time to talk."

She nods as she takes a deep breath. "I'm sorry."

She races off to the office, and I turn to the girls, still a little stumped. "We can't corner her about it here, so before work on Friday, come to mine. We'll order in and have a few drinks to get her talking."

"You are on," Gabby agrees.

"Fuck!" Olivia hisses, staring down at her phone. "It's my brother, Lee. He's got into another fight at school. I've got to go."

"I'll come with you," Gabby offers, before turning to me. "We'll see you Friday."

I leave after them, my mind still on Emily. She's been through a lot over the years. Her grandma isn't getting better, and on top of that, she's been raising a daughter alone.

I don't know where her head is at right now, but she has us, and we'll stand beside her though everything she goes through.

2

RIVER

Annoyance flares inside of me as I pull up outside Harvey's gym. Colin, one of my first serious sponsors before he took me under his wing and became my manager, is calling for the millionth time today.

I owe everything to the man. He helped me get to where I am today. However, the past year has been draining. Not only with the training, but with the extra tournaments and endorsement commitments. I need a break after the tournaments this year are done. I want to start enjoying life instead of being stuck travelling. I've been to America, Australia, and other beautiful places yet never had the chance to stop and enjoy them. I'm forever moving from one place to the next. The UK is my home though. It might be a shithole most of the time, but it's home. I love it here. Colin, however, has other plans and is doing everything in his power to try and get me to change my mind. And maybe at the beginning, I might have. I was on the fence for a while, but once I ran the idea across him, he pushed me to finally make a firm decision.

With all the conferences, red carpets, meetings, training, and then the endorsement commitments, I've not had a chance to really enjoy anything. And when I get close, he steps in and puts a stop to it.

And then this morning, he decided to punish me and tell me I can't train with Drew Harvey anymore.

Drew Harvey is the reason I started this career in the first place. He's the only person who saw where my life was heading and made me change it. Training with him is gruelling, but it doesn't feel like a chore, unlike with Cian, my corner man and day-to-day trainer.

Colin can keep pushing and pushing me, but there's only so much I'll take before I finally tell him I'm done. The only reason I haven't done it already is because of a sense of obligation. I'm grateful for all he's done, but the past year, he's turned into someone I don't like.

I ignore his call. I don't want to deal with him until I've at least gotten some of this frustration out. When I slide out of my car, I'm surprised to see groups of women and men leaving the gym.

Drew has always done well, but in the seven years I've been coming here, I have never seen this many people.

On my way to the entrance, a guy runs into me, knocking my keys and duffle bag to the floor. As I kneel to snatch my keys up, the scent of vanilla and sweet perfume rolls over me. It's a perfume I've smelled once before, and the woman wearing it left quite an impression.

It's not the first time the mysterious woman I met at a charity event I headlined for last year has been on my mind.

It began the same as any event. The atmosphere was charged, my blood pumping. I won every fight that night. It was during the last fight that I saw her. She captured my attention from the corner of my eye. She had just spilled a drink over Colin, and instead of doing what all the other women do—cower and apologise—she told him to fuck off before leaving. Seeing Colin's expression red with embarrassment and shock had been amusing, to say the least. I fought harder than ever after that.

After the fight, I went up to meet a nutty chick who had been cheering me on the entire fight. Or rather, that's the reason I used to go up instead of going out back and leaving. The promise of seeing her again hung in the air. I was shocked when I found her with the very group I went to see.

It wasn't her beauty that enraptured me, although that—and her foul mouth— is what drew me to her at first. Then I finally met her, and up close she was even more beautiful. She looked at me, sultry and seductive, and my dick hardened.

The night went on, and like a creeper, my eyes stalked her the entire night. It's then I knew I couldn't leave until I got her number. I've never seen anyone dance like her. She didn't do it to give a show. She didn't do it for attention. She was dancing in a room filled with people, but the moves were all for her. She carried herself with grace and elegance, but when she danced, it was seductive and sexy.

Her confidence and wit made me want more.

A smile tugs at my lips at the reminder of how she left me. Without a name or a number, she told me she'd only go on a date if we ever met again. And until now, I've had no luck.

As I stand, I scan the area, but I don't see her in the groups of people leaving. Accepting she isn't here, I carry on inside, moving through the reception area to the main room.

Drew is holding the door open, his head bent as he kisses a redhead. It's the same redhead who cheered me on during the charity event.

"Hey, man," I greet.

He pulls away from his girl, and his lips tug into a grin. "You back to training?"

"Yeah, it was meant to be next week, but Colin started me back up two weeks ago," I reply, before turning to the redhead who's admiring my arms. "Hello again."

"Hi," she breathes.

"You look tired," Drew comments on a grin, tucking his girl into his side.

I run a hand over my face. "I feel it, but with the biggest tournament coming up, I can't exactly afford to drop the ball."

"Is it true there's a five-hundred thousand pound, bonus?"

"Yeah, then just over a hundred thousand for each fight we win."

"How are you handling it with Fracture?"

Fracture is Dean Mole's fighter's name. He got it after fracturing his opponents' bones during three of his fights. He's ruthless, cunning, and the biggest prick I've ever met.

We all start this gig as naïve young men looking to make a name for ourselves. I fucked a lot of chicks back when I first started and kept at it until I hit the big fights.

At my first live televised fight, I met Marlene, a ring girl who I immediately went for. We hit it off, and she came to every one of my fights. It was good, until it wasn't. The stress the endorsements and fame brought, got to me. I was exhausted, frustrated, and a little overwhelmed. And more times than not, we got into arguments because of it. By this point, Dean was making his way up. Managers and trainers were talking about him. He had a few people who wanted to take him on as a client.

We were due to fight for a massive charity event, and leading up to that night, we had interviews, meet and greets, and other meetings.

We nearly got into it during one of the meet and greets, which is strictly forbidden in the industry. I let him get under my skin after he made some disparaging comment about Marlene. I knew he was doing it to get a rise out of me, and I let him.

The night before the fight, Marlene found out she was pregnant. We got engaged the same night, and by morning, it was all over the papers.

That's when the bad blood started between Dean and me.

During the fight, he revealed he fucked her. He taunted me with the knowledge he knew she had a tattoo under her bikini line. No one, other than someone who has seen her without her knickers on, could have known that.

I lost the fight that night, and the next time I was up against him, we got into an altercation. The board were left with no choice but to disqualify us for the entire year. He cost me thousands, and now, after another three years, we're at war again.

I shrug. "I'm level-headed now. He can't get to me anymore, but it will be fun to watch him try," I admit. "I'm hoping Karma will be on my side and he'll hit me and get disqualified from the entire tour."

Drew frowns. "You can't let him get to you this time. This will be the biggest fight of your career."

"I won't. I've been working with a martial arts teacher for three years. He's been helping me focus, and I've not lost it like that, since. I've had other fighters try to taunt me with the same shit as Dean, and it hasn't gotten to me."

"All right. I've got some tips that will be sure to help too."

"I bet," I reply, then look around. "I see business is booming. I saw the crowd leaving."

He rubs the back of his neck. "We've got some women in to run a pole fitness class. Since word got out, we've been rammed with clients. I've had to hire more staff, and I've got work going on upstairs to expand."

I chuckle at his expression. "So, things are going good. Happy for you, mate."

"It is. And thanks to Landon, I don't have to deal with everything on my own."

"I owe him a sparring match. I've been trying to learn his foot technique, but I'm not as good as him. I'm hoping he'll teach me."

"Landon is awesome," Charlotte agrees. "And I'm sure if I ask him, he'll be happy to show you."

Drew chuckles and leans down to press a kiss to the top of her head. "I'm not sure if you missed it, babe, but Landon doesn't like teaching. He doesn't have the patience for it."

"He will," she stubbornly replies. "He's always helping people."

I never had someone like Charlotte in my life growing up. I never had someone who cheered for me, or supported me. And even now, with Colin, my trainer, and all those in between, I still don't have that kind of person. It's kind of sad when you really think about it. I have friends all over the world but they're mostly acquaintances.

Which reminds me. "Hey, have you heard of a place called Tease? A bunch of guys from the office are going to celebrate and I have to tag along. We've gone into business with the owner."

Drew grimaces. "Maybe go somewhere else."

"You are going to love Tease," Charlotte beams. "Just don't go on the pole unless you are trained. I'm learning and—"

"Babe," Drew calls in amusement, his shoulders shaking. "You took her eye out."

"I didn't know she was here. She wasn't invited, and if she was, she would have known to stay out of the circle."

"So, it's not a shithole? I can't afford bad press this close to the fights," I admit, hating that I sound like a snob.

"I have to go," Charlotte groans, pocketing her phone. "You'll love Tease. I have friends who work there, and I promise, they give the best lap dances; although, Gabby only gave me one to cheer me up. She doesn't normally do them."

My lips twitch in amusement. "I'll keep that in mind."

I step away to give them privacy as they say their goodbyes, but I'm unable to stop watching. Drew is one lucky fuck.

I'm happy for him. He's a big guy, and his appearance is intimidating to some people, but not Charlotte. She sees the real him and loves him for it. I know it's bothered him in the past that people have crossed the road to avoid him. He grew up with a mum who faulted him for every choice he made. I've only met her once, but five minutes in her presence and I had to bail. She didn't hold back. She let it be known that she thought I was a criminal and that she didn't like her son hanging out with me.

It didn't matter that I've earned more than she's worth. Even as rich as she is, I doubt she's ever worked for it.

Drew ties his hair up as he begins to make his way over. When he reaches me, I ask, "What do you have against Tease? I saw your expression."

"Nothing. Charlotte's right. Tease is a good club," he comments, before lowering his voice. "Don't share this with anyone, but some of the girls from the club come in and teach pole fitness. We let them rehearse here in return, and I've promised I'll keep their anonymity. Since you'll be here a lot, I don't want you to run into them and accidently call them out."

"If I do, I'll keep quiet. I know what it's like to want to keep something private, remember."

And he does. He's the reason I'm not behind bars.

"Is this to celebrate the launch of the new whiskey brand?"

I nod. "Yeah. I didn't think we'd get where we are, but the team

I've hired know what they are doing. I have to hand it to Kim; she gets things done."

My phone blasts once more, and without looking, I reject the call and switch it off.

"Everything okay?"

"Colin," I tell him, and I don't need to say more. Drew hates the guy and has warned me from the beginning to drop him as a manager.

He jerks his chin in acknowledgement. "Go change and I'll get the space ready."

I leave, going to do just that. I'll be training for nearly two hours with him, and then two with Landon. If anyone can help me get this frustration out before I kill Colin, it's them.

SWEAT COVERS my entire body as I sit down on the bench. Drew didn't take it easy, and then when Landon joined, it got more gruelling.

I grab my phone and sigh at the list of missed calls and messages that appear when I switch it on.

He rings again. If I don't answer now, he'll start searching for me, and seeing him in person will only make it worse.

"Colin," I greet.

"Where are you? I've been calling you all day."

"I've been training with Drew—"

"I told you I didn't want you training with him anymore. He's not in the same league as the team I've hired."

"No, he's better. I didn't get this far on my own, Colin. He's the one who taught me. I'm not going to tell you again, he's staying."

"You are making a mistake."

"No, a mistake would be getting a new trainer right before a big tournament. Drop it, Colin."

"We need to go over your schedule. Are you going to be home tonight?"

"Can we do it tomorrow. I'm wiped. I want to hit the sauna for a bit then get some sleep."

"No, we have a function Friday night with the UFT. The press is going to be covering the event and you'll get a chance to promote the new sports line as well as the upcoming fights."

I pinch the bridge of my nose. "I have other commitments Friday. It's on the calendar, Colin, and I told you on Monday *and* Tuesday."

"It can be cancelled. It's not important. This is. You have no idea what these men can do for you. You need to start talking to them. They need to see you are serious."

"It is important. It's my business, one that is running successfully," I bite out. "And before you go on, you're wasting your breath. I'm not cancelling something I'm committed to. I don't need to be at the UFT function. It's just a bunch of people wanting to show off their wealth."

"Need I remind you they are who pay the bonuses to the winner," he snaps.

"I know, but the point is moot. I don't have to be there, and you should know by now that I don't kiss arse. I don't suck up to people. If you want to go, go, but I'm not, and I really do have to go. I'll speak to you tomorrow," I tell him, and before he can try to manipulate me to get his way, I end the call and drop the phone back into my sports bag.

I shove my face into my hands, growling. He'll never learn. I once loved fighting, but he's slowly sucking the joy out of it.

My phone lights up, and his name appears on the screen.

I reach down and zip the bag back up. Instead of going home like planned, I grab my gloves and return to the punching bag.

The sound of my fist hitting the bag slowly helps me forget about Colin and our conversation.

Instead, I think about the mysterious girl, and wonder what she is doing now.

3

HARRIETT

Tonight's the night me and my girls will get to debut our first dance routine together. Normally, there's only one or two of us working the pole on the main stage, but after hounding Dave for months last year, he finally gave in and is letting us perform as a group. He's given us one chance, but we only need one. The performance speaks for itself. After he's done watching us, I can guarantee he'll want us to do more.

Dancing isn't as lewd as people think it is, or it's not at Tease, where Dave runs a tight ship and looks after us girls.

I set the food down on the table as I reach my living room. It's quirky with its two-seater, a swivel love chair, and a handful of beanbags and large pillows. Candles of all shapes and sizes are scattered around the room. Some are lit, some aren't, but I love the vibe it gives off. Everything in here is dark, with a grey/bluish sofa and love seat, a dark oak mantelpiece, shelves, and the TV stand I use for my stereo since I don't own a television.

To finish off the look, I have pillows of various sizes, material, and shapes in the colours sandy and tan beige. I have throw blankets to match.

In the winter, when the Christmas decorations and twinkly lights go up, it all feels cosy, especially when my log burner is on.

I'm hoping to one day own the small home. When I began to rent it from my uncle, it was only ever meant to be temporary, but I fell in love and now I can't imagine living anywhere else.

Gabby makes her way down the staircase leading to my bedroom, and stops at the bottom, striking a pose. She's wearing the black leather two-piece I purchased a while ago for this very night.

She yanks the material from her arse. "The zipper goes from back to front and it feels weird."

"But you look hot," I point out as she steps further into the room.

The two piece is one of my favourites. The top is less revealing than Olivia's and mine, but sexy nonetheless. There's a thin strap of leather below the boobs, and aside from the nipple area, the rest is a black patterned lace that lifts into a halter neck.

The bottoms, however, are all leather and tight up the arse. The zip goes back to front, and on the side, there's a bit of a lace fringe to match the top.

There's less material on Olivia's, and although hers is more of a simple bralette and brief look, the black straps make it sexier. Her bralette shows off her nipples, and instead of sticking tassels there like she normally would, she leaves it how it is. The briefs have four black straps holding them up, and with her hourglass figure, they look hot. She'll be pairing hers with black leather boots and a small hairpiece.

Mine is a criss-cross black one-piece that complements my curves and tan. The back is my favourite—and the reason I bought it. There are strings of rhinestones that fall from the straps at my hips to the thong down my arse crack. It's hot and makes my arse look fuller.

Luckily, we only need them for the routine. Normally, I'd keep whatever outfit I'm wearing on the stage, on, comfortable in my own body. That said, I've only been wearing it thirty minutes and it's not exactly comfy, but then, none of the best outfits are. I might have to remove the rhinestones and slide on my red-checkered skirt or the black leather hot pants that may as well be knickers.

"Any arse play I thought I might have in the future just vanished. There's no way anything is going up there," she firmly states, shoving her hand down the crack of her arse again. "Which is a tragedy because I've been wanting to try out the new arse bullet."

Olivia crooks her finger. "Let me put some talc up there. It will stop it from chafing."

Gabby snorts. "You just want to cop a feel. Admit it."

"Dude, you had no problem with me waxing you down there the other night," Olivia argues.

"Only because I don't like doing it," Gabby fires back.

"Stop arguing," I demand, laughing when Gabby slaps Olivia's hand away.

"I'm sorry I'm late," Emily calls, letting herself in. "Poppy wouldn't settle, and I didn't want to leave until I knew she was okay."

"Hey, we're in the living room," I call out, and slide on my dressing gown.

"Your timing is perfect. The pizza arrived a few minutes ago," Gabby says as she drops down onto one of my beanbags, not bothering to cover up. I think we're that used to each other's bodies, none of us are shy anymore.

Emily flops down on the cushion beside me on the floor, her back resting against the sofa. She's wearing the basic uniform for the club, which is a black and white, low cut T-shirt with the club's logo on, and black booty shorts. I love the knee-length socks with white stripes at the top so much I've stolen a few pairs out of the supply cupboard at work. "Did you all get the message from Woods?"

"I think he secretly chose our group," Olivia comments, grabbing a slice of pizza. I've been wondering when someone would bring it up. With the new safety procedures going in place, the security has had to pick groups they'll be responsible for. "He acts annoyed, but really, he loves us. We make his night."

"Is he still annoyed that you gave him a black eye?" I ask, staring directly at Olivia.

She holds her hand up in the air. "It wasn't my fault. I threw my shoe to try to break up the fight. It's not my fault he got in the way."

Laughter spills out of me. "His expression was so funny. I think he was still shocked when the shift ended."

"Hey, you not eating?" Emily asks, watching Gabby down half a glass of wine.

Gabby shakes her head. "You know I get wind after pizza. It's funny when I'm working with Trixie, 'cause I can blame it on her, but I'm with you guys tonight and I don't want to fuck up your tips."

I hold my drink up and she clinks her glass with mine. "I'm glad I'm not the only one who does that."

"I can't do that behind the bar. There's a fifty-fifty chance someone might smell it, and with only Matt working with me, it's uncomfortable," Emily remarks.

"I don't give a shit," Olivia comments. "Last week I was on all fours twerking my arse in a guy's face when I farted. If he gets pink eye, he only has himself to blame for getting that close."

I spit my drink out everywhere and fall off my bean bag, laughing hard. "Stop, my stomach hurts."

Gabby hasn't stopped staring at her. "I want to be grossed out, but we all do things when we think no one is looking."

"Like what?" Emily asks, munching on some chips.

"Remember when I had that sequinned bra and pants on? It was itchy as fuck, so I kept scratching my fanny when no one was looking," I admit.

"I've fanny farted whilst doing the Falling Genie," Gabby reveals on a shrug.

"Same, and doing the drop splits," I admit, struggling to keep my laughter in.

Olivia pauses mid-chew and turns to Gabby. "Wait a minute! You blamed Trixie last week for farting. I swear, I could taste it in my mouth for hours, it stunk that bad. Was that really you?"

Gabby lifts her drink to her lips, looking away. "No, that really was Trixie," she lies.

"Bitch," Olivia hisses. "I nearly threw up on that old dude with the wig because it stunk so bad."

"Why are you bringing up old shit? Get over it," Gabby argues.

"Don't start," Emily and I yell simultaneously.

They stop bickering long enough to yell back, "We aren't."

"We aren't here to listen to who farts the most. We are here to listen to Emily, remember," I point out, bringing up the elephant in the room.

Emily groans and drops her head back on the sofa. "I had hoped you'd all have forgotten by now."

"How could we forget. I'm a little hurt you didn't tell me," Olivia fires back.

"I didn't know how. It felt weird bringing it up when he didn't know, so I kept it to myself."

"I don't mean who the father is—we get it. But you could have told us you fucked him. He's seriously fucking hot. And the way his R's roll off his tongue gets me wet," she admits.

I throw a pillow at her. "Dude, that's Poppy's dad."

She shrugs, uncaring. "I'd have written a blog post about it, or at the very least, made a TikTok. He's fucking hot. Was he good? Did he make you come?"

"Olivia!" Gabby snaps, but then turns to Emily with hopeful eyes. "Did he?"

Emily cuddles a pillow to her chest. "It was great. He was being sweet and caring, and then the next thing I know, he's sliding my knickers over my thighs and fucking me on the lounge chair in the staff room."

My nose scrunches up. "I take naps on that."

Gabby considers the situation. "And he doesn't know he's the father?"

"No. I never saw him again. When I went into work the next night, Dave pulled me aside and told me I was no longer a dancer. I thought I was fired, but then he told me the owner wants me at the bar and that I must have really impressed him." She pauses to make sure we are following. "I asked who I impressed, and that's when I found out Cole was the owner."

"He didn't come back that night, if I recall," Olivia comments.

"No, he didn't. And aside from fantasising about him, he didn't really cross my mind until three months later, when I found out I was pregnant."

"Did you try to find him?" I ask. "'Cause I swear, if he knew but didn't do anything and let you struggle all this time, I'll kill him."

"I swear, he didn't know. I was shocked when I found out. When things started to feel real, I tried to fish for information about him, but I got nowhere. I'm sure Dave thought I was a stalker."

"I'm still in shock over it," Olivia comments. "Poppy is gorgeous, and it makes sense. You pair are hot so it's understandable you'd make a pretty baby."

"Aren't all babies pretty?" I muse.

"Nell looked like an alien," she retorts, talking about her little sister, and I choke on my drink.

"That's mean."

She shrugs. "She makes up for it now, so it doesn't matter."

"Wait, let her finish," Gabby orders, before asking, "What made you not tell him?"

Emily takes another slice of pizza. "A lot of things really," she answers. "Do you remember Mel, who left just before my maternity leave?"

"The woman with two kids?" I ask.

"Yeah."

"What about her?" Olivia asks.

"She was going through that custody battle. She had to prove to the courts she could provide for her kids since the dad worked full-time. We were in the staff room when she was telling me about it. She thought because he worked and she didn't, it would look better for him, which is why she got the job that paid enough to cover house and bills. But he somehow found out she worked at the strip club and used it to get custody. It scared me. It still does. I work in a strip club, and he owns it. He slept with me, and I barely knew him. I was worried he would think I did that all the time."

"But you only had that one disaster of a dance," I point out.

She shrugs. "It doesn't matter. You know how people will react if they find out. They say stripper like it's a dirty word and we're all slags."

"I wouldn't care if I actually got some," Gabby points out. "I don't think I've had my fanny licked for over a year."

"Because you don't shut up," Olivia points out.

"And you don't let people finish," Gabby fires back. "We all have faults, *Ollie*."

Emily ignores them. "I didn't want him to take her away from me because he saw me as an unfit mother. Time passed by quickly, and now I don't know how to tell him or even if I should. I'm still scared he'll take her, but I'm more frightened of his reaction. He might be angry he missed so much."

"Or he might not like kids," Olivia tries to comfort.

"Did he say anything to you yesterday when you went into the office?" I ask.

"I felt him staring at me the entire time, but I got out of there as quickly as possible whilst Dave had his attention."

"What are you going to do?" I ask.

Gabby leans forward. "Why does she have to do anything? He's never gonna know."

"He might," I add.

"I really don't know what I'm going to do. She's my life. With my nan getting worse, I can't handle losing Poppy too."

I wrap my arm around her in comfort. "It's going to be okay."

"How? He knows I have a daughter now. It's not going to be long before he works it out," she explains. "We have that family barbeque at Dave's coming up, and if I don't take her, he'll put two and two together—if he hasn't already."

"Do you think he knows who her dad is?"

She shrugs. "No idea, but thinking back, it seems strange that he kept asking about her father."

"He asked us at work after you found out you were pregnant. We didn't know, but if you had told us not to tell anyone, we wouldn't have anyway, and I think he knew that."

Olivia pours herself another drink. "He'll be gone soon, and things will get back to normal. None of us will say anything."

"This secret is eating away at me, and this might be the only time I get to tell him. Who knows if we'll see him again."

"Then tell him. You have us to stand by you if he tries anything. We'll back you one hundred percent," I tell her.

"And if you don't want to tell him, we'll back you over that too.

There's no judgement. We might not have a baby, but we're women in the same line of work, so we can relate to your fears. Look at Harriett, she wears wigs and heavy makeup so no one finds out who she is. Her job will be at risk if she's found out."

"Legally, it won't be, but yeah, it's a risk. It's my dad I'm worried about the most. I'm not ashamed of what I do, but I know him. He'll think he let me down in some way, and I don't want him to think like that."

"He loves you," Gabby comments.

"And I love him, but I don't want anyone treating him differently. And life is easier this way. I haven't got to break people's noses every time I leave the house."

"True, although it's always fun to watch," Gabby comments.

"I reword my job description to social services as well," Olivia adds. She got custody of her siblings as soon as she turned eighteen, but she had been raising them long before that. Her mum was never there, which was actually doing them a favour, but that's a different story. "I don't think it's a requirement to have a suitable job, but our case worker is a snob and would jump at the chance to get the kids taken from my care."

Gabby nods in agreement. "I've met her. Since she found out I'm gay, she can barely look at me."

One by one our phones begin to ping with a message alert. I reach mine first to find a message from Dave.

Dave: After the performance, Harriett will be working the VIP and working shots. Jane is off sick, and I'm left with no other fucking choice. We've got a celeb coming in so don't fuck it up. Em, you are working the VIP bar. Olivia, try not to give anyone a black fucking eye tonight, otherwise you're fired.

Olivia snorts. "He says that at least three times a week."

I glance at the time. "We'd best start to do our makeup. We have to leave soon."

"I'm having another glass of wine," Emily comments.

"Everything will be okay. You'll see," I promise.

"He has a right to know, but I'm just so fucking scared. She's my world, aside from you guys."

"You have every right to be. You don't know him," Olivia advises. "But we'd never let him take her from you."

"And he might not even be there," I point out.

"I just need to get my head wrapped around it all. I'll tell him when the timing is right."

As I leave to grab my makeup from upstairs, I have to wonder who the celebrity is. It's not the first time we've had high-profile people come in, and honestly, they are all entitled pricks. The reality stars are the worst. It's like they think they can get away with shit because they are on television.

And Dave must be crazy for putting me in the VIP section. The last time I was in there, the place closed early, and the police were called.

It's only for one night. What's the worst that could happen?

4

RIVER

Music blares as Cole, a manager of multiple successful strip clubs, pulls open the door to his office. He steps aside, holding his hand out to Kim.

She shakes it. "Thank you for meeting with us."

He pulls his hand back, shoving it in the pocket of his trousers. "The VIP area is closed off tonight to other members, so you and your guests have it to yourselves. If you need to add anyone to the guest list, please talk to Woods. He's a part of our security team and will be watching over your section tonight."

"Will you not join us?" Kim asks, lowering her halter-neck top.

He glances down at the floor, struggling to hide the twitch in his lips. "Not tonight I'm afraid. I have business to attend to before I leave."

"You know where we are if you change your mind. It's been a pleasure doing business with you," Kim announces, before turning to me. "I'll meet you in the VIP section with the others."

I jerk my chin, and with one more hopeful glance in Cole's direction, she leaves. I have to hand it to her, aside from the little trip she did when she first met him, she's kept it together. She's good at her job, very focused and committed, which is why I didn't take offence to some of her actions tonight. It's been good to see her let her hair down, so to speak. At the office, she goes above and beyond. She's worked hours after her shift has ended and doesn't leave a task unfinished. She's worth the money I put in to hire her.

I turn to the man who snared her attention and made her lose focus. My first impression of him was wrong—and I'm normally a good judge of character. He comes across stoic, aloof, but he's pretty laid back and easy-going, even if he is business orientated. He even looked past Kim's stumbling behaviour like it never happened.

"I really appreciate you seeing us tonight. I know you are a busy man," I tell him, and he moves back into the office, sitting on the edge of the desk.

"She's good at her job," he comments, and I know he's talking about Kim.

"She is. I'm glad I hired her."

"Your brand will go far with her running it, and if you ever change your mind about being exclusive to Tease, the offer is there."

My lips tug into a smile. "We'll see. I'm still new to this and learning. I didn't think it would be this popular."

"I heard you are thinking of leaving the fighting scene. That true?"

"I'm on the fence," I lie, not wanting the information leaked before I'm ready. "There's so much I want to do with my life. I have opportunities, which is something I never had before. Fighting is my passion but it's not the same anymore. Times have changed."

"You've got the championship this year, right?"

"I do."

"You're doing a lot for your age. You're only twenty-eight."

"I could say the same to you. You're what, in your thirties, and you've got a dozen strip clubs over the entire UK and own a dozen more nightclubs."

"I like being busy," he answers. "You have a good reputation behind you, and after meeting you tonight, I can see why. You have your head screwed on."

"Do you want to be my new promoter?" I tease.

"No, but I'm in the early stages of opening a new club and I want you to help me promote it."

A little taken aback, I reply: "I'm sorry, I don't have any expertise in advertising."

His lips twitch. "You are misunderstanding me. I want you to be the face on the posters. We don't want a random model. We want it personal, and I think you'll be the perfect fit. We want a new crowd, a new theme, and with your following and reputation, we can sell that."

I rub the back of my neck. "Normally I'd tell you to go through my manager. He's the one who manages the endorsements. But I can already tell you now, he'll say no."

"I don't want the fighter; I want the brand. Knight Whiskey is going to be on shelves before the end of the year. And I don't have to point out how beneficial this would be for you and your brand. You'll get to promote it through one of the most popular clubs in the UK. You'll also sell you, and that's something your manager doesn't do. I've seen it in your other endorsements."

"Is this another strip club?"

"Originally, it was meant to be a nightclub, but we're changing things up. Girls come from all over to strip at my clubs, and there's a waiting list. This week, however, it's been brought to my attention that there are some girls who want a change. But like I said, it's still in the early stages. Once things are confirmed, I can present you with an offer. I just wanted to see how you'd feel about it before we start putting things into motion."

"I want to say yes to you, but I'll have to run this by people first."

"Run it by people hypothetically. I'm not ready to go public with it, not until things are confirmed and there's no chance someone else jumps in."

"Then why tell me at all?" I muse.

"Because I trust you'll keep this to yourself."

"Ah, that's why you brought up fighting," I guess.

A slow grin tugs at his lips. "I'm a businessman, but you have my word I'll keep it confidential."

"Thank you."

"Storm, stop sticking your fucking fake tits to every surface," Dave yells. Cole pointed him out to us at the beginning of the night. "And for God's sake, someone move these fucking chairs."

"Dave, there's someone I'd like you to meet," Cole calls out as a man not much smaller than me walks past.

I step away from the doorway to let him through. He takes a double look when he spots me. "Shit, you're a big motherfucker."

I grin, not offended. I get it a lot. "Thanks."

"I'm Dave. It's good to meet you."

"I'm River," I greet, holding my hand out.

He gives me a firm handshake. "Never work with women, son. They're fucking crazy."

"I'll keep that in mind," I muse.

He turns to Cole. "I quit."

"No, you don't. You love it here," Cole muses.

"No, I fucking quit. Misty just *accidently* kneed a guy in the balls. This isn't good for my health."

"You're thirty-five," Cole mutters.

"Not now I'm not. They've put years on me," he whines. "Lin's gonna start looking for someone younger and fitter."

Cole rolls his eyes. "If she leaves you, it's because you moan too much."

Dave turns to me. "I came to help out for a week when the place first opened. It's been seven years and I'm still fucking here. Don't work with family."

I'm surprised by his declaration. Neither of them share any similarities. Dave is rugged looking, with blonde hair and brown eyes, whilst Cole has darker hair and bluey-grey eyes. Dave's also shorter than Cole, who is tall and quite built. They share no facial structure or accent. Cole sounds more like a Londoner, whereas Dave reminds me of a Brummie.

"You two are related?"

"Not by DNA. We were in the same foster home," Dave replies, then glances up at the clock. "Shit! The show starts soon. If I don't go out there now, I'll never hear the end of it."

"Show?" I ask.

"A few of the girls are putting on a show. You don't want to miss it. It's meant to be good," Dave comments as he gets to his feet.

"I do have to get back out there. Kim is probably wondering where I am," I admit.

"Hopefully I'll see you again soon," Cole tells me, and after another handshake, says, "I'll email you with details."

"It's been good meeting you," I tell him, then head to the VIP section.

Kim and a bunch of others are sitting in the section cornered off for our team when I make my way up to the platform.

Elliot, our design manager, spots me, and begins to make his way over.

He's an alright guy and runs a tight ship in the office. His reputation precedes him. I had to beat the competition to get him to work for me. He's a short guy, a little round around the middle, and at times, a little weird. I think he tries too hard to get me to like him. I'm hoping once we get to know each other more, it will calm down. He doesn't need to impress me; his CV already did that.

"Hey, man, it's pumping in here tonight, right?" he yells, holding his hand up. When I don't high-five him, he drops it to his side. "It's cool you picked this place to kick off the celebration. I think we all needed a night out, and if it were left down to the women, we might have ended up somewhere boring."

I pull back a little but keep my voice loud so I can be heard over the music. "I didn't pick it. Kim did. She thought it was fitting since they're the first biggest consumer."

"Oh. Huh, forget I said that then," he calls back. "It's great here. And we get VIP treatment, which is something I've never had before."

"Hey," Harry, another member of our team, greets. "It's going to be a blast tonight. I can't believe you picked this place. I thought it would be seedy but it's classy in here."

"God, Kim picked this place," Elliot tells him, rolling his eyes. "Women can be cool too."

"Have you all been here long?" I ask, changing the subject.

Elliot answers first. "I got here twenty minutes early. You know what I'm like about being punctual."

"Not long," Harry replies, shifting on his feet. "I know this is unprofessional, but, urm, my girlfriend wanted me to ask you for an autograph."

He hands me a pen and an old promo photo from a fight a few years ago. "Sure," I agree and take the pen, scribbling my fighter's name across the photo.

"You have a girlfriend?" Elliot asks. "And she's okay with you coming here?"

Harry ducks his head. "Yeah, she's cool with it."

Kim sidles up to us, her composure cool and content. She doesn't seem fazed by the scantily clad women walking about around us.

"Hey, guys, did you meet with the manufacturing team? They'd love to meet you," she greets.

Both Harry and Elliot turn to the large group that has not long arrived. "I'll go over now."

Both leave and Kim turns to me. "What took you so long? I thought the meeting went well. Did something happen?" she asks, shoving her glasses up her nose.

"Everything is fine. We were just talking," I reply.

Her nose scrunches up. "What were you talking about?"

"He offered me a job to be a model promoting Knight Whiskey and a club."

Her eyebrows shoot up. "Really? What club?"

"I'm not sure," I lie. "But I'll explain more Monday."

She takes a look at my jacket, and there's a question there. "You aren't leaving, are you? They're bringing out three bottles of our whisky and I thought you'd stay for it."

"No, I'm staying, but I can't stay long. I have to get back soon as I have training in the morning."

She nods, happy with my answer. "We've invited some potential investors. I'm not sure when they'll come but it's not an official meeting, so you won't be missing anything if you leave before they arrive."

"Thank you for understanding."

She waves me off. "It's fine. Your training schedule kind of scares me. I only go to the gym three times a week and it kills me."

I laugh at her answer. "I'm used to it."

"Tonight, we bring you a performance of a lifetime. It's something different, something you've not seen before here at Tease. I bring you, Candy, Misty, and Storm."

The crowd roars with cheers as the lights dim. Kim bounces on her feet. "I'm looking forward to this. The bouncer over there said it was a performance we don't want to miss."

My phone vibrates in my pocket, and I pull it out. "I'll be over soon. I just have to reply to these," I explain, holding my phone up.

She nods before taking her exit, sitting with the others. As I take a seat in a booth set apart from the others, a song I recognise from a Christina Aguilera movie blares from the speakers.

Colin: Where are you? I wasn't joking when I said you had to be here.

The sound of lights flashing on has my attention, and I look up to find three girls with their backs to the audience, sitting in single wooden chairs under a spotlight. I tuck my phone into my pocket, the message long forgotten.

One is in leather, the other in a more subtle yet still sexy outfit, but the one in the middle, the one who has a one-piece that criss-crosses over her slender body, is the one who has my attention. There's something alluring about her, something familiar. It has the hairs on my neck standing on end.

Slowly they rise off the chairs, clicking their fingers in time to the song. Every man in here is silent, transfixed as the women really get into the performance. It's sexy, riveting, and when the one in middle swings her chair around, I lean forward, wanting to get a better look.

She's fucking gorgeous, with long legs, round arse, and a generous amount of cleavage. Her blonde hair stands out, and for some reason, I'm not sure it's her real colour. She strikes me as a brunette, and someone who is confident in her own skin.

My cock hardens as I watch her move, graceful and fluid, over the chair. She turns her back to the audience, and her arse—which is only covered with rhinestones—jiggles with the move.

I can't look away, not even when another dancer places a drink on my table. "They told me to bring you a glass of whiskey. If you need anything else, just give me a wave."

I don't reply, and from the corner of my eye, I see her leave.

My attention is pulled back to the stage when they kick the chairs back. The three move in sync, and it's breath-takingly beautiful. The promise has every man and woman on the edge of their seats, and if the men are anything like me, under a spell.

But I only have eyes for the one in the middle, the one who dances effortlessly like it takes no practice at all. There's a natural sultriness that seems to hit her in waves. When she turns once again, with her back to the audience, she shakes her arse in a way I can't help but imagine my dick between her thighs.

Gliding across the stage until they are together again, they drop down in a line. The way her back arches and the way her hand runs up the leg of the woman in front of her… I need more.

As I stand, moving to the bar that separates the VIP lounge from the main floor, her head tilts towards me. I lock gazes with her, and that's when it hits me.

She's the mystery woman.

The woman who wouldn't give me her name.

I'll never forget those eyes.

And I'll never forget that body or the way she moves.

"Fuck!" I hiss, gripping my drink.

As the song comes to an end, the crowd goes wild, men and women hollering for more.

I leave, finding Dave straight away. "The girl in the middle, the one with the rhinestones, I want a private dance with her."

"She's working the VIP today."

I shake my head. "I want privacy."

"Like I said, mate, she's working VIP. I can't pull her off here. It will cost us too much money."

"I'll pay triple to whoever I need to. Money isn't an issue."

His brows rise, and just when I think he's going to argue, he surprises me by nodding. "Head over to curtain one over there. Once she's off the stage, I'll have her brought over to you."

"Thank you," I reply.

"There are rules here and we abide by them. If anything fishy happens over there, I'll personally put you in the ground myself."

"I just want a private dance," I lie, since it's better than the truth. I know what he's hinting at, what he's implying, but I've never hurt a woman in my life.

There are things I want to do to her, but hurting or disrespecting her isn't one of them.

The girls leave the stage as I make my way over to the curtain Dave pointed out. Am I surprised she's a stripper? Yes and no. She has the confidence and allure to do this job to perfection.

And now, she owes me a date.

5

HARRIETT

These are the moments I live for. The kind where the rush of it has your blood pumping and your pulse racing. It's giving it my all and feeling good about it.

Choosing a burlesque song for this performance was the perfect fit, and the men were eating it up.

People think men come and stare at nothing but the women, but that's only half true. Men just want to feel like men. A majority of the time, they barely look at the main stage, too uncomfortable with women flaunting their goods. Us dancers have to work harder to get their attention, to make them want to put money in our pocket or buy another shot.

It's how we earn so much. Not only do we get a fair wage, but we get a percentage of money from the shots we sell. We make a majority of our earnings from doing lap dances. Other places don't offer that, so we got lucky working at Tease.

And I have a feeling tonight is going to be a good one. The crowd aren't only cheering, but they are asking for more. It couldn't have gone better.

That is, until I nearly missed my cue.

It's very rare I get taken off guard, but when I saw hot, tattooed, and lethal—also known as Rampage—sitting in the VIP area, I was taken back to the night I met him.

There's no way he is here for me. I never gave him my name or number. And with my blonde wig, heavy makeup, and from that distance, there's just no way he's recognised me.

I've run into this problem a few times during my time here, but whenever someone we know comes in, us girls work together to keep you from being in their section. There's less chance of being recognised or being put in an awkward position.

The last time one of the girls ran into someone they knew, it happened to be their high-school teacher. He wasn't my teacher, but even I felt the horror of it all. It took me months to stop seeing my sleazy math teacher in every rounded guy who came in.

As the crowd cheers and the lights dim, I chance another look in his direction. He's no longer there, and I'm beginning to wonder if my mind was playing tricks on me. The lights are bright tonight, so it could have been anyone. He's starred in many of my fantasies since the night I met him. And if I'm honest with myself, there have been times I've regretted not giving him my name and number. It's been a long time since I let myself have something for myself. I've been so focused on school, work, and friends, I haven't had a chance to do much else. It's not like I'm short of company. I have my friends and I love them, but I do miss the intimacy of a sexual relationship.

I'm the last off stage, and as I hit the back steps, Dave is there, his expression blank. I know that look. It's the look he gives you right before he lets you down. It's the look he gets right before he fires someone.

"If you are here to moan, email it to me and I'll get back to you in five to seven business working days. That performance was awesome, and nothing you are going to say will change that. Listen to the crowd, Dave. They want more. It just proves you don't have to take your clothes off to turn a man on. It's all about the visual. I've been telling you that for over a year."

He arches an eyebrow. "Are you finished?"

I cross my arms over my chest. "If you say something that's going to put me in a bad mood, I've got a lot more to say to you, yeah."

He rolls his eyes, but his posture relaxes. "I came to congratulate you and to give you a heads up; you'll be doing it three times a night on the weekends from now on," he demands.

The girls behind him begin to jump up and down, clapping.

"I knew you loved me," I cheer.

"Well, you are going to love me even more. You're off VIP for a bit. Instead, you'll be with the gentleman in curtain one for a private performance."

That actually sounds good. If Rampage *is* here, then I want to be as far away from the VIP section for as long as possible.

Gabby pulls my attention away from Dave, and I begin to worry something is wrong with her. She looks constipated, and then she begins to cut her hands over her throat in a 'no' gesture. My brows pinch together. What on earth is she doing?

Instead, I answer Dave, ignoring the crazy woman. "I'll head over there now."

"Storm, go take Candy's place until she's done," Dave orders, and Gabby's shoulders drop at her stage name being announced.

She trips as she grabs his shoulder, stopping him from leaving. "Wait! Why don't I go give the lap dance?"

"The last time you gave a private dance, the punter got taken to hospital."

"Hey," she retorts, straightening her outfit. "I take offence. It was an accident. How was I meant to know he had a big dick?"

"Go. You don't have time to change," he tells me, and before Gabby can say anything else, he points her in the direction of the VIP lounge. "Storm, don't make me fire your arse."

"Like you would. This place would be boring without me," Gabby grouches as we both head off in separate directions.

Lionel is at the curtain when I arrive, and I inwardly groan. Out of all the bouncers/security personnel, he is one of my least favourites. So many girls have been groped under his watch because he's more bothered about getting some pussy than he is about our safety. The only thing he's good for is breaking up fights. He doesn't fuck around, but I think that's mostly because he wants to act hard and manly instead of looking out for us.

"Where's your mask tonight?" he asks when I reach him, and his eyes run over my figure. "Are you sure I can't change your mind for a private performance at my place?"

"Shit! I'll be two seconds. I have one in the hallway."

"What about that dance?"

I walk backwards and give him a sweet smile. "When the world rotates clockwise."

I leave him confused and turn on my heel, rushing to the corridor where I keep spares. The girls know not to steal them anymore, and any newbies learn after the first time one goes missing. I grab it off the hook and am about to head back when Emily calls my stage name from a door not far away.

A huge smile stretches over my face at the sight of her. "Did you see our performance?"

"It was hot. It made me wish I didn't have two left feet," she muses. "Storm wanted me to give you a message. She was talking too fast, so I didn't catch it all, but she swore you'd know what she was talking about."

"Go on," I push.

"She said, tell her to trot into a vibe and that, sharks fall legal—or legally, I'm not sure. Then she kept yelling, 'snort ignition', at me."

The girl is whacky as fuck. "How much did she drink?"

"I only saw her have the one, but, babe, she had that crazy look in her eye."

I chuckle. "I'll ask her later. I really do need to go. I have someone waiting in a private booth."

"Have fun."

"Always do," I reply and make my way back to the private booths.

Lionel jerks his chin up as I tie the lace face mask around my eyes. It gives me a little more anonymity when I'm going to be up close and personal with a punter. It also makes me feel like I'm somebody else. It's like an actor playing a role. This is my role and I'm damn good at it. I can be whoever I want to be with the mask on, and once it's off, along with the costume, I'm back to Harriett. Candy is left inside the strip club, waiting until the next shift.

"He's paid for an hour," he reveals, and I nod, taking a breath to compose myself and get myself into character.

Lionel slides back the curtain and I step inside, my gaze to the floor. Men love it. I'm not sure if it's the submissive gesture, or the revealing of the eyes, but men go crazy for it.

The curtains fall closed behind me, and the first thing I see are his black leather shoes, his feet spread apart.

I run my gaze up his body, noticing his thick, muscled thighs, and then his crisp, white shirt.

I've seen all sorts of men working here. From doctors, businessmen, and lawyers to men who have nine-to-five jobs. From all walks of life, I've met them all. They all give off a distinct body language, and as I continue checking him out, my pulse races. I know this man.

This is the same man I fucked myself to. It's the same guy I've imagined lifting me at the waist and fucking me against a wall. He's starred in many of my fantasies, but this is a new one.

"Fuck," I rasp, knocked off my feet. Literally. I grab the curtain to stop the fall and hold my hand up when he goes to reach for me. "I'm good."

His expression is blank, but his dark, piercing eyes have me anchored to the spot. It's like he can see through the mask, through the costume I'm wearing, and he's seeing me.

The real me.

It's hard not to react any more than I already have, and to keep myself composed before him. I should walk back out and ask someone else to do this, but instead of leaving, I head over to the speakers, pausing with the tip of my finger on the play button.

"No touching. I can touch you, but you can't touch me. I'm a dancer, not a prostitute," I tell him, and there's a pitch in my tone. "Do you understand?"

"Yes," he rumbles, and there's a roughness to his voice that turns me on.

I hit play on the stereo, and Selena Gomez, *Wolves*, blares through the speakers. The lights dim, and I hit the platform under a ruby-red light. As soon as my hands hit the pole, I kick my leg out and wrap it around the silver metal.

I can't meet his gaze, not even as I slide down the pole, my back to it, and spread my thighs, exposing the thin scrap of material covering the most intimate parts of me.

Unless I know the guy is going to give a good tip, I don't really try much in here. I use it to relax my muscles, a way to stretch down after a stage performance. But with him, I want to give it my all. I want him to want me until he can't think straight.

Stripping has always given me a sense of power, but as I spot him watching me, a dark gleam in his eyes, I feel invincible.

Every song that plays, I let the lyrics flow through me. I use the dirty, sensual, and lust-filled words to my advantage, and I know it's having an effect on him.

The tension is thick and the clock in the corner—to remind me of the time—moves slower.

Using my legs to hold me up, I drop back, letting the blonde tips of my wig sweep across the floor.

He lounges back, his arm going over the back of the sofa as he runs his tongue over his bottom lip. He's as hot as I remembered, and when I finally crawl off the platform to kneel in front of him, I realise there's something wrong with me.

I've done this for countless men before. It never affected or bothered me. But here and now, doing it for him, my entire body buzzes with excitement. I'm pretty sure if I were to slide my hand into my knickers, I'd be wet.

There are rules in here. No touching or going beyond what people would count as prostitution. But as my barely covered breasts rub over his thighs and along the hardness of his cock, I can't help but want to fuck the rules off.

He inhales as I come to stand in front of him before straddling his thighs, something I normally avoid if I can, but I can't help but fall into the moment.

I roll my hips as I push up, shoving my chest into face. He grips me, and I'm glad the music covers up my moan.

He does nothing but watch me, his gaze filled with lust.

"No touching," I rasp, continuing with the dance.

My lashes flutter as he drops his hands to his sides, clenching his jaw.

I'm not sure how long it's been, or how many songs have passed. The silence is louder than the music. Normally, I'm used to a guy talking my ear off, too nervous to do anything more.

I get to my knees once more, spreading his thighs apart. He's big, really big, and so very hard under those black slacks. I gulp and turn my back to him, unable to go another minute with his hot gaze on me.

I sit back, grinding against his cock whilst running my hands up his thighs.

I want to touch myself, to come undone in front of him. If I have to go another minute, it might just happen anyway.

He feels good, so fucking good.

"Five more minutes," I warn him, a little breathless.

I could tell him who I am. I could let him slide my knickers to the side and fuck me, and no one would know.

Lionel's boots are no longer visible under the curtain, which means a chick with a nice pair of tits or arse has pulled his attention away.

I keep dancing, and this time, unclasp the strings holding my bra up. His hands reach up to stop me, but it's too late. The bra cups fall to my waist, and his hands are on my tits.

I shouldn't moan, but I do. They feel good on me. *Really* good.

"Fuck!" he growls, thrusting up.

"I'm finished," I whisper, not entirely sure why I'm not leaving. I should remove his hands, call out to Lionel, but I do neither.

"Lift your top back up," he rasps.

My arse grinds against his cock as I reach for it. His growl vibrates against all the sweet spots, and the atmosphere in the small room changes.

"I have to go," I tell him, my voice low.

Get up and leave, Harriett.

He leans in, his lips at my ear as I finish clasping my bra. "You're forgetting something."

"If you want to pay cash, I can take it now, but I assumed you'd be paying by card. I should have made you aware, but there's a fee when you use a card."

"I'm not talking about that, but I'm happy to pay whatever you want."

My body tenses when I ask, "Then what do you mean?"

His hands run down my sides, to my thighs, and I hold my breath to keep back the moan. God, why does his touch set me alight like this?

"You aren't leaving here until you give me what you promised."

"E-excuse me?" I go to get up, but he pulls me back down.

"Don't act like you don't remember me. I know you do. I could see it the minute you walked in and your eyes landed on me."

I stand, but quicker than anyone has ever moved, he has me back in his lap, straddling his thighs.

Holy fuck that was hot.

I'm damp with desire when I meet his gaze. He doesn't look repulsed, or put-off over my occupation. If anything, he seems riveted by it.

"You continue to surprise me. I never pegged you to be someone capable of being lost for words," he huskily states, before his brows pinch together. "You do remember me, right?"

I finally find my voice and tilt my head. "You are kind of hard to forget."

His lips tug into a smirk. "And you are a hard woman to track down."

"You found me here?"

He pulls off my mask, and I let him. "No. It was pure coincidence, which I won't complain about. I nearly gave up searching for you, but here you are, working at Tease."

"If you think I'm a dirty skank, you're wrong. I might strip, but it's not who I am. It doesn't define me. And it doesn't give you free rein to treat me like a prostitute. So if that's what fantasy you have of me now, then I'm sorry to crush it. I'm—"

His hand runs over my flesh until he's cupping the back of my neck. "If that's what I wanted, I could have pulled you into the bathrooms the first night I met you. Or invited you upstairs into a room I had booked."

"How did you know it was me?" I ask, and I can't help but dig my fingers into his shoulders.

He brushes my hair over my shoulder. "I'd never forget the way you move. And I'd never forget those eyes."

I chuckle. "You are so cheesy."

He shrugs, uncaring. "Go out with me."

"What are we, in year five?"

His lips twitch. "I mean, go out on a date with me."

I'm surprised by the offer. "You want to go out on a date with me, even after knowing what I do for a living?"

His brows pinch together. "Why would that matter?"

"You are a pretty well-known fighter and have an image to uphold."

He grasps my arse, sliding me further up his lap. "Like you said, it doesn't define you. And seeing you dance, I wouldn't call it stripping."

"What would you call it?" I rasp, barely holding it together.

The intensity of his stare almost has me ducking my gaze. The only reason I don't is because no man will ever get me to submit. It's the stubborn in me, something my dad tells me I got from my mum.

"I call it art."

Okay, that kind of has my heart hammering against my chest. I never expected him to be sweet. And the way he says it is seductive and awestruck, like what I do is a talent. I guess for some, it is.

"What if I say *maybe* to the date?"

His smirk is dirty as fuck and holds promise. He reaches into his pocket and pulls out his phone. "I never pegged you as a girl to go back on her word. You wouldn't go back on your word, would you?"

Shit!

I never go back on my word.

Ever.

I snatch the phone from his hand and save my number. "Just one date, that's it."

"I only need one."

I hand him his phone back, arching an eyebrow. "You think I'm sleeping with you after that comment?"

"No. I mean, I only need one to convince you."

I cross my arms over my chest. "Convince me of what?"

"To go on a second date," he reveals. I get up, ignoring the smugness in his tone.

"Pay Dave before you leave."

I hear him get to his feet. "Wait, what's your name?"

I stop at the curtain and turn, dipping my chin to my shoulder as I stare at him. "Maybe you'll find out on the first date."

"And what am I meant to call you until then?"

It's my turn to smile. "You can call me Cinderella."

With that, I leave.

6

HARRIETT

The nights here are getting longer, and my addiction to high shoes isn't going away any time soon. I never learn. I see a pretty pair of heels and I don't think of the height, or how badly my feet will hurt after the first few hours. All I can think about is how good they'll look with my outfits. Outside of work, I dress down. I love my comfy clothes too much. But nights out, and nights like tonight, I like to go all out.

My feet are throbbing as I hit the dressing room, and maybe when they stop hurting, I'll be able to say it was worth it. Right now, however, I can't wait to get the shoes off.

Aisling, pronounced Ash-Lin, is the only girl in the dressing room. She turns at the sound of me dropping onto the small, two-seater sofa.

She gives me a knowing look. "Sore feet? It must've been a bad night for ya," she states with a thick Irish accent.

"Aisling, you have no idea," I reply as I finish removing my shoes.

"Me Ma always tells me to soak 'em in cold water. You should try it."

"Your mum knows you strip?" I ask, wincing when my tone comes out judgemental. "Sorry, that sounded like you have something to be ashamed of. You don't."

"Aye, she does. She's come in a few times to support me. Your ma don't know?"

"It's just my dad," I admit. "But I've always been scared he'll hit the roof. You know?"

"Aye. Me Da went mad, but then, that's nothing new wit' 'im. He moved back to Ireland not long after and we haven't seen him since."

"Jesus," I comment. "How long you been living here?"

"Since I was fifteen. I got into dance school, but just when me career was taking off, I tore the ligament in me knee during a car accident. Being here, it gives a little of it back. I get to perform and still do what I love, even if it isn't the most glamourous," she reveals. "A guy tonight slobbered all over me. Luckily, Dave let me use the shower to clean up."

I grimace. "Those guys are the worst," I admit, and swallow back bile. "And the sweat…"

"Aye."

"I get it, by the way. The dancing. I used to perform professionally too, but after I lost my mum, I couldn't do it anymore. It's something we shared together. I could have done any other job whilst going through school, but I guess a part of me missed dancing, which is why I chose here."

"Aye. Same. I felt like I lost a limb, which sounds stupid 'cause I didn't lose anything. I'm alive. I got depressed after the accident and I struggled to pull me-self out. I'd just turned nineteen and lost me dream. But me ma never gave up on me. She gave me options, and then I made a joke about being a stripper 'cause no one will care about me knee, and it just happened."

"I'm sorry. I know it's not going to give you your dream back, and I know being here isn't what you pictured, but it's a start. Not many find their way back. But you did," I tell her. "And it doesn't have to end here. You can teach. Have you ever thought about starting your own dance school?"

She ducks her head. "You really think I could do that?"

"Babe, I've seen you dance. You are amazing. If it's something you want, go for it, and if you need help, just let me know. If I'm able, I'm there for whatever you need."

"Thank you. No one but me Ma has ever believed in me before," she admits shyly as she grabs her bag.

"Then you never had the right people around you."

"I'm sorry about your Ma, by the way. I can't imagine me Ma not being here," she tells me, just as there's a knock on the door. "Come in."

Lionel pops his head around the door. "You ready to leave, Red?"

She grabs her bag from the chair. "Yeah," she replies, then turns to me. "T'anks for talking to me."

"You're welcome," I reply.

The door closes behind her and I drop back. Our conversation has left me a little off-kilter. Emily, Gabby, Olivia, and Charlotte have been my friends for so long, I never really got to know many of the other girls working here.

Growing up, making friends didn't come easy for me. Their jealously caused them to be bitchy or start rumours. Being a teenage girl who developed early and got blessed in the tits and arse department brought attention I didn't ask for with the boys. The girls around me hated it, and the friends I did make soon turned on me as quick as the last lot. It left a bad taste in my mouth, so after a while, I learned to put walls up. That's not saying I was a loner. Far from it. I had the girls I danced with, and although there was competition, it never turned ugly, not like it did at school. I also had a mum and dad who loved me unconditionally. When Mum passed away, I didn't want to be around anyone.

Olivia got through those walls first. Any chance I had to keep her at arm's length went out the window the minute she ignored subtle cues. She had this vibe about her that pulled me in, and we've been friends ever since.

Our group of friends thrive together. We straighten each other's crowns. We are all free to be ourselves and there's no judgement. It's one of the things I love about them. The good and the bad, the crazy and the heartache, we are there for each other. If one of us needs an alibi, they've got one. If a boyfriend or girlfriend cheats, we get revenge. And if there's a body to buried, we'll be there with shovels. It's how we roll.

But maybe we've turned into girls who are so set in our ways, we're ignoring other potential great friendships. I've never gotten to know Aisling. I've spoken to her plenty of times but tonight is the first night she's ever given up something personal. She keeps to herself, much like the groups that have formed here.

I have no idea why I'm feeling so sentimental; it's so unlike me. It could be from lack of sleep, sore feet, or my encounter with Rampage that has left me reeling.

The chances of Rampage finding me were slim to none. I'd never met him before that night, so I knew my proposition to him had been wishful thinking on my part. I believe in luck. I believe in Karma. And I strongly believe we meet people for a reason. Whether it be for them to change my life, or for me to change theirs, it doesn't matter.

For him to find me, today of all days, has to be a sign. The odds were against us, but here he was, getting a lap dance from me. And although I'll never admit it, especially not to Gabby, I feel giddy inside.

And speaking of Gabby, she has a lot to answer for. It took me a while, but looking back, I think that's why she acted so weird earlier. She could have warned me, but instead, she said nothing. I nearly made a fool out of myself, and if it wasn't for pulling myself together so quickly, it would have been worse.

Reaching for my bag, I pull out my phone to check my emails whilst I wait for the other girls to finish their shift.

There's a message from a number I don't recognise. Opening it up, an involuntary smile spreads over my face.

River: So, Cinderella… Does this mean you think I'm Prince Charming? I'm flattered. Really flattered. But something is bothering me. Cinderella leaves the party at midnight, and I don't peg you as the girl who leaves because she's been warned to.

The message was sent five hours ago, so the chances of him being awake this early are slim. But I know if I don't message him back, I'll never get to sleep when I'm home. My mind will be constantly replaying it in my head. I'm not expecting a reply, but still, it will be something to look forward to when I do wake up.

Harriett: Don't be. Prince Charming was kind of a dick. He thought because of his good looks and status, a girl shouldn't run away from him. And he rode a horse. For some reason, I can't imagine you on a horse.

I place my phone down and lean back to close my eyes. Not even five minutes pass before there's a reply.

River: Then I guess you should call me by my birth name: River. I don't ride horses, but I do have a black beauty: my bike. Don't worry, when I pick you up for our date, I'll be driving my car. Also, it's good to hear you've been imagining me. Tell me more…

River. For some reason, it suits him. It's sexy, unique, and strong.

Harriett: In your dreams, buddy. And I've been wondering… Are you psychic?

River: Not that I'm aware.

Harriett: Then, pray tell, how are you going to pick me up for our 'date' when you don't know my address?

River: You aren't backing out, are you?

Harriett: No…

River: Then you can message me your address. Are you free Monday evening?

Harriett: No, I have an assignment to finish, but I am Tuesday evening, if that works for you?

River: I'll move stuff around. I have training so I need to go, but hopefully you aren't too busy to message me later.

Harriett: At five in the morning? Why? Why would you do that to yourself?

River: * Laughing * I'm not going to win this year's championship unless I apply myself. I need to keep fit.

I can think of a few things he could do to keep fit, and none of them involve lifting weights.

Harriett: Well, good luck, I guess!

This time when I put my phone back, it doesn't beep with a reply. I'm going on a date with a hot guy, and later, when I'm not this exhausted, I'll message to find out what I should wear.

The girls are going to go crazy when I tell them. They know all about him since I spent two days kicking myself for not giving him my name and number. I thought I let a good thing go, even if it was only going to be for a night. And I hate to let good things pass me by, which is why I never skip dessert when it's offered, or ignore a sale on shoes I can't really afford. Not many opportunities come around again, so I live life to the fullest.

Olivia steps inside, immediately kicking her heels off. "If it wasn't for the three-hundred-pound tip, I might have put that guy in the hospital."

"What happened?"

"He liked to talk smack about women. He paid me to throw abuse at me. I swear, why they get turned on by calling you a little slut, I'll never know."

"Men," I murmur. "Hey, have you ever gotten to know Aisling?"

"Not really. I keep meaning to. I feel kind of sorry for her. She's not in our group, she's not in the nice girl's group, and she's not in the bitch or whore group. She's kind of on the fence."

"Yeah, we spoke tonight, and I came to the same realisation," I admit. "Did you know she only does this to stay connected to dancing?"

Her brows rise. "A bit like you."

I ignore the comment. It's only part of the reason. I'm good at dancing, and when I was looking for a job to help me through school, I thought, why not put my skills to use? Plus, what I make on a weekend, most people make working full-time for two weeks. "She's nice. I think we should invite her to the next girl's night."

She shrugs as she slides on some joggers. "I'm cool with it."

Emily walks in and takes a seat as the door closes behind her. "I had to clean diarrhoea up in the ladies' room tonight. Would it kill them to clean up after themselves?"

Olivia snorts. "I'm all for women, but even I have to admit, the toilets are vile."

"I draw the short straw because I have a kid. I swear, Matt gets out of all the gross jobs," she announces, before turning to me. "Hey, did you ever decrypt the message Gabby gave you?"

I stand, frowning. "Nope, but I only need one guess, and if I'm right, I'm gonna kill her."

Olivia grins. "What did she do?"

"Remember the fighter I met last year?"

"The one with the hot bod, covered in tattoos, and too good fucking looking to be a fighter? The one you wouldn't shut up about for days?" Emily asks, swinging side to side in the chair.

"The very one. He was the guest in the private booths tonight."

Olivia sits forward. "You gave him a private dance?"

"I bet that was hot," Emily states. "Especially since he has no clue who you are in this get up."

I'm about to tell her he does, but the door opens, revealing Gabby, who is picking the material out from her crotch.

"I'm not wearing this again. My fanny flaps aren't big, but this fucking thing is acting like they're suction cups. Dave asked me if I had it on the wrong way because the material kept getting wedged into my flaps."

Unable to hold it in, I dive on her, and we both tumble onto the sofa. I rub my knuckles over her scalp. "How could you?"

"What are you doing, you crazy woman?" she screams, and rolls until we land on the floor, her on top. "It's not your vagina that's been tortured all night; it was mine, and not in a good way."

I push her to the side, straddling her as I mess up her hair. "You knew Rampage was here and you didn't tell me."

"Yes, I did," she yells, slapping my hands away. "It's not my fault your dumbass can't understand my signals."

"You looked constipated," I growl as she knocks me to the side, straddling me this time.

"I even gave Emily a message to give you."

I roll over her, shaking her shoulders. "Because trot into a vibe and that, sharks fall legally and snort ignition makes a lot of fucking sense."

Her nose scrunches up as she tilts her head to meet Emily's gaze. "What the hell did you tell her?"

Emily throws her hands up. "I just repeated what you told me."

"I said—"

I poke her in the ribs. "It doesn't matter. He took me off guard and I nearly landed on my arse. You didn't warn me."

"Hey, I take offence because before I gave Em the message to relay, I tackled Dave to the floor trying to get to you. He tried to fire my arse. Twice," she argues, holding two fingers up.

"I don't care. He knows I'm a stripper now."

Her expression softens. "He recognised you? That's so romantic."

"Yes, and we have a date."

"Aw, that is so sweet."

I pinch her nipple, and her cry is deafening. "Ow, that hurt. Do it harder."

"You are supposed to be my friend."

"I told her to tell you not to go into VIP, and that dark, tall, and lethal was in there. And screamed to abort mission about four times."

Emily chews on her thumbnail. "Okay, that makes a lot more sense."

Gabby pushes me off her and I land on my arse in front of the sofa. "I'm sorry."

She grins. "So, you've got a date, and he knows you're a stripper."

"I thought you didn't like to date guys who found out because they treated you differently?" Emily asks.

"He didn't tonight, but we'll see."

Gabby holds her hand up for a high-five. "Bit of a good job you didn't listen to me, right? Am I right?"

I gently slap her hand away. "I'm not high-fiving you. I should have been prepared."

The door bangs against the wall and Dave heaves out a breath. "What happened?" he asks, but the minute his eyes drop to Gabby and me on the floor, he growls low in his throat. "You lot are going to kill me before my time."

"Don't be so dramatic," I scold.

"I don't give a shit what it's about this time, sort it out."

"Okay, okay, sheesh. How does Lin put up with you?"

He glares down at Gabby. "I'm going to radio through to Woods not to call the police. With all the screaming, we thought someone had found their way back here, but I should have fucking known it would be you four."

The door slams shut behind him and Olivia drops down on the chair. "What's his problem?"

"Wait, what are you wearing on this date?" Gabby asks.

I get up, brushing dust off my arse. "I don't know." I sniff. "He hasn't said where we're going."

"I hope it's somewhere nice. It's not like he's short of cash," Emily dreamily replies. "Maybe the new steak house in town."

"Fuck that, you know Harriett doesn't do well with boring. He'll have to have a *really* interesting conversation to keep her attention," Olivia announces.

"Hey, I can do dinners," I remark.

"Babe, we went to watch Nell's play and you fell asleep before the end."

"I had been awake for three nights straight working on my assignments. And at least I didn't miss the end. I cheered her on more than any of the parents were cheering their kids on," I argue.

"Oh, remember the time Charlotte wanted to go to church? You got so bored you began to argue with the priest."

"I wanted answers."

"You asked him why he believed in a book that could be just another work of fiction," Emily replies.

"It's a valid question."

"Babe, you insinuated he was brainwashed."

"Again, a valid theory."

"And there's a reason you don't have a television," Emily murmurs.

"Because I have more important things to be doing and it's a distraction. I watch movies with you guys."

"Yeah, but we don't exactly sit in silence."

I grab my T-shirt and pull it over my head. "I don't even know why we are talking about this. I can sit through a dinner. It's not a big deal."

But as I slide on some joggers, I have to wonder how true that is. It's not that I get bored easily, but I prefer to have my mind stimulated. I prefer keeping busy, which is why I work three jobs and attend school full-time.

Sitting through a dinner will be a breeze for me. It's about time I slow down a little.

Maybe.

And it's not like the evening will be boring. I'll be there, and I'm fucking awesome.

We're going to have a great time.

7

RIVER

Every Monday morning, I wake up and remind myself it's a new week, a fresh start to fix the previous week's mistakes. It's a time to reflect, to organise, and prepare for the week ahead.

It's also nicknamed Meeting Monday because it's the day I'm mostly stuck inside doing all the boring stuff. Since I began the whiskey brand, I've been renting an entire floor of offices in a high-rise building for me and my team. It beats working in my home office, where Colin and the others can corner me at every turn. It's a place I can work in peace, without interruption, and somewhere my training team and manager don't have access to. They have to be given permission, and since I have a great team working on the whiskey brand, I'm pre-warned and given the option to lie and tell people I'm not in.

This Monday, however, I turned things around between meetings, so tomorrow evening I'm free for my date. The photoshoot for the new sports brand I'm endorsing is now today, and they didn't mind the last-minute rescheduling. The only downside to moving things around is we are shooting at my home, but my date with Cinderella—Candy, they called her at Tease—is worth a few distractions.

My training for the morning is over, and freshly showered and dressed, I step into the garden and take a seat under the canopy by the pool.

I reach for my phone, wanting to read over the messages between me and Cinderella once more. Even apart, she has my full attention. I've not been able to stop thinking about her since I left Tease Friday night. I'd like to say it's normal for me to obsess like this over a chick, but it's not. This is the first woman in a long time that has captured my attention. And for a man who loves sex and has used countless women to get off, it means something. Or at least, it means something to me. When I decided to give up the women, sex, and drink last year, it made me realise why I filled my time with relationships that were never going to go anywhere. The one-night stands, the friends with benefits, they were like a plaster covering what the real issue was.

I'm lonely.

I have everything I ever wanted out of this career. Growing up with a mum on benefits, who drank and had abusive boyfriends, one after the other, I just wanted to get out of that life. She wasn't like other mums. She didn't make the best of what was handed to her. She didn't make it a home or even put me first. And the trouble I got into to rebel against the life I lived, led me down the wrong path. Being a professional fighter, having all this money, I thought it was what I wanted. I thought a nice pad, money in my pocket, food at my disposal, and clothes that fitted, I'd be living the good life. But they are just material things. What I miss is having someone to spend the holidays with, to celebrate a birthday or celebrate achievements with. People I'm not paying. I want a life, and for some reason, when I laid eyes on her at the charity fight, all of that flashed before me. I wanted to know her story, hear her voice, see her smile.

I went in the private booth to surprise her, to see if that night at the charity event was a dream or a figment of my imagination. I wanted to see if those feelings weren't a fluke, and I did really feel them.

And I did. She took my breath away all over again.

I thought for sure she'd ask me what I was doing there, but she didn't say anything. She knew who I was. It was in her expression, in the way she tried to duck her head to keep me from meeting those hazel eyes.

And then she danced, and the breath got trapped in my lungs.

I couldn't keep my eyes off her the entire time. She was gorgeous, elegant in the way she moved, and she had me hard as a fucking rock. The sensual way she rolled her hips, and the way the tips of her fingers glided over her bare flesh… She knew how to work a man into a frenzy. But it wasn't in a sleazy way. The last time I went to a strip club, I felt uncomfortable. The advances had been over the top, and honestly, the entire time I was there, I had to wonder what happened to these girls for them to degrade themselves like that.

Tease is different. It isn't creepy, and every girl looks like they're having as much fun as the punters.

Back to the messages, I scroll to the Saturday evening.

> River: I'm not good with the whole waiting for someone to text me. I was going to message you sooner, but it occurred to me after we spoke that you were most likely coming off a shift and were going home to sleep. I didn't want to chance waking you up. Hope you got some rest. And thanks; the opponents are good this year, so I'm gonna need all the luck I can get.

> Cinderella: I sleep like the dead. Nothing would have woken me up. I'm just grabbing some food before I have to start all over again. Hope you got some rest after your workout.

> River: I'm sorry if I surprised you last night or made you feel uncomfortable. And I know you probably won't believe me, but I need you to know, I didn't go into the private booth for a dance, I swear. You walked in, and I couldn't take my eyes off you, and well, you know the rest. I don't want you to think I'm a creeper.

> Cinderella: You certainly surprised me, but it takes a lot to make me feel uncomfortable. What were you doing there?

> River: I had a business meeting with Cole Connor. And to celebrate, me and my colleagues reserved the VIP section. You said you had assignments, does this mean you are at college?

> Cinderella: Ah, that makes sense. Dave did tell us someone big had reserved the VIP section. And I go to the local university. Are you surprised?

My lips twitch at the message. I think working as a stripper, she has dealt with judgement and snide remarks. She won't be getting any from me, so hopefully once she realises this, she'll relax a little and stop being defensive.

Who am I to judge how she makes her living, or how she gets by? It's a job, one she is good at and shouldn't be ashamed of. As I continue to read, I still can't get over the contradiction she is. Just when I think I have her figured her out, she surprises me.

> River: Let me guess, you are doing some sort of art performance?

> Cinderella: I actually work with dead people, but I guess me being a stripper would make you think I'm a dancer.

> River: Should I be scared? Dead people? What do you do? And no, you'd be wrong on that. It's the way you move. It reminds me of an act at a talent show I attended for a meet and greet. They had ballerinas performing, and I don't know why, but the way you hold yourself, and the way you move, it reminds me of them.

> Cinderella: Only if you do me wrong, LOL. I have a Masters in Applied Science, Biomedical Science, and a Doctoral in Pathology. Then you have a good eye. I did dance once upon a time, but it's something I didn't continue. I guess a part of me uses stripping to stay connected to it in some way. But that's heavy shit. I'd ask what you do, but I've seen you fight.

> River: I do a bunch of shit, but nothing near as important as what you do. I would never have guessed that's what you study, and I'm not being judgemental. You are the first person I've met who has ever told me they study that.

> Cinderella: It's okay. I get it a lot. You'll have to tell me more about what you do on our date.

> River: I'm looking forward to it. I really didn't think I'd ever see you again.

> Cinderella: I'm unforgettable so that's understandable. But then again, I didn't think I'd be seeing your face again either. If it wasn't for my friend, I would have thought I drank too much and imagined you. LOL.

> River: Yeah, you really are. And you didn't. I'm here. And looking forward to our date.

The doorbell rings, so I scroll to the bottom of our messages, quickly typing out:

> River: Good morning, beautiful. Thought I'd message you and remind you to get your morning coffee.

Getting up, I head inside and through my kitchen. I can cook, but this kitchen is wasted on me. With a marble island, stainless steel appliances, and utensils I have no idea how to use, it doesn't get used to its potential. I make my way down the hallway, ignoring the framed pictures of my victories. I still find it weird having pictures of myself hanging on the wall. I asked the designer not to, but Colin had them put them up and has used it as a gallery to schmooze potential sponsors.

Reaching the front of the house, I immediately spot the squad running today's shoot through the partial pieces of glass on the door.

I've worked with Fletcher for a few years now. He oversees the entire department that consists of design, merchandise and buying, stylists, photography, graphic and design, art direction, PR marketing, and digital and social media. He basically makes sure everyone is where they are supposed to be, and everything runs on time.

Allie, who runs the PR marketing, digital and social media, normally only stays to shoot some promos to give people sneak peeks. We first met at a red carpet. Her husband, Mel, is a movie producer and came to watch one of my fights. He came backstage, offering me some tickets. I went, and although I wouldn't say we are best friends, I have been over to their house a few times for dinner. They're a great couple and have a two-year-old at home.

And today, the stylists and photographers are the same squad I worked with last time. I've worked with a lot of stylists and photographers over the years, but this team is the best. One, they are more direct with what they want, and two, they don't have me holding up some random prop or getting me to pull stupid faces. I find them easier to work with. The only downside is the vice stylist, Larissa. I slept with her once, and ever since, she's been clingy as fuck. She touched my dick during a fitting once, and even came into my dressing room with nothing on under her coat.

I pull open the door, greeting them with a smile. "Morning, guys, come in."

Fletcher steps inside first and immediately starts directing people to the garden. Allie smiles warmly at me. "We're glad you picked today. It's going to be rain and cloudy tomorrow, and he was already fretting about lighting since you know he loves to have natural light."

"Well, the sun is out this morning. I'm glad it hasn't messed you around."

"Never. Do you know how many others have let us down in the past? Loads. We had a shoot with the reality stars of that new dating show, and, oh my God, you wouldn't believe how long it took us just to get them ready for the shoot."

I grin as we move through the house. "I can believe it. I met a few at last year's charity event."

"Anyway, what plans do you have tomorrow? Please don't tell me that manager of yours has you doing something else?"

"No, I actually have a date."

Allie stops with her arm covering the door, blocking us from going outside. "You have a date?"

"Who has a date?" Larissa asks, popping up behind us.

Allie's eyes widen. She's aware Larissa and I slept together, and once, even revealed Larissa has posters of me up in her office. I thought it was a joke, but after getting to know Larissa more, I'm wondering if Allie was telling the truth.

"River," Allie reluctantly replies.

Larissa huffs. "You can't call a one-night stand a date. Dating requires going out somewhere."

"We are," I answer, before I can think better of it.

She forces out a laugh. "You said you wasn't ready for a relationship. Has that changed?"

Shit!

"Larissa, why don't you get the clothes ready for River. We don't want to delay Fletcher. He has another shoot this evening," Allie warns her.

Larissa's violet eyes water. "Call me if you ever change your mind. You know I'll do anything for you. We have a great connection."

"Larissa," Allie snaps, giving her a pointed look.

I rub my hand over the back of my neck. "I'm sorry. I really put my foot in it there."

"The girl is a hopeless romantic. Before you, she fell in love with the guy who brought her pizza. She thought because he kept delivering it to her, it meant he wanted to go out with her."

"She's crazy."

"She's Larissa," she replies. "I'll meet you outside. Shelby is bringing in refreshments and food."

I nod as my phone beeps with a message. I pull it out, a smile lighting up my face.

Cinderella: My coffee goddess has already caffeinated me up for the morning. You are in luck. Have you started the shoot you mentioned?

River: Everyone just arrived, but I'm a little worried for my safety.

Cinderella: Do tell…

River: You might not like me after.

Cinderella: If you are going to tell me you've got a bullet stuck up your anus, then I'm your girl. You really should get to the hospital.

River: LOL. No, nothing like that, and I'm afraid to ask why you seem so calm about it.

Cinderella: There's no point dwelling on the past. Why are you worried for your safety, because I'm gonna tell you now, I can hold my own. If you don't stand a chance, then you are shit out of luck with me.

River: You are one crazy woman.

Cinderella: Even crazier if you don't tell me. The suspense is killing me.

River: And you won't cancel our date if it's about a girl I once, um, fucked?

Cinderella: You didn't know me then, so why would I? It's not like you're doing it now. That would be stupid. For you. I work with dead bodies, remember; I know how to cover up your death.

Laughter spills out of me as I read over her message.

River: First, how do I get a girl to stop liking me?

Cinderella: Okay, now I have to know. What's going on?

River: A girl I once fucked is acting weird. I think there were warning signs, but I just ignored them. She happens to be one of the stylists here today and she heard me telling Allie, the PR manager and friend, about you. Now I'm worried LOL.

Cinderella: What signs?

River: She has posters of me in her office. Or so Allie said. She could be messing with me, but for some reason, I have a feeling she isn't.

Cinderella: And? I had a bunch of Ryan Gosling for years.

River: She's previously turned up wearing nothing under a coat.

Cinderella: Wait! Were you an item?

River: No. I told her it was a one-time thing.

Cinderella: Then a little desperate but not enough to say she's obsessed over you.

River: At the clothing launch last year, they put my body onto a cake. She licked my cake dick whilst staring at me.

Cinderella: I need to meet this girl.

River: Why? Are you going to scare her away from me?

Cinderella: No, I'm going to give her a reality check, so she stops embarrassing us girls. But to answer your question: if she is obsessed, don't give her attention. It will only make it worse. Trust me.

River: How do you know this?

Cinderella: Because I met Ryan Gosling at an event I attended, and my stalking skills have no limits. I camped outside his hotel for two nights. It turned out, he wasn't even there.

"River, I need you to put these on," Maggie, another stylist, orders, handing me some clothes.

"I'll be five minutes," I reply.

River: I have to go. But thanks for the pep talk. Hopefully when we are doing the swimwear, she won't try to grab my dick again.

Cinderella: Do you have a whistle?

River: No, but I have a party horn left over from a New Year's party in the garage.

Cinderella: If she touches you, blow on it and make a scene. She won't do it again.

River: I'll keep that in mind. Speak to you later.

Cinderella: Later, handsome.

Allie walks back in and snatches the clothes from my arms. "Stop grinning like a freak and put these ones on instead," she orders.

"Bossy."

"Move it before I send Larissa in to dress you."

I take the clothes and rush down the hall to my bedroom, unable to keep the smile from my face. I hope Cinderella is as good as I've imagined. She's funny, smart, and gorgeous. It would be a damn shame if tomorrow goes bad.

Because after three days of exchanging messages, I feel like we already know each other. But it's not enough. I need to see her, touch her, and smell the sweet perfume she wears.

Now I just need to get through today and tomorrow without caving and asking her to meet up sooner.

8

RIVER

After twenty wardrobe changes, eight scenic changes, and a lot of hair and makeup, today's shoot is finally over.

The last of the team are packing up their cars, ready to leave, which gives me enough time to make it to tonight's training session with Drew.

Allie stands at my side, watching Larissa. She's sitting in the back of Fletcher's car, staring right at us, her expression downcast.

"I worry about that girl. I know she's harmless, but she was unprofessional today. Don't be surprised if Fletcher doesn't give her a written warning or even fires her. He has every right to do that."

Earlier, to wash off some of the oil, I went and showered between sets. Larissa, still harbouring feelings about my date, snuck into the bathroom. We still aren't sure how long she watched me in there. By the time I got out, she was sat on the vanity, her legs spread.

She attempted to talk me into going out with her and did everything she could to try it on with me. I pushed her away and said things in the heat of the moment. She took me off guard, and a few of the others overheard the ruckus and came to investigate. In that moment, with five people's eyes glaring at her, I couldn't help but feel a little sorry for her. She seems lost, and ever since, hasn't been able to muster a word. I think if Fletcher wasn't her ride, he would have asked her to leave hours ago.

"Don't. This is my fault. I got drunk and slept with her. I knew better than to mix pleasure with business, but I was too goddamn selfish back then to care. I guess Karma really does come around."

"You've come a long way, River, so don't take on all the blame. She knows better than to get mixed up with clients too, but she did it anyway. It takes two, so don't you dare shoulder all the blame," she argues, before taking a breath. "I've watched people come and go in this business. The fame gets to them, and when they hit the drink, partying all the time, it's very rare they come back from it. They start chasing other highs, and before you know it, an addict is born. Their career, at that point, is rarely salvageable. You didn't get to that point. You stopped as soon as you realised it was getting too much. You saw what most people don't; that it's all glass mirrors. Every party is the same. It's a popularity contest and you were just another pawn. You've made mistakes, but we all have. You just learned by yours. I've watched you become a man over the years, and I know we aren't related, and this will probably not mean anything, but I'm proud of you. That girl tomorrow is lucky to have you."

I'm stunned speechless for a moment. I didn't realise. I guess a part of me always thought she saw me like everyone else.

I clear my throat. "Thank you."

"You're welcome," she replies softly.

"If she loses her job, I'll never forgive myself. I should have made it clearer from the beginning," I admit, rubbing the back of my neck. "And I hope you're right about my date. I don't want to mess this up. When you meet her, you'll understand why."

"You couldn't have been any clearer with Larissa. She knew from the beginning what it meant so it's not your fault she isn't registering it. I'm just really sorry it happened."

I nudge her shoulder playfully with my arm. "Is that why you stuck around?"

She chuckles but doesn't conceal the truth. "Yeah. I can upload the content later. I just feel awful about it all. She's been acting strange for weeks now. I should have kept a better eye on her."

"What do you mean?"

She sighs and turns until her back is to the car, and I'm sure it's so no one can read her lips. "I heard her telling people she's dating you. And after the last shoot, we noticed one of the tops went missing. It could have gotten lost during transit, but the way she rushed out of there... It made me think it was her."

"We're leaving," Fletcher announces, and Allie quickly steps up to my side, forcing a bright smile. "Are you coming, Allie?"

"I'll see you back at the office," she tells him. "I just need five minutes."

He turns to me, his expression apologetic. "I really am sorry about today. It should never have happened. Rest assured, I'll be talking to Larissa when we get back to the office. I'll have to take it up with the board first, but she'll be fired."

"Please don't do that for me. I know what she did is out there, and I know that had it been the opposite way around, things would have gone a lot differently, but we've all made mistakes. Larissa will get over this obsession in time. She's good at her job. So please, if you're firing her for my benefit, don't."

His brows pinch together, as if he's thinking about it. "I can't make any promises, but at the very least, I'll still write her up for today. Again, I'm really sorry."

"It's fine," I promise.

He jerks his chin in reply before turning his attention on Allie. "I'll see you at the office."

We wait for them to leave before dropping down on the step, looking out at the scenery.

"That could have gone worse," she muses.

My lips tug up into a grin. "Yeah, that's for sure."

"So, this girl... What's with the mystery? What's her name?"

"I don't know."

Her lips pucker. "You don't know?" she deadpans.

I grin wider. "It's not as dodgy as it sounds. Remember I asked you about the girl at the charity event last year?"

"The redhead who started the conga line?" she asks excitedly. "Because she is gorgeous and so my kind of person. I think I fell in love with her."

"No," I chuckle. "But I'll let Charlotte know you said that."

"Oh my god, the girl who told you that if you wanted to know her name, you'd have to find her?"

"Yep. The one and only."

"Good for you, buddy," she cheers. "How the hell did you find her?"

I bite my lip to stop myself from blurting it out. I don't think she'll judge her, but I don't want to take any chances. I respect her opinion, but without all the facts, she'll think the worst.

"Please don't tell me it's an online date thingy," she muses.

"No. Nothing like that. She's different, so before I tell you anything more, I want you to meet her first before making a judgement."

"Oh, sounds interesting," she jokes, but then turns serious. "Just make sure it's you she wants and not this life. I know you hate me bringing Marlene up, but all that girl ever wanted was *the life*. She fucked up big time with Dean. And I know he's bringing in money, but he isn't you. I've seen him a few times and he's with a different girl every single time. I don't want you to find another Marlene."

"Marlene made her bed, now she can lie in it. This girl, she's different. I can't explain it, but she is. And for once, I'm not thinking with my dick—although, she's very easy on the eyes."

"Then I can't wait to meet her," she tells me, and leans over, kissing me on the cheek. "I do need to get back though."

I stand, helping her up. "Thanks for staying and for having a word with Larissa. I meant what I said: please don't let them fire her because of me."

"I can't make any promises. It's not the first time she's messed up. If she wasn't so damn good at her job, I think they would have fired her years ago."

"Still…" I shrug. "And thank you for always looking out for me. I don't think I've told you before, but you and Mel, your friendship, it means a great deal."

She claps with a big smile on her face. "I've been waiting for the day you admit we are friends."

"So you can tell all your friends and family?" I tease.

She punches me in the shoulder. "No. Because no one should be alone in this world. We've always felt like you keep us at arm's length, too afraid to get close, so it's good to hear."

I rub the back of my neck, a little uncomfortable. "Well, fuck, now I feel like shit."

"Don't. Big things are happening for you. I can feel it."

The sound of an engine pulls my attention. I make my way down the third step and onto the gravel.

Living away from civilisation has its perks. My hillside bungalow is enough to keep me out of the limelight and allows me to live comfortably. And since I own the land, photographers and reporters aren't allowed on here unless they want to be charged with trespassing. I don't have to risk them snapping a photo of me whilst I'm in my pool or undressed. The downside is that there's no gate to keep visitors out.

"Fucking hell," I groan when I spot Colin's black Mercedes driving up to the house. "I thought I had dodged that bullet today."

Allie grabs her bag from the unit behind the door before meeting me at the bottom of the steps. "I'm saying this as a friend; I know you think you owe him a lot, but he wouldn't be where he is without you."

I duck my head, glancing down at her. "What are you saying?"

"I'm warning you to be careful. Mel doesn't like him, and I trust his instincts. After years of working with celebrities and their managers, he knows what to look out for. And that guy is a shark, only out for himself. I've heard him tell you you'd be nothing without him, but he's wrong. He's nothing without you," she tells me, her tone no longer playful and teasing. "I know it's not public knowledge, but word gets around, and there are whispers that you are thinking of leaving the fighting world."

"How did you hear that?" I ask, pulling my eyes off the car.

"It doesn't matter. But a man like that, he'll do anything to keep living this kind of life. You're his meal ticket to the rich and famous. Just be careful not to turn your back on him," she warns.

"Please don't tell anyone about those whispers," I ask her, keeping my voice low.

"I won't. But you should know, Mel's offer to train movie stars in action roles is still available. You can do whatever you want in this life. You don't need people like that," she tells me, then pastes on a smile as the car gets nearer. "I'll see you soon. Don't forget to bring the girl around for dinner one night."

"I won't," I reply, left reeling over her words. As I watch Colin slide out of his car, his expression stormy, I have to wonder if she's right.

Do I need to be careful of him? And I don't mean psychically—I could squash him like a bug and not break a sweat.

How much do I really know him? Because beyond our business exchanges, I've never really been invited into his life. I've been to parties he throws, but that's only because he needs me there to show me off. Anything personal like his family, or friends, I'm left in the dark. But he knows things about me. Things I don't want getting out. Allie doesn't know it, but Colin has the power to destroy my career, the life I've built, and the connections I've made.

And until she just pointed it out, I didn't even realise. I always thought he had my back. Maybe I should have been watching my own.

Everyone else on my team, I've gotten to know. I've bought birthday gifts for their kids, signed merchandise for their family, and even did a surprise meet and greet at one of their sons' birthdays.

"What are you playing at? Any changes to the schedule need to go through me," he barks as he reaches me.

I hold my hands up. "It was a last-minute decision. And they didn't mind."

"That's not the point," he growls. "I should have been informed."

"I don't appreciate you coming here and yelling at me, so I suggest you take a step back," I growl, and he has the sense to heed my warning. "I didn't see the harm in moving it. You don't stay at these things anyway."

"No, but I wanted to talk to Fletcher about next season's clothing. I thought we could—"

"I'm going to stop you there. I've already told you; I don't think I'll be fighting next year. They aren't going to want to endorse a retired fighter."

His jaw clenches as sweat drips down his temples. "You aren't serious. You love fighting."

"I did love fighting."

"You have commitments."

"That I'll fulfil before my contract runs out. It's not your decision."

"Yes, it is. As your manager, I'm telling you, this isn't going to happen. You're at the peak of your career. I won't let you throw away everything I've built."

My spine stiffens. "I know you are upset, Colin, so I'm going to let you off with throwing that in my face. I'm grateful for everything you've done, but don't forget, without me, you wouldn't be here either," I tell him, throwing Allie's words back at him.

He clenches his fists. "Since you rescheduled the shoot today, I've got a meet and greet lined up for you tomorrow evening."

"Then cancel. There's a reason I rescheduled. I need tomorrow evening free," I tell him, trying to remain calm.

"Is it to do with the upcoming fights?"

"No."

"Then it's not important. Whatever it is, you can reschedule," he orders, like he has every right to control every aspect of my life.

"No."

"What do you mean, no? You are doing it. I control your schedule and any changes should have been brought to me."

"I don't give a fuck. I'm taking someone out tomorrow and I'm not cancelling on her."

His lip curls. "For a girl? You are going to let down one of the most prestigious groups for a girl?"

"No, you'll be letting them down. I didn't agree to it, you did. Now, if you don't mind, I have to go train with Drew. I don't want to be late."

"I'm not going to have you disrespect me like this. I've done everything for you. I made you who you are. Without me, you'd be some low-life still serving his prison sentence. Without me, people would know about your mum, what she did, and where she is. The media would have a field day with that information."

"Are you threatening me?" I growl.

"No, merely stating the facts. But you do this, if you keep falling out of line, then everything will come out. I'll no longer be your manager to ensure it doesn't. And I don't want that for you. I think of you as a son. Now, I'll leave, and if you are going to train, do it with Cian at the new gym."

With that, he leaves, and I'm stuck, watching as he pulls off. It's all I can do to stop myself from going after him.

Because that was a threat.

One I should heed.

9

HARRIETT

Music plays in the background as Emily finishes putting my hair up into a sleek ponytail for my date tonight. She's always been the best of us with hair. We've encouraged her more than once to get into hairdressing. Her talent is wasted on just us.

Olivia is lounging on the grey pug sofa opposite my bed, flicking through a magazine that's probably months old. Gabby's on the bed, occupying Poppy with some colouring.

All of them are here to give me support, or at the very least, to make sure I look good enough to get laid tonight—like that's going to happen. I never give it up on the first night.

Gabby puts down her crayon, glancing at me through the mirror. "Tell me again why you won't dress up, 'cause it's your first date in, like, forever. Don't you want to make a good first impression?"

I swing around in my chair, arching an eyebrow at her. "Who do you take me for? I did make a good first impression. He found me, didn't he."

Olivia drops the magazine into her lap. "Yeah, but, dude, you're wearing leggings. I agree with Gabby."

Gabby grins. "Thanks."

Olivia arches an eyebrow. "Don't get used to it."

"And I made a great second impression. I mean, I couldn't have made a better one. I had on the sexiest outfit in the world."

"Exactly," Gabby points out, jabbing her finger in my direction. "You don't want him to think it was a fluke, do ya. You want to give a little more, not make him think he's been catfished."

"Are you saying I look ugly?"

Gabby covers Poppy's ears. "You look hot as fuck. I'd do ya," she admits, before dropping her hands. "But—"

Poppy, with her blonde locks, tilts her head up at Gabby. "Up."

Gabby lifts her up, settling her back down in her lap. "But I'm just saying, leggings… They're plain and you wear them all the time. You could make more of an effort."

"He told me to dress casual with comfy shoes I didn't mind getting dirty, and to make sure I'm warm."

"I think you look amazing. You could turn up wearing a black bag and you'd still look good," Emily replies as she sprays some hairspray on my hair.

"Thanks, Em," I reply, before sticking my tongue out at the others. Poppy copies with a giggle, blowing a raspberry. "Even Poppy agrees."

Olivia glances at her phone. "He should be here soon."

"And you guys need to leave. I'm not having you embarrass me when he arrives," I warn.

"Would we do that? Really?" Gabby asks, feigning hurt.

I arch an eyebrow at the nerve. "You all followed me on my last date wearing Halloween masks."

She grins. "That was such a good night."

"And we did you a favour. The guy was a dickhead," Olivia reminds me.

"Language in front of Poppy," Emily scolds.

"Sorry," Olivia grimaces. "Luckily she's not at the age where she copies everything you say."

"She will be soon enough. She's already growing too fast," she answers, and there's a sadness in her voice. I place a comforting hand over hers.

As I go to reply, my phone beeps with a message. I lean over and grab it from my dresser. "Oh my god, he's here. He's early."

"By five minutes," Gabby deadpans. "Not hours."

The doorbell rings, alerting us of his arrival. Olivia rolls off the sofa and crawls to the stairs. "I'll get it," she yells as she gets to her feet.

Gabby jumps off the bed, and before she can make it to the stairs, I race ahead, scared of what they'll do or say. It's too soon to scare him away with our crazy.

As we reach the bottom, I jump, landing on Olivia's back. She trips, and we both fall forward, landing on the sofa. "Don't you dare answer that door!"

"You crazy bitch, you could have killed me."

"Better than you scaring him off," I yell.

A fist starts banging on the door. "Hey, are you okay? Answer the door," River yells.

"Just a minute," I screech as Olivia rolls us off the sofa.

I grunt at the fall and let out a breath when Olivia leans into my face. "Let us meet him. It's not fair Gabby is the only one who has seen him."

"He's not dating you, he's dating me," I yell, pinning her to the floor. "And he won't want to go on this one if he meets you before getting to know me."

"Hey, we come as a group. Hoes before bros, remember."

"You'll scare him away," I argue. "Are you going to do as you're told?"

"Are you going to get off me?"

"You two really need to start acting your age," Gabby scolds. I lift my head and blow out a breath, ready to argue.

But standing next to Gabby, is River, smiling down at us. "I thought you were being attacked."

I loosen my hold on Olivia and duck my head. "This can't be happening."

I feel a touch on my hand, and I lift my gaze to his. He smirks and helps me to my feet. "Are you okay?"

"I swear, we're not crazy," I argue as I straighten my jacket.

"We really are," Olivia tells him as she gets to her feet. "Jesus, you really are hot."

"River, I swear, I don't know these girls," I lie.

Olivia punches me in the arm. "Bitch!"

"Okay, I know them, but I swear, this isn't the norm for us," I lie again.

Emily sits down with Poppy in her arms. "She's lying. They're always like this."

"So are you," we yell simultaneously.

She looks up at River. "It's nice to meet you. I'm Emily."

Olivia gives a wave. "I'm Olivia."

"I'm Gabby, the sane one."

Olivia snorts. "She's the worst of us all."

"And you?" River asks. A shiver runs down my spine at the heated look he gives me.

Olivia wraps her arm around my shoulders. "This is Harriett, and if you hurt her, we'll show you how crazy we can get."

I smack the palm of my hand to my forehead. "Not helping."

I feel the heat of his presence and lift my head. Standing in front of me, he holds his hand out. I take it, feeling all sorts of feelings as electricity passes between us.

"Harriett. I like it."

My name running off his tongue does all sorts to me. If the girls weren't standing so close, scrutinising every move we make, I'd probably kiss him.

Maybe.

"So, now you know my name," I tell him with a slight tease to my tone.

"But something tells me the mystery still isn't over," he replies with a rasp.

For a moment, we stay locked in each other's gazes, and a feeling, something I've never felt before, passes through me. It's strong; more than desire, more than lust. It's just more. And something I imagine not many people feel in their lifetime.

"Okay, this is getting *really* uncomfortable," Olivia announces, breaking the spell between us.

River clears his throat. "We should go before we're late."

"Late for what?" Emily asks.

He grins. "It's a surprise."

Gabby groans. "She hates surprises."

"No, I don't," I argue.

"Yes, you do. Remember the surprise party we threw for you a few years back? You broke Dave's nose."

"That wasn't a surprise, that was an ambush. And in my defence, I had been watching a horror movie with Charlotte. I was on edge and thought you were zombies ready to eat me."

"It's not that kind of surprise," he promises.

"Then we should get going," I reply, and turn to the girls. "Lock up behind you."

"Can we—"

"If my snacks are gone, I'm making you buy me more," I warn Olivia, and grab my bag from the side before leaving. I hope tonight will be a good night. As the door closes behind us, I turn to River. "Please forget everything you've seen and heard so far."

His grin is dirty and full of promise. "Never."

RIVER TAKES my hand as we trudge through the forest, leaving the car parked behind us. The only reason I'm not stressing is because it's parked with hundreds more. Which doesn't help since the last horror movie I watched started with them parking in a forest.

They all ended up dead, aside from the blonde.

And let's not forget the most recent murder happened in a woodland area.

"So, um, hiking? You didn't get my distaste for exercise when I messaged you before?" I ask, keeping it light so I don't come across as rude.

He chuckles as he twists his cap so the beak is at the back. Fuck, he could dress like a chav and I think I'd still be hot for him.

"We aren't hiking. I thought we'd be able to park closer, but I saw a sign saying the main car park was full. It shouldn't take us five minutes to get there," he promises.

"To where? My grave? Because I'm telling you now, I'm not going down without a fight. There's so much more I want to do, and I haven't bought my holiday home in Spain yet."

"I have a holiday home in Spain," he reveals in amusement.

"That doesn't comfort me. I just hinted you're going to murder me and instead of assuring me you aren't, that's what you have to say? You do realise there's a murderer on the loose?"

"Listen," he orders gently, hiding his laughter as I listen. "See, I'm not a murderer."

Until he ordered me to listen, all I heard was the sound of our voices and our shoes stepping on leaves and twigs. It reminded me too much of the gruesome horror we watched for Halloween last year, in which a group of people were trapped in the woods. Now, however, I can hear voices, *a lot* of voices, and faint music.

"What's going on? Did you throw me a party, because the girls weren't lying, I'm not good with surprises. I'd hate for you to get hurt this close to your fights."

Laughter spills out of him. "You really are nuts," he teases. "There's a fair, arcades, and an outdoor cinema up ahead, but the movie doesn't start until half eight. You said you have classes tomorrow, so I didn't want to do anything that rolled on late into the night. I'll have you back before midnight, Cinderella."

And there he goes again, showing me he isn't like the other guys I've dated before. None of them gave a shit that I worked my arse off twenty-four-seven. I had to work around their schedules and fit into their time. Because I don't take any shit, they were given a month to change. If they didn't, they were gone, and I never lost sleep over it. Not even with Eddie, who knew how to give a girl an orgasm.

We're only on date one and he's thought of everything.

"I *feel* like Cinderella," I muse as we step into the clearing. "This is amazing for a first date. Who gave you the idea?"

He pushes the cap back around to shade his face. "You did. I listened to everything you said in our messages. You told me you don't have a television because it's a distraction, but you never said it's because you don't like movies. You said you don't get time to do much in your free time, and the time you do get, you spend it with friends. So, I thought I'd do something for you to relax and have fun."

"Are you not scared about being noticed? It's packed here," I point out as we make our way up the bank to where the arcades and fair are.

"It's rare I get recognised in a setting like this. Unless there're some fans here. But even then, I can still go on my way unnoticed. It's not like I'm splashed on every newspaper and magazine. I'm just an ordinary guy, not some movie star with paparazzi following me around."

"See, now that's a lie. I did some digging on you after the club, and you're in the papers and magazines a lot. On one, it said you used to be a partier and ladies' man."

"You didn't look me up sooner?"

"I had to believe the universe would bring us together. If I went looking, it wouldn't have happened naturally."

He stops, then pulls me against his chest in a bold move. "I'm really glad I met you."

I dramatically flick my ponytail over my shoulder. "I know. People tell me that all the time."

"But I bet they don't see you like I see you."

"And how do you see me?" I flirt, fluttering my lashes.

"Like I found something rare and unique. You're not like any other person I've met, and I think that's why I can let my guard down with you," he admits, before dropping his head back. "And that sounds cheesy as fuck."

"No. I've been called a lot of things, but rare and unique aren't one of them," I share.

Three kids run past us, screaming with excitement. A mum is next, yelling their names. River chuckles as he takes my hand, and together, we continue up to where the fair is.

To fill in the silence, I ask, "What's the craziest thing you've been asked to do by a fan? And is it true women get your name tattooed on them?"

"Probably, but I'm not sure. And the craziest thing to happen is during the meet and greets. I get asked a lot to lift the guy's partner while he stands to the side, frowning for the picture."

I laugh. "No…"

"What about you? What crazy thing have you been asked to do at work?"

"Well, a guy paid me to talk to him in a baby voice and call him a naughty boy," I answer truthfully.

He chuckles, and the roughness of it makes me tingle in all the right places. "That's weird as fuck, but I meant at the hospital. You said you work with dead bodies."

"Oh. I had to dissect a penis once," I reveal. "I think that beats anything I've ever had to do."

He groans. "Yeah, I didn't need to know that."

I grin up at him. "Scared?"

"Terrified," he murmurs as we come to a stop near the game booths. "You really are a mystery."

My grin spreads. "Stick around and I might just let you be the one to figure me out."

"I plan to learn everything about you."

Once again, I'm locked under his spell. If I'm not careful, I might just get stuck there.

I'm better than this.

My father *raised* me better than this.

I'm a woman, hear me roar, and all that crap.

Being this woman, a woman lost for words, without a sassy comeback, isn't who I strive to be. It's new territory for me, and I'm not sure how I feel about it. I've turned into the girl I make fun of during a romantic movie. I'm the girl who swoons for a gorgeous man. I'm that girl.

Or at least, I am with River.

A booth to the side catches my attention and a thought comes to my head. "How good are you at losing?"

He arches in an eyebrow in question. "I rarely lose."

I put some space between us to gather myself. "Then prepare for me to pop that cherry. We are going to play darts."

He glances over his shoulder at the booth in question. "You're on, gorgeous. I hope you are wearing waterproof makeup 'cause you'll be crying when you lose."

I laugh, glad he isn't one of those guys who lets a girl win because they are female or because they want to make a good impression. He's all in. I see the competitive gleam in his eyes.

10

RIVER

I've gone through life mostly alone. I've kept friendships at arm's length, too afraid to let anyone get close. It's lonely at times, but it's better than the alternative. I'm too afraid of people finding out the truth about me, so I let my busy schedule be an excuse to not form true bonds.

There are people who say I brood a lot because I'm quiet, and if you can believe the headlines, I have a speech impediment. It's better to let people think you're those things than to let them know you're hiding something. There are snakes in this world, willing to strike at any given moment. Being kind of famous comes with a price. There's no privacy. The entire reason I went to great lengths to hide my past is so I could reinvent myself. I didn't want to be the fighter with a shady past. It would be all the papers wrote about during upcoming fights. I wanted people to talk about my skills, about the fight itself. I'm not the boy I once was, and I'm not the guy I was when I first started out. I've changed. Grown. And that's all that matters to me.

Drew is the only other person, aside from Colin, who knows where I come from and the secrets I've kept buried.

Being with Harriett tonight has opened parts of me I kept locked inside. I'm seeing the world through her eyes, and it's made me realise just how much I've missed out on. The last time I went to a fair, I was eight, and I spent the entire time watching other kids have fun. I watched adults buy their kids food. I watched them win prizes at the game booths. I was on the outside looking in, never able to join in.

And the last time I played games like this was when I got invited to a celebrity's carnival-themed party.

I never had fun though.

Not like this.

I pull my cap down a little more, shielding my face from the crowd forming around us. "Are you sure you don't want to admit defeat now?" I taunt.

Harriett wiggles her arse as she lines up her shot but pauses to look up at the guy waiting in anticipation inside the booth. "Mate, I hope you have tissues handy because I'm going to make him weep like a baby."

The guy grins at me. "She's so going to kick your arse."

"It's not over until it's over," I muse.

Silence falls amongst us, and in perfect form, Harriet lets go of the dart. I hold my breath as the dart soars through the air, towards the spinning wheel with red and yellow balloons tacked on. When it hits the red balloon perfectly, the crowd cheers. I reach for her and swing her up into my arms as I twirl us around. "Holy fuck, you did it."

"Did you ever doubt my skills?"

"Gorgeous, I play darts in my free time. I thought I had this, but I can see I got played."

She swipes a fake tear under her eye with a sniff. "Aw, you wound me."

"No, I don't," I state.

"No, you really don't," she chimes. "Your expression is priceless."

I grab the rainbow bear from the guy running the games booth and hand it to Harriett. "Let's get some food and grab a spot to watch the movie. Hopefully, you don't show me up on the way."

She laughs. "You really did think you were going to win. That's so sweet," she tells me, and it's almost patronising—in an amusing way.

"Has anyone ever told you, you gloat too much?" I tease.

"All the time," she jokes as we hit the burger stand. "I'll have the jumbo hot dog with onions and cheese sauce, a tray of chips, and a bottle of coke please."

"I'll have a water," I add, and take a twenty out of my wallet.

"Are you not eating?" she asks. "I thought we were ordering food, or do you have food in that bag? Oh shit, you have food in that bag."

"Relax, we are here for food. I'm training so I have steak, potatoes and veg ready made in a tub in my bag. And you said you love food, but just in case you didn't like anything, I brought a few other bits."

"Salads?"

"I've got a chicken one."

Her nose scrunches up. "I'll stick with my hot dog, but thank you."

I chuckle as I hand over the money and then grab her food. "It's fine. Come on, I heard they're playing the new Cruella movie."

She makes a small, squealing noise. "Are you pulling my leg?"

"No," I reply, fighting back laughter.

"I've been dying to see this. 101 Dalmatians was my favourite movie as a kid, so much so I drew dots on my nan's white Jack Russell."

"You did not?"

She nods. "Every time we visited."

"Is here, okay?" I ask. She nods and takes her food from me.

At the bottom of the hillside, a huge screen is hung up. I slide the strap of my bag over my shoulder and unzip it to pull out a picnic blanket and a few throws the house cleaner advised me to bring.

"You thought of everything," she muses.

The music behind us is muted just in time for the ads to start. "Not everything. I should have brought chairs."

She waves me off. "Too much to carry. This is perfect," she tells me, before digging into her hot dog.

I drop down next to her on the blanket. "Good."

Girls I've been around in the past never ate like this in front of me. She has cheese and ketchup smudged on her upper lip, and instead of running to the bathroom crying over it, she simply picks up a tissue and wipes it away. It's cute, and kind of endearing. The more time we spend together, the more I feel like me again. I don't have to play a part or watch my back. I can just be me.

"You are missing out. This tastes so good," she tells me between mouthfuls.

I laugh when she takes another large bite. "I can see."

For a few minutes we eat in silence, both watching the people milling around us. "As first dates go, this is pretty amazing," she tells me, and I notice her rub her arm.

"Come here," I order, patting the space between my legs.

She complies and sits between my legs. I pull the two throw blankets over her, and she sits back against my chest.

"Thank you."

"You're welcome," I breathe out. Her perfume is intoxicating. God, she smells so fucking good. "I should have brought thicker blankets, but I wasn't sure if I'd get them in my bag."

"Honestly, I'm good now," she murmurs, and turns until she can see me. "Thank you for bringing me here. You surprised me. I don't think I've ever been on a date like this before."

"I wanted to do something fun but still have a chance to talk to you. Going for a meal seemed too boring, and something you do often with your friends. At the cinema, I wouldn't have had time to speak to you. And I wanted you to relax, since you have school tomorrow."

"I only have a few weeks left for this term, and I'm not going to lie, I'm going to enjoy the short break."

"Do you not pick up extra shifts at the hospital?"

She shakes her head. "I'm on set hours right now, but once next term starts, I'll be mostly at the hospital. I'm doing a five-year specialist training programme."

"How do you function with the late nights at the club?"

"I think my body is used to it now. It's weird on the weekends we have off. At the beginning, I'd stir all night, too wired to sleep, but now, me and the girls always do something," she explains. "What about you? Do you not get hungry?"

"Not really. When I'm training, I commit myself to it. I'm not saying it's as easy as that, but I work hard for it."

"Is fighting something you always wanted to do?"

"Not really," I answer, then divert the line of questioning. "You said you used to dance. What's the story there?"

She gauges my reaction, and I know she wants to ask more. "Alright, simple answer, but I'll let you have it because you're cute."

I duck my head a little. "I just don't like talking about my past."

"Now who's being mysterious," she muses. "But it's fine. Maybe in time you'll trust me enough to tell me."

"Yeah, maybe."

"And to answer your question, I used to dance in recitals. It's something me and Mum shared together. She loved to dance, too, but never got to make a career out of it. When I showed an interest, she did everything to support me. She took me to recitals, lessons, competitions, and shows. She was my biggest supporter."

"Was?"

"She died of cancer when I was younger. I didn't continue with dance, even though my dad stepped in and did all he could to try and get me to love it again. But it wasn't the same without her."

"I'm sorry about your mum. That must have been really hard for you."

"It was, but she didn't want me to be sad. She used to tell me there's an upside to having cancer: getting to say goodbye to me and my dad. It didn't matter how long we had, or the goodbyes we got say, we were never prepared."

"Is your mum the reason you work at the hospital?"

"A little. I don't think I could be a doctor. Seeing sick patients, dealing with grieving families, it would bring up too many emotions. But when she got sick, I researched every treatment I could, and I guess I fell in love with medicine."

"So, dead people?"

"It's too much to explain, and I swear, it's not as creepy as people think. I get to give families closure. And the tests we run might one day save a life."

"What about stripping? What made you get into that?"

"During the last few months of my mum being sick, they took some equity out on the house to help with the bills. After she died, my dad went back to work and got into an accident. He used my mum's life insurance to pay back the equity, so he didn't have to worry about losing the house. He lives off his disability allowance now, but it was tight for him. He never said it, but I know university was something he couldn't afford. I watched them get that house and everything they have by working their arses off. I saw what debt and the rise of living costs did to them. I didn't want to do that. My mum had been a teacher before they closed all the middle schools in 2015. She got laid off, and the only job she could get after was a teaching assistant. The pay wasn't good, and with student loans, a mortgage, and a kid, they struggled to get by. But they did. I wanted to be prepared. I don't want a mountain of debt after I leave school."

"Fuck, that's a lot. So that's why you strip?"

"No. I worked every goddamn night and any day I had free. When I moved here four years ago, the adrenaline, working all night and day, it caught up to me. So when Dad came to visit me, I had a breakdown. I was exhausted, and he told me something had to give. He was going to sell his home, a home he shared with my mum, a place I grew up, but I couldn't let him do that. I told him I'd start working weekends only after I took a break."

"Babe, no job is worth killing yourself over."

"I know. But you don't understand. I grew up with the best life. I had parents who gave me everything I ever needed. But I saw the toll it took on them. They bent over backwards to give me the things I needed. I wanted to make them proud."

"I bet you already have," I tell her, and brush her ponytail over her shoulder.

"Until he finds out where I work. He'll probably hate me, or worse, be disappointed in me. When I started looking for a new job, Tease just stood out to me. I don't know what it was, but something inside of me was compelled to apply. So, I did. And although it was hard at the beginning, it's one of the best decisions I ever made. I've made friends for life there. I made a family. And when Monday rolls around, I'm not exhausted. I don't have to work myself into the ground or worry about bills."

Hearing her story has made an impact. What she's been through, how she's survived, I have a deep reverence for her. But instead of feeling good about it, it only makes me feel worse. It highlights another thing I failed at. Growing up the way I did, I acted like the world owed me. I had been selfish and so fucking angry. Yet Harriett managed to make something good from all the shit in her life. She turned it around and carried on living.

Yet it took Drew to keep knocking me on my arse for me to open up. I yelled, screamed, and fought until I could no longer stand. And although at that time it was a safe place, how I did it before, wasn't.

He jump-started my career, Colin made it soar, and I worked my arse off to make sure I didn't let any of them down.

She doesn't know it, but she's the strongest person I know. I can knock a grown man out, but her strength, it comes from within, and that's pretty damn incredible.

"I've lost you," she murmurs, looking a little disappointed.

I tug her closer and feel her shiver against me. "You haven't. I, um, I didn't have the best upbringing. It just made me think about things. I like that you haven't let any of it jade you. Losing your mum, and working at a strip club, it didn't change who you are."

"How do you know it hasn't?"

I run my hand around to the back of her neck. "Because you made something beautiful. Your mum's death was hard, and to keep her memory, you went into medicine. You strip so your dad doesn't lose his house and you don't go into debt. And you made friends and a family. I admire you for it. And you can tell me I'm wrong, but I don't think I am."

She scrutinises me for a moment. "You really don't have a problem with me being a stripper?"

"No. Why would I?"

"Well, from experience, men either think I'm scum or they treat me like I walked into a porn set and they've got free rein to treat me like shit."

"I'm not like most guys," I tell her, running my hand over her shoulder. "And those men are dickheads."

"I know I'm getting ahead of myself, but I'm a planner. I like things organised. It's who I am," she admits. "But down the line, you'll have a problem with it. I need you to know, if you can't take me as I am, then don't ask me out for a second date. I'm not quitting, not yet anyway."

"You aren't getting ahead. I want to see where this goes. And I'll never tell you what to do. I had…" I trail off, wondering if telling her is the right thing.

"You had…?" she pushes.

"My mum dated a lot after my dad, um, *left*. I had to listen to them tell her what she could and couldn't do. I watched her lose more of herself after each man. I won't do that to you. To anyone."

"That sucks. I'm sorry."

"She never learned. She had a chance not long after my dad left to make a fresh start. The guy she met was a good guy, with a great job, but he was too nice for her."

"It sounds like she was punishing herself over something."

"Maybe," I reply, lost in thought.

My mum had a lot of problems. Most of them her own doing. She spent years fighting with my dad. They yelled and hit each other so much it became the norm for me.

Harriett might be right, but any memory I have of my mum… she had been too selfish. I can't think of anything she might have done to want to punish herself.

"Alright, enough with the heavy shit. Let's watch Cruella kick some arse."

I tuck her against my chest and lift my knees up on either side of her. "Alright, boss."

And whilst she's watching the movie, I'm watching her, growing more enthralled with every laugh, smile, and frown.

11

HARRIETT

Stepping off the ride, I can't help but feel exhilarated. Being here, I feel like a child again. The stomach turning, the wind blowing in my face, and that rawness in the back of my throat from screaming, brings back happy memories. It's an incredible feeling, one I know I'll be smiling about in the days to come.

"That was awesome," I yell, letting out a laugh. "God, I feel so good."

Looking a little green, River takes out a bottle of water from his backpack. "I think I'm gonna be sick."

"Not a fan of fair rides?"

He takes my hand without hesitation, which I happen to like. Whether it's the bold move, the sweet gesture, or just the feel of his touch, I don't know. It makes me feel giddy inside, which is a foreign concept for me. He doesn't shy away from affection. It's not just in the small touches, but in the way he looks at me, like I hang the stars and moon or something.

"Until tonight, I've never actually been on one?"

Okay, that's kind of sad. *Really sad*.

"Why?"

He shrugs, and I can see the question has made him uncomfortable. "I didn't have a lot growing up. This isn't something I was blessed to have."

He talks to me like I'm the mystery, but he's the mystery; one I'm having fun trying to figure out. My mum used to tell me I should become a detective. My brain was always looking for answers or clues. I need explanations, reasons, causes. It's why I love medicine so much. It keeps my mind occupied.

"Well, get used to it because I plan on taking you to a theme park one day. You just need to build up the stomach. My mum used to tell me life is a funfair. We go through the fun bit, go on rollercoasters, and then ride the ghost train. Life is made for living, and if this is still not your thing, we can ride a different train."

His lips press together, and he does this sexy thing with his jaw, his eyes molten as he watches me.

He tugs me close, cupping my jawline. "You, Harriett Sparks, are a remarkable woman."

I wrap my arms around him. "And you, River Knight, are making me regret telling you my full name."

He grins. "You've got an awesome name."

I sniff. "I know, but when you say my full name, I'm supposed to run like I would as a kid when my mum or dad used it. But you… You don't make me want to run away."

Heat engulfs me, and my heart skips a beat as he leans in.

"I'm going to kiss you," he rasps, his lips only a breath away.

My stomach flutters. "I'm not going to say no," I whisper.

"Excuse me, Rampage," a child's voice calls, breaking the spell between us.

River's eyes clench shut. "Later."

"I'll hold you to it," I tell him, before stepping back to clear my throat.

"Hey, little man," River greets.

A little boy about six or seven is standing next to us. A harassed looking woman rushes over, a man following, wonderstruck, behind her.

"Can I have a photo with you?" the little boy asks.

The mum places her hand on the boy's shoulder. "I'm so sorry. We told him not to disturb you."

"Please," the boy pleads, pressing his hands together.

The guy, who I'm assuming is the dad, steps forward, holding his hand out to River. "It's really you. Milo said it was, but I couldn't be sure. It's good to meet you, man."

River shakes his hand then grins down at the boy. "I'll take a picture with you."

Milo fist pumps the air. "This is so cool. Everyone will want to be my friend at school now."

"Do you have a phone, Mum?"

Pulling herself out of a daze, his mum nods. River kneels down, and the mum snaps a few photos.

Seeing the dad is still wonderstruck, I step closer. "Let me take one of all of you," I offer, and take her phone.

My lips pull up into a smile as River easily swings the little boy into his arms. The parents stand on either side of him. The mum looks like she wants to pass out, and the dad looks like he's met his idol and is about to do some cartwheels.

"Thank you so much. He accidentally watched one of your fights that Dill recorded and has been obsessed with you ever since. He even has one of your doll figures."

"Yeah, it's really cool of you to do this, man. Looking forward to the next fight."

"He stays up and watches them all," the mum adds, rolling her eyes. "We'll let you get back to your night."

"It's lovely meet you all," he tells them and holds his fist out to the kid. "Keep it real, little man."

"And pummel that dude into the ground," Milo yells, and people walking past begin to stare. Whispers start, and it's eerie, like it's been passed along. Before we know it, people are taking photos. I move closer to River, and he immediately takes my hand.

The mum takes Milo's hand when thunder crackles above us. "Come on, Milo."

"Knock him out," Milo screams, shaking his fist as his mum pulls him away. "Bam, bam, bam."

"Come on, let's go," he tells me, and slides his cap back on. We weave through the crowd, and I keep my head down as people continue to hold their phones up to either take photos or record.

The heavens open and our walk turns into a sprint. I laugh as we hit the path to the forest that leads to the car park.

"Oh my god," I cry, unable to keep the smile from my face. "I'm gonna break my neck."

He stops suddenly and quickly sweeps me up into his arms. My legs grip his waist, and my arms go around his neck.

"Sorry," he calls out as the rain falls harder.

"Don't be," I whisper, and hold him tighter, shielding my face from the rain.

I've been on so many dates, but this has to be, by far, the best one. There's been no first date awkwardness or forced conversations between us. Everything has come easy, like we're long-time friends reconnecting. We've laughed, we've talked, and the connection between us has only burned brighter. It wasn't a fluke or lack of sex. It was him.

And having a connection is so important to me. We live in a world of algorithms, hashtags, and social media. So when I capture moments like this, that connection, the contact, I treasure it. It's not something I'll post on social media, or hashtag it for the world to see. It's for us, and for us only.

We reach the car park, and when we get to his car, he slides me down his body. I feel every ridge of muscle as I go.

"Get in," he orders, his hand going behind me to the handle of his car. "You'll catch a cold."

I grip his wrist, stopping him, and since he's leaning forward, I don't have to yell when I say, "Kiss me."

"What?"

I run my hands along his jaw and lean in closer. "I said: Kiss me. I won't ask—"

He gently shoves me against the door of his car, and my heart skips a beat.

He's going to kiss me and there's no little kid here to interrupt. He grasps the back of my neck and tugs me towards him.

The moment his lips touch mine, I press myself flush against him. Heat rises in my stomach at the feel of him leaning into me.

He isn't just kissing me.

He's claiming me.

Every flick of his tongue, every caress, he does it with passion. We stand under the pouring rain, uncaring that someone could be watching or taking photos.

He kisses me like I'm his next breath.

And I kiss him back like he's mine.

I run the tips of my fingers down his abs, feeling his muscles tense beneath my touch. I'm wielded to ground, to his touch, and when he pulls back, taking a breath, it takes the last bit of strength I have not fall into him.

I blink up at him, raindrops dripping from my lashes. "You were holding back in the taxi."

He smirks as he steals another brief kiss. When he pulls back, there's a heat in his eyes, something he's had a few times tonight when I've caught him watching me. "That's because when I kissed you, and I mean really kissed you, I didn't want it to be a stolen moment. I wanted to take my time, savour it, and make you feel it in ways you'd never forget."

"Mission accomplished," I reply, trying to hide how much his words have affected me.

He pulls open the door to his car. "Let's get you home."

In a lust-filled daze, I nod and slide into the car. My fingers twitch to reach for my phone, to share with the girls how fucking hot that kiss was. But I know if I message them now, they'll be hounding me all night.

IT DOESN'T TAKE us long to get back to mine. Rain pelts against the car, and the radio is playing softly, but for the most part, it's just us talking.

I like listening to him. Although I feel like he's holding something back, I still feel like he's giving me all that is him. I understand secrets. I have one myself, one I keep from family and friends at school. My family might judge me, but they wouldn't love me any less. The same can't be said for the friends at school. I've heard them judge, I've seen them exclude others from sitting with us because of something or another. I have friends, best friends who are my family now. The only reason I keep the friends I do at the school is because it's not easy being there. Does it make me selfish? I don't know and I don't care. I'm not hurting anyone, and I don't pretend to be anyone other than me. Being a stripper is what I do, not who I am.

So, I get why he wants to keep stuff private or not share. In time, he will come to trust me.

Unless he's hiding the arsehole in him; then I won't care what the big secret is. Now is now, though, and I'm not going to think on the what if. The good and bad come and go in life, so when something good happens, I take my mum's advice and enjoy the ride.

And if he's hot, has two legs, and knows how to use his dick, ride *him*.

Because life is a journey, one to be enjoyed.

"We're here," I muse, and smile at the outdoor light the girls have left on.

"Let me walk you to the door," he offers, and jumps out of the car.

By the time I've got my things together, he's at my door, pulling it open. My smile is wide, and my stomach does a little flip. "Look at you being a gentleman."

He takes my hand as I jump out. "I think I watched it in a movie."

He keeps a hold of my hand as we head up to my front door. "And what else did you learn from this movie?"

He flashes his teeth when he smiles. "That I should kiss you at the door."

"Did you also learn the rule of the third date?"

"What's that?" he asks, as I push open my door.

I step inside the doorway and turn to face him. "A lady doesn't sleep with a guy on a first date."

"And what if I said this was our second?"

"Then I'd ask what made you come to that conclusion."

"The club, tonight," he replies, and his eyebrow shoots up, daring me to argue.

I take a step down, standing in front of him. "Then I guess if you were to come inside for a coffee, I could class that as a third date."

"And what about school?"

"I'll go in tired. But you'd better make it worth it."

I'm not sure who moves first. Him or me. But within a second, I'm in his arms, his hands gripping my arse as he heads inside. I vaguely hear the door clicking shut, but then my attention is on him.

All of him.

His lips find mine, and in a frenzy, we go at each other like the night has an expiry date. I tug his jacket over his shoulders as my back hits the wall before the living room. He lowers me and lets his jacket fall to the floor.

"Are you sure?"

I grip the back of his neck, bringing him down until we're eye level. "Fuck yes."

He removes my jacket, and the off-the-shoulder top I have on is yanked down to my waist, exposing the sports bra barely containing my tits.

His eyes blaze with heat. "Fuck, you're beautiful."

I lose control of every inhibition as I lean up on the tips of my toes, kissing him until I feel light-headed.

I am completely lost in him. In the kiss. In the moment.

He kisses his way down my neck and along my breastbone. He tears the fabric down, baring my tits to him. He groans as he sucks the hardened tip into his mouth.

"Fuck," I rasp, arching my back.

I surrender to his touch, to it all, as he lowers himself to his knees and rips my leggings down my thighs.

"Yes," he growls, and seconds later, my thong is torn from my body.

I moan, running my fingers through his thick locks, tugging when I feel his hot breath on my groin.

"More," I plead and make the mistake of glancing down.

His dark eyes meet my hazel ones, and staring back at me is want. Pure want. A want so strong not even sex will quench it.

He grabs my round arsecheeks as he brings me closer. And unlike the kiss, he doesn't savour it. There's no holding back as he goes down on me. Every fibre of my being is on fire. Every lick, every caress, has my nerve endings burning for more. He's eager, fast, as he licks my swollen clit.

And when he thrusts two fingers inside of me, it takes everything not to come undone.

I reach up, groping my own tits as I feel him working me down below.

And he knows how to work me, or at the very least, a woman's body. He takes me by surprise when he lifts me and throws my legs over his shoulders. I use his head and the wall to keep me balanced.

And in all of this, he doesn't stop torturing me with his tongue.

This is honest to God the hottest thing to have ever happened to me. Which is saying a lot, because I like to be adventurous and live on the edge.

Each nip, lick, and caress has me going wild, and I can no longer keep quiet. My moans of pleasure are loud enough for the neighbours to hear.

It's never been this good.

It's never felt this intense.

I've never felt this alive.

When my orgasm tears through me, it's not for a split second, or a stolen moment, it's wave after wave, setting me on fire on the inside.

He manoeuvres his hands once again, sliding me down his body. The roughness of his shirt rubbing against my clit has me wanting more.

Needing more.

"Holy fuck!" I rasp.

He drops his head against mine, breathing heavily. "You are amazing."

"I know," I tell him, keeping my voice low. "Now, it's my turn."

"Your turn?"

I look up at him through my lashes. "I need you inside me, handsome."

His pupils dilate as he bends, lifting me at the thighs. "Where's your bedroom?"

"Upstairs," I reply, running my fingers through his thick hair.

He heads up the stairs, and at the top, he drops me to my feet. My bed, with a soft, cotton, beige comforter and tons of pillows, lies in wait before us, the twinkle lights still on from earlier. He tears off his T-shirt using one hand, baring every ridge and line of muscle. I don't know where to focus; on the deep V leading to his dick, or on his expression, where all I see is want.

I admire his firm body for a moment longer before I finish what he started downstairs. Removing the last scrap of clothing, I stand naked before him, uncaring, and not shy.

As he kicks off his jeans, I step up to him and push him down on the bed. I grin. "You have no idea how badly I want you right now."

I crawl up the bed until I'm straddling his thighs, then something on my dressing table catches my eye.

"Are you okay? If you've changed your mind, we can wait," he assures me.

I lean over him, dangling my tits in his face as I reach for the folded piece of paper. He turns, spotting the strip of condoms.

I unfold the note, chuckling.

Give him a night he won't forget. Jealous! Olivia.
Only 'cause she isn't getting any. Fuck him so he never forgets, Gabby.
Ignore them. Be safe and text us with the deets. Love, Emily.

"What's it say?" he asks.

I throw the paper to the floor and smile as I take a condom from him. "My girls want me to have fun."

"Mission accepted," he states, before doing some fancy leg move that has me on my back and him looming above me.

Gone is the playful glint in his eyes as he settles between my thighs, his erection rubbing against my clit.

His hands slide up my sides, before cupping my tits. His touch is light, delicate, like he's afraid he'll break me. "You don't have to be gentle. I can take a little rough," I croak out, my voice filled with lust.

His fingers pinch my nipples as he inches towards me. He covers my mouth with his, smothering the moan.

God, he can fucking kiss.

I feel the condom tugged from my fingers, before I hear it tear. My fingers are back in his hair, and I grind against him.

"Let me know if it gets too much."

I meet the challenge in his eyes, but I shiver despite myself trying to keep it together. "I never back down."

As he rolls the condom over his cock, I'm already aching for him. And when I feel the tip at my entrance, I meet his gaze.

A part of me wishes I hadn't.

There is so much there. And for the first time tonight, I don't feel like he's holding back from me. He's giving me everything.

He slams inside of me, the intrusion taking me by surprise. He's big, really big, and tension radiates through my core.

"You okay?"

I grip the back of his neck and bring his head down until our lips are a breath away. "I will be when you fuck me."

His kiss is bruising, and fire scorches through my veins. Everything between us feels like a battle. One where we are both winners. The touching, kissing, and the little nips he gives before soothing them with his tongue… Neither of us can get enough.

Every thrust has my nails digging deeper into his shoulders.

Every kiss has the hairs on my neck standing on end.

Every touch has my skin burning for him.

And I know, when our sweat-glistened bodies are spent and truly satisfied, it still won't be enough.

When he slams inside me, fucking me like he hates me, I know I'll be feeling him for days.

And as I run my hands down his spine, I know I'll never forget.

Even if this is a ruse and only going to be a one-night stand, it doesn't matter. It doesn't matter who came before him.

I only feel sorry for the fucker who will come after him if he isn't who he says he is, or if this is a play to get me into bed.

Because they'll never live up to this moment.

They'll never live up to him.

12

RIVER

The sun is rising as I pull on my T-shirt. I'm reluctant to leave but unwilling to rouse her from sleep. Not when only an hour ago we finally stopped fucking. We talked until I felt her fall asleep in my arms, and then I watched her sleep, wondering what I did to deserve her.

Men have told tales that their girl isn't like any other girl. But in theory, they are. It just doesn't stop a man from cheating or moving on. Sometimes, forever doesn't mean forever.

Harriett, though, she is different. There's a quality about her that is rare. She sees the world through her eyes and not social media or what the papers print. She doesn't see status or gain. She's funny, caring, and sharp with her words.

The dim light shines on her slender form. With only a comforter covering her arse, it's making it harder for me to leave.

Last night was phenomenal. I've had workouts that weren't that taxing. And it wasn't a fight to keep up. I had the stamina. It was the fight to keep my hands off her that was the hardest. She's a drug, one I keep needing more of, one I've become addicted to.

There's a presence inside me, one I haven't felt since I was eight years old and I watched my mum's first boyfriend after Dad, beat her. I want to protect Harriett, to shield her from the world around us. I want to protect the life she carries like an essence.

I want to protect her.

And the selfish part of me, the part that takes what he wants, doesn't care that it might be me she needs protecting from.

I carry a darkness. My last fight with Dean proved that. But more than that, I have baggage not even the strongest could carry.

It's been a long time since I opened myself up to have someone. Girls have come and gone. They were faceless chicks I fucked and left before they even had a chance to clean themselves up.

Harriett is different. Since Marlene, something inside of me snapped. I told myself good things weren't meant to happen to me. I was a fraud in sheep's clothing. I followed the masses, followed Colin's rules, and worked my arse into the ground. I wanted to prove myself, to show the world I'm more than some low-life off the street. But that toxic voice inside my head kept telling me I don't deserve what I have.

But for Harriett to come into my life, to be all that she is and still smile each day, I must be doing something right. It must be I've paid my dues and I'm getting rewarded.

Unless she's another part of my life that will get ripped away from me.

I can't let that happen.

I grab the notebook on her nightstand and flip through until I reach a blank page.

Gorgeous, it kills me to leave you sleeping, but I wanted you to get some rest. Last night was incredible, and I know you hate it when people are presumptuous, but I want to do it again.

Spend time with you, that is.

If you are free Thursday night, I'd like to take you to mine and cook you dinner. Message me when you are up. Have a good day,

River.

PS. You mentioned you hate having to wait for your morning coffee, so I went ahead and made you a fresh pot.

Enjoy, gorgeous, and hopefully, I'll see you soon.

Leaving it on the pillow next to her, I head downstairs, my lips tugging at the small home. It suits her. From the cushions to the candles and to even the artwork on the walls, it's all Harriett.

It feels like a home, somewhere you'd feel comfortable and invited. Going home to mine is going to feel like stepping out into a blizzard. Cold, unwanted, and plain.

My phone beeps with a message alert.

Drew: Meet you at the gym in ten. Running a little late.

River: I guess Charlotte woke up with you?

Drew: LOL My girl is a spitfire. See you in a few.

River: On my way.

As I stand with my hand on the door, I take one more look to the platform above where I know she's sleeping in her king-size bed. I don't want to leave, which is new for me. I normally can't get out fast enough. I want to wake up next to her, hear her voice, and the way my cock is still hard, fuck her again.

At first, I thought being drawn to her was about being so alone in my life, but thinking on it, I'd be content going about my life the way it is. It's Harriett I want. It's her company I seek. Her presence I need. I could tell myself it's wanting what Drew has, but the truth is, I can keep being single. I've not been looking for a relationship or companionship. But Harriett makes me want it all.

And I want it with her.

Gently closing the door behind me, I sneak down the path to my car. If I have any hope of getting rid of some of this pent-up tension before I next speak to her, I have to train.

Training clears my mind. It resets my muscles and wakes me up.

And if I don't want to scare Harriett off, I'm going to need all of that. Because whilst I want to give her all of me, I need to trust her first. Owning up to what I'm feeling will give her power. And although I don't think she's like the other girls who come to me after a fight, or I pick up at a club, there's still a chance.

There's always a chance.

I learned that the hard way with Marlene.

My entire body aches as I step out of the sauna. With no sleep, only a shake when I arrived, and a full-on work-out, it isn't just my body that's tired. My mind is too.

Luckily, I'm my own boss and messaged Kim before I hit the sauna to take over any appointments I have with today's potential clients.

Drew is putting on a shirt as I hit the locker room. "You are getting seriously quick on your feet."

"I was taught by the best."

"Is that why I just got faxed a termination letter?"

I pause with my hand grasping the towel. "What?"

He pulls open the locker and brings out a piece of paper. I take it, scanning over the formal letter firing Drew from his duties. "I wasn't even aware I was on your payroll."

"You aren't. My membership is done through the same channels as everyone else who walks through the door. The same with my PT membership. The money I sponsor to the gym is also done through the correct channels that have nothing to do with my payroll."

"Then what's his game?"

"I told you what he said. I guess this is his way of enforcing it. But I ain't doing it. I didn't get this far by getting too big for my boots. I might have nice cars, nice things, food and a house, but I never forgot those who got me here or where I came from. I didn't move on to bigger things. Because whilst they might be bigger names, they aren't better. I've told him this."

"I know you don't want to hear this, but just be careful. This letter means shit to me. If you want to train with someone else, I'm good with that, or if you want to stay, I'm good with putting up with his shit. No matter what, we're cool, and I hope you still keep coming around. Aside from Landon, it's hard to find someone I'm evenly matched with."

I snort. "Evenly matched. I'm pretty sure it was me who had you tapping out in there."

He grins as he grabs his deodorant. "I had a long night."

I grab my shower bag. "So did I."

"Oh? Do tell."

"Nope."

He straddles the bench. "Oh, come on, River Knight has a girl. You have to tell me about her. I don't think you've been in a relationship since Marley."

"I haven't. This girl is different."

"Would I know her?"

Come to think of it, he might. "She actually works at Tease. Her name's Harriett."

He whacks his chest as he begins to wheeze. "Are you sure?"

"Yeah, why?" I ask warily. If he's fucked her, I might not go as easy on him in the ring next time. And it would be a shame, since I'd like to say we're mates.

"She's Charlotte's mate. They're a lot to take on."

"Who?"

"Harriett and her friends."

"Isn't Charlotte her friend?"

He gives me a pointed look. "The last time they were together, I got hit with a baseball bat. They watched a horror movie and thought I was some zombie coming to eat them. I was getting a glass of water."

I laugh. "I've only met her friends once. They seemed, um, friendly."

He arches an eyebrow. "Wait for it. Before you know it, there will be car chases, fires, dildos, and fucking glitter."

"I'm not even going to ask."

"Better off, bro," he replies. "I didn't picture you with someone like Harriett."

"What do you mean by that? She's a great chick."

He holds his hands up. "I didn't mean anything bad by it. You're really quiet, and they're full on."

"She's different. I like it. And it's cheesy as fuck, but I've not met a girl like her."

He gets a dazed look in his eyes. "Same with Charlotte. She's fucking loopy as fuck, but it's one of the things I love most about her. She's strong too."

"How did you two meet?"

There's a darkness in his expression. "Not my story to tell, but I can tell you, it was rough. She got through it though. Harriett's a good one. She looked after Charlotte when she was going through something. Do right by her."

"It's new," I tell him, shrugging. "Look at us having a heart-to-heart like we're some chicks on a coffee date."

He chuckles. "It's talking, man. Nothing girly about it."

I grab my pile of clothes, deciding to skip the shower to have one at home. "I'd best get going. It was a long night."

"You're thinking about your mum and dad, aren't you?"

I slam the locker shut, letting out a dry laugh. "I hate that you can do that."

"Do what?"

"Read my mind."

"She doesn't need to know. Not yet. Like you said, you're still new."

"Shouldn't she know before? Doesn't she deserve to know what she's getting into?"

"You said yourself, she isn't like other girls. She won't care for shallow reasons. She'll care because she has a good heart."

"Maybe."

"What about your mum? Have you seen her?"

I duck my head in shame. "It's best I don't. She does better when I'm not there. She blames me for everything."

"She's the one to blame. Not you. You were just a kid."

"We all make choices," I murmur, and as I reach for my bag, the door to the changing room clangs against the wall.

"River?"

I grimace at Drew's expression as Colin rounds the corner. "What are you doing here?"

He holds up the newspaper. "What the fuck is this?"

I grab it before it falls to the floor. Plastered over the front cover is a picture of me and Harriett about to kiss. The angle is done so you only see a little of Harriett's face, but all of mine.

Drew glances down, reading the headline: **Who's the Mystery Girl that's Captured Rampage's Attention?**

It goes on to read: '**Is this the girl to win Rampage's heart before going into the drama Dean caused with Marlene?** Seeing it brings back memories, but unlike before, I don't get angry. I don't feel anything. I knew a long time ago I had moved on, but having this closure, knowing for sure, there's a weight lifted.

"Give us some space please," Colin spits out.

"Don't," I quickly tell him.

Drew waves me off. "I've got things that need sorting," he tells me, before turning to Colin. "I'm letting you off this time, but speak to me like that again, and I'll put my fist through your face."

Sweat trickles down Colin's temples as Drew shoves past him. "Are you going to let him talk to me like that?"

"You deserved it."

"Who is that?"

I grit my teeth. "None of your business. It's mine."

"You're my business. I'm not having some money-grabbing whore take everything from you," he bites out, and I see red.

I grip his neck and slam him against the locker. "You ever call her a whore again, and I will end you. I will walk away from it all."

"Hit me and see how well it ends for you. I dare you."

I grip him tighter, fighting back the urge. "Then don't push me."

He shoves me away, and I let him. "Do you want this splashed all over the papers when it goes to shit? You've got the championship coming up and they'll already be focusing on the conflict with Fracture. You can't afford to be distracted. This fight will make or break your career. You lose this, all those endorsements, all your contracts, they'll be gone."

"I've told you I'm done after this."

"No, you aren't. You are nothing without this. You'll go back to your estate, eating scraps you get from the foodbank, and have no choices. You have no education. This is what you do. This is your career."

His words ring true, and for a moment, doubt sets in. "I have choices now," I tell him, although there's no conviction in my tone.

"No, you don't. This is it for you," he tells me. "As for the girl, get rid of her. Now is not the time for you to be distracted. If you need girls, there's a service."

My lip curls in disgust. "Prostitutes?"

"Escorts."

"Yeah, a hard pass. I like this girl. She's not a distraction."

"I'm telling you, ditch her," he warns.

"Fuck you! And this bullshit. I don't have to listen to this or to you. This is my life. Mine. Not yours."

"It's going to end badly. I can promise you."

"No, it's not."

"And what if she learns your secret? Do you think she'll stick around then?" he spitefully remarks.

"She has her own secrets. I think I'll be fine, and honestly, she wouldn't do that," I reply. "Look, I'm done arguing with you, Colin. I'm grateful for everything you do and for looking out for me, but I'm getting tired of the same bullshit."

There's a look in his eyes, one he gets as he approaches a new resource, someone to use.

"I'm just looking out for you. You know I think of you as a son. I know what you went through. I helped, remember. I don't want you going back there, and I don't want some woman coming in and threatening to take it all."

"She really isn't like that, Colin. I know you don't want me to stop fighting. I get it. But I need a life, Colin. I see people getting married, having kids, going on holidays, and all I do is work. My life revolves around fighting, but it's time for more. I need more."

"That's why you want to leave?"

"It's *why* I'm leaving."

He shakes his head, disappointment clear on his expression. "Then you're a fool. You've got plenty of time to settle down. Ending your career after you've worked so hard for a woman is foolish. Women come and go, but this, what you have, it's once in a lifetime. It's an opportunity many don't get."

I lean down, done with his bullshit. "Let's get one thing straight; it's mine to lose. Not yours or anyone else's. Mine."

I begin to dress, turning my back to him. "You'll see. Before the end of this season, you'll change your mind. You'll see life doesn't get better than this. And I hope you do. I'm the one who has stood by you. I'm the one who has kept your damn fucking secret. And I'm the one who gets you the best deals. If it wasn't for me, you wouldn't be here. And if you do this, if you throw all this away for some girl, you can forget ever working for me again."

I slam the locker shut, not even glancing at him. "I'll prove you wrong."

With that, I walk out, leaving him to stew on his words.

Is Drew right? Is Allie? Because I finally feel like I'm seeing his true colours. This isn't the man I met when I was a teenager. I'd like to think I wasn't blind to it, but thinking back, I think I saw what I wanted to see. I had been too grateful, relieved, to have food in my stomach, clothes on my back. I had been fortunate meeting him the day I ran into the gang I hung out with. By then, I was out of that life, or as out as someone can get. They wanted blood, revenge for turning my back on them. Colin had been there, like he was waiting for me, and when he told me he saw me fight and wanted to take me to the next level, I believed him.

Now I'm left wondering if he just wanted to take himself to the next level.

13

HARRIETT

There's a skip in my step as I make my way to the coffee shop. With only a few hours of sleep, and every inch of my body aching in the best way, I should be dragging my feet.

It's amazing what one night of good sex can do for you.

And the fresh pot of coffee he left me.

Waking up alone after the night we shared had been the only let down. But in a way, it made it a little easier if he didn't mean what he wrote on the note he left me. I didn't want to face that kind of awkwardness. Not unprepared anyway.

I push open the door and the smell of coffee beans nearly knocks me off my feet.

"She definitely had sex," Milly yells. "You go, sister."

I take a double look behind me, seeing nothing but the door. "How the fuck do you know?" I yell back, uncaring about the bystanders.

She points to the far wall, and sitting at the table against the window looking out onto the street, are my friends. "I'll bring your drink over."

"And a bacon sandwich please."

She grins knowingly and gets to work. "Got ya."

Reaching the girls, they all grin up at me. "Why are you here?"

Gabby looks confused. "You wouldn't answer our messages. And we knew you'd be here."

"Because I was getting ready to go to class."

"From the glow, I take it he was good," Olivia comments.

"Is he big?" Gabby asks as I take a seat next to Emily, who looks ready to fall asleep.

Olivia nudges Gabby. "Why do you care? You are gay."

"So I know what size to get my next dildo, duh."

Olivia goes into a haze, staring longingly at Gabby. "Right."

Gabby grins, unaffected as she turns to me. "So, spill."

"He licked me out," I state.

Her shoulders drop. "Well, that's not exciting."

"Whilst my legs were around his neck and he had me against the wall, standing."

She drops her chin into the palm of her hand, dazed. "Now it's getting interesting. Getting licked out whilst up in the air. That's new."

"And he fucked like a rock star. We only tried two positions but fuck me, he perfected them both."

"Missionary and doggy. I like it," Olivia grins.

"How do you know?" Emily asks over a yawn.

"I know Harriett."

Emily wakes up a little to understand. "Ah, the last guy didn't make it past missionary."

Remembering Carl, I groan. "God, he was a lousy lay."

There's a ruckus by the door, and we turn to see Charlotte trip into the building, the contents of her bag falling at the guy's feet in front of her. "Did I miss the sex?"

I rush over to help her. "You've not missed anything."

Straightening her jacket, she grins. "Thank God. I didn't mean to fall back asleep, but I woke up with Drew, and you know how I get when he touches me. Before I knew it, we were having sex on the stairs. I think I scarred Katnip for life."

Laughter spills out of me as I help her to her feet. "Good to know you had a good morning."

She blows out a breath, shoving her thick red hair from her face. "It was awesome."

"Um, your bird seeds," Neil declares, handing her a packet of seeds.

She sighs with relief. "Thank you. I'd hate to have been unprepared later when I go to feed the birds."

"You feed birds?" he asks, as the others hand her things.

"Sometimes. I carry a bit of everything. You never know what you'll run into."

Neil glances at me questioningly. "She likes being prepared."

"Okay," he replies, struggling to hide his grin.

"This is so cool," a boy cries.

A chair scrapes along the floor. "Darren, put that down," a woman screeches. "Oh my god."

I turn to the boy and see he's waving around a bent dildo. "Shit," I whisper and quickly rush over to snatch it. "Thanks, little man."

The mum gives me a dirty look, but I return back to Charlotte, handing her the toy. "Oh crap, I'm sorry, Gabby, it's bent."

"Her favourite position," Olivia retorts.

Gabby takes it from Charlotte. "It's fine. I can order you a replacement."

Charlotte tucks her hair behind her ear, smiling softly. "Drew said I don't need them anymore."

"I bet," Gabby muses. "Did he like the cock ring?"

Charlotte's eyes light up. "Loved it."

The guy Charlotte ran into hands her a sachet of cat food. "Well, I'll be a regular here from now on. Has anyone told you, you're gorgeous?"

Charlotte's brows pinch together. "My boyfriend tells me all the time, but I'm confused what the two have in common."

"I think he's hinting you're hot and wouldn't mind seeing you again," Emily states, her voice low.

"Oh, I ran from the car park to get here. I didn't want to miss anything," she tells him. "And that's sweet, but it's actually my first time here."

"Never mind," I declare, and tag her hand, pulling her over to our table.

She takes a seat from the empty table across from us. "So, what did I miss?"

"Harriett had mind blowing sex," Gabby pouts.

"You'll find someone soon. You never know, you two might finally get together," Charlotte states, eyeing Olivia and Gabby.

It's something we all want and dread. The former because the sexual tension between the two is off the charts, and we want them both to be happy. The latter because we'd never hear the end of it. The two can bicker on a good day, and I'm worried if they ever did, it would ruin the dynamic we all share.

"Not likely," they both mutter, but there's no conviction or earnestness in their words.

"Are you seeing Rampage again?"

"His name is River, and yes, he's invited me to dinner at his place tomorrow."

"I'm so happy for you. I told you you'd find your happy, didn't I," Charlotte dreamily replies.

I wink. "I find my happy every time I get my toys out."

"Here's your order," Milly tells me. I duck my head, wondering when I'll ever find a filter. "We don't normally do table service, but any friend of Harriett's is a friend of mine. What can I get you?"

"I'm good, thank you. I can't stay long. I have to get back to the library."

"Alright," Milly replies. Before she can leave, the newspaper tucked under her arm catches my eye.

"Holy fuck!" I rasp as I snatch it. I open it to see the page fully.

It's me and River from last night. My name isn't mentioned, but once they find out, this might not be good for me.

Milly grins. "Neil isn't into fighting, but he likes this one. Watches most of his matches," she states as Neil walks past.

He glances down at the paper. "Looks a bit like you too, H."

Wide-eyed, and still a little shook, I manage to reply, "My arse is better."

Emily, catching on, agrees. "Way better."

"And if I was on a date with a famous, hot fighter, Harriett wouldn't be wearing leggings," Gabby adds, and I narrow my gaze at her dig.

"Well, whoever she is, I'm happy for him. With what his ex did, I'm surprised he's put himself out there."

"His ex?" I ask before I can question myself.

"She really did a number on him. Went after his opponent, who he had bad blood with. Got pregnant and everything, but told Rampage it was his. It wasn't. She had been sleeping with the other fighter for two months on the press tour. They got engaged the night before it all came out. I'm surprised you didn't read about it. It was all over the papers."

"Holy fuck!" I whisper. "I tend to stay away from these kinds of papers. I mostly listen to a radio station called Loop Love Live. The chick is funny as fuck, and I'm pretty sure they've gone through a least a couple dozen male hosts since it changed."

"I love that show," Gabby announces. "She reminds me of Hayden."

Charlotte begins to mooch through her bag, which reminds me. "Will you mind bagging my lunch ready today? I only have a twenty-minute break, so I won't have time."

"Sure. You keep the paper. I'll grab it once you've gone."

When she leaves, all the girls lean in. "Shit, you are famous now," Gabby mutters.

"And probably get some haters. Every girl I know wants to fuck him."

"Not every girl," Gabby retorts.

"He is very handsome," Charlotte agrees.

"Fuck that, I'm more bothered about them finding out who I am."

"Why?" Charlotte asks.

"Because of my job. You know that will get plastered all over the place and my dad will read it."

"It will be fine. We'll make sure of it," she replies.

"Doesn't he have some sort of PR team who can, you know, get rid of it?" Gabby points out.

Olivia snorts. "He's not Brad Pitt."

"Just saying."

"Oh God, what am I going to do?"

"Well, you only have half an hour to decide."

Emily smothers a yawn. "You could talk to him. Be more careful. We only know because we know you went on a date with him. But you aren't recognisable from this picture."

I eye her. "Are you okay? You look like shit."

She gives me an eye roll. "Love you too."

"I'm being serious. Are you okay?"

She runs her fingers through her hair. "Just tired. Poppy didn't sleep well last night. The neighbours were arguing again."

"You look pale," Olivia comments, worry in her tone.

"I'll be fine, but if it's okay with you guys, I won't stay long. Poppy finishes nursery in three hours so I want to get some sleep before I pick her up."

"Go. And if you still feel tired later, call me. I'll take her out for the day."

"You have a shift at the hospital," she reminds me.

"I'll call in sick."

She places her hand over mine. "Thank you, but I'm good. I promise."

"Come on, I can drop you off on my way home. Or did you drive?" Charlotte asks.

"No, Olivia picked me up."

I reach over, giving her a hug. "Go get some rest. I'll fill you in on the rest later. Okay."

"You sure?"

"Positive."

We say our goodbyes, and once they are gone, I start to dig into my food.

"I'm worried about her. She's taking too much on," Gabby comments.

"I think the stress of boss man coming and going is stressing her out too. With her nan and Poppy, working nights, and the shifts she pulls at the gym, she's not giving herself enough time to rest."

"Holy fuck," Olivia gasps. I lift my head and find her looking over my shoulder. I turn, and the television on the wall shows a reporter outside a run-down house. The volume is too low for us to hear, but reading the subtitles, and the message board below, we don't need to.

Another murder.

When the screen moves back to the main reporters, a picture of a young woman appears on the left-hand side of the screen.

"Is that…"

"Keeley," Olivia finishes.

"Who's Keeley?"

"She used to work at Tease. She left before you started," I answer sadly. "She was really nice."

"How haven't they caught this person?" Olivia bites out. "We aren't in the stone age now. We have technology, science, but this person has killed how many now?"

"Five that we know of."

Gabby rubs up and down her arms. "This is starting to worry me. The details the police are releasing give us nothing. They aren't telling us who to be vigilant of, or if there's a pattern. We could walk past this person and not know it."

Olivia, in a rare form of serious comfort, takes Gabby's hand. "It will be okay. We always stick together, no matter what."

"She's right. We do. The last I heard, Keeley was moving for university. She doesn't live near here."

"But it's not that far. I'm pretty sure it's only an hour's drive," Gabby explains, as the area is announced on the television.

"Two strippers can't be a coincidence," Olivia mutters.

"I'm beginning to think there is a pattern, one they aren't sharing," I agree. "Or I do now. We're taking self-defence, we don't go off on our own, and we're careful. We've got each other's backs."

"Let's talk about big dick and how many times he made you come," Gabby announces, and the guy walking past, trips over his own feet.

I turn away. "I didn't tell you his size."

She grins. "The way you walked coming in said it all."

I laugh, throwing a crumb of bread at her. "Bitch."

She shrugs. "I'd say I care, but I'd be lying."

"Shit, I have to go. I've got a meeting with the school principle about Lee," Olivia announces, grabbing her bag. "Do you need a lift?"

"Do fish swim?" Gabby retorts.

"I hate it when you do that. Just say yes."

"Don't ask stupid questions then," Gabby fires back.

"Stop," I warn through my laughter. "Let me know how it goes."

Gabby gets her stuff together. "The same as it normally does. Olivia will sit there staring the principle down until she gets uncomfortable. It's unnerving as fuck. And then after, Olivia will give her a piece of her mind and she'll walk out with no answers nor a solution."

"Then you deal with the stuck-up bitch," Olivia argues.

Gabby pauses. "Actually, I will."

I give them both a hug, and we share our goodbyes. Once they are gone, I lean back and pull out my phone, debating how I'm going to tell River about the photo.

And the headline.

His ex was a fool to do what she did. I don't know the other guy, so I can't make any assumptions, but I can say if River doesn't like them, there's a reason. He seems like a laid-back kind of guy. A little quiet, but it's what I like about him. When he speaks, it's because what he has to say means something.

I'm surprised to find I have a message waiting for me. Clicking on it, I then read over it.

River: There's an article in the papers about me. About you. Someone snapped a photo of us last night and sold it to the paper. I'm so fucking sorry. We didn't get any warning, but my PR assistant called me not long ago, and her phone's been blowing up for a comment.

Harriett: I've seen it. I didn't prepare for this so I'm at a loss for what to do. People can't find out about me. This would break my dad's heart.

River: He won't. I've told my PR team not to file a statement. I won't be revealing your name to anyone. I swear. This will blow over soon. With the fight coming up, they'll focus on that.

Harriett: Are you sure? I've read about reporters hounding celebs. Keeping quiet might make things worse. They'll think you have something to hide. And I know you said it's the worst part of what you do—having your life plastered over the papers.

River: I'll sort it if it ever comes to that. I swear. I'm just really fucking sorry you are involved. I didn't think I'd be seen.

Harriett: I know. I trust you. I'm just worried about my family finding out.

River: They won't. Aside from the paper, how are you doing? Did you get my note?

Harriett: I did. I can do Thursday as long as it's after eight. I have a shift at the hospital.

River: Sounds great.

Harriett: I have to go, but speak to you later?

River: Any time, gorgeous. You know that.

Harriett: Later, handsome.

After finishing my lukewarm coffee, I leave the half-eaten sandwich on the table, pay, and then leave.

Nothing will ruin my mood today.

Not the papers.

Not the newest murder.

And neither will the arsehole professor I have today.

Today is a good day. A really good day. And the countdown for tomorrow ticks on. Nothing can ruin that. Nothing.

14

RIVER

As I turn onto my drive, I don't gun the engine like I normally do. With precious cargo in the car, I take it easy.

The road leading up to my house is quiet, and some of the turns are narrow. And since she seemed like a nervous passenger during our last car ride, I don't want to spook her.

"I'm beginning to think you like scaring me," she muses.

My hand is resting on her thigh, and at her words, my fingers flex. "Come again?"

"Middle of the woods, and now the middle of nowhere. I'm beginning to worry."

"Horror movies?" I guess.

"Charlotte finds joy in them. For someone so sweet, she can be a little psycho. We were watching the new Halloween movie and ninety-nine percent of it she spent laughing until tears rolled down her face. The only time she showed any other emotion was at the end. She felt sorry for Michael."

I nod, thinking the same. "He is misunderstood."

I feel her stare on the side of my face. "He's murdered innocent people. Okay, one kid was questionable, and some of the others had it coming, but, dude, Laurie didn't do shit to him other than defend herself."

I struggle to contain my laughter. "I'm kind of joking. The story can be hard to follow with all the spin-offs. I watched the new one though. It was great."

"Nah, he moved too fast. He's a legend for his slow-paced walk, but he moved like he had been sniffing coke all night."

The car swerves at my laughter. "I'm never gonna unhear that."

"Then don't ever watch a romantic film with me. I get judgey," she jokes.

"Here we are," I announce.

The leather seat squeaks as she sits forward. "Holy fucking shit. This is so not what I was expecting."

"What were you expecting?" I ask as I put the car into park outside. Since I don't know whether she's staying or not, I decide to wait to put it in the garage.

"At first, a top floor condo, or penthouse—whatever people call them. But then the further we got from town, I started to think a shed of some kind."

"Well, it's not a shed, and much nicer than any penthouse. I lived in one before, but it wasn't for me. I like being outside, where I can't be disturbed."

She whistles. "Nice."

I slide out and walk around to meet her at her door. I pull it open, and she throws her bag over her shoulder, still looking up at the house.

"Welcome to my place."

I take her hand, and together, we walk up to the door, where I pull out my key to open it. I step to the side to let her walk in first, but she's not paying attention. She's staring at the floor by the entrance. "Everything okay?"

"I feel like I need different shoes. Or slippers," she replies. "Dude, you have marble flooring. I bet that's freezing in the winter."

"It's heated flooring," I tell her, and tug her hand. "And don't worry about your shoes. You should see what I bring in when I return from my runs."

We step into the short hallway, and I take her jacket, before hanging it in the cupboard. "I'm not going to lie, I had too many meetings today to prepare anything. But a cook I hire during events fixed me up and has a dumpling stew going in the slow cooker."

"I thought you had steaks and shit?"

"I've got a chicken and veg one," I answer as we hit the living room.

This room is more modern, and not a space I really enjoy or sit in. The large corner sofa surrounds a glass coffee table, and there's a TV mounted to the wall. The home designer I hired had free rein in this room and said it's what was in at that time. She forgot to mention the sofa is uncomfortable, something you can't really lounge on, and the table is a bitch to clean. Not that I do most of the cleaning. I have someone come in a few times a week to sort it out.

"Want to see the view?" I ask.

Looking away from the decor, she nods. I slide open the glass door that leads out to the patio.

"I can't believe you live here. This is like a dream home," she states as she walks around the pool to the outer decking, which looks out to an incredible view. Trees, greenery, and the sun setting over the horizon... It doesn't get better than this. She stops at the decking panel, her hand on the wooden top. "How fond are you of this house?"

For a split second, doubt about bringing her here sets in. Women before have tried to use me for money. At first, it was subtle hints about wishing they could afford something, then manipulation when the hints didn't work.

It's why I never got serious with anyone after Marlene. I saw them for who they are. But maybe deep down, Harriett is like that. Maybe she sees the big house, the nice things, and wants it for herself. Or maybe I'm too jaded to even see what's truly in front of me.

"Very fond, why?"

"Because this is a great place to play Murderer in the Dark. And have water fights. Just think of the games you could play without worrying you'll lose a ball over the neighbour's fence or the neighbours complaining about the noise. It's just a shame you're fond of the place. The last time we played Murderer in the Dark was at an old mansion hotel. We accidently broke a few things, but luckily, they were props and not the real thing."

Once again, she surprises me. "Any time you want to bring your friends to play... whatever it is—"

"Murderer in the Dark and water fights," she quickly rushes out.

I wrap my arms around her stomach as we continue to face the sunset. "Well, you are welcome here with your friends any time."

"It's a beautiful offer, but we only get one weekend off together. It's at the end of every month so we try to make the most of it. We're actually planning to go away this time. Poppy, Emily's daughter, breaks up from nursery, so we want to take her to the beach. Next time though."

I turn her and cage her in against the decking panels. "I have a holiday home not far from here. It's on the beach. It's not being used, so you're welcome to use it." I run my hands down her sides to her arse.

"As lovely as that sounds, it's probably out of our price range, but thank you."

I run my finger over the crease lines between her eyebrows. "No charge," I firmly state. "It will be good to see it get used. I have a few acquaintances that rent it out now and again, but other than that, it's empty. I try to go up there as much as I can, but I've been busy lately."

Her eyes widen. "That's really generous of you, but we can't impose like that. And I wouldn't feel right accepting it."

"Why?"

She lists off reasons using her fingers. "Because we are new. You don't know me that well. It's a big thing to offer. And I'd like to hope you don't offer it willy-nilly because you don't know who you can trust. Not that I'm saying I'll trash it or rob it. I love my life. I'm not cut out for jail. Although I'd probably succeed at it. I can picture it: I'll have my own group, and prisoners will come to me and offer something up in exchange for me and my group's protection. And I'll be like—"

"Gorgeous, take a breath. If it will make you feel any better, why don't I rent it to you?"

She bites her bottom lip. "I might consider it if it's reasonably priced."

"Twenty-pound a night."

She arches an eyebrow. "Really?"

"Just take it. And if it makes you feel any better, I don't do this willy-nilly. You are actually the first friend I've offered it to."

Her arms go around my waist. "Is that what I am to you—a friend?"

"Nope. You are more than a friend. Way more. But I'm good to wait until you're ready to put a label on it."

"Thank you," she replies. "I'll talk to my friends and get back to you."

"Good. And I have a boat you can take out. There's a guy who tends to it. In return, I let him use it for his business to take people out to sea."

"Awesome."

"Now kiss me. I've been dying to kiss you since I picked you up."

I don't have to wait. She reaches up at the same time I lean down. Our lips meet, and the second they connect, electricity sparks between us. I tag her around the waist, pulling her closer.

Her fingers slide underneath my T-shirt, lifting the material as she goes. I pull back, arching my brow in question.

"Take it off, handsome."

"Here?"

She grins and turns a little to the sunset. "Where else? The view is perfect."

I rip my T-shirt off before undoing my belt. She kicks her leggings off, so she's standing before me in black lace underwear, and a crop top that shows off her midriff.

The tips of my fingers dig into the palms of my hands as I step forward. In a quick motion, I lift her up until her arse is on the ledge of the decking panel. She's at the perfect height. I press my cock against her pussy, kissing her once more.

I'll never get tired of kissing her.

Her fingers move from my shoulders, and she leans back, removing the flimsy material barely containing her tits.

I had been right. No bra.

She is sweet torture, someone I can't get enough of; someone I don't want to get enough of.

I suck her hardened tip into my mouth, and as I reach between her legs, I bump hands with her.

I groan, my legs trembling at her touching herself. "You are killing me."

"And you should be fucking me," she rasps, bringing her fingers up to her mouth. "I'm already wet."

"Fuck," I growl, and shove my jeans down my thighs. I move her knickers to the side. My tip rubs against her wetness, and I hesitate. "Condom."

"I'm clean and on the pill. And in your line of business, I know you get tested regularly."

As badly as I want to, my mind flashes back to the moment Marley told me she was pregnant. The only reason I believed that fucked up lie is because there was a night we got lost in the moment and forgot to use protection.

But this is Harriett. She wouldn't lie about this. She has a career, a job, and I know having a baby right now, just when she's finishing her major year, would be stupid. She wouldn't risk it.

"I'm clean, but I'll pull out."

Her pupils dilate at the image, and she spreads her thighs further apart. "Fuck me, handsome."

I slam inside her, and her back arches, a cry echoing into the dim evening. The balcony shakes with each thrust, but I can't get enough.

I don't care if it breaks.

I don't even care if there's someone in the distance who might hear, or if someone turns up.

Leaning back, she grips the posts on either side of her. I grip her tighter, so she doesn't fall back, but I needn't have worried. Her thighs grip the railing with sheer strength.

I groan at how tight she feels around my cock, and needing more, I fist her ponytail, pulling her head back as I kiss and nip down her slender neck.

"Harder," she cries.

If I go any harder, the decking posts will break. I reach under her, taking her over to the bed lounger I have near the pool. Lowering her down onto the soft, thin mattress, I order, "Turn around."

She does, and I tear her knickers down, letting them pool at her knees. She moans as I grip her hair once more and slam inside of her.

I glance down, watching my cock slide into her.

Fuck, so tight.

I reach around, grabbing her tits as she sits up, giving me better access. "Fuck, you feel good."

She cries out when I pinch her nipples. One thing I've learned, is she likes a little pain with her pleasure. But only a touch. Which is great, because every time I've been inside her, I've not been able to contain myself.

I slide out and turn her until her back flops down on the mattress. Her tits bounce, and I groan. I always thought I was an arse person, but seeing her tits has my cock swelling.

"Fuck me," she moans, massaging her tits. "Harder."

With a groan, I place my hand gently below her neck and shove my cock inside her. I impale her until her moans turn into cries and her body trembles.

She takes all my cock. Every inch.

And if she doesn't come soon, I'm going to shoot my load inside of her.

I thrust harder, stretching her tight cunt more than it's ever been stretched. And from her moans, whimpers, and the grip she has on the cover, she's enjoying every minute of it.

She meets every thrust, her tits bouncing wildly.

"You feel so fucking good."

"I'm going to come," she cries. "Faster."

I grant her wish, slamming inside of her, rocking her further up the lounger. Each stroke has my cock swelling further, and sweat beads down my spine.

She climaxes violently, her head tilting to dig her teeth into my arm.

The roughness of the bite, the wetness rubbing against my cock, and her pussy clenching around me, undoes me.

I don't slow. I don't savour. I chase the orgasm like it's my last, fucking her thoroughly. She slams down on my cock, and my balls tighten.

And I feel like I'm going to lose all control.

I pull out with enough time to shoot my load. I grip my cock, coating her fair skin with my cum. Seeing her pussy glistening with my cum makes me want her all over again.

And again.

And again.

I drop down over her, supporting my weight with my forearms on either side of her. I kiss her and pour everything I'm feeling into it.

She whimpers, her slick cunt rubbing against my cock, seeking more.

I pull back and grin down at her. "Ready for dinner?"

"I'm gonna need a minute," she tells me, out of breath.

I drop down next to her, and she rolls, pressing her arse against me. Her fingers run lightly over my arm that's covering her waist, both of us spent and content to watch the sun setting.

This is what I've been missing.

Not just the intimacy, but these moments. I've never had anyone to share this with before, and I never pictured it either.

But now, I want all my moments like this to be with her.

15

HARRIETT

If I hadn't seen this with my own eyes, I would think it's a fantasy. This isn't a dream home. It's *the* home.

And I love my home. I made something simple into something spectacular and it's one of my favourite places to be. But I would die for this room.

The rest of the house, I'm sad to admit, lacks character. It doesn't hold the same warmth mine or my friends' homes do. There's nothing personal about it. It doesn't give me any insight as to who River Knight is.

But a cinema room...

It's like a fucking room dreams are made from.

The entire bottom row is one massive seat—or more like a gigantic bed. The row behind has five wide recliner seats that could probably fit three of my friends on one.

I turn to the back corner of the room, where sweets and popcorn are in glass containers. "I'm scared to breathe."

He chuckles as he steps up behind me. "It's my favourite room."

"Or touch anything," I continue like he didn't speak.

"Make yourself at home."

I drop down on the bed, my arms spread. "I want to take this home. Who needs a bed when you can have this?"

He crosses his arms over his bare chest. "I'll wait to show you my bed then."

My eyes widen as I sit forward, ready to get up. "Is it this big?"

He laughs, pushing me back down as he drops down next to me. I snuggle into his arms. "Not this big. It's half the size but so damn comfy. I swear, the first night I slept in it, I missed my morning alarm."

"I'm glad you have all of this."

"I guess I got lucky," he replies.

I shake my head as I run my hand down his chest, touching the ridges of his muscles. "Luck has nothing to do with it. When I look around and see the things you have, I feel proud—which I know sounds ridiculous since we barely know each other. But I love that you worked for it. It wasn't handed to you."

He tenses beneath me. "I've never really looked at it like that before. Sometimes I feel like an intruder here, like it's not real."

"It is real. Very real," I state. "I know my place is nothing compared to this, but I love everything about it. When I see the smallest of things, pride wells up inside of me. I worked for it. I worked for everything I have and I'm proud of that. You should be too."

"I guess. It's still a lot to get used to," he declares, hesitation in his tone. "This place might be big, but it isn't home, not really. After walking into yours, I finally realised what it's been missing. It's missing the personal touches."

"I didn't want to sound snobbish, but I came to the same conclusion. And I'd like to point out that I love cleaning, but this place would give me anxiety. I just keep imagining you having window cleaner stockpiled in some cellar."

He laughs, and his hand goes to my bare thigh. After fucking each other's brains out once again in the shower, he loaned me a pair of his boxers and a T-shirt. He doesn't know it yet, but he isn't getting the T-shirt back. It's soft as fuck, and I love that it reaches above my knees.

"I don't have window cleaner stockpiled in the basement."

I shudder. "But you have a cellar?"

"No. I don't even have a shed. Everything is stored in the second garage."

"Good, because a cellar is a deal breaker for me."

"It is, is it? Bit of a good job I don't then," he teases. "I'm a little afraid to ask, but why?"

"Me and the girls went on a ghost hunt a few years ago. We scared ourselves so much by trying to freak each other out, that when we heard a noise, we all lost it. We split from the group we'd also terrorized with our babblings and got trapped in a basement. It took six hours for them to get us out, and I think that had more to do with us freaking out. A police officer gave us his CS spray and baton in the end. Emily still hasn't forgiven herself for accidently spraying it in Gabby's face."

"How did you manage to get yourselves in that kind of predicament?" he chuckles. "The other day, Drew tried telling me you get into car chases and fires, but I'm starting to wonder if he wasn't playing."

"Oh no, he definitely wasn't. That was during Charlotte's ordeal. It was seriously fucked up, but I'd do it all again."

"Drew mentioned something but wouldn't go into detail."

"He wouldn't. Charlotte has accepted it, but she doesn't like talking about it. But I'm glad she has Drew. He's good to her and doesn't treat her like shit, like so many others have."

"He's a great guy."

"How did you two meet?" I ask, and he leans over, taking a remote off the side.

He leans back, bending his leg up to rest his arm across it. "We should pick a film."

"You do know there might be a time where you can't avoid the questions I ask. I want to get to know you. Not judge you. Or get the inside scoop."

He lets out a breath, keeping his gaze on his knees. "I'm not ready to dish the dirt. I'm not saying I won't ever open up to you; I'm just saying not now."

"Alright. I can live with that," I murmur, feeling sorry for the guy, and not in a pitiful way.

Going through life not knowing who you can trust, not being able to open up to those around you, stems from somewhere. It means he's been burnt before. He put trust into someone who soiled it and threw it in his face. It must be lonely to live like that. I can't imagine keeping anything from my girls. Even if I tried, they'd hound me until I opened up. I'd accuse the ex for being the reason, but something tells me it burns deeper than a scorned heart.

"Drew helped me," he blurts, and I still, waiting for more. "I won't tell you why, but he helped me. He gave me a safe place, trained me, and when things got bad at home, he offered to take me in. But I told him no. Until Colin. When he turned up at my door, things were as bad as they'd ever been. I let him guide me, and for a while, he let me sleep in the back of his shop. Back then, he owned a supply shop for athletes, and was working his way up to managing trained fighters. In exchange for a safe place to sleep, and food, I did everything he told me to. My career soared after that. And now here I am."

"I'm glad you had people looking out for you."

He lets out a dry chuckle. "It wasn't always like that."

"Everyone starts somewhere. My dad had been working site to site in construction before he met my mum. He worked for basically pennies. Then he went off on his own, became a contractor, and made a living from it. Even when business got slow, he still kept going."

"What did he do after his accident?"

"An uncle took over. They worked through word of mouth, so Dad signed everything over to him. If he didn't, he wouldn't have been able to live. He didn't want to take money from the business he didn't work for. He gave a fair wage, and to take a cut when he didn't do anything didn't sit well with him. He helps my uncle from time to time, but only when his back isn't playing up."

"It sounds like you have a great dad."

"I really do. He's been there for me through everything. And raising a teenager without a woman, to guide her, must have sucked for him. His sex education talk didn't go so well so he just threatened any male who went near me."

He gets lost in his thoughts for a moment. "I guess he doesn't like your boyfriends then."

"He's only met a few. He gives them a fair chance because he wants his girl happy, but once I'm hurt, all bets are off, and he puts them in their place."

"Can't wait to meet him," he muses.

Something that has been on my mind, something I've been dying to look up on my phone since the coffee shop, springs to my thoughts, and before I can stop myself, I'm talking. "Is your reluctance about talking to people something to do with your ex?" I ask, and inwardly groan.

I don't believe it is, but I had to bring it up. I need to know if he still has feelings for her; if I'm chasing waterfalls.

"You read about that?"

"I didn't. Someone I know was talking about the front page and happened to bring it up. If you don't want to talk about it, it's fine. I shouldn't have brought it up."

"It's fine. Marlene isn't the reason. She didn't know much about my past. I don't think she ever asked, if I'm honest. And I never offered it up because it really isn't something I like talking about."

"I get that. I really do. But just so you know, you can trust me. Even if this doesn't last or you cheat, I'd never reveal something like that. I prefer my revenge up close and personal. Not hiding behind words."

"Good to know," he replies, and the corner of his mouth kicks up.

"It must have been devastating to go through all of that."

He tenses. "What do you mean?"

"With Marlene."

He relaxes and gives me a careless shrug. "At first, all I felt was rage. I nearly lost my career, everything I've worked for. What she did hurt, and I stewed on it for a while. I thought I loved her. She was everything to me and she needed me. But looking back, I think I just wanted to feel that because I had never had it before. I wanted her to need me because no one has ever needed me. Once I came to that conclusion, I made peace with it."

"So, you aren't in love with her?"

His hand runs up my thigh, under his T-shirt I'm wearing. "You wouldn't be here if I did. You have nothing to worry about where she's concerned. I don't feel anything for her. I don't feel hate or sadness towards her. Her guy, the one she cheated on me with, is in this year's tournament. I'll probably have to go up against him at some point, and I've known this for a year."

"Do you think he'll try to piss you off?"

He grins. "It won't work. As soon as I realised she didn't mean that much to me and I was better off, I worked with groups of different people, under different occupations, to help me centre my emotions. When it got announced last year that he'd be rising to this year's tournament, I picked it back up. But until recently, I didn't realise I had nothing to worry about. He's got nothing to use against me. He thinks he does, but he doesn't. He thinks he's won some great prize."

"Men who brag like that, rile me. But if you think about it, he's basically bragging he took a cheater off you. I'd say he did you a favour."

"He did. A big one. But that doesn't mean I'll ever thank him for it."

"You should, but then, I'm a little twisted like that."

"Is that what you wanted to know; if I was still in love with her?"

"Yes, it crossed my mind a few times. I like you, and it would really fucking suck if we had to finish this so soon. The sex is great."

His lids lower lazily as he leans in closer. "The sex is great? Is that all?"

I playfully roll my eyes and shove him back. "You are okay, I suppose."

"You suppose?" he asks, reaching for me as he presses his lips to my neck.

I pull back, running my hand along his jaw. "Yeah, I mean, if you grew your beard, you'd be perfect."

"My beard?" he chuckles.

"I don't know why, but you kind of remind me of Derek Hale from *Teen Wolf*. When he grew his beard, he became ten times hotter. It did things to me."

"Most girls like guys in suits or a uniform."

I scoff. "Puh-lease. You wear shorts for your job. That beats any fucking uniform. Although, you do look good dressed up."

"Well, I'll make sure you get a front row seat at my next fight."

I sit up on my elbows. "I can come?"

"Yeah. I'll even get you and your friends backstage passes. First one is the middle of next month. Everyone will be there. The first fight is one all fighters attend. It's a show of respect," he explains, before his expression drops. "Shit! It's on a Saturday. Will you be able to make it?"

"Oh crap. I'm working, but I'll see if I can swap with someone."

"What about your friends? I don't want you to go alone. They can sometimes get a little heated, and I know I'll spend the whole night worrying about you."

"I don't think Dave will give us *all* the night off twice in a month, but I can ask Charlotte to come. The last time I saw Drew, he was telling me Charlotte is thinking of taking up boxing."

"She's a character, that's for sure. Drew has tickets to every game, so run it by him too. He might tag along."

As I go to ask for more information on the fight, the doorbell rings. "You expecting someone?"

He doesn't meet my gaze as he slides off the couch. "It's probably about the meeting I missed earlier."

"You missed a meeting?" I ask, then groan. "Please don't tell me it's because of me."

He shrugs as he grabs the T-shirt tucked into the back of his shorts. "It's not like I have an input. I'm there for show, and training is more important."

"River, don't change your schedule because of me. If you want to train, I'm cool to hang out and wait."

He grins. "For four hours?"

"Yeah. I'd be bored shitless, but I could bring my coursework."

"Next time," he promises. "Get comfy. I'll be back in five."

He still doesn't meet my gaze as he leaves the room. I sit up and shuffle over to where I threw my bag earlier and grab my phone.

As I scroll through my messages, I keep an ear out. The cinema room is on the other side of the house that leads down to another floor.

What if it's a booty call showing up for a good time?

He said he hasn't slept with anyone for a while, and I believed him, but then, what guy will admit to sleeping around?

As the minutes tick on, I get up, telling myself it's to make sure he's okay, but really, I just want to make sure he's telling the truth.

Heading out, I follow the path he walked us down earlier, jogging up the eight steps to the main floor.

Voices echo as I hit the kitchen.

"You have responsibilities, River, and you will abide by them. Because as of today, I'm sorry, but I'll have to give you a penalty charge."

"What the fuck? I missed a meeting, one I'm never a part of anyway. You can only fine me for the training and missed fights, and I've done neither."

"I am. You have been too lax recently and I won't stand for it."

"I work my goddamn arse off," River bites out. "I do everything you fucking ask, including photoshoots I tell you I'm not up for."

"Don't make me raise the fucking fine," a guy snaps.

"Do it. I don't give a fuck anymore," River argues. "Why don't you just say what this is really over? It's because I want to leave, and you don't like it."

I audibly gasp at the news. He never mentioned this to me. Not once.

They both turn at my gasp, and my eyes widen when I recognise the man from the charity event.

"You!" he bites out.

16

HARRIETT

The older man hasn't changed a bit since I last saw him. Still in what I assume is the same suit and blue tie, and giving me the same glare, I can't help but dislike the man even more. Something tells me he wears the same suit as a costume, to assert himself into a world he doesn't belong. Being a stripper comes with its perks. It gives you a chance to really see into a person. I've met men like him before. The suit makes them feel powerful, untouchable, but inside, he's just a scared little boy, and a snake.

Pretending to not know him, I pinch my brows together. "I'm sorry, do I know you?"

"You know very well who I am," he snaps.

"Colin, don't," River warns.

"Is this who you're choosing to spend your time with? Really?" he argues, the veins in his temples pulsing.

"I'm sorry, have I done something to upset you?" I ask in a sickly-sweet voice.

"Don't play coy with me. You know who I am. Like I know *who you are*."

River wraps his arm around my waist, and to add insult to injury, I cuddle up to him, placing my hand over his pec. "I'm really sorry, I don't recall. And I'd appreciate it if you could refrain from being rude to me."

"You spilled your drink all over me at the charity fight last year."

"I'm sorry, I don't recall."

"I warned you to stay away," he replies, his voice growing harder with frustration.

I tap my finger to my upper lip before pointing it at him. "Oh, I remember now. You thought you could order me around. I didn't like that," I admit, and then tilt my head. "I'm sorry your nose didn't mend straight."

I feel River's chest rumble against my cheek, and I know he's fighting back laughter as Colin's hand goes to his nose.

He drops his hand quickly, before remarking, "I know your game, and you won't get what you want here."

"I already did. Multiple times," I answer.

"Do you know who she is?" Colin bites out, addressing River now.

"I do. It's *you* who doesn't. I don't appreciate this visit or you attacking my guest, who, I will remind you, was *actually* invited."

Colin takes another step up, pointing from River to me. "This is over between you. After tonight, I forbid you to see her. You forget who runs this show. She'll ruin you, you stupid fucking boy."

River lets out an exasperated breath. "What the fuck are you talking about Colin?"

"Do you care?" I mutter under my breath, and his hand tightens around me.

Colin glowers at me, having heard my remark, but it's River he replies to. "She'll try to take everything we have. Our reputation will be ruined because of her, and there will be no more endorsements or deals. They'll never want to work with us after the scandal she'll create. Do you want that? Do you want us to lose everything?"

"Are you his dad?"

"I'm his manager, and I'm not talking to you," he snaps.

"Enough," River dangerously barks. "She's staying, Colin, now I suggest you leave."

"No, she isn't," Colin grits out, and the look in his eye has me stepping further into River, seeking his safety. There's disgust when he looks at me, but more. There is no doubt in my mind that if River wasn't standing next to me, this man would go for me. "She goes, or I'll make her go. And don't push me, boy. I will walk and take everything with me. I didn't want it to come to this, but you've left me no choice. I'll tell everyone. You'll no longer be worshipped by fans, you'll lose sponsors, endorsements, and every contract you have active. You'll be cancelled, and everyone will come after you. The world will know who you really are."

I feel River tense beneath me. "Harriett, can you give me a minute please?"

Sensing the seriousness of what is about to transpire, I gently step out of his embrace. "I'll wait in the garden."

As I step into the house, he closes the door behind him, and it leaves me with an ominous feeling. I make my way into the garden, no longer feeling smug about getting the guy riled up. I'm also concerned about what he has on River to make him react the way he did.

Should I be worried?

As I take a seat on a lounge chair, I can't help but feel like I shouldn't. I might not know everything about him, but I feel like I'm a good judge of character. He's not a bad guy. He might have done some shit when he was younger, but as far as I can see, he worked to change it around. I could be wrong, but there's not even a small hint inside of me that's telling me I am.

We might have only gone out a few times, but I've been with him intimately. It opens your heart and your eyes, and builds a connection, whether it's one night or ten. I might not know everything, but I know him. Or who he is right now. There's no way I would be here if I didn't. I'd sense something is wrong or off about him.

About fifteen-twenty minutes later, he steps through the doorway, running his hands through his hair. The tension pouring off him has me sitting up in the chair.

"Are you okay?"

He lets out a dry laugh as he takes a seat on the edge of the chair next to me, facing me. "Far from it."

"I'm sorry if I made things difficult for you back there. I didn't think it through."

He scrubs a hand over his head. "Don't do that. Don't apologise. He was rude and a prick."

"What did he mean when he said he'd tell the world? What did you do?"

He tugs at the strands of his hair. "I can't tell you," he chokes out, his voice breaking.

I get up and pull his hands away so I can straddle him. He grips my arse and rests his forehead against my chest. "Is this about what you mentioned inside?"

"Yes."

I run my hands over his jaw, tilting his head back as I do. I wait for him to meet my gaze. "Then you don't have to tell me. I can wait."

His brow arches. "Just like that?"

"Believe it or not, I trust you. I have a feeling you did something you aren't proud of, and because you've built it up in your mind to the point you can't even talk about it, you've made it out to be worse than it really is."

"You can't possibly know what it is," he replies, his voice low. "And now your mind is probably going over a shit ton of scenarios."

"It's how my mind works," I lightly tease. "Have you ever raped someone?"

His lips twist. "No."

"Killed a child?"

"No."

"Then I can wait," I reply with conviction. "But if you want me to leave, to comply with his demands, just tell me. You aren't going to break my heart, but I do think you'll be making a mistake."

"It's fine. I sorted it," he replies, looking lost in thought.

"How?"

He looks ashamed when he averts his gaze. "I threatened him back."

"With what?"

"He cheats on his wife. I told him I'm not the only one with something to lose. He has kids and a home. And after the first time he did it, she threatened to take everything and the kids and leave him. He won't risk losing that, not when her parents are wealthy as fuck and she's an only child."

I can feel the guilt he's feeling over doing it. "I'm sorry you had to do that."

"He needed to be brought down a peg or two."

"And you think it's enough to stop him from revealing your secrets?"

"No. I reminded him of what he has because of me, and I made a wager with him."

"A wager?" I repeat, wondering what they could possibly wager.

"I reminded him of what we've achieved together and what he would lose without me. He pointed out that you could take everything from me and reveal my secrets yourself for money. So, I told him if he trusts my decisions, and be the man I think he is, I will give him a bonus when I leave."

"And what does he get if he doesn't?" I ask, not liking where this is going.

"Me. If he's right about you, or if things go to shit before my last fight, I have to fight for another year."

"You don't need to do that, not for me. I don't want to be the reason you don't get to do what you want. And this isn't me saying I will do any of those things because I won't. That's not me. But it's a lot to lose on a chance."

"If that's the price I have to pay to be with you, then I'll give it all to him. You're worth it to me. And I don't think you will either. Trust works both ways."

"It's been two dates."

The intensity in his eyes has a ball of emotion building in the back of my throat. "When something feels right, I hold on to it. Two dates, two hundred dates, I don't give a fuck. It feels good to be lost in the right direction."

"Lost?"

"We're just beginning. We're in the unknown, but for the first time, I feel like I'm finally heading in the right direction. And I'm hoping you feel the same way. I want exclusivity, I want it all… with you. If you want."

My shoulders drop at his sweet words. He's summed up everything I've been feeling in just a few words. "I do, and I would hope we were exclusive without labels, but it's good to know. I'm all in too," I tell him, but then broach the other subject. "You said you didn't want to fight anymore. I heard you before, you said you were leaving."

"I am. I love what I do, but I want more. It's why I've worked so hard for the past year. If I leave with the championship on my belt, I'll have achieved everything I've worked for. But I'm also good if that doesn't happen. I still got here. I still competed," he explains, gripping me tighter. "I'm tired though. The training is gruelling, and I'll be thirty in a few years. I want to live, not constantly be on the go and missing out on so much."

"Then do what's best for you, no matter what," I plead.

"I will," he tells me, and his eyes heat. "Starting now."

He lifts me in his arms and takes me inside. "Not outside? Mr Knight, I'm disappointed."

He chuckles as he heads back in the direction of the cinema room. "No. Since you dropped down on the sofa, I've been imagining fucking you on it."

Wetness pools between my legs. "Then fuck away."

There's no warning when he kisses me. No build up. No words. And he doesn't just kiss me; he devours me as we reach the cinema room.

He lowers me onto the sofa, his body engulfing me. I reach up to touch him, but he pins my wrists above my head, holding me captive.

And I don't mind one single bit if it means he keeps kissing me like this.

He frees my hand so he can reach under the T-shirt, snaking his hand up to cup my bare breasts. I moan into his mouth, and he pulls back with a wicked grin.

He sheds his shirt and boxers, and my attention is drawn to his dick. I lean up, shedding mine, leaving me in nothing but his boxers. "I never thought I'd find this sexy."

"What?"

"You, wearing my clothes."

I let my hands travel down his chest as he pulls out a condom. I arch an eyebrow. I don't find it arrogant; I find it sexy that he thought to come prepared this time. It means he doesn't want to keep his hands off me, just like I don't with him. "Impressed."

His lip kicks up at the corner. "I live to impress."

He rolls the condom on, and surprises me when he doesn't immediately start fucking me. Instead, he caresses my tits as he grinds into me, and I find it hard to be quiet. I know what it feels like to have him inside of me, how good it feels when he fucks me. The tease, it is torture. And I'm a willing captive.

He bends his head, licking and sucking my nipple into his mouth before pulling back and lightly blowing over the tip.

"Fuck," I hiss, arching into him.

I need more.

He leans back and grips the elastic on the waistband of the boxers I'm wearing, before tugging them down my legs.

When his fingers run through my pussy, he finds how wet I already am, and his hooded eyes turn molten.

God, that look. It does dirty things to me.

"I need to be inside you. I wanted to savour the moment, to tease you to the brink of an orgasm over and over until you begged me to fuck you. But I can't wait. I need you."

He gets no argument from me, and it's the best decision I ever made. He slams into me like a feral man and my back brushes against the soft fabric beneath me.

With gritted teeth, he leans up. "God, you feel so fucking good."

I tighten around him as I drag my fingers through his hair. He fucks me like he hates me, yet he never pushes me past my limit. Whenever it's too much, he pulls back, using enough strength to please me.

"My turn," I whisper, and shove him away.

He slides out of me, and I'm unashamed with the wetness between my thighs as I straddle him. This position brings him deeper, so I lower myself down slowly, keeping my hands on his chest.

He groans, one hand gripping my hip, the other on my thigh. "Fuck!"

I continue to go slow, getting used to his size and enjoying the torturous feel of him inside of me. He grunts as I begin to rock faster, and I glide my fingers up my sides and over my chest.

His gaze never wavers.

Because if there's one thing I've learned, men love visual. It's why they watch so much porn. They love the sensual touch, and the vision of what they want but can't have.

I pinch my nipples, tugging at the tips.

"Oh fuck, enough play," he growls ,and keeping hold of my hips, he sits up, spreading his thighs.

I'm no longer in control. With my legs behind him and nothing to use as leverage, I'm at his mercy.

And he easily grips my hips, rocking and lifting my weight on his cock.

He's deeper, hitting the right spot inside of me. "Oh fuck," I breathe out. I'm lost for words.

He cups my tit and lifts it to his mouth. He sucks on the tip, keeping up with the pace.

Needing more, I maneuverer my legs until I'm on my knees and griping his shoulders. I ride him until my muscles feel weak. I fuck him until I can't remember my own name.

So many sensations…

So many feelings.

I lean down, taking his lips with mine, but it's all too much. All I can feel is him. I pull back until our lips are only a breath away. I grind down even harder, and my moans and his grunts echo in the quiet room.

When he grips my arsecheeks, one in each hand, and begins to bring me down harder on his cock, I come undone.

I cry out, my hands tightening around his shoulders as my orgasm tears through me.

He grunts, his movements ragged, hurried, as he chases his own orgasm. "Yes," he growls, as he drops his head back.

It's a beautiful sight seeing him come undone.

When he drops back, I follow, wincing as he slides out of me. I feel sore, but in a good way.

I place my hand over his chest, completely spent. "I don't want to be high maintenance, but I'm staying here. I don't think I can move."

He turns and runs his hand over my hip. "Why would you want to?"

I peel open my eyelids. "Because I'm cold."

He shuffles over and grabs a remote off the side table. He presses a button, and a drawer slides open at the end of the sofa. He takes out a few blankets and throws one over me. "See, you don't need to move."

I groan. "Why do you do that?"

He looks a little taken aback by my remark. "Do what?"

"Spoil me. I'm going to get used to it and it's not a good thing."

"If this is what you think spoiling is, then I can't wait to see what you're like when I really do."

"What do you mean?"

"I plan on spoiling you often."

"I was playing."

"I know, but I'm not."

I run my hand along his jaw. "Why do you have to be so perfect?"

"I'm far from it," he tells me, his voice darkening.

"You're right," I tease. "If you were, I would have snacks and some drinks in front of me. I need the sugar after that."

He grins. "Let me go get cleaned up and I'll be back with snacks," he tells me, and hands me the remote. "You find us a film. Won't be long."

I snuggle back into the sofa, taking the blanket with me. It's really fucking soft, softer than any of mine. As I flick through Netflix, I can't help but think on what he said.

He doesn't know it yet, but I plan to be the one doing the spoiling.

From what I've learned, he hasn't had the best upbringing. He admitted he had never been to a fair before our first date, and the little things he's commented on, I can tell it's always been like that.

He might have nice things and has been to many places, but something tells me he's never really lived. He never got to enjoy them. So I'm going to make it my mission to give him a piece of my world.

I might not want to admit it out loud, but I seriously like him.

And for him to risk everything for me, I want him to know I'm worth it.

17

RIVER

Kicking the stand of my bike down, I shut the engine off and rip off my helmet, letting the breeze flow over me. I didn't sleep much over the weekend because I spent it being worried about Harriett working at the club. I meant what I said about being okay with what she does, but until this weekend, I didn't realise how much it would affect me—how much she affects me.

Knowing men get to see what I now class as mine, infuriates me. Not because I want to get my dick out and measure who's is bigger, but because she deserves better than sleazy guys gorming over her.

The only thing that kept me in my bed was knowing what working there means to her. I know she's created a family and has kept her identity a secret. She's Candy there; it's only me who gets to see Harriett take off her clothes.

Still, my mind ran over things that might happen to her. Would someone get rowdy, touch her? Or worse, would she get stuck in the middle of a brawl?

Fortunately for me, Harriett loves to text, so we've been exchanging messages all weekend.

Never in my wildest dreams did I ever think a chick would get to me like this. She has me tied up in knots, and I don't want to get free. I like this new-found feeling, this relationship that doesn't even have a label. It doesn't need one. She's mine and I'm hers.

Now, as I stare up at the building where Colin awaits to start the morning meetings, dread hits me.

Threatening him didn't feel good, even if it was deserved. He's been a father figure—a crappy one at that—and this bridge between us keeps growing.

And something inside me knows the minute I see him, he's going to try again and turn what I share with Harriett, ugly. He tried to do the same thing with Marlene, but not to this extent, and he gave up once he realised he wasn't going to get his way.

Maybe he will again this time.

I swing my leg over the bike and head over to the front doors. The minute I step inside, staff begin to greet me, and I greet them back with a jerk of my chin or a short, 'hey'.

As I hit the elevator to go up, a woman steps out, pushing her glasses up her nose. When she looks up, she stumbles at the sight of me. I reach out, steadying her. "Fuck! I didn't mean to scare you. Are you okay?"

"Thank you. I'm fine. I just wasn't expecting someone to be outside."

"You're welcome," I reply, holding the doors to the lift open.

"You are River Knight, right?"

"You are?" I ask, as the elevator door next to us opens. Colin steps out, taking a double look at the woman next to me before his expression tightens.

"I'm—"

"River, my office now. Tell your lady friend to leave," he orders sharply.

I grimace as the woman stares at him in shock. "Sorry, I have to go. Again, sorry for scaring you."

I don't wait for her reply. I shove past Colin and step into the elevator. I push the fifth floor, uncaring that he's probably going up too.

He might be my manager, but he works for me.

As the door closes, I clench my hands into fists and count to ten as I take slow, steady breaths in and out.

Hitting him won't solve anything. It will make me feel good for a few beats, but after, the guilt will set in, and a shit storm will brew. He has friends within our local police station. He knows every law to rule a trained fighter, and he knows every loophole in the business to get what he wants. I don't doubt for a minute that he won't hesitate to sue me for everything I'm worth.

So yeah, hitting him won't solve anything. And as long as I remain calm, there won't be a problem. Doesn't mean I have to like it, and it certainly doesn't mean I can't picture him later when I punch the fuck out of the punching bag.

The doors open on the fifth floor, and I'm immediately greeted by Hetty, an older receptionist who I personally feel is overworked and overlooked. When I leave after the championship, I'll be offering her a promotion to come and work for me, for as long as she wants. Or if retiring is something she wishes to do, I'll make sure she's well compensated for the shit she has endured working here.

"He's not in a good mood this morning," she explains.

"I'd be worried if it was a good mood," I comment, making her laugh. "Hey, I don't suppose you know why I wasn't given today's itinerary? It's normally emailed to me, but I've not had anything all weekend."

She looks to the elevator doors, before scanning both ends of the corridor. Once it's clear, she reaches under the desk and hands me a bunch of folders. "That's everything you need to know for today's meeting. If you need anything else, just let me know," she offers, taking another look to make sure no one is listening in. "I offered to send them, but Mr Andrews… he was in a bad mood and said he'd do it himself."

I place my hand over hers. "Don't sweat it. I'm sure he would have gotten around to it," I tell her, knowing full-well he wouldn't have.

Suddenly, her posture changes. She sits straighter in the chair, her expression dropping. "If that is all, Mr Knight, I must be getting on with my work."

I hear the footsteps behind me before he announces his presence. "Change of plans. I'll see you at the first meeting in an hour."

"What about our meeting?"

"I don't have time. I have business to attend to. You can wait," he tells me, and doesn't wait for a reply before he's storming down the hallway to his office.

"This is going to be a long day," I groan.

"I bought some pastries. They are in the staff room. Go, eat and read up on today's meetings."

I lean over the desk and kiss her wrinkled cheek. "I don't know what I'd do without you."

She brushes me off with a blush to her cheeks. "Get. You need to eat if you want strength to deal with Mr Andrews today."

"See you later, Hetty."

"Good day, Mr Knight."

"Call me, River, please," I offer, and when she goes to argue, I continue. "At least when Colin isn't around."

"Alright," she agrees, before the phone rings.

I leave Hetty to her work and make my way down to the staff room, where I know I won't be disturbed. Colin runs a tight ship here, and no one is found slacking off in the staff room, since they are too scared they'll be fired.

Just like I guessed, it's empty when I walk inside. It's a simple room. Half kitchen with a table and only two chairs. With all the money he earns, he couldn't even splash out on a decent seating area.

I drop the folders on the table and pull out a chair. I might as well get comfortable since I'll most likely spend a majority of the day in here.

My phone pings with a message and I quickly pull it out, a smile lighting up my face when I see it's Harriett responding to my morning text.

> Harriett: Morning, handsome. I slept like the dead, as always. How was training? I still find it weird you get up that early to train.

> River: I don't get this body by doing nothing.

Harriett: Well, since you put it like that, train away. I wouldn't want you to pull your back the next time you fuck me against the wall.

River: We wouldn't want that, now would we, especially since I enjoy fucking you until you scream my name.

Harriett: Keep going… What else do you like?

River: I love your taste.

Harriett: Yes…

River: And the way you clench around my cock.

Harriett: Keep going…

River: And I love your little throaty moans, and the way you run your fingers through my hair.

Harriett: You do have great hair.

River: But most of all, I enjoy the way you look at me.

Harriett: And how do I look at you, River Knight?

River: Like I gave you the world. And like I invented sex.

Harriett: Well, you are a new experience.

River: When can I see you again?

Harriett: I was about to invite you to dinner, but then you got me horny and distracted me.

River: Well, I know a cure to fix that. When?

Harriett: Tonight? And promises, promises.

River: I never make promises I can't keep. I'll be at yours tonight around six. I'll shift some work around.

Harriett: Don't do that. Bring your work here. I have an assignment to do, so we can work together, if you want. And I know what you are thinking: how will I get work done with Harriett looking so hot? But I have a solution for that. We can't touch until after we've finished our work. I can't think of better motivation. And I promise, the reward will blow your mind. I mean, you can't get a better reward than me.

River: Deal. And you're right, I don't think there is a better reward.

Harriett: I know. So, dinner is a go?

River: Yes, I'll be there for six, but if I finish earlier at the gym, I'll message you beforehand and see what you are doing.

Harriett: Sounds like a plan. See you there, handsome. Anything you prefer to eat before I head back into class?

River: Protein, veg, but for you, I'll eat whatever you put in front of me.

Harriett: Now I'm picturing me laid out on my dining room table, legs spread, cream…

> River: Not an image I needed before I have to go into a meeting.

> Harriett: Then it's a good job you are well endowed and have nothing to be ashamed of.

> River: Minx.

> Harriett: Later, handsome.

> River: See you later, gorgeous.

Putting the phone face down on the table, I push images of Harriett naked on a table aside and get to work. If I'm going to get through today without another confrontation with Colin, I have to get reading.

SOMETHING IS MOST DEFINITELY UP. Colin has avoided speaking to me unless he has no other choice, and has barely looked in my direction.

The meeting comes to an end, and the sponsors are the first to leave.

"Colin, can I talk to you for a moment?"

"I'm busy," he tells me, without meeting my gaze.

Picking up on the tension, the others are quick to leave. I place my hand over the stack of folders, stopping him from picking them up. "Look, I get you are mad at me, but we need to sort this out if we are to continue to work with each other."

He sighs and drops down in the chair. "I don't know how it's come to this."

I take the free seat to his right. "Me either. But we're better than this, Colin. We've been working together for a really long time, and I hate it's come to this."

"Me too. I should have kept my reservations about the girl to myself. But I need you to know, I was only trying to protect you. I still am. But until you see for yourself, there's nothing I can do."

"Colin," I warn on a plea. "I don't want to keep going around in circles with you."

"I'm not. I promise, I won't get involved again. I only said what I said because I care about you a lot and I think of you as a son. I was just trying to protect you."

"And I appreciate that, I do, but I can take care of myself."

"Then there's something you should know. At the charity event last year, it was brought to my attention that she was working the room. When I saw her sights on you, I had to step in. I don't know whether it's true or not—you know how parties like that can be—but I thought you should know in case there's some truth to it."

"What do you mean?" I ask, not believing it for a second, but anyone could have gotten the wrong impression.

"I didn't get the gentleman's name, but when he saw her, he panicked. Apparently, he had been seeing her, even paid for her bills and stuff, and he fell in love. Until he got warned about who she was. He called things off, but she started blackmailing him. She sold stories to the press and nearly ruined his career."

"Are you sure he was talking about Harriett?"

"I assumed so, but then, you wouldn't risk everything for a stripper. Whoever this guy was talking about, was a working girl," he explains, before waving me off. "Ignore me. I've already overstepped where she's concerned, and I've been on your back a lot lately. I don't want anything else to come between us."

There's an inkling of doubt inside of me, but then, I think of Harriett, and everything we've shared, and I can't see her doing that. It must be a mistake.

"For what it's worth, I'm really sorry for what I said the other night. She means a lot to me, and in time, I know you'll like her too. But let's move on from this. I don't like the tension and I think everyone has picked up on it today."

He ducks his head in shame. "Same, boy, same," he tells me as the door is pushed open, revealing his personal assistant, Marco.

"You have Tempro waiting on line one."

"I'll be just a minute," Colin replies, gathering his stuff.

"I'll see you Wednesday for the press tour meeting," I tell Colin.

"Yes, I'll have a list of questions for you to prep for by then too," he tells me.

"I'm glad we could sort this out," I admit.

"Me too, son, me too," he replies, but doesn't meet my gaze.

He leaves, and I grab my stack of papers and exit the room. As I do, Marco is at the end of the corridor, head bent as he talks to Colin. They both stiffen at my presence, and Colin leaves abruptly, without another word to his assistant.

Shrugging off their weird behaviour, I head to the elevators and begin to wonder about what Colin said.

The charity event tickets weren't cheap. They were in their thousands, and although Harriett isn't poor, I can't see her forking out tickets for an event like that, nor the friend she had been with.

I don't want to question her, and I feel like a prick for even having an inkling of doubt, but I didn't make it this far in life trusting everyone. And those I did trust, always threw it in my face.

Now I have to wonder if Colin told me this so I can twist it in my head, or if he merely means no harm.

The only person who can answer the questions I have is Harriett, and I don't know how she'll take being judged. Because that's essentially what I'll be doing. Judging. Judging her by other people's standards and not the standards I've come to learn and love.

Talk to her.

The voice inside the back of mind knows I should.

Deciding to not let it twist into something ugly inside of me, I decide to ask her about it later. If there's one thing I know Harriett appreciates, it's honesty.

The worst outcome is Colin being right. But it's better to know now rather than later down the line.

I hope.

18

HARRIETT

I've always loved the smell of a Sunday roast cooking in the oven. It reminds me of my childhood, back when my mum was alive. It was the one day we sat down at the table together without the stress of schoolwork, dance, or other commitments that had us rushing through dinners. Sometimes it was just us, but other times, we'd invite family or friends to join us. Both were as equally enjoyable. We'd eat, laugh, and talk, and after we all cleared it away and washed up, we'd spend the evening playing board games until it was time for me to finish any homework or have a bath before bed.

Since university started, and with the extra workload, my Sundays now are mostly spent sleeping or catching up with schoolwork. I never have time to cook a roast for me and my friends, but Dad and I always make sure to have one at least once a month. I missed last month's since he had been visiting relatives, but I'm glad I get to do one today, even if it isn't a Sunday or with my dad.

River has been here awhile, but now we are in my small but practical kitchen, he seems rigid and tense.

I've got a sinking feeling it's because he doesn't like roasts and is too afraid to tell me. I remember as a kid when I went through my fussy eating stage. If I was invited somewhere and I didn't like the food, I got too nervous to speak up. He reminds me of me at that time.

As I dish up the last of the food, I turn to him. "Hey, if you don't like anything, I can cook you something else. I don't mind," I assure him, but then drop my shoulders, and in a light tease, admit, "Okay, I'll make you cook it yourself, but the thought is still there."

He grabs the gravy, pouring it over his chicken and potatoes. "No, this is great. It smells amazing."

Taking a seat across from him, I take the gravy from his offered hand. "Then what's up? Did things not go so well with Colin at work today?"

He clears his throat, unable to meet my gaze. "We actually cleared things up."

Then maybe it's something I've done or said. "Then what's up?"

"You're going to think it's ridiculous," he states, rubbing over the clock tattoo on his forearm.

"The only thing I find ridiculous is Gabby trying to do handstands. You'd think someone as flexible as her would have nailed it by now, but apparently, she still needs work on her balance."

He leans back, gesturing to the plate of food. "I've never had anyone cook for me before. And I don't think I've ever had a traditional roast like this before."

I'm taken off guard by his response. I thought for sure he didn't like it, or maybe I cooked too much for him. Never this.

"Not even one of your ex-girlfriends?"

"My only ex is Marlene, and she didn't even know how to cook toast," he admits. "Which is a dick thing for me to say, but it's the truth."

I'm actually surprised. "She took you out for dinner though, right?" His expression says it all. "Well, get used to it, because I was eyeing up your kitchen. I might not be the best cook, but I've had no complaints."

He grabs his forks. "Thank you, but next time, I'm cooking."

"You can cook?"

"Like you, I'm not the best, but the cook I hire to prep meals has taught me a few dishes. I couldn't exactly live off Pot Noodles or sandwiches."

"Hey, you'll get no complaints from me. My first year at university, I lived off Super Noodles, Pot Noodles, and cups of soup."

"Did you have to share a room?"

I roll my eyes at the guy question. "Yes, for the first year, and she liked to hum show tunes a lot."

He laughs at my reply. "What about after?"

"I stayed in shared accommodation for a year, but the guy who lived with us had a revolving door. I rented privately after that, but it wasn't for long. When I had to move schools for the next level of my course, my uncle offered this place. It used to be a drive and garage until he got planning permission to build. He planned to use it as an extra income, but his first tenant was a nightmare. When he got rid of him, I had just come home and was looking for temporary accommodation until I got on my feet, so when he offered it to me at a family rate, I said yes. I fell in love with it and decided to stay here. He's hardly home cause he works away a lot, so I keep an eye on his place for him. I think when the time comes, he'll move in here and he'll rent the main house out."

"I did wonder why it was such a small house. It stands out from the rest."

I laugh 'cause he isn't wrong. "It's quirky, that's for sure."

"What have you got planned for the rest of the week?"

That reminds me. "I had actually meant to bring this up when you arrived, but then you kissed me, and I got distracted."

"Sounds ominous."

I arch my brow at his teasing. "Alright, it might not be your thing, and I'll understand if you say no, but Thursday, we're going to a drag bar and I was wondering if you want to go. We know a guy who works there, and he's finally hosting this week. He's funny as fuck and does a great Dolly impersonation. The first half is filled with different performers, and then he'll go on to do a comedy set. It's a great night and we promised we'd go and support him if you're up for it. My friends really want to meet you too, but if you prefer something lowkey or whatever, I understand."

He squeezes my hand. "You're cute when you ramble," he states. "And I should be okay to go. What time do you want to be there?"

"It starts at eight."

He sits back, his expression dropping. "Shit, I have an interview, but I can see if it can be moved around. It starts at seven, but it can last a few hours with the photographers."

I wave him off. "Come after. Unless that's your polite way of not accepting the invitation. I mean, my friends can be a little full-on."

"No, I want to come. If you don't mind me showing up a little late, I'm up for it."

"Alright. Well, I think Drew is coming this time. The manager told us Charlotte wasn't allowed to go without supervision. She got drunk, wanted to dress up as a Drag queen, and we didn't realise until it was too late that she couldn't walk in high boots. She tripped and pulled down the backdrop, which somehow broke the lights."

His raspy chuckle runs down my spine as I take a bite of the food. "I think you are all a little nuts and need supervision. I have to go, even if it's just to make sure you don't get into trouble."

I shrug, uncaring. "We live life, and we aren't going to apologise for it."

"Did you speak to your friends about the place I have on the beach?"

I drop my fork. "Shit, I'm sorry, I forgot. I'll see them Thursday, so I'll mention it then and get back to you."

"No rush. The offer doesn't have an expiry date."

"How about you; how was your day? And truthfully. Don't spare my feelings."

"It actually wasn't that bad. Boring to the point I wanted to fall asleep."

"You said you made things up with Colin. How did that go?"

"Tense, but I think he's seen the error of his ways."

I doubt that. "Do you feel okay now?"

"A little but it's still not a great position to be in. I'm not saying I'm a golden boy, I'm not. I've done things I'm not proud of. But I got a second chance in life, and I don't intend to spit on it. I've worked hard to be the man I am today, and I've come a long way. I'm not proud of what I did, but he left me no choice. He had no right to speak to you like that or demand I stop seeing you."

I reach for his hand. "It will be okay, you know. I know it doesn't seem like it now, but it will. You'll see."

"I just wish it didn't have to come to that."

"You said he has been on your back since you told him you wanted to leave last year."

"Yeah, I actually told him at the charity event last year. It sucked it came out the way it did, but I'd just had enough. We argued a lot that night."

"It's not your fault he can't handle not getting his way. If it's any consolation, you handled it the best you could. I just hope everything calms down for you now," I tell him, meaning every word. "I am surprised he gave up just like that though. I would have thought he would try again. He really doesn't like me, and I have no idea why. Not that I care."

"He has a lot to lose," he explains, but there's a note in his tone that tells me there's more. It's the same tone my dad and mum used before they told me about the cancer being terminal.

"Okay, I know there's more. Just spit it out. What did he say?"

He lets out a dry laugh. "Nothing gets past you, does it?"

"Not even spiders, now spill," I warn, my tone gentle.

"Okay, but I want to start by saying I don't believe a word of it. He told me he has reservations about you because a guy he met at the charity event said you were an item once. He told Colin that he paid your bills and stuff and fell in love with you."

"What?" I ask, completely flawed. "No one has ever paid my bills. And the last guy I dated didn't last long enough for him to be invited inside my house."

River shrugs. "Told you it was unbelievable. Colin said the guy called it off with you when he found out what you did for a living, and that you started blackmailing him afterwards. Oh, and you leaked stories about him."

"Convenient," I mutter, a little angry about the lie.

"Gorgeous, I thought the same thing. Things didn't add up, but the guy did say you was a stripper. Colin doesn't know that, so this guy must have been trying to twist shit. Or maybe he recognised you. I don't know. And don't worry, I didn't confirm your occupation to Colin. He didn't believe it anyway, but none of it matters. Whoever told him all this was trying to stir up shit."

I don't reply for a minute, too livid over what I've just heard. Colin knows exactly who I am and where I work. The fact he hasn't told River makes me wonder if he has something up his sleeve. But for him to spread shit like this, to taint my image and who I am, yeah, I'm not down with that.

I go to tell him about Colin and my concerns, to let him know some random guy didn't make this up. Colin did. Colin knew exactly what to say to mess with River's head. And I wouldn't even fault him for doubting me. I probably would too if I heard that story. A good lie or a good story always works if there's a bit of truth to it. But I'm a woman, and I can do crazy shit when I'm upset or angry. And right now, I'm fucking furious.

"Let's forget about it. I don't believe it, so there's nothing to worry about. It's just a misunderstanding."

"Yeah," I agree, pasting on a fake smile.

Once I get time off, I'll be paying Colin a friendly visit.

I'VE ALWAYS BEEN a believer in keeping it real. Be who you are and not what others perceive you to be. And when a time calls for it, fake it till you make it.

And tonight, I've had to do the latter—or I have to an extent. I just couldn't stop thinking about what Colin told him or wonder if River truly didn't believe it. And I don't understand why I care. If he does, it won't be the end of the world.

But it will be the end of us.

And I like us.

I love that we haven't known each other long but the connection is strong like we've known each other a lifetime. We just click. And it would suck if tomorrow I woke up and had to pretend like the past few weeks haven't been the best weeks of my life.

And I'd miss the incredibly hot sex. No one has ever managed to fulfil my every need the way he does. He gives as much as he takes and I'm all for that.

I peer over the top of my textbook to where he's sitting in the corner, using my desk chair to work. He has one leg crossed over his knee, a binder resting on his thigh, and a notepad in his hand.

There's nothing sexier than a guy who works.

I tug my glasses off and bring the ear part to my lips, chewing on the end as I watch him concentrate on the papers in front of him.

My heartrate picks up, because watching him, imagining his lips are on me and not on the pen he's tapping against his lips, is more proof it would suck without him in my life. No one has ever revved me up like this before, especially without even touching me.

When he moves, I duck my gaze back to the papers, mindlessly tapping the tip of my pen on the corner of the textbook. I feel his gaze burning into me, and a part of me hopes he's feeling the same ache I'm feeling.

Because I want him.

I want him so goddamn bad.

I've always had a strong appetite when it comes to sex, or at least I thought I did until River. I had been sore over the weekend, something I hadn't felt since I lost my virginity at seventeen. And not once did it ever stop me from fantasising about him or wanting him again. Just like now.

I'm not even sure a marathon of sex will ever quench the need I have for him.

I chance a peek over the textbook and our gazes meet. The desire in his gaze has me crossing my legs.

"How important is that assignment?"

"I have two days," I tell him without hesitation, lowering the book to my lap. "How important is your work?"

He drops his work on the desk before standing and removing his T-shirt. "Fuck my work."

I place my laptop on the bedside table and sit up, pushing the work to the side. Stripping down until he's naked, he crawls onto the bed. I unbutton the silk pyjama top I put on after I cleaned up, and finish with the last button just as he grabs my ankles and drags me down the bed.

Wetness pools between my legs when he roughly spreads my thighs apart. "So much better than work."

I shudder at the feel of the silk shorts running over my thighs. He discards them, throwing them over his shoulder.

"By the time I'm done, you'll be writing about me fucking you 'cause it's all you'll be able to think about."

As he runs his fingers through my wetness, I know he isn't wrong.

He's all I think about now.

I crave his touch, the feel of his hands, and I know when my body's to the brink, and I can't take much more, I'll still crave those things.

Because when he fucks me, he does it with everything in him. He does it with passion, with skill, and brute force that has me screaming out his name.

And when it's all over, I want to experience it all again.

Because he fucks me like it's our first time, every single time.

And a girl will never tire of that.

19

HARRIETT

There are a few things I like about working on the lower floor of the hospital, and that's that I don't have to run into visitors or grieving relatives. And not because I don't care, but because I care too much. But where there's an upside, there's a downside, and one of the downsides is the creep factor this entire floor holds.

Down here, it's like death runs down the walls from above and the smell has seeped into every stone and fitting. It's a smell you learn to ignore the longer you are down here, but not one you get used to.

It's the same with blood. After working down here for so long, I should be used to it, and maybe with a few more years on my belt, I will be. But it always makes me nauseous for the first hour or so.

But that isn't what creeps me out. I can live with that, no matter how uncomfortable it can get.

There are no windows down here, and it can feel suffocating at times. And the only light is from the florescent lights hung above on the ceilings. There's no chatter to cover up the silence, and although only a few of us work down here, there's still a strong presence. Or at least, it can feel like that.

And like now, as I walk down the corridor towards the room I work in, the only sound is my shoes tapping along the flooring. Gone are the bustling voices from upstairs, and the birds tweeting, and cars revving just outside.

It's just me in the Hallway of Doom.

Or as another student refers to it, the Hallway of Death. More than once, Cat—another student—has argued she has heard voices talking to her when she walks along these halls. And I've lost count of how many times she's locked herself in a room because she swears someone is down here with us.

And speaking of Cat, she's at the end of the hallway I turn down, pacing outside the room we are examining today's body in. I've questioned her education so many times since we started working together. If I hadn't watched her answer our mentors' questions to the textbook, I would think she cheated to get into this course. But I've come to learn Cat is eccentric and too brainy for her own good. It's probably why she lacks a filter or has trouble compartmentalising her thoughts as to what is tactful or rude.

"Please don't tell me you dropped an organ again," I call out as I near her. I watch the blood drain from her face when she jumps.

She stops pacing and brushes her vibrant pink hair back. "No, but I think I heard my nanna scolding me from heaven."

"I've only had one cup of coffee so I'm sorry, but you've lost me."

"He has a boner."

"Who has a boner?"

"The hot dead guy."

"You think a dead guy is hot?"

She arches her eyebrow in frustration, and that's when I notice her mascara is smudged beneath her eye. "He's dead. Dead is dead. But Dr. Aubrey told me to wash him down. I got to the legs, and I wasn't looking. I had my headphones in, my tongue hanging out 'cause I was concentrating, and then bam!"

I jump when she slaps her hands together. "What?"

She points to her eye. "I noticed his boner, jumped at the size, and forgot to clean up the water I spilled."

"Oh no," I gasp, scared of where this is heading.

"I fell, and his dick poked me in the eye. Now my nanna is screaming in rage from the grave because I'm an unmarried woman and I got poked by a dead guy."

"Cat, you aren't a virgin, so why would your nanna care?"

She lets out a breath. "Look, I'm just saying, I'm done dealing with boner patients. I moved from upstairs because I was done dealing with old, wrinkly penises. Don't get me wrong, I'm happy he died happy, but I'm not going back in there. I can't look at him the same way again."

"He's dead," I deadpan.

"Not the point."

"No, clearly his dick is."

"It's massive," she explains, holding her hands out wide.

I peek through the window at the corpse lying on the metal table. The sheet is over him, but she isn't wrong. But still, it's not our first rodeo and it's not like we have to deal with this sort of thing daily. "I'd take this over someone who has passed gas through their mouth."

"I don't know. Have you smelled Todd's breath?"

"The cleaner?"

"Yeah. It's like something died in there. I'd take the dead body gas over that."

"Didn't you date him?"

"Look, we all have our faults."

"Ladies," Dr. Aubrey greets, but pauses when she catches sight of Cat. "I'm too afraid to ask why you have mascara running down your cheek."

Cat sniffles. "It's a big loss in there. I got a little overwhelmed."

Dr. Aubrey pauses with her tag over the fob. "You knew the young gentlemen?"

"Personally," I mutter.

Heels clang on the floor before I hear, "Miss Sparks, can I have a moment please?"

I smile at our supervisor. "Hey Doc, how are you?" My smile drops at her expression. "Is everything okay?"

"I'm not sure how to bring this up, so I'm just going to hand it to you," she explains, and hands me the paper.

My stomach drops at the title. **Rampage's Affair with a Stripper.** And below is a picture of us at the fair, and another of me from Charlotte's Facebook page.

I scan through the article, and the speculation goes from River paying me to me fooling him, just like his ex did. I've even been labelled a gold digger.

"Is that you?" Cat asks. "I didn't know you were a stripper."

I ignore Cat, and address Lilian, a doctor I've known for a while since she treated my mum. "Is this going to be a problem?"

"Why would it be a problem?" Cat asks.

Lilian lets out a breath. "You know I don't have a problem with it, but board members might. This could tarnish the hospital's reputation."

"Which means I'm fired," I guess. "I've worked so hard to be here."

"Hey, you are one of our best residents. You aren't leaving," Lilian promises. "This will blow over, and I'll do everything I can to make sure your job is secure."

I turn to Dr. Aubrey, fighting back emotions. If I let them in, I won't be able to concentrate. "I'll understand if you want me out of your programme."

"Sweetie, no. If I don't kick this one out, who talks to the corpses like they are still alive, I won't kick you out for making a living."

Cat flips her hair over her shoulder. "Hey, it gets boring, and I have no one to speak to."

"You had a conversation with an old man because you thought he'd be a good match with your nanna. Who's dead," Dr. Aubrey remarks.

"I promise, this isn't what you think. I know how people perceive strippers, but I work in a high-end club. I don't have drug issues, daddy issues, or whatever other issues people think strippers have. I love dancing, and this, for me, is a way to pay off those student loans. I have dreams for the future. It doesn't involve working every minute of every day. I want holidays, my own home, and maybe children. This isn't who I am, it's just what I do on weekends, and something I won't be doing forever."

"I'm a little upset you've never invited me," Cat mutters, still reading the paper. "I've never been to a strip club."

"You haven't been to a nightclub," I tease, before turning to Dr. Aubrey, waiting for her to answer.

She places her hand on my bicep. "I know who you are. You have graduated at the top of your class each year. You come in early, you leave late, and you never hand in an assignment late. You are bright, loving, and this doesn't change my view on you. I've had students come and go with this course. It's not for everyone. But you treat these remains with dignity, and I hear you after every procedure. You say—"

"May God light your way, and your family be waiting," Cat finishes in a soft tone.

"And you guys don't see me differently?" I ask to be sure.

"No," Aubrey and Lilian reply.

I glance at Cat, and she startles at the attention focused on her. "Oh, I was picturing myself as a stripper and wondering if I had what it takes. But then I remembered the time I tried to do a TikTok dance and tried to be sexy. I ended up breaking my wrist and needing surgery on my nose."

I laugh, pulling her against me. "Thank you," I reply, and meet Lilian and Aubrey's gaze. "All of you."

"Now everyone knows, you'll have nothing to worry about," Lilian comments, and the blood drains from my face.

I feel like the ground beneath my feet shift. "Oh my god, my dad!"

Lilian places a hand over her mouth. "He doesn't know?"

I shake my head. "No. I've been too scared to, and now he'll find out through this."

"Go," Lilian orders, pointing to the door.

"Are you sure?"

"Yes," she replies.

"Thank you," I declare, before rushing off down the hall.

"Wait, what about boner guy?" Cat calls. "You can't leave me. What would Nanna think?"

"Stick a needle inside to withdraw the blood," I yell back. "You'll be fine."

I get to the lift and hit the button for the first floor. My dad is going to freak. I always thought I'd be prepared and always planned out what I'd say. But now the time is here, I don't have a clue.

'Hey, I dance like Mum wanted,' doesn't seem appropriate now it's happening. I know my dad loves me unconditionally, and I know this won't ever change that, but that's not saying our relationship won't change or that he won't be disappointed in me. And I'm not sure I can handle that. I don't give a fuck what others think or what people will say.

But my dad matters. His opinion matters.

And now thinking on it, picturing the look he'll most likely give me, I feel a little hot.

Really hot.

I step off the lift, and it's like the world's eyes are on me. Every person who meets my gaze, I fear they know and are judging.

The girl held by her mother who watches me over her shoulder.

The old man in the wheelchair.

The young lad in scrubs at the coffee counter.

And the old woman at the flower stall.

Thousands of voices echo in my mind, and I hear them.

"Is that her?"

"What a hussy."

"Gold digger."

I hear it all—or I think I do—until the room starts spinning. I move through the crowd faster and take in a lungful of warm air when I hit the outside.

Someone leaked the information. Someone who knows me. Someone close.

A hand touches mine and I jump, surprised to find River looming above me. His lips move rapidly, but all I hear are the voices around me. All I feel is the stares at my back.

My dad might disown me.

My anonymity is over and every sleazebag or man who thinks they have a right to touch me, will hound me to the brink of insanity.

My god, it's so fucking hot.

Why am I hot?

River lifts me in his arms, and I wrap my arms around him, a little dazed by his arrival. People watch us and cameras immediately begin to flash.

I think I whimper.

Not long after, I'm placed down onto a chair, and River is there, gripping my face, concern written all over him.

I blink out of my daze, and I hear him. "Scaring me."

"W-what?"

He lets out a breath, his shoulders dropping. "Are you okay? You scared me?"

Everything around me settles and the voices I thought I heard, disappear. Cars, people talking, and the occasional horn blares, but the attacks and insults are no longer there, and I begin to wonder if they ever were.

"What are you doing here?"

"I got the paper. You weren't answering your phone and you said you were here today. I came to find you."

I push myself to smile. "That's really sweet of you."

His large hands grip the back of my neck. "I think you were having a panic attack."

I snort. "I don't get panic attacks."

"Gorgeous, you were having a panic attack," he tells me.

"Shit!" I groan. "My dad. I need to go and see my dad. He can't find out this way."

He reaches around me and grabs my belt, strapping me in. "I'll take you. I'm so fucking sorry about this."

"It's not your fault."

"It is. If you had been with anyone else, this wouldn't be splashed all over the papers."

"Maybe, but I don't blame you. We both know who did this."

His brows pinch together. "You can't possibly think Colin would do this."

"Who else would care? You said yourself, he doesn't want you to stop fighting. And this is the publicity he didn't want you to get. He won. And now you'll be working for him for life."

"No, I won't. You've done nothing wrong. People will always have an opinion. I can't stop them, but I also don't care. I know you. And this," he tells me, holding up a paper from the floor of his car, "means nothing to me. I don't care what this does to me. It's you I'm concerned about. You shouldn't have to deal with this, but, gorgeous, Colin wouldn't risk this even if he did know."

"He does know. Why do you think I punched him the first night I met him? He knows exactly what I do for a living, or at least, the stripping part. I've been wondering why he hasn't brought it up to you, but now I know why. It's so he can claim he's innocent when it's conveniently leaked."

"I don't think it's him," he tells me, but there's no conviction there. I know I'll not get anywhere, but it doesn't mean I'm wrong about Colin.

He did this. Or had some part in it.

And once I'm done making things up with my dad, I'll be paying Colin a little visit. He'll soon see I'm not someone to fuck with.

"I'm not going to argue. We'll never know who leaked the information, and maybe it would have always come out. But it's done now, and the world knows. So I'm not going to stew on it."

"I really am sorry."

I run the palm of my hand along his jaw, the stubble rough against my skin. "It's not your fault. But I really do need to go see my dad."

He stands and leans forward, pressing his lips to mine. I moan at the peppermint on his tongue. "I didn't want to meet your dad this way."

"I didn't want it to be like this either, but it will be fine."

"Are you sure?"

I take a breath as I meet his gaze and answer truthfully. "I really don't know."

20

RIVER

Harriett has always reminded me of someone who has her shit together. She looks okay from the outside, but I saw her at the hospital. Inside, she's a mess. She can tell me a thousand times that she's okay, but I know better.

I wanted to protect her from this, from all the attention and vile, money hungry, reporters. They see a story, something that pays their wages, but they have no idea of the ramifications it can cause a person with their twisted words and lies. And with the internet expanding all the time, they'll use anything to get a story published.

I want to be supportive, to be there, but I keep picturing her stumbling out of the hospital—looking as white as the coat doctors wear—and I'm doing all that I can to keep it together. Her anonymity means everything to her. She's told me how people change when they find out. Guys have treated her like a willing porn star, or they've ended it because of disgust. She's had women hurl abuse at her and people she called friends ghost her.

Harriett has spoken fondly of her dad. Their relationship has always been close, but after her mum died, she told me he became her best friend. She respects him, and I know his opinion means everything to her.

"I don't know how to make this better," I comment as she continues to stare out of the window.

We aren't far from our destination, but I can hear her thinking.

"It's done now. All I can do is beg for forgiveness and hope he doesn't hate me."

"I don't know him, but from what you've told me, he could never hate you."

"I'm so freaking nervous, and I never get nervous. I'm sure there's a rap song about how I'm feeling right now."

"Palms sweating?"

She laughs. "Weak knees too."

I rest my hand over her thigh. "It's going to be okay."

We pull up onto the road, and I take note of the numbers on the door.

"It might be best if you wait outside so I can judge his mood."

"I'd prefer to be with you?"

"He won't hurt me. He might yell. I don't know."

I nearly give something away by saying all parents yell, but who am I to assume. My parents weren't the best role models, and I found that out when Drew took me to his dad's. "Are you sure?"

"Positive."

I put the car into park at the end of the driveway. "I'll come to the door."

I slide out, and by the time the door is closed behind me, she's closing her own. Still in scrubs, she makes her way to the end of the driveway and takes a deep breath as she stares up at the house.

I take her hand and we make it halfway up the driveway when the front door opens. A stocky, built man with greying hair and eyes much like his daughter's greets us, a phone to his ear.

"Benny, I'll call you back. Harriett has come for a visit," he states, before ending the call.

His expression doesn't give anything away, and it's unnerving.

Benny, I know, is her uncle, the one who owns the house she lives in.

"Dad, can we talk inside for a moment?"

He glances at me, running his gaze from head to toe. "And your friend?"

"I'll wait out here until she's ready," I explain.

"Come on then, sweetheart," he states, and she follows him inside, not closing the door behind him.

I step closer, listening in. I promised to stay outside, but I didn't promise I wouldn't overhear. I know he's her dad, but I won't have him talking to her like shit. If that's how it goes anyway.

"Tell me, was it something I did? Is it about money, because I have some. Not a lot but I have some," he offers.

"Dad, it's nothing you did, I promise. And it's not about money either. Well, it is, but it's only to pay off my student loans until I graduate. I'm working at the hospital full-time next term so it's not forever."

"Harriett, why did you never tell me? Why would you do this to yourself, to your mother's memory? She wouldn't like this for her daughter."

"She would want me to be happy," she points out, her voice breaking. "It's not what you think, I promise. It's not sleazy, or degrading. You know my friends work there, and you know it's not who they are."

"You're my daughter."

"I know, and I love you. But I like dancing. It might not be the dancing you or Mum had hoped but it makes me feel close to her again."

"Then take up teaching. You know your old school want you there."

"I like my profession, Dad. Working at the hospital is what I want to do. It's what I think I'm meant to do."

"Then why this?"

"It really is about not wanting to be in debt after leaving school. Do you think less of Emily?"

"No," he replies with conviction.

"Gabby or Olivia?"

"No, they're like daughters to me."

"Exactly. I'm sorry this is how you had to find out," she explains, and I take that cue to step away. I have phone calls of my own to make.

I dial my publicist first. She'll be able to help me. "Lara, I need you to make a statement about today's headline. Harriett doesn't deserve this, and they shouldn't have invaded her privacy."

"River, I've been calling you all morning."

"Can you do it?"

"Making a statement now will be suicide. Reporters will be following you everywhere and you won't get a moment's peace."

"They were outside the gym this morning. I want it taken down."

"It can't. Not unless what they are saying is false."

"She works there, but they're making out she's a prostitute doing all she can to make money for drugs."

Her sigh is heavy. "It's not as easy as that. I can try to do damage control, but right now, I'm telling you, keeping your head down is the best way to go. We can turn this around and explain you aren't dating her."

"I am dating her."

"A stripper?"

The judgement in her tone has my hackles rising. "Lara," I warn.

"Sorry. Sorry," she rushes out. "Just do what I said."

I pinch the bridge of my nose. "And can you find out who leaked her information?"

"Her information isn't leaked. They don't have a name, just an occupation."

"Someone leaked it, and I want to know who."

"They won't reveal their source. You should know that by now," she argues.

"Just try, please. This is important."

"Alright. Look, I have to go. My phone hasn't stopped all morning and I've got clients calling me for answers."

"Fuck. Will they be okay with this?"

"Probably not, but you've worked with these men longer than me."

They'll probably give me a pat on the back and tell me I'm the man. Still, this whole ordeal is fucking shit.

"Alright, I'll talk to you later."

"Keep your phone on," she orders, before ending the call.

The next person I need to speak to is Colin. If Harriett is right, and he does have something to do with this, not even the law against trained fighters getting into fights will stop me from decking him.

Fuck the championship. Fuck the contracts. And fuck him if he has anything to do with this.

The phone rings once before he answers, not even greeting me. "This is exactly what I warned you about. A stripper. I knew that guy was right about her. Now can you see why I'm so protective."

"I already know what she does on the weekends, Colin, and I've just learned you did too," I bite out, unable to hide the viciousness in my tone.

He splutters. "I don't know what you mean."

"You knew exactly what she did for a living on the weekends. I know everything."

"This is the first I'm hearing of it," he snaps.

I don't believe him.

"Did you inform the press about her?"

"River, I know I've pushed you to stay on next year, and I know I've said some things that I'm not proud of, but I wouldn't do this to you. Your image and privacy are important to me. You know that," he explains. "Have you asked her if she leaked this, hoping to get money out of you?"

"Wouldn't she have done that before going to the papers?" I question, livid he'd even ask that.

"I don't know. But you can't see her again now. I've been talking to Lara, and we are going to work on damage control. We can say she tried to steal from you to get on the public's soft side."

"You aren't going to do a thing. Harriett isn't going anywhere," I tell him.

"You cannot be serious," he bellows, and I pull the phone away from my ear for a moment.

"Deadly. Whoever did this, did it with malicious intentions. They aren't going to win. I'm not going to let this drive us apart."

"I won't have this," he barks.

"It's not your choice," I reply harshly. "And Colin, if I find out you had something to do with this, I'll make sure you regret it. She means a lot to me."

"I understand," he tells me, his voice low. "She really does have her nails sunk into you."

"No, she doesn't, and I wouldn't care if she did. What has happened today might have caused her problems. It's put her at risk. And she's still here. She hasn't ended things or told me to fuck off. She's here. So, you, Lara, and whoever else is doing damage control can forget about me going anywhere. Nothing will make me walk away, not even her."

"Lara is calling me," he replies, sounding like a scolded child.

"I'll speak to you later," I tell him before ending the call.

When I reach the front door, I listen in to Harriett and her dad. "So, you aren't mad at me?"

"I could never be mad at you, sweetheart. I just got scared you were in trouble."

"If, by chance, me and the girls couldn't handle it, you would be the first person I call if I had a problem."

He laughs. "That's my girl."

"Love you, old man."

"Love you too, darlin'," he replies. "Now, who's the young gentleman outside?"

"That is River."

"The guy from the paper?"

"Yes."

"They said he was some famous fighter. That true?"

She chuckles. "Yes, so why do you have a frown?"

"Because how the hell am I meant to scare a professional fighter if he hurts my girl?"

"He isn't like that, I promise."

"So invite the poor sod in. He's probably worried I'm going for the kitchen knives."

I hear footsteps before Harriett reaches the door. "You okay?" she asks, when she sees my expression.

I place the phone in my pocket. "Yeah, just had to make some calls. Did everything go okay?"

"Do you really want to pretend you weren't listening?"

"Only the first bit and just now," I admit sheepishly.

She grins, placing her arms around my neck. "It went good. He wants to meet you now."

"Do you think he's got the kitchen knives?" I whisper.

"Get in here, boy, before I actually do get them out," her dad calls.

She grins and I lean down, pressing my lips to hers. It's good to see colour back in her cheeks and a smile on her face. "I'm meeting your dad."

"You're meeting my dad," she repeats firmly. "You okay with that?"

No, but I have to meet him at some point. I've never had to meet a parent before. Marlene's mum ran off to live in Greece, and she never knew who her dad was.

"Yes."

"It will be okay," she promises, keeping her voice low.

She takes my hand, and together, we step inside and head into the room on the left, where her dad awaits in front of a brown, worn-out leather sofa. His voice is deep as he appraises me. "So you're the boy who got my daughter on the front page of the paper."

"And I'm truly sorry. It was never my intention for her to get caught up in a media storm."

"And what do you plan to do to protect her?"

"I don't need protecting," Harriett scoffs.

"My PR team seem to think this will blow over and has advised us to keep a low profile and not to make a statement."

"They are calling my daughter a whore online."

"You have the internet?" Harriett teases.

He gives her a stern look until she clamps her lips shut.

"I truly am sorry, and I will do everything to make sure nothing else happens. And please know, the things they are saying about your daughter aren't true."

"Well, I know that. I'm old, not senile."

"I wasn't implying—"

"Dad, stop playing him up," Harriett warns.

I feel nervous under his scrutinising gaze.

"I'm Stanley, but you can call me Stan."

Holding my hand out, I give him a firm handshake. "I'm River."

"Take a seat. You can tell me how you met my daughter."

"Crap," Harriett whispers. "I'll go make drinks. Be back in a second."

"I can do that," her dad offers.

She waves me off. "I've got it," she promises, and then turns to me. "Water?"

"Please," I reply with a nod.

I take a seat on the single chair, gulping as her father takes a seat on the sofa behind him, not taking his gaze off me.

I know what he means to her, so getting on his good side and making sure I can turn this visit around, is vital.

"Relax. The only time you have to worry is if my girl gets hurt."

I run my hands down my thighs. "Sorry, I don't want to mess this up. You mean a lot to Harriett, so this is important to me."

He sits back with a grin on his face. "Good answer, son. Good answer," he praises. "Now, tell me how you met my daughter."

And that is how it begins. I tell him how we met, and how I thought she was beautiful dancing, which in turn, gets him to tell me about her dancing. Photographs are brought out, much to her dismay, and the more he speaks, the more they laugh together at their inside jokes, the more I realise how much I missed out on as a child.

I wish I had this. I wish I had a mum who cared enough to make me succeed. I wish I had a dad who stuck around after things got tough. I wish I had parents who thought of someone other than themselves.

Now I'm more determined than ever to get the best out of life. And I'm going to start by making memories; memories I want to share with Harriett.

21

HARRIETT

The sun begins to set over the horizon, leaving that gloomy, grey feel to the air. Rain splatters against the window screen of Emily's ugly green banger of a car, only adding to the dreary night. As the car back fires, making a popping sound, I can't help but feel for my best friend. Her pride and joy, which she named Betty, got ruined in a crash we were involved in last year. The insurance wouldn't pay out and the car was a total right-off. Charlotte offered to compensate her for the loss, but Emily refused, wanting to wait until she could get one on finance. It gets her from A to B, so she isn't bothered, but I know she hides the fact she's ashamed and worried when her daughter has to ride with her.

I'm not complaining. This evening, it got us to Colin's offices, a place I've been determined to visit since the news broke yesterday about my occupation. There're a few cars left in the car park, and it's eerie and still, but this is what I wanted.

After extensive research on Colin, I found his home and work address. Going to his home will be too easy. And he has kids and a wife I don't want to scare or worry. I also don't want to cause a scene so big it makes trouble for River. Which is why I opted to wait until this evening to go inside, knowing from my chat with River, this will be the best time.

Gabby leans forward from the back, sticking her head in the middle of the two seats. She chomps down on a crisp, staring up at the building. "Tell me again why we are waiting?"

"I'm waiting for River to message that he's at the gym," I remind her. "As soon as he does, that means their meeting is over and Colin will be driving back here."

Olivia clears her throat. "Are you sure he's driving back here?"

"Yes. Because I heard him telling Colin he wasn't going to push back his training. He's with his coach tonight."

"My stomach is turning," Emily comments, her voice filled with nerves. "I don't want to get arrested."

"We aren't going to get arrested. Not after what we found out. He won't want that getting out, and once it's on record with the police, the press will get hold of the information and leak it," I point out.

I knew I had Colin pegged the minute I first met him. I'm rarely wrong. Which is why I questioned the affairs River mentioned. There had to be more than he told me about. And I was right. The second I started asking questions, people began talking.

"Anyone else still shocked over Trixie's entire family being centred around stripping?" Olivia asks, munching on her own snacks. I lean over the seat, grabbing a bag of Haribo from her lap. "They could start their own reality TV show. They could name it Keeping up with the Strippers."

I hide my laughter. "Her nan even teaches it. I'm still in awe. She's eighty-two."

"And her brother is hot," Emily comments. "It's a shame he follows his sister with the arrogance and bitchiness."

"I'm still processing the fact she offered that information up freely," Gabby comments.

I turn a little in my seat. "Are you actually surprised though? She likes being involved with everyone."

"Okay, when you put it like that, no. But I thought for sure she'd make a few digs, not admit her cousin used to sell her va-jay-jay before she got into stripping."

"She can try to make a dig, but she'll get a chicken fillet shoved in her trap," Olivia retorts.

"I'm surprised she admitted it too. But I've always said, there's a softness to Trixie; she just doesn't like to show it," I admit. "And that girl loves her family."

"Yeah, buried, deep, deep down," Olivia declares. "I'm all for fixing each other's crowns, but not to bitches who try to steal them."

"She's not a bad person though. She just says and does shitty things, but I think that's more to do with the way she's programmed. She's learned to survive by being that way and she doesn't know any other way," I offer as explanation.

Olivia taps her chin. "Okay, now you've put it like that, I can understand, but it doesn't mean I have to be friends with her."

I laugh at the face she pulls. "No one is asking you to."

Gabby sits forward. "Us being here, does it mean you and River are getting serious? You only go to this much trouble when you get even."

"I like him. Like, really like him. And I don't want this prick making it harder for us," I reply.

"We won't let him," Olivia promises.

"So, serious, huh?" Emily questions, arching an eyebrow.

"I think so. It doesn't feel like a fling or a good time until something better comes along. We both agreed to exclusivity, but it wasn't expanded on. You know me, I don't like to get my hopes up, but they are. I do want this to work. I like spending time with him."

"And the sex is hot," Gabby adds.

"The sex is phenomenal," I amend. "But this prick is out to put a pin in it before even giving us a chance."

"We won't let him," Gabby promises. "We've never let you down before and we won't start now."

My phone goes off. It's River, letting me know he's leaving for the gym and will call me later.

"Showtime?" Emily asks, her hands gripping the steering wheel.

"Yes, but, babe, if you want to sit this one out, it's okay. We've got this."

She shuts off the car and unclips her belt. "Yeah, fuck that, I'm coming," she declares, but then turns in her seat, pointing at Gabby. "Do not get me fucking arrested again."

Gabby rolls her eyes. "It was one time."

Olivia pins her with a look. "One? Really?"

"Okay, but in my defence, we were all involved. You can't blame this all on me."

I push open my door as laughter spills out of me. "Let's go."

We make our way into the building, and the inside is just as grim outside. The place is dead. Only a security guard and the receptionist are on the lower floor, and both are occupied in conversation.

We continue without making eye contact. We've learnt over the years that when you want to get in somewhere you aren't invited, you have to act like you are. Confidence, with an air of belonging, gets people to look past you. They don't question your presence or arrival. It's how we've always got into the best parties, backstage at concerts, and one time, on a set for a TV show.

It's a skill we have down, which is why we make it to the elevators without being called upon or stopped.

"Is it me or does this get boring now? There's no rush when we do it anymore," Gabby admits as the doors close.

"My stomach is still turning," Emily replies.

"I'm with Gabby," Olivia adds. "I still think we should try Buckingham Palace again."

"Charlotte got us arrested," I remind her.

"She needs a little more coaching is all. The girl wears her emotions on her face. And in all fairness, she was yelling 'God save the Queen'. They probably thought she was there to assassinate her."

We arrive at the office floor, and we're immediately greeted by an older woman who looks tired and ready to drop. I know who it is from her reddish-grey hair, green eyes, and the laugh lines crinkled at the corner of her eyes. Hetty. River's talked about her with affection, but I always got the feeling he's never let her get close. Which I've found is a pattern. He has so many people he talks about with love and affection, so many he admires and respects, and yet when I ask about his relationship with them, he plays it off, saying they don't want to be those kinds of friends.

Given the chance, I reckon all these people would make him family. He just has to see that people like him for him and not what he can do or give them. He has to take the plunge and let one of them in, and I mean really in.

Hetty looks up, startled by our arrival, but then her shoulders relax. "Good evening, ladies, welcome to Andrews Management and co. How can I help you this evening?"

"You know what to do," I whisper under my breath, before pasting on a smile. "Hi, you must be Hetty. River has told me all about you."

She's utterly shocked by the comment, and she places a hand over her chest. "River talks about me?"

I beam with pride. "All the time. He showed me the picture you got framed for him. He loves it."

"He does?" she asks, and her eyes glass over. "Mr Andrews said it was tacky. Me and my husband don't make much, but James, he's good with his hands. He made the frame himself, and when River won that award, I knew it had to be framed. I know Mr Andrews had his fight stills framed, but I think Mr Knight is more than a fighter."

"He really is," I agree. "And the frame is seriously beautiful. I asked him where he got it because my dad's birthday is coming up and I wanted to get a frame done. My mum passed away when I was younger, and when he was decorating, their wedding photo got smashed. It means a lot to him, and so I've been searching for the perfect frame. I was so upset when he told me he didn't buy it himself."

"Oh dear, I'm awfully sorry for your loss. I lost my ma at a young age too. It never gets easy," she admits, before pulling open her desk drawer and grabbing a card. "Call me. My James will be happy to help you. And maybe you and River can come over for dinner. I've offered before. The boy doesn't have family, and I sense he's alone on the holidays. But he never accepts."

That sounds like the River I know. "He's probably worried he's putting you out, but don't you worry, Hetty, I'll get him there whenever you want us."

She hands me the card, and I take it. "If you're looking for him,

I'm afraid you've missed him. He left for a meeting earlier and won't be back in tonight."

"We're actually looking for Colin," I tell her, and let out a dramatic sigh. "I'll be straight with you because you seem like a woman who appreciates honesty. He's done something that's seriously pissed me off and I want to get a few things straight with him."

Realisation dawns on her expression. "The papers," she guesses.

I nod because there's no point lying. "I think he did it, and I just want to warn him before he tries to do something else. My dad read that paper. He thought his highly educated daughter had packed in her doctoral degree and fell in with a bad crowd. But it's not because of that. And it's not as sleazy as the papers have made it out to be. And my dad didn't have to find out that way. He deserved to be told by me."

"His office is down the hall, but he's not here. If you want to take a seat over there, he won't be long."

Emily is the only one left with me. Gabby and Olivia used the distraction to find his office to complete phase two of the plan.

Phase three is just about to start. I turn at the sound of the lift arriving, and Emily reaches out, giving my hand a squeeze before giving me room.

As I had hoped, Colin is alone when he steps off the lift. He doesn't even hide the resentment or disgust when he spots me.

"You won't be getting a penny from me," he spits, but drops his expression when he spots Hetty still at her desk. "What do you want?"

I don't go for him, and I don't react in the way he hopes. Or in the way I want to. "I don't want your money. I want you to stop this vendetta you have against me. I want you to end this game you're playing because it won't work. Leaking that information wasn't clever. Did you think I would keep it from him? How do you think we met the second time?"

"You all want money," he berates me. "You think you can come in here and tell me what to do, but I have news for you, lady: River belongs to me. I own him. I made him who he is, and I won't have some slut coming in and trying to get him to question everything. Especially not some stripper who doesn't know her left from her right.

And while you are here, don't think it didn't pass my notice that the night you first met him is the night he decides to throw away his goddamn career."

I have to bite the inside of my cheek at the snub, and to stop the scream threatening to escape. "One, I don't have to explain myself to you, but I'm a very nice person, so I will. I know it was you who leaked my occupation to the press," I tell him, and his cheeks redden, ready to argue. I hold my hand up, stopping him. "But let's get one thing straight. I'm not just a stripper. I have a doctoral degree. I have a Masters in Biomedical Science and Applied Science. I'm kind, caring, and I'm fiercely protective of those I love and am close to. You don't get to fuck with my life, and you most certainly don't get to fuck with his. I won't let you. So whatever creepy notion you have about him belonging to you, you can forget. He doesn't belong to you. He doesn't belong to me. He is his own man. He's a man who is generous with his time even though he's busy, a man who is loyal to even those like you, who shit on him, and a man who is fantastic in bed. Everyone has told me it's not about me, but after this little informative conversation, I'm starting to believe otherwise. Maybe you do think he belongs to you. Maybe you've had some weird-ass crush on a guy more than half your age, and you don't want him to be with anyone. You want him all to yourself. Is that it, Colin? Are you in love with River, and that's why you don't want him near me?"

And there he is, the man behind the mask. "You little fucking whore," he spits, ignoring Hetty's gasp of horror. "You think you are clever and smart, but I have your number. I made him. He was a no start, going nowhere, and I gave him *everything*. I don't fucking love him. I don't care about him at all, but he owes me. He owes me everything, you stupid fucking bitch. I didn't work this hard for him to walk away. And you'll be gone soon. I'll make sure of it. You'll be crawling to me begging me to help you, and I might have, but now you can crawl back under the rock you came from."

"No. What you are going to do is stop meddling in business you aren't a part of. River isn't the only one who can fight. So can I. And unlike him, I don't fight fair, and I don't have some unnecessary notion that I owe you. I'm not him. So take this as your warning. You keep making things difficult, and you will lose. You will lose it all because I won't stop until you do," I threaten.

"You have no idea who you are messing with."

My lip curls. "You don't get it. I don't give a fuck."

"You will. I won't have you coming into his life and ruining everything I've built. He wouldn't be where he is without me. He would be probably be in a prison cell, or worse, living on the streets, or working some dead-end job. I made him. Me," he yells, jabbing his chest. "And you think he'll pick you over me. Over my dead body. He knows he owes me. I made him."

He's spluttering the same nonsense.

"No, *he* made *you*. You were just some shop owner who couldn't make ends meet before you met him. You cheated on your wife with prostitutes because no other woman would look at you. You like tying them up because it makes you feel manly. You smack them around a little because you need to show them who's in charge. Well, I'm not one of them. I'm not someone who will be fucked with," I tell him, and step closer, getting in his face. I ignore the girls sneaking out of his office and continue. "From now on, you keep your mouth shut. You leave River alone and you stay the fuck away from me."

He grits his teeth and raises his arm. "Mr Andrews," Hetty gasps, standing from her chair.

The steam might as well be coming out of his ears. "I will ruin you."

I smile sweetly and straighten his tie. "No. I'll ruin you. You won't see me coming. You won't get a warning. And you won't know what's hit you when I'm done. Because you see, I have people who love me as much as I love them. They'll do anything for me."

Olivia steps to my side, startling him. "Including being the perfect alibi."

Gabby is next, and a whimper escapes him. She has a small spade in her hand, one you take to the beach. "And burying the body."

Emily rests her elbow on my shoulder. "Wouldn't be the first time, right, girls?"

"See, it will be easy. This is the only warning you'll get from me."

"Get out!" he roars. "Get out, you stupid little whore."

"Mr Andrews, please accept this as my resignation," Hetty announces, grabbing her bags.

"You can't leave," he tells her, and there's panic in his eyes. "You have a contract, and we don't have anyone trained for your position."

"Mr Andrews, I have worked within this firm for a long time. Before you, I worked for Mr Smith. He could be rude, but he treated his colleagues fairly. Then before him, I worked for Mrs Brown, and she was a hard woman who could be cold. But never, in all my years, have I ever watched a man threaten a poor woman, much less raise a hand to her."

Colin splutters. "She threatened me."

"No, she is standing up for herself. They are two very different things, Mr Andrews."

"Hey, cute lady," Gabby cheers. "Let me help you with that bag."

His face is red when he turns to me. "You might think you have won but you haven't. Not by far. Coming here today was your mistake."

"No, it wasn't," I state calmly. "Your mistake was thinking I was Chelsea."

The blood drains from his face and Olivia chuckles. "See, Chelsea is a chatty Cathy and remembers you well. Not because you were good but because you were the worst person she ever slept with."

"So you see, you aren't the only one who can fight dirty," I tell him with a smile in my voice.

He looks at the others, then at Hetty gathering her stuff. "Get out," he grits out. "I'm calling security."

I wiggle my fingers as I watch him storm off down the hall to his office.

"I'm sorry you had to endure that," I tell Hetty.

She takes my hand. "He's the one who has to be sorry," she promises, before biting her lip. "Now I need to find someone who will hire an old lady like me."

"Do you like books?" Gabby asks, jumping off the desk. "Because we have a friend who owns a library who will hire you."

"Oh, that would be amazing, but I'm not sure how good I'll be lugging books around."

"That's okay, she has a boyfriend who does all that."

"I'll give her your number," I promise as the lift opens.

"Where on earth did you get a spade?" Olivia asks.

Gabby beams. "From one of the other offices. I've never seen a gold, glittery one before."

"That's an award, dear. You really should leave that on the desk," Hetty replies.

A scream echoes down the hallway as Gabby drops the spade on the desk before rushing to usher Hetty into the lift.

A smile spreads across my face at the sound. It's the sound of a man falling from the chair Olivia dismantled. And when the other scream comes, I know the last leg of his desk has collapsed on top of him.

"Bit of a good job he's calling security," Emily assures Hetty when another scream echoes along the hall. "They'll be able to see what's wrong."

Tonight was a good night.

A really good night.

As the door closes and Gabby gives me a low-five, I can't help but feel good about it. I had been worried and clouded with guilt that this might fall back on River.

But I think Colin and I are on the same page now.

He doesn't fuck with me, and I won't fuck with him.

22

HARRIETT

The drive back home is much different to the one we took getting to the offices. There's no pop music blasting from the stereo, there's no arguing from the two comedians in the backseat, and there's no idle chatter. Instead, it's silent, everyone lost in their own thoughts, or in Gabby's case, reflecting on her behaviour.

I feel her knee knocking into the back of my seat, and I know the silence is killing her.

"Gabby, just spit it out."

She wastes no time. She sits forward and grips the back of my chair. "I didn't do anything wrong. I was being friendly, and I resent the fact you guys are in a mood with me for it."

"You invited an old woman to a strip club," Olivia retorts.

"I was being kind," Gabby scoffs.

"And the free lap dance?" Emily adds on.

"Well, I didn't want her night to be boring. I give a good lap dance," Gabby argues. "I don't see the issue."

"She's only ten years younger than my nan," Emily points out.

"Harriett, you get me. Tell them. I was being nice."

"Dude, you offered it to her husband," I remind her, before adding. "But that's not my issue."

She scoffs. "Look, we didn't get arrested, so I don't see what the big deal is."

I turn in my seat now. I'm not mad, but getting arrested when I have so much attention on me at the hospital and in my private life is a bad idea. "You are going to pay for that ticket."

"I didn't park in the disabled parking. Emily did."

"And he was going to let me off with a warning until you asked the community officer if he had handcuffs."

"I like to be in the know. I've never seen a set of police issued handcuffs before. I wanted to see them, maybe bribe him into giving them to me."

"Again, he was a community officer, not a police officer, and he was ready to call the police."

"That guy couldn't tell his left from his right. It's not my fault we are so damn hot and he thought we were coming onto him."

"You tackled him to the floor because you thought he was lying," Olivia argues, fighting back laughter.

"He shifted weird, like your siblings do when they're hiding the last bar of chocolate."

"Are you surprised? You eat us out of house and home. I don't know how you stay so skinny."

Gabby snorts. "Are you really going to stick up for them? The other day you pretended to be on the phone to Santa. You'll give that girl PTSD. And let's not forget the night you locked yourself in the bathroom because you wanted to eat the pizza you ordered to yourself."

I turn in the seat, smiling. "Wait, go back to the Santa. What did you do?"

Olivia rolls her eyes and begins to pick at the rip in her jeans. "Nell wouldn't finish her food, and I'm worried she's not eating enough so I got my phone out and pretended to call Santa. She thinks she's on probation. She has to eat most, if not all, of her food if she wants to get back on the good list."

"You do realise one of the others will dob you in," I tell her.

Gabby laughs. "Are you kidding? She took the WIFI box to bed with her the other night and threatened to get rid of it for good if they didn't get their shit together."

"Wait, how do you know?" Emily asks, her gaze flickering in the rear-view mirror.

Gabby sits back, sighing. "The landlord moved his nephew in to the flat across from me and it's been a little tense."

"He put shit on her doormat," Olivia puts in.

I growl low in my throat. "The cute one with the kittens?"

"Yes," she replies, sounding depressed about it.

"I'll get you another one the next time I pop into the Range," I offer.

"No point," she replies. "He'll only fucking do it again."

"What's his issue?" Emily asks.

Gabby doesn't answer, it's Olivia. "He asked her out, she said no, and he didn't like that answer so kept asking. She told him she was gay, and he's been treating her like fucking shit ever since."

"Hence, the shit on my doorstep," Gabby adds.

Emily grips the steering wheel. "And that's why you went to Olivia's?"

"Well yeah. She told me I could go there any time I wanted."

"I thought I'd get warning. She let herself in and crawled up the stairs."

Gabby chuckles. "I was so tired, I walked into Nell's room. I'm not sure who scared who more."

"And this nephew guy? When are we sorting this out?" I ask.

"No point. It will only make it worse."

"Gabby, that doesn't sound like you," I tell her softly. "We don't take shit, remember?"

"She broke into his flat and cut holes in all his jeans."

A smile lights up Gabby's face. "And sequined a few of his tops. I didn't get chance to do more. It takes time and effort, and his clothing didn't deserve the Gabby glam."

"And stuck a dildo on his door," Olivia admits.

"It was a broken one," Gabby rushes to explain.

"And stuck the pride flag to his window."

"With super-duper glue," Gabby cheers. "He's still trying to peel the yellow off. He'll be there awhile."

"We need our next girl's night at yours. Let us deal with him," I offer, angry on my best friend's behalf. She might be nutty, and can be bitchy like the rest of us, but she isn't mean. She doesn't have a mean bone in her body. Shit like this, it shouldn't be happening. We live in a world where smart phones, internet, and cars exist. We've adapted, or at least, our ancestors did before us. But we did. Yet, the world still can't seem to accept the LGBT community, and it's been around for longer than most people have been alive.

"I love you guys," she gushes. "We could even record it."

"Or do a TikTok like the coffee guy has started," Emily declares.

"Oh, just think of what we could name the account," Olivia excitedly retorts.

"Finding a douche bag," Gabby replies.

"Who to avoid," Emily adds.

"Revenge served sweet," Olivia offers.

I laugh, adding, "Queens of revenge."

"Um, Harriett," Emily calls, and there's hesitance in her voice.

I straighten in my chair, and when I glance through the window screen, the blood drains from my face.

Photographers and crews are camping outside my home. There are cars pretty much blocking the street, and some are parked over my uncle's drive.

"I feel like I need to ask for an autograph," Gabby whispers.

"You definitely shouldn't have worn leggings," Olivia comments.

"There is nothing wrong with my leggings," I argue. "What the fuck is happening?"

Emily slows the car down. "Do you want me to keep driving?"

"And go where?" I reply, a little shaken by the amount of people here. Even my neighbours are outside, some in dressing gowns, some pretending to take out the rubbish, and a few have lawn chairs out, setting up camp to watch the show. "You have a daughter to get home to, Olivia has her brother and sisters, and Gabby…"

"I have my cat to get home to," Gabby finishes.

"You don't own a cat," Olivia argues.

Gabby clears her throat. "I could. I've been thinking of getting one."

"Pull in behind my car. I'll call River and see what he suggests I do," I order, gripping my handbag.

"All right. Girls, be quick, and whatever you do, do not answer their questions," Emily orders.

The second we pull in, people are surrounding the car. Bright flashes light up the interior, and I duck my head, blinded.

Everyone races to get out of the car, and I'm left struggling to push open the door with the media crowding in on the other side.

"Move; let her out," Emily yells, and the door flies open. She takes my hand, and as I step out, Gabby throws her jacket over my head.

"No photos, no photos," she yells.

"She isn't making a statement," Olivia calls. "Stop taking photos."

"Why are you acting like I'm a celebrity?" I grumble as we step inside. I throw the jacket off and turn back to see my girls, women I consider sisters, posing for the cameras.

"Rock on!" Gabby hollers, throwing her hand in the air.

Both Emily and I step forward. Emily grabs the back of Olivia's top and I do the same to Gabby, pulling her back. I slam the door closed behind them and then take a breath.

They all stand there, grinning. "You are famous," Emily comments.

"I've always pictured myself being friends with someone famous," Gabby adds.

Olivia shrugs. "And when you get haters, that's when you know you've made it."

"I need to call River," is all I can get out, reaching for my phone.

"You need to call River," they all affirm.

I SHOVE Olivia away from the curtain. "Stop doing that," I demand.

"I can't help it. If I end up in the papers tomorrow, I want to be memorable."

"Why? So you can be some Facebook GIF people use on posts?" Gabby replies.

Olivia snorts. "I'd still rock that GIF."

Emily steps back into the kitchen, her face red. "I've run out of tape and the guy is determined to get a photo through the letter box."

Gabby falls off the chair and rushes to the hallway. I let her, my headache getting too much for me to handle. I don't have it in me to give her another list of reasons of why pulling faces isn't a good idea.

"You can stay at mine. They don't know who I am," Emily offers.

I give her a small smile. "We should have kept driving," I utter. "Now if I leave, they'll probably follow, and I don't want to put your nan and daughter in the middle of that."

Gabby sticks her head back around the corner. "Stay at mine."

"And get caught on camera kicking your neighbour's arse? Yeah, that's not going to help anyone."

"Then what about mine? The kids won't care," Olivia offers.

"They will. Do you really want their friends to find out you strip? You said it yourself; kids can be arseholes and you don't want to give them more ammunition."

"We're your friends. We aren't leaving you here to deal with this."

"You aren't. River is going to be here soon, and he said he'll sort it," I point out, but there's no conviction. I've seen celebrities hounded by the media. There's no stopping them and no getting away from it. But I have to believe River knows what he's doing.

Olivia peels back the netting. "Well, I think he's here."

I rush to my feet, squeezing by the sink to look out. Sure enough, the media have moved away and are now surrounding the car. "Shit."

"Why is he alone?" Emily asks.

"Gabby, get the door," I yell, and step away.

The door closes, and the second I hit the hallway, River is there, pulling me into his arms. "I'm so fucking sorry. I don't know how they got hold of your personal information."

"It's fine," I reply. "Are you sure you should be here? I thought you said we had to keep a low profile?"

"I'm not leaving you to deal with this. I've spoken to the PR team, and they are trying to sort it. But in the meantime, I need you to pack a bag."

I pull back. "Why? Are we giving them my clothes?"

He laughs. "No, I want you to come and stay with me until this dies down. I understand you have friends and family but none of them have land the media aren't allowed to trespass on."

"I don't want to put you out," I whine. "This is such a mess."

His expression softens as he pulls closer. "You aren't putting me out. I did this. I caused it. Let me fix it."

"It's not yours to fix. You had nothing to do with this," I assure him.

"I did."

Gabby sighs, stepping close to us. "Let him fix it."

I glance her way, my brows pinching together. "Why are you so close?"

She steps away, shaking herself out of it. "I got lost in the moment."

"This is crazy. Are they always this bad?"

"Not normally, but I never give them anything to print. I'm kind of boring, remember."

"Wait, can we come visit her?" Gabby asks.

"Any time you want," he assures her. "Just treat it like it's Harriett's home."

Gabby grins. "I'll bring my swimming cossie."

I roll my eyes. "You aren't coming to use his pool."

She looks completely put out by the comment. "Why not? He said to treat it like yours, and if you had a swimming pool, we would totally be going in it."

"I don't think that's what he meant," I tell her, pinching the bridge of my nose. I have a migraine coming, and this back and forth isn't helping.

"It's fine," River quietly tells her.

"Score," she whispers. "And I want to see the cinema room where you had hot sex."

I smack my forehead. "Gabby, you aren't meant to tell him you know."

"I didn't."

"You did," I argue.

River laughs, pulling me against his chest. "It was hot."

"Not helping," I grouch, but can't help the flutter in my stomach.

Emily comes down the stairs with a case I use for holidays. "I threw a bunch of stuff together."

I arch a brow. "I can do it. I know what to pack."

"What's to pack? You have about thirty pairs of the same leggings, and we threw in a range of tops and PJ's, but I can't see you wearing many," Olivia muses, her gaze catching River's.

"I need makeup."

"All packed, including all your toiletries. This isn't our first rodeo, remember. We can pack in a flash. It's what we do in a crisis."

"Are you ladies okay to lock up? I want to get this over and done with before the police are called. Then we'll be stuck making statements."

"Go," all three order.

"You sure you have everything you need? We can come back if you don't, but it will save you from getting stuck in the middle of this media storm again."

My jaw drops. "How long do you think I'll be staying with you?"

He comes to my side and leans down, cupping my cheek. "If you don't want to do this, just say the word. I won't be offended, and I can hire security for you until it blows over."

"You don't want that. I've read too many romances where they fall in love with the bodyguard."

"I'm not going to fall in love with the bodyguard," I snap at Emily.

She holds her hands up. "I'm just saying."

"I need my schoolwork," I tell him.

"Already packed," Emily promises.

He takes my hand. "I'll get you in the car first and put your stuff into the back. Then we can get out of here, okay?"

"Okay."

He leans down, capturing my lips with his, and everything but him is forgotten. I no longer hear the click of the cameras, the calls of his name, or the knocking on the door. He makes it all disappear.

A throat clears, and I pull back to find my friends, arms linked, beaming at us. "Should we leave?"

"Sorry."

River grabs my suitcase with one hand and then my hand in the other. "Close the door behind us and wait for us to leave before you do."

The girls nod, then give me a quick hug goodbye, making me promise to call them if I need them. And this is another reason why I love them so much. No matter what, they are there for me. Through thick and thin, they have my back.

Gabby takes a breath with her hand on the door, and with a chin lift from River, she opens it.

The sound that greets us is like the beginning of a concert when the singer enters the stage. It's deafening and not in an exhilarating way.

"Rampage, is it true she's your paid girlfriend?"

"Harriett, did you trick Rampage into your relationship?"

"How did the two of you meet?"

"Is it true she's blackmailing you?"

"Did you meet at the strip club she works at?"

"Why are you here?"

"Is she really taking you to court?"

"Is she carrying your love child?"

I hear River curse under his breath as we reach his car. Instead of opening the door, he turns to the waiting crowd. I grip him, unsure of what is happening and why we have stopped.

"I understand the fascination with Harriett," he begins, and at the sound of his voice, the crowd quietens. My friends step into the doorway, frown lines clear on their faces, and at Emily's questioning look, I shrug. "Believe me, I get it. She's different. But she is not your story. She's new to this world and I would like her to stick around, which will be difficult if you scare her away."

A few laugh at his not so subtle way to ease the tension. A woman no taller than five-foot squeezes through the crowd. "Are you together?"

He looks down at me, smiling. "Are we together?"

"Well, I don't want to get rid of him," I joke, and they laugh.

"We're together," he confirms.

Another steps forward, holding out a recorder. "Then tell us: are what they saying about her true?"

"Is she a stripper?" he asks, just to make sure that's what she's asking.

"For starters."

"I am," I answer before he can. "And I'm not ashamed of it. I do it because I love to dance. I do it because I can't work twelve-hour shifts, which is what I'll need to do to afford bills and my school grants. It will also get in the way of my school timetable. But I shouldn't have to explain myself. Not to you or anyone."

"I get why people want to make assumptions about my relationship, but they are wrong. So very wrong. There isn't some big story here," River declares. "There isn't some huge secret we don't want getting out. Harriett might dance, but it's not who she is."

"And who is she?" a guy asks near the back.

River grins as he stares down at me. "She's the woman who formed a crowd when playing darts because she's competitive. She's a woman who took me on a fair ride and didn't think I was a wuss for feeling sick after. She's the sort of person who doesn't see my home for what it's worth but sees the fun she and her friends can have with water fights and hide and seek. She's a woman who knows her mind and is caring yet not afraid to speak out. She's everything I aspire to be. She's a woman who isn't afraid of living or showing the world who she truly is. Life is a fun fair. We go through the fun bit, go on rollercoasters…"

"And then ride the ghost train," I whisper.

He heard every word. He understood every word. But more, he understands me. He sees me, not the girl working the pole, or the girl in the blue scrubs. He sees me. And for that, I think I'm falling for him.

He clears his throat before turning back to the crowd. "Now, if you don't mind, we need to leave. I understand this is your job, but please, be mindful and respectful and don't camp out outside her house."

He ushers me into the car before closing the door behind me. The cameras are going wild, and when he slides into the driver's seat, I take his hand. "You are so getting fucked tonight."

He grins, shifting the car into reverse. "I'm not complaining."

There's something different about him. I can't quite put my finger on it, but it's like he's finally at ease. There's no tension clogging up the air, or a reserve he seems to hold himself back with.

He's relaxed.

I suck on my bottom lip, afraid it won't last. I've never lived with a guy, even if it is only temporary. But if we can survive my job, his manager, and the media outside, how hard could sleeping in the same house be?

23

RIVER

Having the lifestyle I do, I'm used to a frenzied rush around me. From media to stylists to meet and greets, I thought I had grown accustomed to it.

Yet none of that prepared me for the storm Harriett can create.

One minute we were having incredible sex in the shower, and the next, she was cursing and rushing around like she was on a timer.

I lean back against the counter, protein shake in hand, as I watch her put her shoes on. She trips, face planting onto the sofa, and I move to help, but then she leans up. She groans, and it sounds more out of annoyance than anything, so I rest back against the counter, happy to watch on in amusement.

Pushing up to her feet, she blows out a breath and finally heads my way. I've been waiting for her to acknowledge my existence since she left the bedroom.

I duck my head to kiss her when she reaches me, but she walks right past me, reaching for a piece of toast without even a glance in my direction. My shoulders shake with laughter as she begins to gather the piles of work she left on the side last night, still unaware of my presence.

I meant it when I told her to make herself at home, and I'm not at all bothered by her confidence in taking it literally. I find it refreshing. I remember the time I lived in the back of Colin's shop. The entire time I had been tense. He told me to help myself to the food in the fridge and to make myself at home, but I never felt comfortable. I was scared to breathe and hesitated over the smallest things. I've seen none of that in Harriett since we got back last night.

"Are you in a rush?" I finally ask, unable to keep the smile from my voice.

"I realised I don't know how to get to the hospital from here. The last time I took a bus unprepared, I ended up three hours away from home."

I laugh as I snatch the keys off the side. "I'm taking you. Stop worrying."

She drops her stuff into her bag, and begins to open cupboards, searching for something. "I've completely trashed your house rushing. I'll fix it when I'm back, I swear. Just don't go into the bedroom until I've sorted it."

When I got out of the shower earlier, I walked in to utter chaos. Clothes were everywhere as she dug through the case, searching for her favourite hoody. I'm actually scared to go back in there, but I know better than to get in the middle of Harriett and something she wants. It was only the other night she nearly bit my finger because I tried taking the chocolate cake away from her. She was feeling sick and complained she didn't have the willpower to stop.

I step around the breakfast bar and pull her away from the cupboard, holding her against my chest. She tilts her head up, letting her hair fall down her back.

"The bedroom is fine. I told you that when you nearly broke your neck trying to clear a space for me to walk. Stop stressing about it."

She groans. "I can't help it. You should have seen your face when you walked into the bedroom. I swear, I'm not a messy person. I'm just used to having a space for everything."

"I looked shocked because I only saw one suitcase packed last night. You have more clothes than I do, and I find it hard to believe all of that came from that one case," I tell her.

"We know how to pack," she rebuffs, and pulls away to open the next cupboard. "I'll clean it when I get back. I swear. I really do need to get going, but first…"

"Grab your things and we can get going," I demand softly, before pressing my lips to hers. "And don't worry about your stuff. I have a housekeeper coming, and she'll hang them in my wardrobe."

Her eyes widen as she freezes with her hand on the cupboard door. "River, she doesn't need to do that. I can throw them back in my case."

"What did I say about stressing," I warn. "If staying here freaks you out, stop. It doesn't have to be a permanent thing if you don't want it to be."

"I need coffee," she blurts out, and I know I've spooked her. "Where is the coffee?"

"I don't have any?"

Not hearing me, she continues to search the cupboards. "I don't even see a kettle. I think it's been stolen."

"Again, I don't drink hot drinks."

She closes the door, her complexion white. "Where's the kettle?"

I grin wider, finding her cute. "*Again*; I don't drink coffee."

Her nose scrunches up. "Like, at all?"

I shake my head. "I don't like the taste."

"But you have a kettle, right?"

I shake my head. "I've never needed one."

"You have to have a kettle. What if guests need a cup of tea, or a Pot Noodle, or fuck, what if you have cramps and need a hot water bottle?"

I tug her against my chest. "Why are you freaking out?"

"Because I can't survive without my coffee. I'm trying to pretend you didn't say all of that, but it's hard. People think I'm weird for not having a television, but this is weird. I mean, are you even a Brit if you don't have a kettle?"

"It's not a big deal," I tell her, shrugging it off.

Her eyes widen in horror. "Not a big deal? I can't survive without coffee. You want me to survive, right? You want me to be happy? Coffee makes me happy. Really happy."

"Then we'll go and get a kettle or coffee machine, like the one you have," I offer, needing her to calm down. I don't want to piss her off by laughing.

She throws her hands up. "You can't keep changing your life to accommodate me. I don't want you to do that."

"Are we arguing?" I ask, a little unsure, and a little baffled as to what she wants me to do about the kettle.

"What?" she asks, utterly confused. "Of course not."

"Good," I reply. "Then tell me, is having coffee important to you?"

"Like my heart," she replies quickly.

"Then it's important to me," I tell her, pulling her into my arms once more. She wraps her arms around me, her expression softening.

"You are sexy as fuck when you do things like that," she gushes.

"Let's get you to work before you have another mini freak out."

She laughs as she moves over to grab her stuff. "That wasn't a freak out. I just love my coffee."

"Got you," I muse as we reach the front door.

She stops and pouts up at me. "But can we please stop at a coffee shop on the way? I won't get through the morning without one. Someone kept me up all night fucking."

"Yes," I tell her, laughing now. "I'll even order you an extra-large."

"And you are now my favourite person ever."

"I thought I was after the two orgasms you had this morning."

"Different kind of favourite," she teases.

"Get in the car," I order, unable to hide my amusement.

"Don't forget we're going to the club tonight. Are you still okay to meet us there?"

"Yes," I reply. "Now are we leaving? You've been ranting about being late for a while. I don't want to be the reason you are late for work."

"Oh, I've got half an hour. I'm never late," she tells me before sliding into the car.

I grip the top of the door, smiling like a cat who got the cream.

Life is never going to be boring with Harriett in my life. She's a firecracker, and for sure going to keep me on my toes.

WHEN I STEP out of my office, a frazzled Loraine rushes in my direction. Her purple hair blows out behind her, and her face is pale.

"Mr Knight, I'm really sorry, but Mr Andrews is on his way up and he sounds upset. I thought he was the ads team arriving, but then Kim heard his voice and informed me it's Mr Andrews. She said you wouldn't be happy."

I place my hand on her shoulder. "You aren't in trouble. Calm down."

"I should have done better. When you hired me, you said you were strict on who could pass security. I should have—"

"Loraine, you aren't in trouble. You're new and still learning your role. Do you think Kye or Libby didn't make the same mistake? They did. I'll deal with him."

"Phew, because I seriously need this job," she breathes out, finally relaxing. "And to warn you, he sounded really angry."

"He always does."

Kim pokes her head out of her office. "Loraine, can you knock on when Colin has left?" she asks, and when Lorraine nods, she turns to me. "I'm sorry, I know he's your manager, but he's a dick."

"He is, don't apologise."

The lift dings, alerting us of his arrival, and Kim scatters back inside her office, firmly closing the door.

"Lorraine, you can take an extra break until he's gone."

"Is he that bad?" she whispers.

"River," Colin yells.

Her eyes widen. "I'll check if he's gone in fifteen minutes."

"Good idea," I mutter, before stepping down the hall to the main reception area. "Colin, what do I owe this visit? And what happened to your face?"

He has bruises and cuts, like someone would get walking into a glass door.

He holds up the paper, the veins in his temples bulging. "You spoke to the goddamn paper? Did you not listen to a word Lara told you?" he yells.

"They were hounding her at her own house. What was I meant to do?"

"Lay fucking low and stay away from her!"

I grit my teeth, already done with the conversation. "And we've been through this. She's in my life, and she isn't going anywhere."

"Are you trying to sabotage your career? Mine? Because that's what you are fucking doing. I taught you better than this."

"Step back," I warn, and he does.

"And you didn't have the courtesy to inform me of this, and I have no doubt that woman is the reason. I had to find out when Marco brought me the paper."

"Get your fucking head out of your arse, Colin. No harm was done, and I don't have to inform you of every aspect of my life. If anyone has a right to be upset, it's Lara, because until you walked in yelling, I forgot about it and realised I didn't tell her either."

"You tell me," he roars, stabbing his finger to his chest. "Me. I should have been prepared for this."

"Why? Were you going to add to it? Run a photoshoot? Why? It was out there and nothing you could have done or said would have changed that."

"You are deluded if you think this is going to end well."

"Who said it has to end?" I snap.

His look of disgust has every nerve on end. "This girl has you blinded, River. She could have called them and given her location. She said as much when she turned up at my office last night and threatened me."

"Clue me in because I have no fucking idea what you're talking about."

"That stripper ambushed me at my place of work. Don't try to act like you didn't know about it."

"Harriett wouldn't do that."

"You want proof? You can take a look at the security footage."

"No, you aren't understanding. I meant, she wouldn't ambush you.

She's not a fragile woman. If she had something to say to you, she would say it to you. And can you blame her? Someone leaked her personal details and occupation. And you've not exactly been the friendliest to her, so I can see why she would presume it was you."

"She threatened me," he snaps. "She came in and told me if I didn't stop trying to protect you, she would get you to fire me. She even offered me sexual favours. That's the sort of girl you are dealing with."

Sheer will is the only thing stopping me from grabbing him around the throat. "You have no clue who she is. I know Harriett. She wouldn't do that."

"Well, I'd tell you to ask Hetty, but Harriett scared her so much she was too afraid to come back to work this morning. That's the woman you are with. You want to keep seeing her, you want to go down this path, keep me out of it. I won't have you tarnish my good name. I was willing to risk it when I first met you because I believed you weren't this person. I thought you wanted to get out of that life, make a new start, but you are willing to lose all that I've built over a girl."

"Get out!" I demand.

Both his brows rise. "So, I'm finally getting to you. You are hearing some home truths and you don't like it."

"No. I need you to leave because it's taking everything in me not to put you on the ground. I won't listen to another line of bullshit from you, not where Harriett is concerned. She's done fuck all to warrant this hostility, but you continue to treat her like she has," I grind out. "Leave, before I make you leave."

"I'm going, but from now on, our relationship is strictly business. You'll attend every event, every meet and greet, and every conference. Failure to do so, and I will terminate all your contracts, which I am legally obliged to do. Your house you so fondly mentioned in this article, will be gone. Because I'll make sure you have to sell every asset you own to cover the termination costs."

He turns on his heels, heading back towards the lift. I head back to my office, doing everything in my power to keep it together.

I hit my office, kicking the door shut behind me, and immediately grab the ball off my desk. I whack it against the wall, roaring in anger and frustration.

That man was born to push people's buttons and test their patience. He knows exactly what to do or say to hit a nerve.

The door behind me clicks open and Kim pops in. "Everything okay?"

"Yes. No," I answer, rubbing the back of my neck. "I know it's a lot to ask, but can you take point on today's meeting? I'm not in the best of moods."

"Sure," she agrees. "Do you need anything?"

"I'm good, but thank you."

Once she leaves, I drop down on my desk chair, grabbing my phone off the desk.

River: I just had an interesting visitor.

Harriett: Please tell me it's Jesus Christ because I have questions. A lot of questions.

River: I'm afraid to ask what. It was actually Colin. He said you visited him last night.

Harriett: Oh, yeah, I went to ask him to stop playing games 'cause I will play them back, and I don't play fair. We messed with his office too, so he might be complaining about a few *accidents*.

Well, that explains the marks on Colin's face.

River: He told me something different. But I'm not going to bore you with the facts since I don't believe a word of it. He's being a dick and clearly got out the wrong side of the bed. He even tried to accuse you of scaring Hetty into leaving her role.

Harriett: Oh, Hetty has left her role. She didn't want to work for a man who would verbally abuse a woman. I was meant to tell you last night when you came around, but the media and the sex kind of distracted me and I completely forgot. I wasn't keeping this from you.

River: I didn't think you were. And she really left? Damn, I was hoping to steal her to come and work for me.

Harriett: I've passed her number on to a friend for a job at the library. Charlotte is excited to meet her. She can't pay her much, but she needs someone like her. She has Drew's sister working with her on weekends and after school but she needs someone else.

River: Is there anything else I need to know before I get some work done?

Harriett: Yes, at some point, we are going to Hetty's for dinner. She invited us.

River: Really?

Harriett: You sound surprised. She said she's offered before.

River: I am. I thought she was asking because she felt obliged. She's a kind-hearted woman.

Harriett: Well, she meant it. I've got to go, but I'll see you later. X

River: Be safe.

I drop my phone back onto the desk, wondering if I should have told her about the threat Colin made. Some women might not like it being kept from them, but then, she isn't like most women. But she does feel things just the same and I know she'll feel responsible and want to do something. It's who she is.

I can't think about it anymore. The season will end in just a few months and then I'll never have to see him again. Harriett won't feel the need to protect me or be worried of what he'll do next.

All I have to do is keep my head low, keep to my commitments, and make sure I don't give him any more ammunition to use against me.

24

HARRIETT

Music blares from the speakers of the club, vibrating the floor beneath us. We've been here awhile, and soon, the show will begin. Shots are passed around, and jugs of Tequila Sunrise are evenly shared around the table.

Hayden—Charlotte's cousin— who surprised us by turning up to girl's night, hands the tray of shots over to Emily, bypassing Charlotte. She doesn't even notice, but then, the girl is already two sheets to the wind. Hayden is a different kind of crazy to us, but then again, her dad is Max Carter, and he is a known legend by reputation. Personally, I think someone was manipulated into not forcing him to stay in a mental institution. Because that's where he belongs.

Hayden snatches another shot off the tray before eyeing me. "So, fighter boy, huh?"

"Yes, and he's coming later, so whatever you have to say, get it out now," I tell her.

She grins at the directness and clasps her hands together. "I bet the sex is rough and hard. I picture it rough and hard."

I grin. "You've pictured what sex with me would be like? Aw, honey."

Hayden is hot in a tom boy way. She acts like a guy, swears like one, yet dresses to bring men to their knees.

She rolls her eyes at my comment. "I get it, you don't want to talk about it, but I'm just saying, I bet it's hot."

"More than," I admit.

"And they are getting serious. She is now living with him," Emily adds.

"Emily," I groan. "Don't say that out loud. And I'm not living with him. I'm just staying there."

"Oh no," Charlotte yells, and I find her facing the entrance. I turn, and my brows lower at the sight of Eloise, a girl I met the same night I met River. She's Drew's sister's friend—or was—and is a bigger bitch than Trixie from the club. If it wasn't for the fact they are both attention seekers and like being centre of attention, they could be friends. Best of friends.

"What is she doing here?" Gabby asks, having met the snide woman before.

Charlotte bites her lip. "She might have heard me tell Drew not to forget about tonight. She's been trying to fix her relationship with his sister, Natalie. I bet she's hoping to talk to Drew and get him to fix it."

"You think she's still trying to get with Drew? She can't be that stupid. Anyone can see how in love he is with you," Gabby declares, narrowing her gaze on Eloise.

The young woman takes a seat with her friends, unbothered by the hostility the table is throwing her way.

"Um, no," Charlotte answers but doesn't meet my gaze. In fact, she goes out of her way *not* to look at me.

"Charlotte, you are terrible at keeping things to yourself. What's going on?"

She bites her lip, her cheeks reddening. "She wants to have sex with Rampage."

"River," I correct, because fighting might be what he does, but he's River. He's still a man. "And she isn't fucking getting near him."

"I heard they had a fling, but you know what women are like," she replies, taking me off guard.

I take a look at the girl once more. She's kind of pretty, so I can see what he saw in her. But she's had so much work done she looks like a clown. More, she's a bitch and I can't see why he would go for that, even if it was a quick fuck.

"Who cares," I shrug. "Let the bitch try. He's had me now, so if it is true, she's no longer a memory."

Hayden grins, holding her hand up across the table. "You are my kind of person."

I slap my hand over hers. "I like you too."

She rears back, like the comment is foreign to her. "Who doesn't."

"Actually," Charlotte begins, but Gabby leans over, covering her mouth with her hand.

"She didn't mean literally," Gabby assures her.

"Back to River," Emily interrupts. "I like him. And he's been kind enough to rent us his holiday home—which is pretty cool of him."

Drew drops a tray of fresh drinks on the table before taking his seat. "He must really like you if he's letting you use that place. It's one of his favourite places to be. I've only ever been there once and that was to help set up the downstairs gym," Drew declares.

"He made it seem like it was no big deal," I reply quietly.

Why would he trust a toddler and four crazy women to stay for four nights at a place that means that much to him? I mean, it's not like we'll leave it not standing. But I can't promise something won't get broken. Gabby likes to mess. She sees a button and has to press it.

And Olivia… there's a reason her siblings aren't coming. They are what I imagine the aftermath is after a tornado meets a volcano. They aren't purposely destructive, but nothing is safe once they start fighting. And since Olivia is a mum to three kids she never asked for or birthed, she deserves a break from them. Their aunt comes down and stays to watch the two youngest.

So why would River give us a place he cherishes?

"Maybe for you, it isn't. But when Colin wanted to use it, he told him no. It means a lot to him because it was a place he could go and not be bothered by anyone."

My brows rise at the comment. "I don't blame him on the Colin thing."

"I still can't believe the bitch grassed on you. What a tattle tale," Gabby scolds.

I take another shot, needing it if we're going to keep talking about him. "I'm not surprised. I knew it would happen. I'm just pissed I never got to be the one to tell River."

"Sex distracted her," Olivia kindly informs everyone.

Hayden grins. "Right on."

"He's giving you a hard time still?" Drew asks, his brows pinched together.

"Yes. And I don't trust him one single bit. I have a feeling this is just the start," I admit.

"Be careful with him, and be careful with River. River is a tough guy, but he has his limits. He has some messed up notion that he owes Colin. He's a man who is grateful, and shows it in any way he can, so if Colin is getting in the middle, he won't make it easy, and River will be torn, especially if he's serious about you."

"A part of me wants to say I don't give a fuck, but I do. I don't want River in the middle any more than you do, but this guy is making it hard for us to be together. I don't give a fuck about him, and if it wasn't for everything you just mentioned, I wouldn't have held back the way I have."

"River needs to learn it for himself. Colin will mess up, and when he does, River won't hold back either. Be patient with him."

That last sentence is said with a warning, like a hidden meaning he wants to tell me about but can't. And I understand that. River has secrets, a lot of them, so I know how hard it must be for Drew knowing them and wishing he could expand.

"Let's drop it," I tell him, not meeting anyone else's gaze. "I'm not comfortable talking about him when he isn't here."

"Alright."

I have a feeling there is more he wants to say, but he knows I'm right. It's not cool to talk about someone like this when they aren't here.

Angelina LeMay, also known as Morgan, rushes over to us with her teased, blonde wig wobbling at the top. Decked out in extremely high heels, a rainbow sequined dress that spreads out like wings when she raises her arms, she looks every bit the part.

"Hey, Angie, you excited for tonight?" Olivia asks, taking a sip of her drink.

"I'm going to be sick," she reveals when she hits the table. She does a double take of Drew, her long lashes fluttering at the sight of him. "Well, hello gorgeous. I've not seen you here before."

"It's his first time," Charlotte announces.

"I love to break in a newbie," Angelina gushes.

"Enough of that," I order, clicking my fingers to get her attention. "What's wrong?"

"Bitches being bitches," she breathes out, taking Olivia's cocktail and downing it. "Sally's mum should have swallowed her."

"Want us to sing My Pet Sally and change the lyrics to Please, go away Sally?" I offer.

"You love me," she reveals.

Olivia snatches her glass back with a frown. "Tell Sally to fuck off. She's so dramatic."

"Babe, I would, but only pushing her down some stairs would make my day right now."

Gabby's nose twitches as she leans forward. "I thought you were friends. You were staying with her, weren't you?"

Angelina dramatically cocks her hip out. "Yes, and the hoe told me to make myself at home."

"So, what's the problem?" Emily asks, her lips twitching.

"I threw her out. I don't like visitors," she explains, and I can't hold it in. I start laughing.

"Angelina, no wonder she's been a bitch to you. I would be too."

"She's probably right though," she replies, taking a shot. "Tonight will be a disaster."

"No, it won't be," I assure her. "And if it helps, we can cheer louder."

"I'm going to need more than cheers," she explains. "The boss is making cuts, and I think these host nights are our auditions. I need to do something different, something to make him want to keep me."

"Todd isn't going to fire you. Stop stressing," I tease. "You'll get wrinkles."

"I'm gonna get grey hair," she stresses.

"I'm going to fire you if you don't get your arse to work," Todd announces, stepping up to the table.

"Sorry," Angelina grimaces, before her attention falls to the stage.

"Tonight, ladies and gentlemen, I bring you, the Queen Bees. Up first is Cheryl Le Voo."

"Oh fuck," Angelina moans. "I have to go. I'm up next."

Todd glares at each of us. "You'd better be on your best behaviour tonight."

"We're always on our best behaviour," I reply sweetly.

He points to Charlotte. "And stay away from the stage."

"I've learnt my lesson," Charlotte promises.

We laugh as he storms away. He acts like we're a problem, but we're not. He wouldn't let us in if we were.

The show begins, and singing *Candyman* by Christina Aguilera, is Cheryl, the queen bee of the set, and one of our favourites aside from Angelina. She is a queen of all queens and doesn't take any shit from people in the crowd. When she got into a fight with a straight guy and won, we cheered and fell to our knees worshipping her.

We all whistle and cheer as she begins. Drinks are brought to the table as requested, and we enjoy the show.

When her set finishes, Angelina steps onto the stage, her pink glitter microphone in hand.

Dolly Parton 9-5 intro begins to blast, but the minute Dolly's voice is about to come on, the speakers cut off, and Angelina's deep voice, off key, echoes over the noise. Her expression pales, and she turns to our table, panic clear.

"Help her," Gabby hollers.

"Charlotte can sing," Hayden offers. "Get up there."

"No," a few yell, but she's already up, excitement on her face.

"I've always wanted to do this," Charlotte gushes, rushing away before Drew can hold her down.

Olivia turns to me, eyes wide. "Go. Help."

"Why me?"

"Because you are the only one who doesn't sound like a suffering cat," she argues and gives me a gentle nudge.

I stand, rushing up to the stage. And even though I don't like it, I will, because I never want to see one of my friends crash like this.

"Can you really sing?" I ask Charlotte as she straightens the dress she's wearing.

"I think so. My mum and dad say I have a voice like an angel, and my family say I'm a star."

Oh God, they could be lying to her to spare her feelings. It wouldn't be the first time. Charlotte loves to bake. But just because someone likes something, enjoys doing it, doesn't mean they're good at it. Everything she bakes should come with a warning label. Me and the girls learnt that the hard way. The first time we got rushed to A&E, we thought it was a fluke and something we had eaten at the club. The second time, Gabby had to get her stomach flushed it got that bad. And when all of us were down with sickness and diarrhoea the third time, we knew her baking was the culprit.

"Girls, you can't be back here," Nico, their stage coordinator, orders.

"We're coming to sing to save the set," Charlotte explains, as I duck my head around the curtain to find Angelina seconds away from turning.

Nico hands microphones to us, then holds out his phone. "Take this," he demands. "It's connected to the sound system, so if I can get it started, it will be in sync to where you are."

"What happened?"

He looks frazzled as he glares at me. "We're in a building full of petty bitches. Someone started a rumour people will be let go so now it's every woman for themselves. One of them tried to sabotage the night."

"So, no one is getting fired?" I ask, feeling giddy now I know my friend has nothing to worry about.

"Of course people are getting fired. He can't afford to keep *everyone*."

My shoulders slump at the news, and I take the phone from him. "Then I guess we're going out there to save our friend's livelihood."

As we head to the stage, I can't help but be grateful River is detained with his meetings. This kind of humiliation I'd rather wait for him to see until he's madly in love with me—if he isn't already. Because I am awesome, and who wouldn't fall in love with me?

Charlotte wastes no time in hitting play. Angelina, in all her glory, gives us a questioning glance. I paste on a smile, acting the part, and smack her around the arse.

"Go with it," I tell her when I step behind her.

Giving the audience the side of her face, she smiles, but the panic and horror is clear. "Why is looney toon up here? The last time I let her on this stage she broke my favourite pair of Cher heels."

"Trust me, she's good," I lie, and carry on so she can't question me further. I have no clue how good Charlotte is. I mean, she sings in the car, but I never hear past the awful squawking Gabby belts out.

Charlotte begins the song, and for a split second, I forget why I'm up here. She's not good; she's phenomenal.

Even Angelina is taken off guard because it isn't until Charlotte hits the chorus that she realises she's standing there gawking. She shakes herself out of it and puts on a show, owning the stage like she was born to do.

And having grown up with an obsession with Dolly, I already know the lyrics and move into action.

Charlotte grins at the sound of my voice greeting hers, and begins to shake her hair. And boy does she have a lot of it.

I sway my hips, dancing next to her as we belt out the next verse. We're just hitting the part about being your own boss when movement at the back of the room catches my attention.

Standing in front of the entrance is River. He arches an eyebrow, yet he's grinning like he's got dirt he can use on me at a later date. I shrug and dance like I'm in my bedroom and no one is watching. Even when the music comes on, and Nico is waving us off the stage from behind the curtain, we continue.

We continue until everyone is on their feet clapping along, and Charlotte hits the high notes.

We're still singing and dancing long after the music cuts off. It isn't until Angelina snatches the mic from my hand that I finally stop.

I'm out of breath, grinning, and nudge Charlotte. She blows out a breath, happiness radiating from her.

"You are so not going to get fired," she assures Angelina, forgetting she still has the mic in her hand.

The crowd starts kicking up a fuss, protesting to keep Angelina. She smiles and hugs us against her inflatable tits. "You girls rock!"

"We know it."

We hand off the mics to Nico and take the stairs down to the main floor. River is at our table, heated desire in his gaze.

And I want him. I so fucking want him.

As I reach the table, I don't look away from him. "Hey."

"You sing too."

"I'm a girl of many talents."

"I'm starting to learn that," he muses.

"Oh God, I'm going to vomit," Olivia moans.

"I think it's romantic that he wants to fuck her. Our girl is hot," Gabby adds.

"I would do her," Hayden announces.

"Me too—if I was into girls," Charlotte admits. "I'd do all of you. Not at the same time."

Gabby laughs. "It's fine. We get it."

The flush to Charlotte's cheeks suddenly drops back to her pale complexion and she drops down next to Drew, panic evident. "I would never cheat on you. I just mean if I was gay and single. Not that I want to be single. I don't. I love you and we have amazing sex. Do we have amazing sex?"

"Are you not going to stop her?" I ask Hayden quietly.

Hayden doesn't lose the grin. "No. Because I took Charlotte's quirkiness for granted once and it wasn't until she lost herself that it made me realise how much it makes Charlotte her. So whenever she has her Charlotte moments, I take them in because it's a reminder she's getting better and she's finally finding herself again."

"You really are a softy."

Her smile drops as she turns to me. "If you tell anyone, hunk behind you won't even save you."

"All right," I reply, then go back to River, who is happily listening to Drew assure Charlotte he gets what she's saying.

"Go," Emily orders, her eyes lit up with happiness. "You know you want to."

"He just got here," I point out.

River lifts me at the waist and takes the seat I left, placing me on his lap. "We're here to spend time with you guys, which is what we are going to do. Isn't that right?"

I reach around, cupping his face. "You are so hot right now."

He grins and leans up, his lips at my ear. "Later, I'm going to fuck you so hard."

"You always do."

"Let's hope we make it out of the car."

"Or through the rest of the night," I tell him, not bothered by the idea. I'm not the girl who fucks in the toilet, but for him, I'd fuck him backstage if it meant having him inside of me.

Because he's the guy I don't need to change for; would be willing to make compromises for.

Although, fucking him is never a compromise. It's a reward.

But first, he has to pass the friendship test. If he can get through the night with my friends, and still want them in my life, he's a keeper for sure. I've yet to meet a guy who has passed the test, but River, he's no ordinary man.

He's a keeper.

25

RIVER

Placing her hand on my thigh, Harriett stops the nervous bouncing. I'm amped up, ready for tonight's fight, but more, I'm anxious, something I'm not accustomed to, during or after a fight.

And Harriett is the reason.

Tonight, all the fighters will be there, which unfortunately includes Fracture. There's no doubt he's read the papers and is planning to use it as ammunition against me. It's what he does. He did it with Marlene and he'll do it with Harriett. The only difference is, I really care about Harriett. I don't want to be the man who lets another person talk shit about his woman, which is what I'll need to do if I want to stay in the competition. She deserves a man who will fight in her corner.

We arrive at the stadium, and Colin, who has done nothing but glare at us from the other side of the limo, moves towards the door. "Let's get this done."

"Give us a minute, Colin," Harriett asks him sweetly. "I want to talk privately to River."

"He doesn't have time to cater to you. He needs to be out there on the red carpet, promoting himself."

"Alright, you go ahead. Let him out there jittery with nerves," she tells him. "I mean, it's not like he'll punch someone over me. He hasn't punched you yet."

"Five minutes," Colin demands, understanding her concern. "I'll be outside."

The flashes of cameras hit us the minute the door is opened, but once they see it's Colin, they stop. He closes the door behind him, and Harriett pushes down the lock to stop him from coming back inside. "Are the windows tinted from camera flashes?"

"They are reflective ones so no photo they take, no matter how close they get to the glass, will penetrate through the windows. Why?"

"Good," she tells me, then slides up her glitter gold dress, with a split down the middle, up her thighs and straddles me. "What's going through your head? I've never seen you like this."

I drop my head back on the seat. "I'm worried we'll run into Fracture and he'll talk shit about you. And it hit me, if I did any other career, I wouldn't hesitate to hurt someone who spoke shit about you. I hate that Colin has essentially gotten away with it. I don't know if I can take someone else. You must think I'm weak."

She runs the palms of her hands along my jawline. "No, I think it shows great strength. If it bothered me, you would know, I promise. But like you, I know how serious the ramifications can be if you did hit someone on my behalf. I wouldn't want you to do that. Because whilst it might feel good for a split second, it won't in the long run. I'd hate myself for being the reason you ruin your career, and you'd eventually resent me for being the reason it was taken away."

"It fucking sucks that my hands are tied."

"Look at it this way, you said you would if you could. That's enough for me. I also know if I was ever in danger, you wouldn't hesitate. I get you, River. I truly do."

I place my hands under her dress, gripping the globes of her arse. "You really do."

"So, if he talks shit, ignore it. I'm the only one who's allowed to be offended by it and I don't know this person or care what he thinks of me. And I'm not saying that to make you feel good about yourself either. I've had people try to bully me. It doesn't work. For it to work, I have to care about their opinion, and I just don't."

I lean forward, pressing my lips to hers. "Have I told you how amazing you are?"

"I already know how amazing I am," she sniffs teasingly.

I grin at her confidence. "Come here," I demand, and pull her head down so I can kiss those red lips she's covered in a glittery lipstick. As soon as she stepped out of the bathroom and I saw her lips, I imagined doing dirty things to her. Things we didn't have time for. But now... Now I don't care if I mess them up. I need to kiss her.

She doesn't hesitate to move, and dives right in, kissing me. I plunge my tongue inside her mouth.

My hands on her arse tighten, and the movement has her grinding down on my cock, which instantly hardens.

She clings to me, her hands greedily roaming over my shoulders and chest before finally sliding down to my belt.

I pull back. "What are you doing?"

Eyes bright with desire, she replies, "You're still tense."

"But there are people outside."

"People you said can't see inside," she argues softly, her fingers undoing my belt. "I've been wanting to get these off you the minute I stepped out of the bathroom."

She's referring to the suit I'm wearing. It's a pointless outfit since the minute I go inside, I'll be changing into my shorts.

"A quickie," I warn, lifting up so I can shove my trousers down my thighs. She grabs her clutch, pulls out a condom, and slides it over my cock.

Once I'm sheathed, I slide her knickers to the side and enter her in one thrust. She grips my shoulders as hers drop back. She moans as she begins to rock.

I run my hand up her back and bring her forward, needing to feel all of her against me. Her movements quicken, and so does her breath, as she forces herself down on my cock.

She's wet. I can feel it on my thighs. "Oh God," she moans.

There's a tap on the window, and I turn, seeing the shadow of a man who I suspect is Colin. It's confirmed when he calls my name.

I grip her hips, thrusting harder. "Quick."

From the corner of my eye, I notice Colin with his face against the window, trying to peek inside.

"He can't see us, can he?" she moans, getting louder.

"No, but he'll hear us," I warn her, and quickly manoeuvre us until she's on her back, and I'm between her thighs.

I push her knees to her chest, and she reaches behind her to grip the back of the seat, her body arching as I slam inside of her.

"Oh God," she cries.

"Shush," I warn, and press my thumb down on her clit. I feel her tighten around me as I hammer inside of her.

In.

Out.

Until she's crying out my name.

My orgasm tears through me, and with a jerking motion, I finish inside of her. "Fuck!" I growl.

"Are you relaxed now?" she asks, a wide smile on her face.

"Very," I assure her, and quickly dispose of the condom and do up my jeans. She's straightening her dress when I take a seat beside her.

"Thank you for being here."

She takes my hand. "I wouldn't want to be anywhere else," she admits, before taking a mirror out of her bag.

I open the door as she's fixing her lipstick. "We'll be out in second."

He pops his head in. "What are you…" His lip curls in disgust at Harriett fixing her cleavage. "Are you fucking serious? Here? Right now?"

"We have a red carpet to walk," I remind him and gently nudge him back. I step outside as a crowd cheers. Cameras begin to flash as I reach in, taking Harriett's hand.

She steps out, immediately taking to the spotlight as she smiles for the cameras. I never had a doubt she couldn't handle this life, but if I did, seeing her shine in front of the cameras and fans would have melted it away. She was born for this.

BACKSTAGE—AS some call it—Harriett and I greet everyone who stops to talk to us on our way to my allocated locker room. Fighters from all over even take a minute to stop and wish me luck. Everyone is buzzed from the atmosphere, and people are bustling about, pumped on adrenaline.

It isn't until we're nearing our corridor that the atmosphere changes. Everyone still milling around in the halls, stop what they are doing. Dean Mole—also known as Fracture—pushes off the wall with a taunting smile when he spots me.

He's not how I remembered. He has more ink, for starters, and no longer has any space on his chest. Why he didn't cover up the Thug Life tattoo when he had a chance, is a mistake on his part. And instead of thick, shoulder-length hair, he is now sporting a buzz cut. He's also not as muscular as he used to be, like he has shed some weight.

However, when I look at him, I no longer see the man who slept with the woman I was with, or the guy who nearly cost me my career. All the rage and tension I had before… it's gone. The hate is still there —he's a dislikeable person—but the reasons why I wanted to smash his face into a brick wall are no longer an issue. All I see when I look at him is pity, and an opponent I will take great pleasure in defeating.

It's more proof that I'm truly over what they did.

Or maybe it was never there to begin with, and I was projecting what I knew I should have been feeling.

I was still trying to navigate my way through life and come to terms with the new lifestyle. I was young, naïve, and didn't think I deserved it. When I started out, I was still learning what it meant to have what I did, and in the process, I partied hard. Until Marlene. Seeing her life, where she came from, it made me start taking stuff seriously. Or more than I already was.

Dean missed that lesson. He didn't learn to appreciate what he has, and instead, began to expect more. It's why I pity him. This could be the height of his life, and he's not appreciating it.

"Hey, new girl," he calls, and every muscle in my body tenses. "When you get bored of being with a boy, my door is always open."

"Don't, Dean," Mark, his manager, warns.

"Listen to your manager," I tell him.

"I heard it never closes," Harriett remarks, already picking up on the tension.

"I hear that doesn't stop you," he replies just as quick. "I'll even pay you double whatever he's paying you."

"Fuck you!" I spit out, but Harriett's hand tightening around mine stops me from saying any more.

"Dean, we spoke about this," Mark declares.

"Let's go," Harriet announces, squeezing my hand.

I want to punch him, to pummel him into the ground, but I know I need to save it for the ring. If he's as good as rumours have suggested, I'll be going up against him at some point. And I can't wait.

He'll pay for that comment.

Fracture runs a hand down his bare chest, his snarly smile still plastered over his face. "I'm going to need entertaining later. How much is your going rate?"

Harriett begins to walk, or tries to, but I hold her back, staring him down. She stands in front of me.

"This is what he wants. To get to you. Don't let him," she pleads, and she briefly glances over her shoulder. "And seriously, I don't get it. She had you but went for him? It's like she had a Rolls-Royce but traded it in for a toy car."

"Hey," Dean protests.

I grin, swing her up in my arms, and move away, something I should have done from the very start. She wraps her legs around me. "Toy car?"

She rolls her eyes. "It was the only thing I could come up with. He's fucking ugly."

"He didn't always look like that. He's lost muscle too. Not much, but enough to show."

"You calmer now?"

"Thanks to you."

"Because I'm amazing, I know," she affirms, flipping her ponytail over her shoulder.

We reach my locker room and Drew is there, waiting. "Hey," he greets.

"You made it," I greet, and drop Harriett to her feet.

His expression is serious. "I've told everyone to come back in ten. We need to talk."

I step inside, and when he closes the door behind us, I know it's serious. "What's going on?"

"You know I train guys at the gym. The circuit is getting bigger, so more and more are canvasing other gyms, trying to find out what works for who and why."

"Yeah, that's new," I point out, taking a seat on the bench.

"One of the guys mentioned something and I decided to get some feelers out. And it's true."

"What's true?" I ask, growing impatient. Harriett takes a seat next to me.

Drew scraps a chair over and straddles it. "You need to be careful. Word is, Dean is going to try and get you out of the competition."

I snort. "We already know he wants to win. We all do. I also know he won't play fair."

"He's already tried to pull him into an argument," Harriett adds.

Drew shakes his head. "You aren't understanding me. Dean risks the chance of ending his career. Sponsors, coaches, they don't think he's worth the hassle."

"I don't blame them," I admit. "He's not exactly made friends."

"No, he hasn't. But one of his major sponsors have told him unless he can beat you this season, then he'll no longer be sponsoring him. Endorsement contracts have pretty much said the same."

Fuck! "Shit!"

I feel Harriett's gaze on me. "What? What does that mean?"

I turn to her. "It means he's going to try and get me fired from the circuit. We aren't allowed to endorse ourselves. We need sponsors. If he's being told he'll lose it all, then he's going to do everything in his power not to go up against me. He knows he might lose."

"He will lose," she affirms.

I turn to Drew. "What else did you hear?"

"This information is the only one I couldn't confirm, but it's not just him you'll need to worry about. The new starters for this year, he's been talking to them. They think you are out for their career and don't intend on letting you win. And tonight, you're going up against Helix."

"The one people are calling Boldor?"

"Yes. I've seen him fight, and he's good. He's quick on his feet. But you've got this. You've been working with Landon on your footwork."

There's a knock on the door before Cian pushes it open. "We need to get you ready," he tells me.

I stand and take Harriett's hand. "Drew, will you show Harriett to her seat?"

Drew nods. "I will, but then I need to go out front. We're hoping to bring in new fighters, so we'll be out front doing sign ups."

Harriett leans up, kissing the corner of my mouth. "Knock them out, babe."

"Have fun, and no starting fights out there," I warn.

She beams, pointing to her chest. "Me, start fights?"

"Oh, Drew filled me in, and I know it was you who started the fight at the charity ball."

"Hey," she scolds, punching Drew in the arm. "That was totally your girlfriend."

He wraps his arm around my girl, tugging her towards the door. "Good luck, man."

They leave, and I begin to strip out of my clothes. My mind drifts back to what Drew warned me about, and I can't help but fret over it. Before, I didn't have anyone I cared about. He couldn't touch me. But now I have Harriett.

I have something to lose.

But I won't go down without a fight.

Whatever happens to him now, he only has himself to blame. And I hope when he looks back on this time, he remembers me. I hope he remembers the man who took it all away from him.

Because I intend to win this championship.

26

HARRIETT

Tonight isn't my first rodeo. I've been to fights before, but this… this is on another level. I haven't seen this many people in one room since Dave, our manager at Tease, put the drinks on offer for buy one get one free. It's rammed in here, and everyone is feeding off each other's adrenaline. It's buzzing in the air. I've not felt anything close to this, not even when we went to the rave we bought tickets for, just so we could wear our rave outfits.

I knew River was popular when I met him. I'm not a naïve girl who hides away from the world. But I never knew it was like this for him. People have his cage name painted on their T-shirts. Some even have merchandise with his face on. *His face* for Christ's sakes. And I'm pretty sure one guy has his face tattooed on his arm.

This is crazy. And people think I'm nuts for sliding up and down a pole.

The ring announcer has just finished introducing Helix when he steps out. The guy has a silk gown on, for fuck's sake, and the only thing that could make this cheesier is… And the *Rocky* theme tune begins to play. I want to roll my eyes, but I'm so embarrassed for the guy, I can't.

The crowd is loud, and the front row seats on the other side of the stadium must be his family and friends because they cheer the loudest and get to their feet.

But the second he starts introducing River, the crowd goes wild. Everyone is off their seat, including me, when Sweet Caroline begins to blast. I scream, cat call, whistle… everything to let him know I'm in his biggest supporter.

He grins as he runs down the line of fans, slapping his hands against theirs as he goes. When he reaches me, he leans down, kissing me.

"For luck," he states.

"You don't need it."

He winks and moves away, lifting his arms in triumph.

I move back over to my seat, keeping my gaze firmly on his ripped back. He steps into the cage; his posture assured and dominant.

Fuck, he is hot.

I'm so focused on him, I don't sense the arrival of a newcomer until they are at my side. I run my gaze over the bleach blonde, noticing a few things. Her makeup is thick, too thick for someone who has fair skin. And her red dress clings to her in all the wrong places due to her round middle. But what pulls my attention are the faint bruises on her bicep and, on closer inspection, the teeth marks that fail to be concealed under the strap of her dress.

We both take a seat before she speaks. "You are here with Rampage?" she asks, her gaze on the cage.

My brows pinch together as I watch her more closely. "I am. Can I ask who you are?" I ask, whilst wondering if this is one of the friends River was talking about last night. He wasn't sure whether or not they'll make it. But for some reason, this doesn't feel like the person he spoke about. For starters, he told me she and her husband are very happily married. This person is someone I don't know, but I have a feeling she knows River. And knows him intimately. It's the way her pupils dilate at the sight of him, the longing in them.

And a gut feeling.

And my gut is rarely wrong.

"A friend."

I hesitate to hold out my hand, but I do, because when someone thinks they have you where they want you, they talk more freely. "I'm Harriett."

She smiles, but it doesn't reach her eyes. She ignores my hand. "I know who you are. I also know you are dating River."

Oh God, this is her.

This is the woman who cheated on River for a man not even in the same league.

"I am."

"Then you should know—woman to woman—he will never love you. He will never care for you. He doesn't know how to."

"And how would you know?" I ask, playing along.

"Because I'm the only one he has come close to loving."

"You're Marlene," I guess, hoping my surprise is believable.

Her thick, dark brows rise in surprise. "He's spoken about me?"

"No, I read about you in the paper," I lie, taking comfort when she scowls.

"He won't love you, you know. It won't go anywhere. He's doesn't know how to. He's never gotten over me and what happened. I broke the last bit of him that might find love."

"It's bitchy and forward of you to come here and warn me away from the guy you cheated on," I tell her, unashamed of my words. "It must suck to see what you lost in the papers every week."

She rolls her eyes. "I'm not being a bitch. I thought, woman to woman, you'd appreciate the warning. I know what it's like to get attached to him. Believe me, I know. He makes all these promises, and they sound believable, but I swear, he doesn't mean them. It's all a lie to compensate for what he needs. He has mummy issues."

"Then it's a good job he hasn't made any. But even if I believed you, why would I care? The sex is phenomenal. But then, you'd know that; probably kick yourself daily for throwing it away."

Her lip curls. "So, it's true, you're a stripper?"

"I am. He loves it."

"Probably because he knows you won't last as an item. I bet he hasn't even taken you to see his mum, has he?" He hasn't. And I think she can tell the truth by the look on my expression because she grins. "And you never will. He told me when we were together that I'd be the only woman who would meet her. She has some kind of mental health issue, so he doesn't tell anyone about her he doesn't trust."

I'm missing the fight for this bullshit.

"Is there a reason you're here?"

"I guess not. You'll learn the hard way; I did."

I lean into her, making sure she hears every word. "No. I won't. Because I'm not you. I won't cheat on him, for starters, and with someone who clearly isn't on his level. You thought you could come over here in hopes I'd walk away from him. He'd see me leave and lose concentration, but I'm here to tell you, it won't work. I've been around women like you before, I'm used to catty behaviour. And woman to woman, all you've done is make yourself look like a desperate, scorned ex."

"It isn't like that. I'm over him, was before it even ended. Dean is perfect for me."

"No, it's exactly like that. And I'm betting you haven't had a day close to what you had with River with your new guy. I bet he treats you like shit, cheats on you all the time, and couldn't care less about you." I make a point of looking at her bite mark. She lifts the strap over it, blanching. "I bet you've seen River and I together, and you hate it. It's eating you up because you are picturing what you may have had with him and you thought coming over here and getting me out of the way, you would have a chance again. And if that isn't the case, then you really are here to try and make him lose this fight."

"You don't know what you are talking about. River treated me like shit. He said things, did things, but he never meant them, not really. He wanted what I could give him without giving anything back in return. He didn't give me the attention I needed, and I bet he does that to you. I know I broke him when I left him, but I had to. I love Dean. He loves me. And we're blissfully happy," she lies.

I shake my head in pity. "No, you aren't. You are miserable. But just so we are clear, River treats me with nothing but respect. And I'll admit, the sex is beginning to kill me, but I'll push through it because the orgasms are great," I declare, and lean in again. "We talk, we share, and he likes that I cook for him. The difference between you and I, is I see him as River. You see him as Rampage, the guy who put money in your hands and gave you a little fame. That's how I know I have nothing to worry about. Now I suggest you run back to that guy you call perfect and leave me the fuck alone because I'm pissed I've missed two rounds of this fight."

Her expression twists into something ugly. "He's nothing. And when my Dean is finished with him, he won't be Rampage anymore. He'll just be someone people used to know. And if you had a brain, you wouldn't stay and be caught up in the crossfire."

I grab her wrist, digging my nails in to stop her from leaving. She whimpers, dropping her arse back in the chair. "Threaten me again, and I won't need a cage to put you down," I warn, digging my nails in deeper. "You should also know I'm not just a pretty face. I work with dead bodies, so I know exactly what artery to nick, and how to make it look like an accident."

Just as I finish, a stunning woman in a black dress steps into the aisle. "Marlene, I think you are in the wrong seat. Yours is on the other side of the room, right at the back," she explains, her voice firm.

I smile sweetly. "Marlene is just leaving. She just needed some advice."

Without a word, Marlene gets up and leaves. The woman steps aside, revealing a man I recognise.

"Holy crap, you're Mel Jacobs," I greet, standing.

He takes my hand, grinning. "And you must be Harriett. River told my wife all about you."

"I'm Allie," she greets, and leans in, hugging me.

I hug her back before pulling away, staring down at my hand. "I'm never washing my hand. I think my dad might kill me if I do. He has followed all your western movies. He's kind of obsessed."

He grins. "Later, I'll sign something for you to gift him. I wouldn't want you to not shower," he teases.

I laugh before shuffling down the aisle to give them room. "River is going to be thrilled you're here. He has spoken fondly of you," I tell her as we take our seats.

"He's a softy," she replies. "After, when the break is on, you'll have to tell me what *that* was all about."

"Of course," I agree, and then turn my attention back to the fight.

My man is sweaty, a little bloody, but on fire as he dominates his opponent. With three rounds down, I'm glad I'm not going to miss the end.

Because I wouldn't miss this for the world.

My throat is raw to the point the alcoholic drink I bought to sooth it is burning my oesophagus. But I don't regret a single thing. My man deserved to be cheered. He waited until the last round to knock his opponent out. The last I saw of Helix, the first aiders were carrying him back to his locker room.

Now, I'm waiting for River in the bar area, and I don't know a single person. Well, that's not entirely true. Dean is in the corner flirting with a few ring girls, and instead of paying attention to the men who are speaking to him, he's looking at me.

Giving him my back, I can't help but shudder. I disliked him the minute I met him, but now, the guy gives me the creeps. He reminds me of the guys who sit in the front at Tease. He's the guy who makes lude comments with his mates and doesn't put money in the tip jar after each stage performance.

He's that guy.

The guy we steer clear from, yet make fun of backstage.

He's also the guy I know I'm going to have to keep an eye on when I attend these things. Because he's out for blood, my man's blood. Not that I'm worried River will lose. He won't. But men like Dean, with not only his pride to lose, will go to any lengths to protect it. We're in the bar area where later, a party will commence. Fortunately, we won't have to stay and watch him fight. River does not plan to give Dean the privilege of his presence. He said it will be a slap in the face to Dean, and he won't like it.

Spotting Drew, I begin to relax at the familiar face. His brows pinch together as he approaches me, before they narrow at the man behind me. "Hey, you okay? I heard Marlene cornered you."

"I wouldn't say cornered but she approached me," I admit. "And I'm good."

He's scanning my arms. "I heard you were bleeding."

"Oh, no, I dug my nails into her wrist to get my point across," I assure him. "But I don't think she'll be bothered by them. She has other injuries to be concerned about."

"You think she's being beaten?"

"I *know* she is. I saw bruises on her biceps, and a faint cut on her lip. But that could be because she applied her lipstick too thick."

"So, you are alright?"

"I'm more than alright," I promise. "Did you see River? I didn't get chance to see him before he went back to get cleaned up."

"He's the reason I'm here. He's showered and now out front watching the next fight whilst they sort his cuts. He wanted me to come back and tell you he'll be here shortly."

"Harriett," Allie calls.

Allie and Mel, hand in hand, head towards us. I grimace when I realise I left without saying goodbye. "I'm sorry I left in a hurry. I had to get a drink before I lost my voice completely. I wanted to be able to talk when I saw River."

She laughs. "I thought for sure you were going to tackle the team in front of us to get to him on that last bit."

"I tried, but my leg got caught in my bag," I admit sheepishly.

"If you plan to come to all his fights, we'll make it our mission to accompany you. Tonight has been so much fun."

"I'm not sure if I'll get time off again for the next two, but I am planning on coming to the last one. Me and my girls are coming. Our boss already cleared it."

"Oh, the more, the merrier. I can't wait to meet them," she tells me.

My brows pinch together. Allie is a great woman, and as much as I love her company, I don't want to tarnish her reputation. I know Mel is a famous producer who has worked on many blockbuster movies. Being seen with a stripper—even as friends—might cause a scandal.

"Um, there's something you should know about me," I begin.

She waves me off. "I read the papers, sweetheart. I don't care what they say. You make River happy and that's good enough for me. We've known him for years, and we see him as a dear friend. It's finally nice to see him let someone in. Because whilst we see him as a friend, he always holds us at arm's length. Don't worry, we don't hold it against him."

Mel rubs the back of his neck. "And trust me, we've tried to get him to warm up to us and come over more often."

"I'm beginning to see a pattern when it comes to that with him."

"Here he is," she announces. "The man of the hour."

"You came," he greets, shaking Mel's hand before placing a kiss on Allie's cheek. "It's good to see you."

"We're actually leaving now. We have another event we need to get to, but we wanted to see your first fight," Mel admits.

As they say goodbyes—Drew leaving too as he has to open the gym in the morning—I'm glad to finally have River to myself.

"You were incredible," I gush, jumping into his arms. "I never saw it before, but watching you fight, it's an art. And you excel at it."

"Enough about the fight," he soothes, lowering me to the floor. He keeps me close, placing his hands at the bottom of my back. "Are you okay? I saw you talking to Marlene."

I roll my eyes. "She tried to warn me away from you, but I honestly saw it coming. I just didn't think it would be tonight."

"What did she say?" he asks, utterly baffled.

"Nothing much. She wanted to press some buttons so I would react."

"What kind of buttons?"

"She mentioned your mum. She said she's in some sort mental institution and has it in her head that she's the only woman you'll ever let your mum meet."

"She's never met my mother," he argues, then takes a look around, noticing we aren't alone. He pulls me away from the small crowd and hides us behind a post. "My mum, she is mentally sick."

I reach up, running my hand along his jaw. "You don't have to explain anything to me. I know what she was trying to do. And it didn't work. I know when you're ready, you'll trust me enough to tell me."

"I do trust you," he replies heatedly. "It's just… My mum, she's complicated. Explaining her health brings up other topics I'm not ready to talk about."

I duck my head to meet his gaze. "It's really okay, River."

"It's not. You'll eventually begin to wonder if she's right."

"River," I soothe. "I'm not her. I'm not judging you."

He seems to be at war with himself, not meeting my gaze. And when he does, there's resolve there, but more, there's fear, like he's worried it will scare me away. "My mum got diagnosed with bipolar not long after she had me. But when she got taken into care, she was diagnosed with schizophrenia. Mild, but with Bipolar, it's a toxic concoction. She's in a facility that monitors her twenty-four-seven. I don't like talking about it because it brings up memories I would rather forget."

"River, you didn't need to tell me that," I tell him, my voice low and filled with anguish over what the boy in him went through.

"I did, because I need you to know you have all of me. You are the first person I've been able to tell. Colin and Drew, they knew because they were there. They saw it. And when the time is right, I will tell you all of it. It's ugly, disturbing, and not for the faint of heart, but I trust you with it."

"Then I'm honoured to be the one you've told," I reassure him. I lean up on my toes and wrap my arms around his neck. He needs a distraction, and I'm happy to be it. "Do we have to wait for Colin to leave?"

He pulls back, his hands on my lower back. "Not really. He's probably trying to schmooze other sponsors."

I run the tip of my finger along his collarbone. "Then let's go make good use of the limo on the way home."

A squeal passes through my lips as he lifts me at the thighs. "What are we waiting for then, let's go."

Laughter spills out of me as we head for the exit.

This is the River Marlene never had when they were together. She never cared enough to make him feel safe enough to be himself. She wanted the idea of him, the promise of him, but she never wanted *him*.

The information he shared may be small for some, but I know for River, that was huge. And I'll never tarnish that. I'll never break his trust or faith in me. He passed the friend test and the girls let him know. But what he doesn't know, is that he's past my test. And now we are on dangerous territory.

Because I never intend to let him go.

Marlene never got this River Knight, but I did.

And now he's all mine.

27

RIVER

Everything is passing by in a blur. Weeks feel like days. Days feel like hours. Hours feel like minutes.

Because every day I get to spend with Harriett goes by in a blink.

I'm happy, blissfully happy, and it's all down to the woman who has stayed in my bed night after night. She hasn't gone home, even long after the media stopped hounding her.

And I've found myself dreading the day those bags get packed and she leaves.

All around there are mementos of her. A coffee machine sits on what is now essentially a coffee bar. There are candles all over the place, and just the other day, she ordered some huge lanterns for the garden.

She's brought colour into my life, made it thrive, and I wake up each morning excited for what the day will bring for us.

Which is why this morning I'm dragging my feet. Harriett and her girls left for the beach house early this morning. They were meant to go yesterday, but the aunt looking after Olivia's siblings got delayed and didn't arrive until late last night. And since Emily has a little one who was in bed at six, they didn't want to disrupt her bedtime.

But now, I have three days without her, and I don't like it. She gives my days meaning, and without her here, it feels empty.

The house feels cold, quiet, and it's just not the same. I keep expecting to see her lounging on the sunbed outside.

My phone beeps with another message, and I lean over the counter to snatch it.

Colin: Where are you?

Not where I'm supposed to be. I should have left forty minutes ago to head to the stadium. We have interviews, meet and greets, and are required but not obligated to be at the weigh in for tonight's fight. And since it's Dean fighting tonight, I wasn't eager to attend before Harriett left. Now that she has, I'm unmotivated to go full-stop.

As I click on the message, my phone rings. My day just got better.

It's Harriett.

As I answer the call, I notice the keys on the coffee bar. Keys to the beach house. "You left the keys by the coffee."

"I know, I know. I'm so sorry. I needed the coffee to prepare me for Gabby's singing."

"I resent that," Gabby yells.

"And then I got so focused on the coffee and how good it tasted, I forgot to pick them back up. We're here, and please, tell us you have a spare set of keys."

"I do. There's a restaurant just on the turning onto the beach road. Did you see it?"

"The one that looks like a beach hut?"

"That's the one," I tell her. "Go grab some food and a drink and I'll be there as soon as I can."

"Wait, aren't you busy today?"

"Nothing that's important," I assure her.

There's a rustling over the phone, and I hear muted voices, so low I can't make out a word. A minute passes before she's back on the line.

"If you're coming, pack a bag."

"What?" I ask, wondering if she's talking to me.

"If you're going to travel two hours to get here, you might as well stay. You said what you had to do wasn't important, so come. It's only right. This is your beach house."

"I have training tomorrow."

"Drew mentioned you have a gym here."

"I meant my training on the night. It's intense training. I don't have those things there."

"Stay the night then, at least. You can go back in the evening after the boat trip," she suggests. "Unless you don't want to. I mean, you'll be stuck with a bunch of girls for the weekend."

"I think there are worse things to be stuck with," I tease.

"True. I got stuck with a snotty nose kid who called his mum every two minutes when I first started my hours at the hospital."

"Are you sure? This was meant to be for you and the girls."

"They are all up for it, and honestly, Gabby is a little apprehensive about the boat trip tomorrow. She's a little wary around men she doesn't know, but she trusts you. And if it makes you feel better, she asked multiple times why you weren't coming. And on the way here, she said it would have been better if you came too."

"And you aren't just saying that? Because I'm good with dropping the keys off and coming back."

"I want you to come. The girls want you here. So, if not for me, for Gabby's sanity because she nervous eats. And she doesn't need a bigger arse."

"I'll do it for you," I tell her with a smile in my voice.

"Yes!" she cheers. "Meet us at the restaurant."

"Alright," I tell her, and end the call. Then I take a massive sigh, knowing what I have to do. I hit call and bring the phone to my ear.

"Where the hell are you?"

"There's been a change of plans. I'm not going to be able to make it. I have to get to the beach house. Um, the boat needs looking at?" I lie.

"Your beach house? You aren't supposed to be there. Why are you there? Someone else can fix the boat," he grits out, and I hear chatter of other fighters and people over the phone. "It's two hours away. You can be back by this evening."

"I'm staying there for the night. Keep track of everything and fill me in over email. I'll be back tomorrow night," I explain.

"No, you need to get back here. Stop letting that girl monopolise your time. River—"

I end the call and take a breath. That felt good. Really good. I should put the phone down on him more often.

Excited to see my girl again since I wasn't looking forward to sleeping in bed by myself, I rush to the bedroom and pack an overnight bag.

PULLING into the car park over two hours later, I find the first available parking space. With the sun out, the holiday resorts are busy with visitors, so I'm lucky to grab the space near the entrance.

Harriett is outside waiting when I get out the car. "I really am sorry. I swear, I did not leave them on purpose."

I pull her into my arms, smiling at her panic. She rambles when she panics, and I find it cute. "And I've already told you, it's fine."

Finally, she leans up, kissing me, something I've been waiting for. I groan at the taste. Kissing her is like finding magic. It's a promise. A declaration of what we share together. She's fiery, cheerful, and lives for the day. I'm kind of broody, and someone who keeps to himself whilst planning for the future. Together, we are explosive, in a good way.

I pull back, brushing the hair out of her face. "It's so good to see you."

She gives me a lopsided smile. "You only saw me this morning."

"And that was hours ago. You were right to leave the keys."

She jabs her finger in my chest. "Hey, I told you I didn't do that on purpose."

"I'm kidding," I assure her. "Where are the others?"

"They're inside. Poppy wouldn't eat her food. She's been grumpy, so we got her something fresh to eat."

"Have you eaten?"

"Yes. What about you?"

"If people don't mind, I could eat a sandwich right now."

"Then you should try their chicken salad one because I swear, it touched my soul it was that good."

I lock up the car as a kid comes running outside. A kid who has shot up since the last time I saw him. I bend at the knee and lift him up in my arms. "Hey, scrapper, how's it going?"

He brushes his dark curly hair from his face. "Mum said it was you, but I didn't believe her. I watched your fights. Mum recorded them for me," he tells me, then continues without waiting for me to reply. "Do you think you'll fight Fracture, because I can't wait for you to knock him out. You are going to knock him out, right?"

"That's the plan," I muse, fighting back laughter at his enthusiasm. "Luke, this is Harriett."

The five-year-old turns to Harriett, his eyes widening. "You are really pretty," he gushes before turning to me, his nose twitching. "Is she your girlfriend?"

"She is."

"Eww," he whines. "The girls try to kiss me at school, but I run away."

"You'll regret running away, kid. One might be the one you'll marry when you're older."

"Nah, I want a girlfriend who looks like yours."

Harriett laughs at his comment. "Sorry, little guy, but I'm a limited edition. There's only one of me."

"Like my Chandelure Pokémon card?"

She smiles wide. "Yeah, something like that."

I drop him to his feet as we head inside. "Do you think you can tell your mum I want a chicken salad sandwich?"

"Right away," he salutes. before running off towards the kitchens.

We move down the line of tables to where Harriett's friends are sitting. Emily is fussing over the young toddler in the highchair who is refusing to eat the food in front of her.

"Hey, how was the drive?" Gabby greets.

"Quiet," I reply, sliding in the booth after Harriett.

"Not like ours then," Harriett teases.

Gabby throws a chip at her friend. "Thanks for coming and saving the day."

"You're welcome," I murmur, distracted by the young girl who has stopped crying to stare at me. "You must be Poppy."

"Up," she demands, lifting her arms in the air. When I don't, she bangs her little fist on the highchair table. "Up!"

"It's okay, I got her," Emily assures me, but the girl wants none of it and starts screaming once again. I've never held a baby, much less been around one, which is why I don't know what comes over me when I lift her from the chair and deposit her on my lap. "Oh my god."

I glance up, seeing Emily watching me, mouth open. "Did I do something wrong?"

"No," Emily whispers, still staring.

"My ovaries just burst," Harriett declares quietly.

"Mine too," Gabby states, staring too.

Olivia has her chin resting on the palm of her hand, and she, too, has a faraway look in her eyes. "Me three."

"Do you want me to put her back?" I ask Emily.

"No!" the girls all yell.

"River, it's so good to see you," Gill, the restaurant owner, greets as she places the sandwich down in front of me. "I didn't think you'd make it down here this year because of training."

"This one forgot the keys," I explain, pointing to Harriett. "Gill, this is Harriett, my girlfriend. Harriett, this is Gill. She owns the restaurant."

"Told you he had a girlfriend," Luke declares.

"And a little girl," she murmurs, giving me a questioning look.

"Poppy is Emily's little girl, not mine," I explain.

Gill holds her hand out to Harriett. "It's lovely to meet you. This one normally comes down here on his own. It's about damn time he stays in that big house with friends."

"It's nice to meet you too," Harriett muses. "Did you two meet here, then?"

"No, we actually met on the beach. He saved my son's life."

"What?" Harriett asks, turning to me. "You saved his life?"

"It was nothing," I assure her.

"It wasn't nothing. I turned to watch my niece for a split second and Luke slipped out of his dingy. The current pulled him away, and I couldn't find him. This one was close by, saw the whole thing, and decided to run in and help. It was a minute, if that, but for me, it felt like a lifetime. He saved Luke, then helped me save my business when it threatened to go under."

I reach out, taking her hand. "You're a good mum. You didn't deserve to lose everything you built because you decided to take care of your son," I heatedly remark before turning to Harriett. "She had PTSD after the accident and didn't want to leave her son. I came back to see how they were doing."

For a moment, she doesn't look away. I can't read her, which isn't new for me, but in this instance, it feels it. There's warmth, maybe pride, shining back at me.

Harriett clears her throat and gives the woman who doesn't give herself enough credit, a warm smile. "I'm glad you had him here to help. I can't imagine what it was like for you."

She waves Harriett's comment away. "He's a hero in my eyes," Gill declares as she lifts her son into her arms. "We'll let you get to your lunch, but pop in tomorrow. Luke has made you a birthday card. We were going to send it but since you are here, we can just give it to you."

Oh fuck!

"Wait, it's your birthday?" Harriett squeals. "How did I not know this? Why didn't you tell me?"

I rub the back of my neck, grimacing. "I don't celebrate it."

"He forgot," Olivia comments. "I can tell by his face. It's the same expression my brother gets when he forgets to do a chore."

Harriett scans my face. "Oh my god, you did. You forgot," she agrees. "When is it?"

"Tomorrow."

"I'll leave you to your food," Gill offers, before scampering off.

"I don't have anything to give you," Harriett stresses. "Oh my god, where is the nearest shop that does cards?"

Gabby already has her phone out whilst I take Harriett's hand. "Will you stop stressing and enjoy your holiday with your friends. When I say I don't celebrate, I don't celebrate. It's just another day for me, so please, don't go to any trouble. Being here is enough, I promise."

She hums under her breath for a moment, then takes a look at

Poppy, who has dropped her head on my shoulder. "She's asleep, so I'll take her whilst you eat, and we can talk about this later."

"Are you mad at me?" I ask, making sure Poppy is steady when I hand her over.

"Of course not. I'm mad at myself," she confirms.

"Harriett," I call through laughter. "I promise, it's not an issue."

"Okay," she tells me, but I can see that it's not.

This has taken her off guard. And I've learned that Harriett hates being taken off guard. She prefers to be in the know.

But now is not the time for us to discuss it. Later, when we are alone and naked in our bed, we can talk about it.

Because from her expression, she has questions.

A lot of questions.

28

HARRIETT

My mind is absolute mush because of the man beneath me. Fucking me in the laundry room wasn't enough.

Neither was in the shower.

He had to fuck me again when we reached the master bedroom.

In his very large, luxurious, king-sized bed that might just be better than his bed at home. A bed I'm dreading to leave when he finally tells me to leave. The only reason I've stayed is because he's not asked me to go. His bed is too comfy, and I've been having the best sleep of my life. And the sex... We can have sex whenever the mood hits us—which is often.

And we crossed a boundary again tonight, one we've not spoken in detail about. He's bare-back, and it feels too good for me to care. Fortunately, we have a backup: my pill—something I take religiously.

His hand slides back up my body to grab my tit, distracting me once more. I roll my hips as he thrusts up, the muscles on his stomach tensing at the strain. He's giving it to me as hard as I'm giving it to him.

My eyes roll as he lifts up, bouncing me up and down on his cock.

He's deeper, so much deeper, and I don't think I can have another orgasm. I'm all orgasmed out. If that's even a thing.

There are no words between us. We don't need them. Everything we want to say is in the way we move, and in the way we touch each other.

Without warning, he rolls us until I'm on my back, and before I can protest, his lips meet mine in a searing kiss that I feel all the way down to my toes. He hammers inside of me, and the pressure of his weight presses down on my clit. It feels amazing. And I know at the first twinge, that little pulse, I'm going to orgasm.

Again.

I'm not going to survive.

He slides the palm of his hand down my thigh, lifting it higher up his waist.

"Oh fuck," I cry as the pressure deepens.

"So fucking wet," he growls roughly.

I touch the rough stubble over his jaw, and when our eyes meet, there's a new kind of tension, one I can't look away from.

It's him.

It's me.

And it's all I can take as another orgasm tears through me. I drop my head down on the pillow, crying out as a powerful release tears through me. My lids fall closed as all the sensations intensely run over me. My entire being shudders with pleasure, and just as I'm about to cry out and make him stop, unable to take anymore, he growls with his own release.

He drops his weight over me, panting for breath. "I think you might actually kill me with sex."

My lids snap open, and I jab him in the side. "If anyone is dying it will be me. Death by orgasm is what my tombstone will read. And you touched me first."

"To kiss you," he argues, dropping down to the side of me.

"No, you brushed my nipple with your fingers. And you know how I get when you play with my tits."

The bed shakes with his laughter. "Are we really arguing over sex?"

I close my eyes once more. "No, but if you touch me intimately again, I'll be exercising my right to say no because I don't think I can take another orgasm."

I feel him move, so I flip my eyes open to see him staring down at me. "Exercising your right?"

"Yep. It's a woman's right to choose what she does with her body. And I'm telling you, I can't take any more orgasms today," I tell him, struggling to hold back laughter. "My god, I need to clean up, but my legs feel like jelly."

He leans over, kissing me, and at first, it seems like it's going to be a quick peck, but then he takes his time pulling away.

And it feels good.

Too good.

"No more orgasms," I remind him, pulling away.

He grins, giving me a peck on the cheek before getting up. "Stay there and I'll go get something to clean you up."

"Hurry up then because if this stains the sheet, you're sleeping on this side." When he goes to reply, I hold my hand up. "And if you say we can put a towel down, we are over."

He grins, confirming that's what he was going to recommend. "Yes, Miss," he salutes, before rushing off into the joining bathroom.

He comes back with a towel and a wet cloth. I take it from him and quickly clean up. Once I'm done, he drops them in the basket near the bathroom door before getting back into bed.

Not wanting to be far, he tugs me to the centre of the bed and holds me against his chest.

For a moment, we peacefully lie in silence. It isn't until the silence becomes too much that I speak. I have questions, a lot of them, and I need him to open up, even if it's just a little bit. But I also don't want to push him or force him to tell me.

"Why did you tell us this was a beach house?"

Running his finger along my arm, he replies, "It is a beach house. It's on the beach, and it's a house."

"It's too big to be a house. A house has a few bedrooms, this has seven, and separate buildings outside. I want to say it's a villa but the villa I stayed at in Spain was nowhere near as luxurious as this."

"I guess when you put it like that..." he muses, shifting a little. "I had the new additions built outside when I bought it. It was run-down for a few years before I bought it."

I take a breath and ask the question that's been plaguing my mind since the restaurant.

"Why here? Why this beach? When we were eating at the restaurant, we got talking to some locals. They said this is the only house like this left here. All the others sold, and big corporations came in and made resorts. But this one is still standing." I rest my chin on his chest and look up at him. "You could have any place in the world, why here? Does it hold sentiment?"

"I have other places. This is just closer," he explains, and although that's probably true, it's not the real answer. He's holding back.

Worry it will always be like this, that he'll never open up, hits me like a train, and I blurt out, "Are you ever going to open up to me?"

He tenses. "It's *just* a house."

"No, I don't think it is, and your body language and the way you tensed up confirms that," I affirm. I lower my lashes. "Please, talk to me."

"Please, just drop it," he tells me, and his voice hardens into annoyance. I sit up and grab my pyjamas I dropped on the floor. I slide into the shorts when I feel him sitting up. "Where are you going?"

I stand, straightening the tank top before leaning over and pressing a kiss to his cheek, hoping I've successfully hidden the hurt. "I'm going to get a drink."

I leave out of the double doors and make my way down the spiral staircase. The marble floor feels cool to touch. I keep going, passing the extravagant living room that leads out onto the patio and down the hall to the kitchen.

I hit the overhead light switch above the huge breakfast bar centred in the middle of the room, when I feel him behind me.

"Why are you being like this?"

I turn after reaching for a glass. "I'm not being like anything. I told you I was getting a drink."

"I could have gotten you a drink."

"You aren't my maid."

He steps further into the kitchen, coming under the light so I can see him. It breaks my heart to see him hurting, but there's a tightening in my chest, a fear in my mind that this is how it will always be between us.

"You said you didn't need to know everything. You said you could wait."

I slam the glass down on the counter because that is unfair of him. "And I can. I'm okay to because I understand, River, I do. But you give me *nothing*. I know nothing about you other than the present."

"The present is all that matters."

"I'm scared you'll never open up. I'm scared you'll always keep your past hidden. I'll never get to understand how you came to be this man. I'll never know the things that made you, you."

"No, you're letting Marlene get to you. What she said, it isn't true. It isn't. I never trusted her the way I do you. And maybe I did push her away by not telling her. Or maybe I was right to not tell her. I'll never know, but I do know I don't regret not letting her all the way in. I let you in. It's a little bit at a time, but I do."

"I know that. I do," I rasp. "Just go back to bed, River. I'll meet you up there in a minute."

I turn my back to him to grab a jug of water from the fridge. I'm pouring a glass when he begins, his voice low, filled with pain and anguish.

"My mum brought me here when I was six. It was the only time I can remember where she spent time with me. We stayed on the beach all day building sandcastles, and then we slept in the car because we had no money. I had the best day," he tells me, his voice drifting off. "I think she was going to leave my dad. I heard them arguing over the phone the next day. And I thought... this is it. This is when we'll finally be free, and my mum can get better."

"River," I soothe, instantly regretting that I pushed him. "Don't tell me like this. Don't tell me when you're hurt and upset. This isn't what I want."

He lets out a dry laugh. "But it's getting between us," he states before continuing. "I didn't know she was having a manic episode.

Our trip wasn't real. None of it was. And we left that evening. Back to our shitty life, in our shitty flat."

"So you bought it because it reminded you of a happy time?"

"No, I bought it to remind myself things could have been different if we had just kept going. That night, I listened to my dad beating her, listened as my mum screamed and hit him back."

"River, I didn't mean… I never meant to bring up bad memories for you."

He leans against the counter behind him, his laughter dry, void of humour. "You don't get it. None of it was good. My childhood didn't consist of parents who loved me. They didn't take me to the park to play football or come to any of my parents' evenings. I didn't have parents like yours, who loved me. I wasn't even a burden to them because to be a burden, they would have to remember I was there. And half the time they didn't."

"And the times they did?"

"I wished for them to forget about me."

"River, I'm sorry. I'm so sorry."

"This is what you wanted. You wanted to know and now you do," he replies, frustration evident in his tone.

"Not like this. Not when you're mad at me," I explain. "You don't tell me much. I don't need you to share everything, but I *needed* something. Just not like this. I wanted you to want to tell me."

"Why? Why now?"

I give him the real reason. "Because you didn't tell me it was your birthday. I didn't even know it was tomorrow. And it made me wonder if it will always be like this. Will I always find out after the fact?" I reveal, letting out a sigh. "I'm scared I'll do something you don't like or say something that might hurt you. And what we have, it's good. It's so fucking good that sometimes I have to pinch myself to see if it's real. But I need it to be real for you too."

"I didn't remember my birthday because it's a day I don't wish to remember. I got told often that I should never have been born. I never got presents or birthday cards. But if you want the truth, if you really need to hear it, I don't deserve to live another year. I don't."

"Don't say that. Don't you dare say that," I argue, moving around the breakfast bar.

How did we go from seven orgasms to this? Why did I open my mouth? I should have left well enough alone.

He holds his hands up, stopping me from going any further. "I need to tell you everything. I need you to know."

"Not like this," I plead. "Please, not like this. You'll hate me for it, and I'd rather never to know, than have you hate me."

"My mum is in a facility because she admitted to killing the man I killed," he states, knocking the breath out of me, to the point I have to grip the counter for balance. "I killed a man because he no longer got joy out of beating me. He wanted to humiliate me. He stripped me from the waist down, and was just undoing his belt when I lost it on him. I hit him over and over, using every technique Drew taught me until he lay there in his own blood. Colin showed up and my mum took the blame."

"This is your secret?" I rasp. "This is what you didn't want to tell me?"

He continues like I never even spoke, lost in his own grief. "They never found his body, you know. Colin said he sorted it since I was a minor, but I never read about it. Never spoke to the police or made a statement. And my mum, she admitted to killing my dad, but they could never find evidence to sentence her, so she got admitted into an institution instead. I'm a coward. I let her take the blame, and all I did was push those memories aside and carried on like nothing happened. I hid behind the cameras, hoping no one would find out my secret."

"River, no," I choke out, but in the back of my mind, a voice is screaming that this doesn't add up. None of it makes sense. However, River is my focus. He's who I care about right now. "You were protecting yourself."

Tears stream down his face as he slides down the wall. "I wanted to wait until you knew the real me before I told you about my past. I didn't want you to run."

How can I run away from the man who has just poured his soul out to me? He's given me what no one has ever been given. A chance to accept him for who he is.

Am I okay with knowing he's killed a man? No, because I don't think he did. And I don't blame River one single bit for hitting back. The man deserved worse for what he was going to do. Way worse. So, if he did die, River did him a blessing.

I sit down in front of him, spreading my legs on either side of his thighs. I grip his face. "I can't sit here and tell you I understand. I don't. I've not lived through that kind of horror. But I can tell you, you did what any one of us would have done. Gabby did it when she got attacked by her old boss. Charlotte did it when her ex-boyfriend raped her. He was hurting you. *Had* hurt you. And you did what you had to."

He swipes at his tears. "I don't even remember it. I blacked out," he whispers, before meeting my gaze. "Why are you not running away? I've told you the worst bits. You should be getting your friends and leaving. You should be running as far away from me as you can."

"Because I know you. You're a man who saves little boys, who makes sure their mum is financially stable. You're the guy who visits children's hospitals to cheer up sick kids. You are the guy who raises money for children living in poverty, and the guy who dates a stripper and treats her like a queen. I know who you are, River. I know exactly who you are."

"And what if I'm not that? What if it's a disguise so no one would find out the truth?"

"Then you would have used media attention to make you look good. But you don't. You do it because it's who you are."

"I didn't want you to find out like this," he tells me, his voice breaking.

"River, I don't think you killed anyone," I blurt out. "I don't. There was no body, no police report, and something like that, the media would have a field day with. But they don't."

"Because Mum hid the body."

I shake my head. "I'm telling you, I don't think that guy is dead. And do you really think your mum was in a condition to hide a body?"

He clenches his jaw, and I can see his mind working overtime to figure it out. I might not know a lot, but from what he has told me about his mum, there is no way someone with her medical condition could do something like that. Kill someone? Yes. But hide a body? No. They wouldn't care.

"He has to be. Otherwise, why hasn't he come forward? Why didn't he come after me?"

"I don't know, but we'll figure it out," I admit, my shoulders dropping. "I'm sorry for forcing you to reveal all of this. This isn't what I wanted."

"You were right though. It was coming between us. It *is* coming between us. Now everything has changed."

"Look at me," I demand, and tilt his chin up until he meets my gaze. "None of this changes anything. I still want to be with you."

"You will look at me differently."

"Probably," I reply, and at his anguished expression I can no longer take, I continue. "But only because I'll no longer see a fighter. I'll see a survivor. I'll see a warrior. I'll see strength that goes beneath the surface and what you can do with your fists. I see you. All of you."

"I can't let this get out. I can't. Not about my mum. Not about her boyfriend. Not because it will ruin me, but because I'm ashamed. I'm ashamed I could fight in the streets, but not at home. At home, I was a scared little boy who just wanted his mum to love him."

"You have nothing to be ashamed of."

"I killed a man. I killed him."

I run my hand down the side of his face. "I don't think you did. And I think somewhere deep down, you know it too. I think you were that traumatised, you suppressed your memories. And I think if you really thought about it, you would realise that too. But we aren't going to talk about this tonight. We are going to get a drink, maybe some snacks, and if you are really lucky, a blow job when we get upstairs."

As we get to our feet, he takes my hand, stopping me from going to get my drink. "If you want to phone the police, I won't stop you. If you are scared I'll do something to stop you from leaving, I promise you, I won't. You can do it."

I take a step until I'm flush against him, running my hands over his chest. "River, listen to me when I tell you I'm not phoning the police. I'm not going to run. Because even if I did believe you did it, I wouldn't care. The guy was beating you. He was going to *rape* you. And if you hadn't stopped him, all those kids wouldn't have got their last wish. Your charities wouldn't have had those donations. And I wouldn't have met you. If that makes me twisted, I don't care."

He lifts me by the waist, and I wrap my arms and legs around him. "Thank you. Thank you for not running."

"I'm not going anywhere," I promise.

And I'm not.

We'll get through this, and now I know where to tread carefully. And I'll do everything to make this right, to find out what really happened.

First though, his birthday.

29

RIVER

A soft breeze wakes me up from an unsettling dream. A reoccurring dream of the night my life changed. The night *I* changed.

I always thought with the good I did, the more I gave, it would make up for that night and the wrongs I caused. I made a mistake, an excruciating mistake that I'll have to live with for the rest of my life. I don't regret stopping him. I don't regret fighting back. But I do regret blacking out and killing a man.

If I did.

Since Harriett questioned it, I have to wonder if she's right. I only had a small television in the back room of the shop, but I watched the news. I watched it religiously every night, wondering when they'd show it or when my picture would pop up in the top corner. I watched it just as much as I did the backdoor, scared the police were going to kick it down and arrest me. And it never came. There was no big announcement or hotline to call. No one ever looked or came for me. Not once. And he was never mentioned.

And the day it all got too much for me, and I was ready to hand myself in, is the day Colin first yelled at me. He told me not to throw my life away for a mother who killed my father. He made good points, so good, in fact, I stayed and followed his every word.

I never wanted to tell Harriett why I was in the back of that shop. It was better for her to think I was there for a warm place to sleep, instead of the truth that I was there, hiding out.

Her reaction isn't what I imagined. I expected her to run, to phone the police and get me arrested—something that should have happened to me a long time ago. But once again, the woman has taken me by surprise by doing the complete opposite.

She stayed.

But more. I took myself by surprise, because the minute she told me it's okay, I desperately wanted to tell her I love her. And how could I not? I'm addicted to the way she makes me feel when I'm around her.

She's everything I'm not.

She is the light to my dark.

The good, the bad, the ugly; she accepts all of me.

And she's Harriett; how could I not love her?

Feeling groggy from lack of sleep, I reach for her and find her side of the bed empty, which is surprising since we stayed up a majority of the night talking.

Lifting my lids, I confirm her side is empty. She's gone. And I don't hear any signs of movement in the house.

Sliding out of bed, I tug on my shorts and then grab my phone from charge before heading over to the balcony doors.

The sea air hits me in the face as I step outside and over to the railing. Seagulls squawk, and I tune them out to listen to the waves crashing against the shore. It's a comforting sound, one I never get tired of.

Being here is bittersweet, and at times, a punishment. I don't get to visit my mum often. My presence unsettles her. But here, I get to be close to the mum I wished I had. Our day here had been my only good childhood memory. I still hear her laughter as she chased me, I still feel her touch when she held me, and I remember the warmth in her eyes as I jumped with joy over building the biggest sandcastle. That day, I felt like a son. I felt like all the other kids at school.

Things got bad after that. Mum's health declined and my dad... he went to prison not long after for drink driving. He crashed into a car that held a family driving back from a birthday party. Luckily, no one died, but he still had to face the consequences. It's how I know my mum never killed him. He had been locked up, and we never saw him again. But that's a conversation for another day. I didn't want to ruin her weekend away even more.

My phone vibrates with a message, and I click it open, seeing it's from Harriett.

Harriett: Are you awake?
River: I am. And you're gone. Are you okay?
Harriett: Come downstairs to the living room.
River: Let me clean up and I'll be down in five.

She replies with a smiley face. A part of me is nervous she's changed her mind, that she's woken up and realised she can't handle the truth about me. They always say things will look different in the morning.

And if she is going to leave, I don't want to draw it out by taking my time up here. Making quick work in the bathroom, then getting changed, I'm out of the bedroom in five minutes as promised.

As I make my way downstairs, Poppy's cries reach me. We heard her a few times during the night, and Harriett left once to go and see if she could help.

As I round the corner to the living room, I startle when everyone jumps up.

"Surprise!"

Hanging from the beam is a happy birthday banner. Balloons with various colours and cartoon characters are strung up. And to the left, where there's a large dining room table, are trays of breakfast foods. From eggs, smoked salmon, and almonds to fruit and veg, she has thought of everything.

"W-what?" is all I manage to get out as I continue to scan the room, inch by inch.

"Happy birthday, babe," Harriett greets as she steps into my arms.

"You did all of this?" I ask, still struck by the surprise. No one has ever done anything like this for me before.

I've never had balloons or banners. And I've never had a cake, even if it is a Spiderman one that has a bright red two and a white nine that has clearly been added on.

"I did. I got up early to surprise you," she admits, then steps back, grinning. "I couldn't get you a present, so I made you breakfast."

"This is…" I shake my head, still in a daze. "I don't know what to say."

"Say thank you so we can eat because I'm starving," Olivia pleads.

I pull Harriett against my chest. "Thank you."

She beams up at me. "My pleasure," she replies, then leans up until her lips are at my ear. "Later, I have a different kind of surprise for you, but it will have to wait until after the boat trip."

As the others begin to take their seats, I pull Harriett away. "Last night…" I close my eyes, ashamed of how I spoke to her. "We should talk."

She leans up on the tips of her toes, pressing her lips to the corner of my mouth. "Not today. Today is about you and celebrating your birthday. Last night… it doesn't change anything. I promise."

"What are you two whispering about?" Gabby calls. "Because if you sneak off to have sex, we aren't waiting for you."

"Harriett is not ditching," Olivia argues.

"How would you know?" Gabby asks, arching her brow.

"Because it's a girl's plus River holiday. You don't ditch unless you have a good excuse. The sex might be good for them, but it's not a valid excuse."

"We need to sit down before they start arguing," Harriett rushes out, tugging me towards the table.

I take a seat at the head of the table, grinning at the birthday cards placed next to my plate.

"Is there something in them?" I ask, holding one up and rattling it, because they look bulky.

"That one has a badge," Emily tells me, amusement in her voice.

"Mine has a gift card for Ann Summers," Gabby adds.

"It doesn't have anything on it, so I wouldn't try to use it," Olivia warns. "I added a tube of lube."

"Why do you have lube with you?" Gabby asks, snatching the bacon off Olivia's plate.

"You don't?" Olivia fires back.

Gabby rolls her eyes. "Not the point. I don't get why—"

"Stop arguing," Harriett and Emily yell simultaneously.

"Thank you, everyone. It means a lot," I tell them, and I mean it. All of this, it means everything.

And as I watch them talk amongst each other, bickering, teasing, and laughing, I can't help but feel honoured to be a part of this weekend. She has great friends, a fantastic dad, and I'm lucky she wants to share them with me.

WEARING booty shorts and a white see-through cover up, my girl looks like a poster girl for a swimming magazine. She tips her straw hat back as she stands.

"Are you ready?"

I adjust my hard-on and walk over to her. "Is it bad I want to make us late?"

Her smile is infectious. "Unless you want an audience, it's probably not wise, 'cause they won't leave us until we get our arses moving."

I groan and wrap my arms around her, squeezing her round, tight arse. "You look so fucking hot in this."

"Then you can peel it off me later," she teases. "Let's go."

"Just so you know, it's under duress," I complain as we leave our room.

The girls are waiting at the bottom of the stairs. Emily, who hasn't changed out of the clothes she was wearing this morning, is struggling to hold the screaming infant in her arms. Poppy's cheeks are red, and tears stream down her face.

"Emily, what's wrong?"

"I'm so sorry, but I'm going to skip the boat trip. Poppy is unsettled and has a fever. I'm going to pop into town and grab some Calpol."

Harriett drops her bag to the floor. "That's okay. I'll go and you stay with her."

Emily's eyes crinkle at the corners with guilt. "No, please, I don't want to ruin your day. You guys go on ahead and I'll be here when you get back. There's no point you being here. There's nothing you can do. I promise, I'll be fine."

"Fuck that, we're staying," Gabby announces.

Emily smiles at the conviction in Gabby's voice as she tries to soothe her daughter. "And I love that you would. But it will make me feel better if you go. You don't want me to feel guilty that you had to stay, do you?"

"Well, no, but you wouldn't need to feel guilty," Gabby replies, her voice dropping. "This sucks."

"I know, but I *would* feel guilty, so please, go have fun and take loads of photos," Emily orders. "And no pushing Olivia into the sea."

"I wasn't planning on it," Gabby tells her, but even I, someone who hasn't known her long, can detect the lie.

I clear my throat, rubbing the back of my neck. "Why don't I stay with Poppy so you can go?"

Her smile is warm, comforting. "That's a generous offer, but I wouldn't be able to relax. I'd be worried the entire time and that's not fair on anyone. I want to be with her," she tells me, before looking to her friends. "I'm seriously good. I'll go into town, and hopefully, the medicine will get her to settle, and we can catch up on some sleep."

Harriett steps forward. "Call us if you need us," she demands softly, then presses a kiss to the crying girl's head. "You get better soon, little miss."

"We'll be straight back if you need us," Olivia swears.

Gabby is hesitant to leave. "Are you sure you don't want us to stay?"

"I'm sure," Emily promises, pressing a kiss to her cheek.

Gabby runs a hand over Poppy's head. "Get better soon, squirt."

The girls make their way outside, but I stay behind, waiting for them to leave before addressing Emily.

"I know a nurse here. He lives close by, so if you like, I'll message him and ask him to come in and check on Poppy later?"

Her relief is genuine. She had been worried for her daughter and didn't want to voice it in front of the girls in case it made them stay. It's written all over her expression. "Please, if he wouldn't mind. I'd really appreciate it. I'm going to head into town with her now and grab some medicine."

Noticing her phone on the side, I reach for it. "I'll programme my number into your phone." I do, then ring my phone so I have her number.

"Thank you."

"I'll message him now and get him to call you."

"Okay," she replies, before soothing her daughter.

I turn to leave and find Harriett standing at the door, her expression soft. "Are you ready?"

"Yes."

"See you later, Em," she calls out, before I close the door behind us. She takes my hand, leaning into me. "That was a really sweet thing you did in there."

"She's a good mum, and you can see she's worried about her daughter."

"She's the best," Harriett agrees, then lets out a sigh. "I know we all want to stay with Em, but she's got this. So let's not make her feel any worse than she already does. Let's have some fun."

Gabby shoots her arm into air. "Yes, queen."

Olivia laughs as she tugs on her arm. "Come on, drama queen."

"Too full on?" Gabby asks.

"Yes," Olivia replies with no shame.

As we head down to the docks, I send out a message to Jimmy, and he replies quickly with a yes.

"Thank you for doing that," Harriett tells me when I pocket my phone.

"What did he do?"

"He's got a nurse friend to go check on Poppy," Harriett explains.

"You think it's serious?" Gabby worries.

Harriett nudges her forward. "No, she's probably caught a bug or something."

"Then why call a nurse?" Gabby argues.

"Do you have to question everything?" Olivia asks her.

"When it concerns my niece, yes, I do."

"Niece?" I question. I didn't think any of them were related.

"We're all her aunts," Harriett answers. "So she's our niece."

"Jimmy is a good nurse. He'll check her over, assure Emily that she's okay, and it will ease her mind."

Gabby groans. "I feel bad. It's like opening presents in front of people who don't have any to open."

"Is that why you open my presents?" Olivia questions.

"Well, yeah, and because you take too long."

"I open them normally."

"A new-born could open them faster than you," Gabby declares.

"I open them normal," Olivia states, and turns back to me and Harriett. "Don't I open them normally?"

"Will you two stop already," Harriett orders, fighting back laughter.

"She started it," Gabby declares.

"You did."

"You pair," Harriett warns.

Olivia holds her hands up. "Okay, okay."

When everyone continues to stare at Gabby, she sighs, "Fine, I'll stop, but I can't promise I won't push her off the boat."

"That's all I can ask for," Harriett comments, taking a breath.

As they walk ahead, I chuckle. "Are they always like this?"

"Yes. And it's worse if one of them is dating. They always find something wrong with whoever it is, and they bicker like crazy."

"Why? Did they used to be together?"

"Oh, if they get together, all their problems would go away."

"Why don't you sound so sure?"

She stops to look at me. "Because it could also mean more crazy from them."

I grin at her answer. "You love them."

"I do. And I want them to be happy. But they are either pineapple and pizza or salt and pepper. There's no in between."

"Hey, Harriett, you think I'd be able to go snorkelling, don't you?" Gabby questions.

Olivia is nodding. Harriett, though, lets out another breath, like a tired mum fed up of answering pointless questions. "No. Because you'd see one fish and think it was a great white shark. You'd freak. Remember the time we went paddle boarding?"

"It was a huge-ass whale," Gabby declares heatedly. "That was different. I feared for my life."

"It was a shadow, and we were on a lake," Harriett reminds her.

Gabby turns and continues her argument with Olivia. It's fun watching them interact. I can understand why they mean so much to Harriett, and why I got put through the friend test.

They aren't just best friends or work colleagues.

They are family.

And I hate that I'm making her keep a secret from them.

30

HARRIETT

We picked the perfect day to come out on the boat. The sun is out, and the breeze is the perfect temperature to keep us from melting or freezing to death.

It's the perfect holiday activity. Peace and tranquillity. I live my life on the go. I'm constantly busy and it's how I like it. But holidays... I like to do the complete opposite. I don't need to go bar crawling, scuba diving, or do things that are strenuous. Site seeing, relaxing, and if the weather calls for it, sunbathing by a pool is what I want. That is my kind of holiday.

Emily is like me, although we adapt to make sure we do fun things with Poppy. Gabby and Olivia are a different kind of breed. They don't like keeping still, especially Gabby, who I think has undiagnosed ADHD. The girl is unable to sit still. She is constantly fidgeting or finding something to do. She excessive talks, acts without thinking, and has a way of changing the subject ten times in a minute. We're all fast-paced, but Gabby, she's on another level.

Five minutes ago, Gary had been talking through the snorkelling equipment, preparing them to go into the water. Now, they're reenacting the scene from *Titanic* at the front of the boat, and Gary has given up trying. It's been four hours since we left the port, five since we left the house, and already, they are finding things to entertain themselves since Gabby is too chicken to go into the sea.

We are far out on the ocean and other boats that left the port at the same time as us, are no longer visible to the eye. They split off, and Gary, the guy who runs the boat for River, explained there are caves not far from here. Tourists like to see them and spend the day on the little alcove beach. The girls had no interest in it, so we opted to stay out on the water.

Movement from the corner of my eye catches my attention. Shirtless, and looking hot with his ripped chest glistening from the sun, he places a cocktail drink down on the table next to my sun lounger.

I sit up, taking a sip, and it feels amazing, soothing my throat. I hum with pleasure, taking one more sip before placing it down. "That is so good. Thank you," I tell him, my voice filled with affection.

He grins as he drops down on the lounger next to me, dropping his shades to covers his eyes. "You're welcome."

"I want to feel guilty for not being the one waiting on you, but these are too good to pass up," I admit, unashamed. "You should have told me you could make these. I would have had you serving them for weeks. Naked."

He chuckles as he removes the water bottle from his lips. "If I gave you all the good stuff, you might have gotten bored."

"Never," I sing. "Where did you learn to make them?"

"I actually had a meet and greet at a cocktail bar in London. You get to learn how to make different cocktails. I enjoyed it. It was the first meet and greet I did that wasn't boring."

"Please tell me you get to drink them after."

"Yeah," he assures me. "You'll have to go there with the girls. I think they'd like it too."

"It does sound fun," I admit. "Speaking of meet and greets, you have something like that coming up, don't you?"

"I do. It's the end of next month. The night before the last fight. If I qualify to the next round."

I reach out, taking his hand. "You will."

He squeezes my hand as he sits up, turning until his legs are between our sunbeds. "About last night. I know you don't want to talk about it, but I need you to know something. That person isn't who I am anymore. I wouldn't hurt you. I wouldn't hurt anyone like that ever again."

I sit up, and he spreads his thighs apart to make room for my legs. He places his hands on my knees. "I know that. If I thought you were a bad person, I wouldn't be here. It's not a case of 'good people do bad things.' You were defending yourself. You were scared, and rightly so. But I wasn't trying to make you feel better when I said it doesn't add up, and I don't think you killed him. I truly do think that."

He ducks his head, and his muscles bulge in his arms. "I want to believe that too. I do. But what if I only want to believe it because it gives me a get out of jail free card?"

I stand, knocking his hands from his thighs to his side so I can straddle him. He leans back, giving me room as he grabs my arse, something he does often. *He's definitely an arse man.*

"You were traumatised. People who live through that kind of trauma, they block things out and they don't see the bigger picture," I explain as best as I can. "But today isn't about that. It's about you. I'll look into it when we are back home, but until then, let's concentrate on the now."

His grip tightens on my arse. "You can't go looking into it. You need to promise me you'll leave this alone. If the wrong person finds out—"

"Hey, shh, it's okay. I'm not going to tell anyone."

"Promise me," he pleads.

"Okay. I promise," I assure him, but deep down, I don't know if I can. This guy has been tormenting himself for years over this. It explains why he never lets anyone close, or why he doesn't form attachments. He's scared to. He doesn't feel like he deserves it either.

All the missing pieces of the puzzle are finally in place, and I can finally understand him better.

It doesn't mean what he's saying is right. For a teenager, going through all that testosterone, and with an upbringing like his, he must have felt so alone and confused. And like a scared, wounded animal, he attacked.

I'm fortunate to not have gone through something like this. I'm lucky. Because it can happen to anyone. It happened to two of my closest friends. So just like I did with them, I'm standing by him. I'm going to be his strength until he can find it on his own.

I'll be here for him. Because he has come to mean so much to me.

"I'm sorry," he sighs, dropping his head between my breasts.

I run my hands over the back of his head. "You have nothing to apologise for."

He looks up, and I melt into his gaze. "You are amazing."

I sniff dramatically. "I know."

He runs his hands to my waist, sliding them up my sides until his thumbs brush underneath my boobs. "And I really do want to thank you for this morning. It meant a lot that you went to so much trouble."

I glance over my shoulder, seeing Olivia and Gabby are distracted —squabbling over who would be Rose. When I turn back, I grin. "Do you think you could be quick? Gabby has the attention span of Dory and might coming looking for us."

"The fish in Finding Nemo?"

I laugh, rolling my hips against his cock, pulling his focus back. "Do you think you could be quick?"

He arches his thick brow. "The real question is: do you think you could quiet?"

I smirk. "I can try."

"Liar," he remarks, and stands with me in his arms.

A squeak slips free, and I press my face into the crook on his neck. "Where are you taking me?"

"There's a small room downstairs," he tells me, then orders, "Hold tight."

He climbs down the ladder, and I hold on tighter, giggling when the boat rocks and we nearly tip to the side.

We move through the small seating area, past the kitchen, and then the bathroom he showed us earlier, to a small room at the back of the boat. He deposits me down on the vanity bolted to the wall, and before any words can be exchanged, he's on me, kissing his way up my neck to my lips.

My head spins when his mouth meets mine, vaguely aware of his fingers at the strings keeping my bikini bottoms up.

I grip his biceps as his fingers lower, finding my clit and driving me wild.

I drop my head back, breaking apart from the kiss as I dazedly enjoy his fingers thrusting inside of me.

He roughly tugs down my bikini top and sucks my nipple. I forget about the girls upstairs. I forget about Gary, who could be using the toilet for all we know.

"Oh God," I moan, and reach forward, pulling at the elastic on his shorts and tugging them down. "Fuck me!"

He grips his dick in his hand, and his eyes turn black as he pins me with that dark, promising look. Pumping his dick once, he lines it up at my entrance. "I can't wait to feel you come all over my cock."

"Now," I demand.

With his free hand, he roughly takes my shoulder, using it as leverage as he thrusts inside me.

My back slams against the glass mirror behind me. He doesn't stop. Instead, he grips the back of my leg, lifting it up until my knee is practically to my chest.

"Oh fuck," I cry.

He's so fucking deep.

With one hand above me on the mirror, and the other holding my leg, I'm caged in, unable to touch or run my hands all over him.

And it only adds to the pleasure.

Closer by Nine Inch Nails blasts from the top deck, and I hope that's not to smother out my moans.

Because that would mean they can hear me.

Not that I care.

This is torture.

Sweet, bittersweet torture.

He fucks me hard, so hard I can't move. I can't meet him thrust for thrust or give him my mouth. I can't touch him and bring him to the same insanity as he has me.

"You are so fucking tight," he growls, his voice rough with desire.

That's because I'm squeezing his dick. Every time he hits me to the hilt, there's a bite of pain. But that pain is followed by pleasure.

Undeniable, intense pleasure.

Sweat trickles down the side of his face, running down until it lands on my chest—which happens to be the side my tit is hanging out.

He fucks me with everything he has, building me higher and higher. Groans, moans, and curse words mingle together as we both near our release.

"Come," he demands, and if it wasn't for the fact he lifts my leg higher, it might have killed my orgasm.

But unable to wait, he drops his hand from the mirror and grabs the back of my neck, slamming his lips against mine.

My head slams back against the mirror as my orgasm tears through me. It's long, intense, and I've never felt anything like it.

"Oh God," I cry, thinking I might die.

"Fuck!" he growls, finding his own release.

He drops his forehead against mine, both of us sweating and panting. And just as I breathe in through my nose, a smell burns my nostrils.

"Do you smell that?"

"W-what?" he pants, still catching his breath.

It smells like burnt toast.

He presses his lips to my neck, and for a second, I forget about the smell. "W-wait, do you smell that? I'm being serious."

He leans back. "Wha—

I gently push him away, cutting off his words, and whimper when he slides out of me. "Something's burning."

He tugs his shorts back up as I do my bikini bottoms. "I can't—" His eyes widen as they hit me, because he smells it too.

Burning.

"Shit!" he snaps, and throws his T-shirt at me before leaving the room.

I follow.

31

RIVER

The smell reminds me of when my first car overheated. For a week, all I could smell was burning rubber. Nothing I did got rid of it. Absolutely nothing.

And this is worse. Way worse. It's burning the back of my nose and making my eyes water, it's that strong.

As we leave the bedroom, I scream for Gary. By the time we are heading through the kitchen, he's coming down the ladder.

His eyes are round with fear when he smells it. He tries to hide it, but it's too late. I've already seen it. "I need you to get up deck and radio this in. The signal has been spotty all day, which it's never done before."

"Are we in range?"

"I always stay in range."

"What are you doing?" I ask when he lifts the hatch on the floor.

Black smoke immediately fills the air, which can't be a good thing. I tuck my face into the crook of my arm, so I don't inhale any. "Fuck. Call it in. Now!" Gary demands. "It's a mayday code."

"River," Harriett calls, tugging on my hand. "Listen to him and let's go."

"Wait, Gary, what are you doing?"

He pops his head back up, exasperated. "I need to see the extent of the damage. Once you've called it in, get the raft out on the water. Now, River! Now!"

Not needing to be told again, I usher Harriett up the stairs, needing to get her to safety. The girls look up from where they're sunbathing at the bow of the yacht. "That was really quick," Gabby states, sounding disappointed as she rolls her head to the side at Olivia. "I'll give you the twenty when we get back."

Olivia pops her hand above her eyes, blocking out the sun. "Harriett? Are you okay?"

Coming unglued, I let go of Harriett's hand and reach over, kissing her quickly on the mouth.

"It's going to be okay. Grab some life jackets. They are under the seats. I'll be back in a second," I order, and the girls, hearing the seriousness in my tone, get to their feet. "And get the raft ready."

I leave Harriett to explain to the others and make my way up to the helm of the yacht where the controls are all located.

I reach the top and glance down at the girls scrambling to get their life jackets and belongings. Concentrating on what I need to do and not what I want to do—which is grab Harriett and get her to safety—I grab the radio.

It's static, like something is interfering with the signal. Still, I press down the side, calling it in. "Mayday, mayday, mayday; this is Hollow Knights. Mayday, mayday, mayday," I call, before reciting the coordinates of where we are.

I'm about to try again when Gary falls onto the deck, coughing uncontrollably. "We need to get off the yacht. The fire has nearly reached the gas line. Get off, now!" he orders, getting to his feet. I drop down and race over to Harriett and the others, helping to drop the raft into the water.

Gary gets down into the raft first and then proceeds to help Olivia, who is shaking, and I think... praying.

Harriett is next. Just as she drops down onto the raft, Gabby freaks out and drops the rope that is keeping the boat anchored to the side of the yacht.

"I can't do it. I can't," she cries as the raft begins to drift.

"Gabby," Olivia screams, hanging over the side of the inflatable raft to try and reach for us. It's too late. They are already out of reach.

"I can't do it. I can't," Gabby cries. "Oh God, I'm going to die."

Needing to be calm, I turn to her, ignoring the girls screaming for us. "You are not going to die," I promise. "But we need to jump. Now."

Her grey eyes dilate and fill with unshed tears. "I can't. What if there are sharks?"

"There aren't any sharks in these waters."

She brushes her hair from her face. "What about whales? They won't even chomp on me. They'll swallow me whole and I could die a long, miserable death in his stomach," she panics, her entire body shaking.

I take her shoulders, giving her a subtle shake. "Nothing is going to happen to you."

She tilts her head up, crying, "You don't know that. I don't want to die."

"You aren't going to die."

"Gabby, get your arse onto this boat, right now!" Olivia cries. "Please."

"Please, both of you, jump," Harriett pleads.

The boat rattles, and a boom sounds down below. Wood creaks, and thick, black smoke fills the air around us. Fear and panic take over, and I know we only have a minute, if not seconds to get off this boat. I meet Gabby's gaze, grimacing when the smoke behind her thickens even more. "I'm sorry."

"For wh—"

I shove us both off the side of the boat. Her squeal is the last thing I hear before I go under. I keep hold of her arm and fight my way to the surface, bringing her with me.

I reach the surface, and Harriett's is the first voice I hear. Her complexion is white as she hangs over the side of the boat, reaching out for us.

"Come on!" she cries. "Swim. Come on."

"I think a shark just nipped at my toe," Gabby curses, trying to hide the fact she's petrified.

"It's probably a fish," I assure her as I try to swim us further away from the wreckage.

"Definitely not Nemo," she mutters, before choking on water. I lift her head higher whilst trying to tread water.

"River!" Gary yells, throwing the ring out to us. It lands in front of us, and I grab it, letting them reel us in.

The closer I get, the more relaxed I become.

Harriett is safe.

We're safe.

Everyone is safe.

Yet, it doesn't feel real. Not even when we are halfway to the raft, there's a massive explosion behind us. The pressure throws us forward, knocking the breath out of me.

A roar slices through the fog in my head as I watch Harriett get knocked back into the raft. I move quickly, tugging Gabby in front of me to cover her from the debris dropping into the sea around us.

Jesus, fucking, Christ.

My yacht exploded.

When the worst seems to be over and the flames aren't kissing the flesh on my back, I look up to the raft.

Harriett isn't there.

When we reach it, I yell, "Is she okay? Is Harriett okay?"

"She's okay," Gary tells me, reaching for me and pulling me up by under my arms.

Olivia reaches for Gabby, and I hear her cough out water. "If you tell me there's no room on this boat, I will drown you myself," Gabby warns, but her words are shaky.

Olivia barks out a laugh. "Don't worry, I won't let go. I'll *never* let go."

"You promise?" Gabby asks as I fall into the raft and reach over to help Olivia pull Gabby up.

Olivia blows out a breath. "Yes, Rose was a spoilt brat who was too selfish to share."

Gabby is barely inside the raft before she has Olivia in her arms, holding her tight. "Thanks for not letting go," she tells her, before pushing away and diving on me. "Thank you for saving me."

"You would never have jumped," I tease, making my own *Titanic* joke.

She laughs, ducking her head in embarrassment. "No, I wouldn't have."

I reach for Harriett, seeing a small cut on her head, and turn to Gary accusingly. "You said she was okay."

"I am," Harriett promises, taking my hand. "I think I'm in shock. Did your yacht really just blow up?"

"It did," Gabby calls out. "And I'm never going out on a boat again. It will be safe, you said. We won't hit an iceberg, you said. Like fuck am I doing this again. I nearly died."

I take Harriett in my arms, finally taking an easy breath as I turn to the disaster that was once my yacht. "What the fuck happened?"

"I don't know. I really don't," Gary stresses, tugging at the ends of his hair. Complete horror and shock are written all over his expression. The disbelief is just as palpable as ours. "I checked everything myself last night. Everything was—"

Gary places a hand over his mouth. "Everything was what?" I push.

He slowly turns to me. "This is my fault. I got distracted last night."

"Distracted?"

"Yes, I was finishing up my nightly routine when a car was set on fire. I went to help the others put it out. And I don't remember if I carried out the rest of the checks. I think I did. But I don't know."

I can't yell. He's already punishing himself. "Did you do all the checks this morning?"

"You saw me do the walk through. I do all my routine checks every time I take the boat out," he promises, falling back on his arse. "I'm so sorry. I'm so fucking sorry."

"You couldn't have known," I tell him, but I can't say more. It's still raw.

Harriett could have died.

We all could have.

And I might not have been here to get them off the yacht quick enough.

"This is my livelihood. Our kids are going to college in September. How are we going to pay for it?"

I reach over, clasping his shoulder. "I'll replace the boat as soon as I can. Right now, let's focus on getting home safely."

He nods, still in shock. "I'm really sorry. This has never happened to me before."

"Never?" Harriett asks, seeming calm.

"Never," he swears.

Gabby lifts her head from Olivia's shoulder. "How are we getting home?"

"You can swim and pull the boat," Olivia offers. "I mean, you're already wet."

"Someone will have heard our call," I promise her, when Gabby's expression is one of complete horror.

"I've seen this movie. We'll end up on some island with a polar bear on steroids chasing us. And what will I do? I'll go crazy if my mind isn't stimulated."

Harriett clears her throat. "You could always spend time making a wooden raft."

"I'm not Moana. I'll get distracted and end up on another island where I'll have a ball called Wilson," she cries. "And who will feed my cat?"

"You don't have a cat," Harriett and Olivia yell simultaneously.

"But I could. Now I won't get a chance."

"Someone's coming," Gary announces, sitting up.

Gabby looks around, seeing what we all see. Nothing. "How do you know?" she asks, eyeing him curiously as she leans forward to whisper, "Do you see dead people?"

He doubles back to stare at her, utterly baffled. "What?"

"Ignore her," Olivia orders, tugging Gabby back.

And that's when I feel it. The vibrations beneath us. "There's a boat coming."

In the distance, another tourist yacht like mine is speeding towards us. Gabby and Olivia rock the raft as they stand, waving their arms in the air to get their attention. "We're here. We're here."

"Do they know they don't need to do that?" Gary whispers.

"Let them feel useful," Harriett tells him, sounding tired.

"Are you okay?"

"I've got a headache coming," she admits, pinching the bridge of her nose.

I pull her closer. "I'm sorry this has happened. I was so scared when I saw you go down."

"Not as scared as I was when that first explosion happened with you on the boat," she tells me. "I thought that was it. You were gone."

I tilt her chin until she can see me. "I'm here. I'm not going anywhere," I soothe, pressing my lips to hers. When I pull back, I exhale heavily. "My yacht blew up."

Her nose twitches. "It could have been worse."

"Worse?" Gabby snaps when she takes a look around. "My fucking favourite iPod is on that boat. It's as worse as it's gonna get."

"Do you want to go and get it?"

"No, do you?" Gabby argues, staring down at Olivia.

"You should have stayed on the boat," Olivia snaps.

"And who would sort your hellions out?" Gabby asks, cocking her hip.

"I'll buy you a new iPod," Harriett promises. "And we can sync your songs onto it."

"Thank you," Gabby replies, then turns to Olivia, arching her eyebrow.

Olivia turns away from the approaching boat, feeling Gabby's stare. "I'm not getting you one. I got you the last one and you left it on an exploding boat. You should have taken better care of it."

As they continue to bicker, and I hold Harriett like her life depends on it, Gary turns to us, utterly discombobulated. "A boat just exploded, and they've gone from making terrible references about the *Titanic* to arguing over an iPad. I think the smoke has damaged my brain."

"iPod, Gaz," Gabby quickly adds. "But I'll let you off since you had to grow up with Walkman's."

He splutters out an inaudible response but doesn't say any more because the boat begins to slow.

As we are helped onto the boat, I can't help but take another look at the burning yacht that, moments ago, I was fucking Harriett on. Even half under water, it's still aflame.

And it hits me, like really hits me.

We were on that yacht.

BACK ON DRY LAND, I scan the area and take in the chaos around us. Paramedics, police, and reporters have filled up the entire carpark. It's like the sound of it all is booming in my ears, but everything around me is moving in slow motion.

I started the day being surprised with birthday banners and balloons. I never expected it to end like this.

I've just finished giving my statement, when the policeman I've been talking to places a hand on my shoulder, bringing me back to the present. "I know this isn't the right time to ask, but my dad will never forgive me if I don't. Can I have your autograph?"

"Sure," I whisper.

I mindlessly take the pen, scribbling my autograph on the pad before I begin to search for Harriett. A paramedic took her aside to clean up her cut, and although he said she doesn't need a hospital, I'm still worried and she's been out of sight for longer than I had hoped.

The adrenaline is wearing off, feeding my restlessness. None of it feels real. I never imagined something like this could happen. I've been on that yacht hundreds, if not thousands of times, and nothing even close to that has ever happened.

And all I keep thinking is, I wasn't supposed to be here. I'm meant to be in meetings, and training. Not here. If Harriett didn't leave the keys, I would never have come. Harriett wouldn't have been down in that bedroom with me, and we wouldn't have smelled that smoke. And they might not have gotten off the yacht in time.

Spotting Harriett sitting on the back end of the ambulance, I rush in her direction, leaving the policeman still talking. I ignore the calls from the reporters who come alive once I step out from between the police cars.

"Are you okay?" I ask when I reach her.

She touches the plaster covering the cut along her hairline. "I'm good. But I need a shower and a bed. In that order."

"This isn't how I wanted your weekend to go," I declare. "I wanted you to have fun and relax, not nearly die."

She rests her head on my shoulder when I sit in the free spot beside her. "It isn't your fault. But I'm grateful you were there. We would have panicked if it wasn't for you."

"Gabby might have. But you and Olivia are good in sticky situations. You would have handled it."

"Don't tell Gabby that. She'll want to prove you wrong, and we'll all be dead," she teases, which is followed by a yawn.

"We'll be able to go soon," I promise her, looking around. "I just want to—What are Gabby and Olivia doing?"

They look like they are having a seizure, bouncing in front of the cameras like they aren't on tarmac.

Harriett lets out an amusement chuckle. "The reporters keep trying to take photos of me. They're making sure they can't use any of them."

"Harriett? Gabby? Olivia!" is yelled.

I turn to the left, spotting Emily frantically searching the area, pushing Poppy in the pram in front of her.

"We're here," Harriett calls out, waving to get her attention.

The other two step away from the cameras and make their way over whilst still managing to block the reporters. Pale and frantic, Emily pulls Harriett in for a hug. "I got so scared. Jimmy was checking Poppy over when it came on the news. They are saying your yacht blew up."

"It did, but thankfully, no one was hurt," Harriett replies.

Emily begins to sob. "You look hurt. I got so scared. I thought... I thought you had all died."

"It honestly sounds worse than it was," Harriett assures her. "It happened so fast. I might feel differently tomorrow, but right now, it doesn't feel real. None of us got hurt, so please, don't worry."

"This one nearly died," Olivia offers, hugging her friend.

Gabby lifts her head out the pushchair after giving Poppy a kiss on the cheek. "No, I did not," she argues.

Olivia rolls her eyes. "River saved her life, otherwise she would have gone down with the ship."

"Feeding me to the sharks is not saving my life," Gabby breathes out. "I swear, I'm lucky I didn't lose a limb." She pauses to lean into me. "Totally grateful you saved my life."

Emily hugs her. "You scared me. I don't know what I'd do without all of you."

"Bet you're glad Poppy was sick now," Gabby announces, and I can tell she didn't think the comment through when her jaw drops, in an 'oh fuck.'

"Oh my god, we were going to be on that boat," Emily states, staggering back.

Olivia steadies her. "It's all good. Don't think about that."

I wrap my arm around Harriett as we get to our feet. "We should be able to go now. Are you all ready?"

"Yes. And I don't know about anyone else, but I think we should order in and not leave the house until tomorrow," Gabby comments. "Or ever."

"Agree. And if everyone is okay with it, we'll leave in the morning. I'm ready to get back to the kids," Olivia admits sheepishly. "They'll freak when they see this on the news. I need to charge my phone to call them."

Harriett looks up at me, biting her lower lip. "Are you still leaving tonight?"

I pull her into my arms. "Nothing could get me to leave you."

She relaxes against me. "Thank God," she breathes.

"Come on, let's get you all warmed up. It's starting to get chilly," Emily offers. "I have my car, and Jimmy is here. He's checking on an older dude with a paramedic."

"I see him," I reply.

"I'm not going to argue," Gabby comments. "I smell like dead fish."

"I wasn't going to say anything," Olivia comments as we begin to head towards Jimmy.

"You're the one who pointed it out," Gabby snips.

"Everyone is okay," Harriett breathes.

I press my lips to the top of her head. "Yeah," I murmur, not telling her I was only worried about one of us.

Her.

If it makes me selfish, or evil, I don't care. I can't imagine the world without her.

I can't imagine my life without her.

And I don't want to.

32

HARRIETT

It's Sunday evening, one day after the yacht went down and we were rescued. One day to process, and it still doesn't feel real. I thought I'd feel different when I woke up this morning, but it only felt more like a dream. It's like I experienced it through someone else's eyes.

I was there.

It happened.

Yet none of it seems real. Things like this don't just happen. It's not something you read about every day—if at all. I've been trying to wrap my head around it, but the more I think about it, the harder my headache throbs.

Olivia and Gabby are either good at hiding how freaked they are, or they really are okay. I'm hoping for the latter. They seemed it when we parted ways. They messaged me earlier to say they were home and doing okay, since I bummed a ride with River. Emily took longer to respond, since Poppy still isn't one hundred percent, but once she could, she assured me they were okay.

I, on the other hand, decided I didn't want to be alone. Just the thought of sitting at home, or at River's alone, made my skin break out in hives. So, I tagged along with River to his training session, and he didn't argue. In fact, he looked pleased that I wanted to tag along.

He didn't lie when he said it's gruelling. I'm feeling hot and bothered just watching him. The heaviest thing I've lifted since I arrived is my laptop.

I'm supposed to be finishing up my dissertation, but I can't concentrate on that, so I decide to look up the murders around the time River said his mum's boyfriend attacked him. I go down a massive rabbit hole, finding absolutely nothing. And without a name to Google, I have nothing more to go on. That said, I haven't given up. Since I've not been able to find anything, I'm hoping that's a good sign and one more step towards confirming my suspicion that he didn't kill anyone.

He might be ruthless in the cage, but that's a sport, not who he is. He doesn't get off on inflicting pain on others. No, the River I know has a deep soul. He's a guy who grew up with nothing but gives everything. And yeah, he might have at one time lost his way, but he didn't kill somebody. I don't believe he has it in him.

And I'd be further along in my search if it weren't for the fact he's half naked and tipping a massive tyre along the gym floor, flexing every muscle he owns.

God, I can't wait until we are in bed tonight. The things I will do to that man...

He's got great abs, but each time he flips that tyre, I can't help but admire the muscles in his back. It's like workout porn. I've lost count of how many times I've had to clench my thighs.

He's sweaty, a little red in the face, yet he's never looked so hot. I can't look away, which is probably why he stops to stare at me.

I lick my lips when he wipes the sweat from his forehead, grinning over at me. "Are you going to answer your phone or keep ignoring it?"

And that's when I hear it. The ring tone I have for my dad.

Oh crap.

I scramble to grab it from my bag, ignoring his laughter as he goes back to working out. I'm surprised he even heard since Cian has him so focused on what he's doing.

My thumb hovers over the green button to answer, and I bite my lower lip worriedly. Through all the chaos, then crashing last night before I could put my phone on charge, I forgot to call him about the yacht. And there is no doubt in my mind that this impromptu call is about the accident.

"Dad, hey," I cheerfully greet. "How's it going?"

"How's it going?" he repeats in frustration.

"Um…"

"A yacht blows up with you on it, you ring *your dad*," he growls, punctuating each word.

I smack my forehead at my own dumb actions. "I swear, I was going to call you, but I fell asleep last night and forgot to charge my phone. And then it completely slipped my mind this morning."

He inhales sharply. "It slipped your mind?"

I grimace. "Do I get points for the fact I was going to call?"

"No!"

I groan at how epically I'm fucking this up. "I'm sorry, okay. I'm fine. I wasn't hurt, and it isn't as bad as the papers have made it out to be. You know what papers are like. They dramatize everything to make money."

"Did the yacht blow up?"

"It did. But not with me on it. I was already on the raft."

"Then it's as bad as the papers have said," he snaps. "Are you okay? Are you hurt?"

"We're all fine. River got us off the boat before it got bad, and he even saved Gabby."

He blows out a breath. "She freaked over sharks, didn't she?"

"And whales," I add, since there's no point in lying. It's Gabby, and we all know she's as whacky as they come.

Although, I think Max Carter has her beat in the crazy department. If he wasn't married or twice her age, and she wasn't gay, I'd say they were a match made in an institution.

He chuckles, but I can hear the breath of relief. "I've been working on your mother's garden. I didn't see the news until now. I almost had a heart attack when I saw the girls blocking the ambulance from the cameras."

"They were looking out for me. I had just finished getting a routine look over," I lie. He doesn't need to know about the cut. It's barely noticeable. "I can't believe they are still showing it. I would have thought they'd move on to some other story."

"They said there was faulty electrics," he tells me. "That true or did Gabby and Olivia press buttons they shouldn't have?"

"So they say," I reply, not believing it for a second. Call it intuition, but I don't believe it was an accident. But who am I to question it? I'm not the professional. "The fire hit the gas line, which is why it blew. It had nothing to do with Gabby or Olivia. They were already warned to stay away from that part of the boat."

"And everyone is okay? You aren't just telling me that to make me feel better?"

"I promise. We're all good."

"You need to keep me informed, baby girl. You'll put your dad into an early grave."

I doubt that. My dad is the strongest man I know. Aside from River. "Nah, you've got years of therapy to go through over me before you kick it."

He laughs. "I'm still saving for the upfront cost. I'll need as much as I can get to afford that kind of time with a therapist—especially with all the trauma you've put your old man through."

"See, there's a bright-side to everything," I tease.

"No wonder your uncle has been calling me all day. I thought he was calling to moan about the new worker he's hired again so I put the phone on silent."

"I'm sorry. I should have called you sooner. I've been a little spacey today, but that isn't an excuse. It just doesn't feel real, you know?"

"I felt like that the day after me and your mum won the lottery."

I nearly drop my laptop, sitting up straight. "What! When did you win the lottery?"

He laughs. "Calm down. The ticket was dated for the week before, but the ticket we had for that week actually won a hundred quid."

"Dad, don't do that to me. I actually thought you'd won the lotto for a second."

"Still, that hundred quid went towards our weekend away. Your mum told everyone who would listen. She didn't care if it was one quid or one hundred."

Thinking of my mum only brings on more guilt. I should have called him. "I love you, Dad, and I'm sorry I didn't call."

"I'm just glad you're okay. That's all that matters," he replies. "Come to dinner Sunday. Bring the boy."

"He's not a boy," I retort teasingly.

"Alright. I won't call him that. But only because he saved my girl," he tells me on a breath. "Your uncle is calling me again."

"I'll let you go so you can explain what happened. Send him my love and I'll see you Sunday."

"Bye, sweetheart, and stay safe."

"Love you."

I end the call and drop the phone down on my papers. If only my dad knew the boat isn't the worst of what I've been through. I never told him about being run off the road and crashing because of a mad woman. And he doesn't know about me being trapped in Charlotte's library when it was set on fire by the same mad woman. He thinks it was just Charlotte. It's better for his health that he doesn't know.

The gym doors creak, alerting us to a new arrival. I twist my head to see who it could be this late, and I'm disappointed to find Colin strolling in. He straightens his suit jacket, and I wonder if wearing the suits makes it easier for him to play pretend. He acts like a big man, someone who holds all the power, but really, he's just a snake, willing to bite anything in his path to get where he needs to.

He only spares River a quick glance before he makes his way over to me. The lip curl at my presence brings me so much joy. In fact, pissing him off will always bring me joy.

When he sits down in the space next to me—awfully close—I can't help but roll my eyes at the intimidation tactic. The guy has a nerve sitting even in the same room as me. He doesn't deserve to breathe the same air, or any at all. I've never wished an accident on someone as much as I have him. And I know when I blow the candles out on my cake this year, that will be my wish.

'Cause if anyone deserves a birthday miracle, it's him. And I hope the accident is painful.

I've never felt like this with anyone. Trixie can get on my nerves, and I've imagined her tripping and breaking a leg on stage, but I've never had this warmth in my belly that is filled with loathing. I can't stand the thought of him, let alone the sight.

And him being this close, it's only heightening that feeling.

Rock begins to blast through the speakers, but the noise doesn't stop him from scooting closer to me.

"You still think you are good for him," he comments, and when I turn, he's facing River, watching him train.

"I don't think that's up to you to decide," I remark.

"You could have gotten him killed."

"Since you've forgotten, that was River's yacht, not mine," I bite out. "And I didn't set it on fire."

"He wasn't meant to be on that boat," he grits out, glaring at me with so much hatred it almost takes my breath away. "You are going to destroy him, and I won't let you. You could have killed my most prized possession."

Is he for real?

"Are you still talking?"

"You little—"

I turn until we are nearly nose to nose. "You are boring me. We've had this conversation before, now fuck off."

He grabs my wrist, tugging me closer. The grip makes me wince. "I can make your life a living hell, young lady. Mark my words, I can. I haven't even begun, and already you are on the defence. That's how much power I already have over you and you don't even see it. You want to stay with him, you want this life, you need to know your place."

I shove him off, and he lets go of my wrist. My pulse begins to race as I mull over his words. He does have me on the defence. He does have power. He holds all of River's secrets. All of them. The bad and the gritty. I understand now what is at risk for River and why he has felt indebted to Colin. And I never want to be the person who jeopardises his future. Because that is what Colin holds. His future.

And worse, he knows it.

"Touch me again, and you'll regret it," I bite out, forcing a tight smile when River finally acknowledges Colin's presence.

"Don't be mad. It was always going to end like this. And if you want to stay happy, you need to make me happy," he warns, getting to his feet before I can even reply. "River, good to see you training."

River is watching me, but I duck my head, pretending to pay attention to the screen in front of me.

"I'm surprised you're back already," River greets. "Did they finish their investigation?"

"Yes. They couldn't find any other faults with the yacht other than the electrics."

River wipes the towel over the back of his neck, his brows scrunched up. "I don't understand. Gary sent me the invoice for the electrics being serviced. It was done not long ago. The works were all above board and documented and signed off by a colleague. He has a file for the entire thing."

Colin shrugs, uninterested, but it's piqued my interest. It's the first I'm hearing about an electric report done. And now that I know, I'm more inclined to think foul play.

I watch Colin closely, wondering if he has something to do with it. He has it in him, but then, why would he try to kill River when he needs him for this fight?

River wasn't meant to be there.

Needing to keep that to myself until I can prove it, I busy myself with my work, or pretend to while I listen to their conversation.

"I don't know, but word on social media is that Dean caused it."

River barks out a laugh. "You can't be serious."

Colin shrugs. "The man is determined to win. I wouldn't put it past him."

I eye Colin, arching my brow. "Yes, I wouldn't put it past anyone."

His eyes narrow. "Moving on, I need you to double up on training. You missed the weekend, and we can't have you slacking off. The fight is a little over three weeks. You need to be ready."

"I am ready."

"We'll see," Colin replies doubtfully. "Be up early tomorrow."

He leaves without another word, and Cian, looking out of place, clears his throat. "He's a burst of energy."

"Sucks it out of you more like," I mutter, making him laugh.

Cian slaps River on the shoulder. "I'm going to clear up. Good work tonight, man."

"You too," River replies, dropping down on the bench next to me. When Cian is busy, he turns to me, running his hand over my thigh. "What did he say to you?"

"Who? Colin?"

"Yes. If he's still going on, you need to tell me. I'm not going to stand for it anymore. He needs to see what you mean to me and start treating you with respect."

I place my laptop down on the bench next to me and give him all my attention. "That man doesn't respect his own wife, so don't hope for something that is never going to happen."

"So he did say something?"

"He loves to hear himself talk, so yeah, but it's nothing. He was making idle chitchat and it bored me."

He drops his head back on the brick wall behind us. "I can't wait for the day I never have to see him again. These months with you have made me realise just how much I was missing out on."

"Great sex?"

He grins and lazily rolls his head to look down at me. "You. All of you. Every day, it's like I have something to wake up to. I didn't have a family, but you… you've become that family."

I run the palm of my hand over his cheek "I hate to break this to you, but you had it all along. You have so many people in your life who love you, and you don't let them in. Allie, Hetty, Mel…" I trail off for a moment, forming the right words for what I need to say next. "I get why you never let them in. You had some misconception that you didn't deserve them. And I think somewhere, you might not have known how to let them in. You didn't have anyone to teach you. But you need to stop that right now. You need to let people see the real you, because, babe, even without the incredible sex, you are one hell of a guy."

He presses his lips to mine, and I moan at the salty taste of sweat still on his skin. He pulls back, searching for something, before finally saying, "Move in with me."

"What?"

"Move in with me."

"Oh, I heard you, but, babe, it might be too soon."

"You're already there every night."

"Is this your way of telling me I'm in your space?"

"No, this is me saying I like having your clothes in my wardrobe. I like seeing your toothbrush next to mine and all your face products on the shelves. I love waking up to you," he tells me. "Move in with me."

I search his gaze for regret but see nothing but determination. "Can I think about it?"

His crestfallen expression has my heart skipping a beat. "It's okay if you don't want to."

"It's not that. I do. But I need to process it. I just need time. This is a big step. It's a big step for me."

"All right."

I take his face in my hands, leaning over to kiss him. "Being with you feels right. It has from the very start. I don't have any regrets, and I don't want us to end. Just… give me a week. Give me a week to process it."

"A week?"

I grin, kissing him briefly on the lips. "A week."

He shakes his head in amusement. "Then I guess I've got a week to sell you on it."

"Will you be living there?"

His brows pinch. "Yeah."

"Then you don't need to sell me on it. You just need to give me time to process it."

"You are one incredible, complicated woman."

I grin back. "I know."

"I'm going to get cleaned up, then we can go."

Once he leaves, I flap my arms and legs in the air, squealing inside. He doesn't know it, but the answer is already yes. But before we can take that kind of step, he needs to know I'm in it for the long haul. He needs to know I'm all in. The good, the bad, the ugly, I'm there.

Which means, he needs to be free of his secrets.

33

HARRIETT

Hitting the dressing room, I don't take notice of who is in the room as I drop down on the sofa. My feet are on fire. This is what you get for going nearly two weeks without wearing heels. Your feet are no longer immune to the aches and pains.

"I'm pretty sure my blisters have blisters," I complain, as I kick my feet up.

Olivia, whose break happens to be at the same time as mine, laughs and throws me a couple of gel packs. "Put them on before your next pair of shoes."

"If I had the strength, I'd get up and kiss you."

"And I'd like it," she teases, as Aisling steps out of the bathroom.

"How's it hanging, Aisling? You doing okay?" I call out.

She looks up from the mirror. "Aye, I'm good. I've been to talk to ya. I took your advice and spoke to Dave," she reveals, and I arch an eyebrow, interested. "He told me to talk to the hot owner."

"Cole Conner?"

"Aye."

"Why don't you sound pleased?" Olivia asks, smirking.

"I get tongue-tied around good-looking men," she reveals, her Irish accent strong.

I sit up, smiling. "What happened?"

"I messed it up, but t'ankfully, he's going to help me set up a business plan and even offered to invest. My appointment is the beginning of next month."

"Oh my god, that's fantastic," I cheer.

"Wait, what did I miss?"

"Aisling used to dance. I told her she should open her own dance school and talk to Dave."

Olivia pouts. "You're leaving?"

"Nay. We're going to brainstorm first. Me Ma is helping look at studios and stuff. But if it works out, I might need to."

Olivia turns her accusing glare at me. "We don't have many nice chicks here and you go and run off the one we like?"

Aisling looks stunned by the comment as I throw a thong at Olivia. "I haven't run her off. It's her dream."

"I dream of being a princess. You don't see me chasing Prince Harry down."

"He's married."

"And there's a thing called divorce," she hisses, before tilting her head up to Aisling. "Don't leave us with those piranhas."

"Ignore Olivia, she can be dramatic," I warn.

"I didn't t'ink you liked me," Aisling muses.

Olivia's jaw drops. "We like everyone but Trixie and her crew."

"Aye, they can be a bit much."

"A bit?" Olivia argues, scoffing. "Try a lot."

"I'm happy for you," I tell her. "We'll have to go out and celebrate."

"Let me know. I'll be there."

"We will," I assure her.

She finishes applying her lipstick before letting out a breath. "I'd best get out there before Dave comes looking for me."

"Have fun," we tell her.

Once she's gone, Olivia turns to me. "Why have we never invited her before?"

"Told you. It surprised me too," I reply, as the door opens.

Gabby eyes Olivia and then me. "Has she told you her decision yet?"

She's talking about the big question River asked.

"No," Olivia replies in annoyance when Gabby drops down in her lap. "Your arse is sweaty. Get off me."

"Because it's been sliding up and down a pole for the past hour," she tells her, before landing on the floor. She huffs out a breath and drops down on the sofa next to me. "Fine. Be like that."

"You made me fall," Olivia snaps.

"It was an accident, and FYI, it's dark out there. How am I meant to know when you are going to move?"

"Stop," I warn.

Gabby stares at me. "So, are you going to say yes?"

"You already know why I haven't," I remind her, which leads me to grabbing my phone. Liam, a guy Charlotte is not related to but may as well be, is a private investigator. He deals with so much, and I knew from recent events, he is good. He managed to uncover some shit about a guy who's been terrorizing the Hayes family. I only know the family through Charlotte, but I like them, especially the women in their lives. Which is why I know he's discrete. Plus, I trust Charlotte—maybe not with my life, but I trust her with everything else.

And she trusts him.

So, after I revealed River's past to the girls, I told him. I had been right to go to him. Once he found out what happened, he looked pissed and angry. And I think it had something to do with the abuse River endured. He's been investigating ever since. He's pricey, but nothing a few weekends in the private booths won't cover. And since he knows I'm a friend of Charlotte's, he's done it for family rates.

I just wish it would move quicker. I thought a week would be long enough for someone as skilled as him, but it's taking him longer than expected.

"What are you going to do if it's true?" Gabby asks. "I know you don't know yet, but what if it is?"

"It's not, so I don't see the point in playing What If?. You know I've never done that."

"But what if it is?" she pushes.

"It's not," I fire back, determined. I'm hoping the more I believe it's not true, the more chance I have of being right.

"Don't you have to tell him tomorrow if it's a yes or a no?"

"Technically today," Gabby corrects, glancing at her phone. "You really should make up your mind."

"I want to move in with nothing between us. And although this isn't about me, it's still there. He'll always wonder if he's good enough, and he is. I just need him to know it."

"Does he know you're looking into it?" Olivia probes.

"No, and I don't want him to," I warn with caution.

Olivia holds her hands up. "I'm not going to say anything."

"Hey, it's going to be okay," Gabby soothes.

"We don't know that," Olivia pushes.

I pinch the bridge of my nose. "I just want him to be free of Colin. I have a bad feeling in my gut, and you know I'm never wrong."

"Hey, we won't let anything happen," Olivia declares.

"I get it. You want him to breathe easier," Gabby surmises.

"I do. I want him to be able to sleep at night knowing he isn't the person he's painted himself to be. I don't want Colin to blackmail him with that knowledge. River thinks he can leave easily, but I don't think he realises just who Colin is."

"Speaking of, are we really thinking he rigged the yacht?" Olivia asks.

I shrug, but I can't lie. "He's pushing the blame onto Dean. And River is eating it up and working harder to win. And since Dean won tonight's fight, that means he's in the championship. He'll be training harder than he already is."

"River can take him," Olivia promises.

"I hope so."

"Back to the boat," Gabby blurts out. "Do you truly believe he did it?"

"I can't say for sure, but I know I won't feel guilty putting the blame onto him. He's guilty of something. And…"

Gabby's eyes widen. "There's more."

"Yes. I didn't get chance to tell you, but he told me if I wanted to keep being with River, I needed to make him happy."

"He's said that before, though," Olivia states.

"There was something different about it this time. He reminded me of the sleazy guys who offer you a ride home."

Gabby gags. "God, I hate those."

There's a tap at the door, and Olivia calls, "Come in."

Woods, our favourite security guy, pops his head through the gap. "Candy, you are being requested in the private booths."

"I'm not in the private booths. I've switched to the red room," I explain.

He shrugs. "I'm just passing on the message. Lionel seems impressed. The guy tipped him for making sure you got the message."

"Oh, big money," Gabby creepily whispers, rubbing her hands together. "Want me to go in your place."

"Short stuff, Dave is looking for you since you aren't where you're supposed to be. Again," he tells her, giving her a pointed look.

"I get bored," she playfully argues, then looks confused. "Where am I supposed to be?"

"The VIP," Olivia reminds her.

She drops back down on the sofa, deflating. "They are talking numbers. They aren't even appreciating the effort I put into this outfit."

Her outfit is hot tonight. She's a lady in white, and with her new tan, it glows on her. The bralette nurse's outfit is one of my favourites too. It's just the hair I don't like since it only looks good with teased hair.

"Move it before I tell him where you are," Woods warns.

Gabby slaps the sofa with both hands. "You wouldn't."

"I would," he confirms. "My jaw is still throbbing."

"I didn't hit you," she harrumphs with triumph.

"No, but you caused the fight with the guy who did," he points out. "I need to get back to my post. Don't make me come back here."

He closes the door as I get to my feet. "He's so grumpy today," I voice.

"I know. I mean, I can't help it when guys fight over me. I'm hot as fuck. It's not my fault it makes them dumb."

Olivia snorts. "Didn't you tip a drink into his lap?"

"Accident."

"It was on fire."

Gabby gets to her feet, fixing her outfit. "Again, accident. Why so judgey?"

I finish applying my lipstick before stepping away from the mirror. "No arguing when I leave," I warn, grabbing my mask.

Neither of them speak, but as soon as the door closes behind me, they're arguing again.

Heading towards the private booth, I spot Lionel outside booth three, bouncing on the balls of his feet. When he meets my gaze, there's something calculating there, something smug. "Have fun, Candy. He's paid for a full hour."

"Okay," I drawl, and push back the curtain.

Without looking at the client, I recite the rules. "No touching. I can touch you, but you can't touch me."

"And where's the fun in that?" a deep voice counters. My head snaps to the man lounging back in the booth, a smug grin on his face. "Hello, Harriett."

"Dean," I bite out, stepping off the podium. There is no way I'm dancing for him. I don't even want to be in this room with him.

"Where's lover-boy tonight? Arriving soon, I hope."

"None of your business," I snap, and turn to leave.

"I wouldn't do that, if I were you," he warns.

I hesitate with my hand on the curtain. "You don't get to tell me what to do."

"Don't tell me you won't dance for me. I would have thought for someone who fucks Colin, dancing for me would be a breeze. I heard he's not very good."

I shouldn't let go of the curtain, but I do, needing him to elaborate. "What?"

He smirks like he holds all the secrets. "It's okay. I can keep a secret."

"What are you talking about?"

He takes a sip of the dark liquid in his glass. "How many times have you fucked him?"

"I wouldn't let that man touch me with a ten-foot pole," I revolt.

He leans forward, resting his forearms on his thighs. "Marlene told me all about his deal. You keep him happy, and you can stay happy with River. River is so far up Colin's arse, the pansy didn't stand up to him."

My mind is blown. Marlene fucked Colin? I mean, I'm not surprised. She fucked the guy lounging in front of me. But Colin? Eww.

You want to keep this life, you need to keep me happy.

I swallow back vomit as realisation hits me. He made her sleep with him so he wouldn't do what he's doing to me. It all makes sense.

What doesn't make sense is Dean. He could have goaded River with this himself. Instead, he chose to come here.

Why?

"Unfortunately for you, I'm not Marlene," I warn, still trying to find a reason for this visit.

His jaw clenches at the insult. "If you don't want lover-boy to find out about your affair with his manager, get up on that pole and give me what I paid for."

"No."

He glares, clearly not used to the word. "You have no idea who I am."

"I know exactly who you are."

"Yeah? Then get on that pole. You need something to do before your boyfriend arrives. So, entertain me."

"Luckily for you, he isn't coming," I snap.

I turn and push the curtain aside. Lionel is there, blocking my path. "You can't leave until the hour's up. Boss's orders."

"Since when?" I snap, trying to push him backwards. Dave wouldn't do this to any of us. He has always let us walk away. Always. If we didn't, he'd be pissed.

Lionel bends until we're nose to nose. "You snotty little bitch, always thinking you are God's gift. You forget your place. Now turn that tight arse around and shake what you're paid to shake. It's about time you got what's coming to you."

My eyes widen at the insult. Lionel has always been a jerk, but this is low, even for him. He's never acted like this before.

When he shoves me inside, I'm taken off guard, so I don't react until I feel Dean behind me, pressing his chest against my back. "Strip!" he orders.

I jab my elbow into his ribs, but he doesn't even grunt. And just as he takes my arms to stop me from struggling, there's a commotion outside. The curtain is pulled back, and there, wearing a burgundy shirt and black trousers, is River.

Hatred, devastation, and betrayal shine back at me.

And I know when he curls his lip in disgust, he's no longer seeing me.

He's seeing the man he hates more than anyone, holding his woman.

34

RIVER

Meet and greets have always been a hit or miss for me. It's a bunch of people who, for the most part, are good people, but then there's the other half, who rile me to no end. They want to pretend you are friends, that they know everything about you, and it's those people… the people who Colin wants for connection reasons, that make these nights unbearable for me.

My wrist is beginning to ache from signing posters and merch. If I hadn't spent the first part of the night signing stuff for Colin's friends, I wouldn't be feeling like the night isn't going to end.

And this is the part I hate the most. All these people lining up to see me are the people who matter. They are the fans who purchases the subscriptions to watch the fights, those who purchase extortionate tickets to come and see me. These are the people who matter, and Colin brushed them to the end of the night so all his so-called connections and friends could see me.

And I'm done.

I was meant to have finished hours ago, but the queue seems to be getting longer.

Harriett hasn't helped my mood. I've been so focused on the fact she hasn't given me an answer that I forgot to take a break.

She said she wants to move in but needs time to process it. And I told her I got it, but I don't. If she wants to say yes, what is stopping her? What does a week change?

I don't get it, and although I've always found it endearing that I never know what she'll say or do, I don't over this.

Because I want her. And I want her to want me just as much.

I don't think she realises the significance of the question I asked. I've never wanted this before. I've never wanted it all. Even with Marlene, it wasn't something I wanted. One day she moved her stuff in and never left. I never asked. There wasn't some big gesture or discussion. She decided and that was that. We never even shared a room most of the time. She said it was because she couldn't handle my early mornings and didn't want me waking her up all the time. It never bothered me once because Marlene and I never shared the same kind of bond Harriett and I do.

With Harriett, I never want to let go. I love waking up to her in my arms, or her mouth around my cock. I love that she's in my space. And not once has she ever berated me for waking her up at four in the morning.

It didn't hit me until that realisation just how badly I treated Marlene, to an extent. Because I know if Harriett ever told me not to wake her, I'd do everything in my power not to. I'd make changes for her.

I never wanted to change for Marlene. Marlene was someone to fill a void. Harriett is the person who has filled the gaping hole in my chest. She's given me everything whilst expecting nothing in return. She doesn't want to be showered with expensive gifts or be spoilt with expensive clothes. She just wants me.

Which is why I don't understand her hesitation.

We both want this. Neither of us want to be apart. Both of our admissions the night I arrived at the beach house confirmed that. Neither of us were looking forward to sleeping apart.

I glance at my watch. Harriett has a break soon, and I want to call her, let her know I'm thinking of her, and that if it's a no, I can take it. Because she's worth waiting for.

Whispers and chatter loudly fill the room. I glance up to see what the excitement is about and find everyone gaping down at their phone. The woman in front of me gets an alert, and when her guilty gaze meets mine, I make a joke. "Did the cameras get my bad side?"

She clears her throat as she takes the merchandise I just signed. "Um, it's Fracture. He's at a club."

"When is he not?" I joke, but she doesn't laugh. Instead, she hands me her phone. Fracture is outside somewhere, walking down a street with people crowding behind him.

He won tonight's fight, which means we'll be going up against each other in the weeks to come.

"Ladies, gents, I'm here," he announces, and turns the camera, showing the neon sign for Tease.

My fingers tighten around the phone, and I sit up straighter.

"I'm going to get me a private dance from a special lady tonight. I hear she's pricey but it's okay, I can afford it," he jokes.

"Sir, no phones allowed," a doorman I don't recognise, orders.

Dean grins, bringing the camera closer to his face. "VIP baby!" he hollers. "A few drinks in me and I'll forget where she's been."

Comments about Harriett fill up the feed, and I grit my teeth at people telling him what they'd do to her.

I push my chair back and hand over the phone to the woman. Colin rushes over. "You aren't finished."

I drop the pen on the table. "Oh, I'm finished," I state, and move out the back, heading towards the exit.

"River, you can't just leave."

I stop with my hand on the door. "Stop me and you'll be on your arse quicker than you can blink. Do not fucking test me right now."

"I'm coming with you," he demands, and I ignore him as I rush out to where my driver is waiting. Cameras flash, and the media fire off questions about where I'm heading.

Colin calls out, no comment, but all I see is red.

Dean knows exactly what he's doing there tonight. He wants a reaction. He wants me to retaliate.

I'm not worried for Harriett. She wouldn't do anything to hurt me. But Dean... he's the one who will try to cross the line.

He wants a fight. He can have one.

The car has barely pulled to a stop when I open the door and slide out. Whispers begin to get louder, and I hear as a string of people alert everyone to my arrival.

"He's going to kill Fracture."

"They're going to get kicked out of the championship."

"There will be nothing left of Fracture to kick out."

"Nah, my money's on Fracture."

I keep going up to the door, until I feel a tug on my shirt. Colin. "River, you need to think this through. You do not want to lose everything you've been training for, for a piece of pussy."

I turn, getting in his face. "Ever refer to her as pussy again, and I'll tear you a-fucking-part."

"Don't do this," he demands. "At a fucking strip club, of all places."

I shove him backwards, and he takes two steps down. "Get fucked," I snap. "I should have told you that a long time ago."

Red-faced and embarrassed, he glances around at the crowd forming. "We'll talk about this later."

"No, we won't."

"We're at capacity," a doorman I don't recognise announces, blocking my entry.

"I don't give a fuck."

He places a hand on my shoulder, and I stare at it, before slowly lifting my head, hoping he can see what he's done wrong by touching me. He gulps but doesn't backdown.

Woods comes barrelling down the main stairs. "Hey, Luke, let him through," he demands.

"Never touch me again," I threaten.

He lets go of my shoulder, and I shove past him to meet Woods.

"Look, man, we're busy. Some celebrity VIP entered not long ago, and it's been crazy in here."

"Yeah, I know. It's Dean," I tell him, and his eyes widen. "Where's Harriett?"

"Fuck, man, she's working in the private booths."

"Which one?" I demand, and take the stairs up. He follows.

"She's in booth three," he yells up to me.

I weave through the crowds and make my way over to the booths. I don't stop until I reach them. The same doorman who had been working the night I was here, frowns when he spots me.

"You can't go in there," he declares.

"Like fuck," I growl, and shove him aside, using little strength to get past him.

I pull back the curtain, and I see red. A haze comes over me. I don't see Harriett, not really. I just see the man holding her.

She danced for him.

Him.

Out of all the people she could have danced for, she chose him. She could have walked away but decided to stay.

"I didn't dance for him," she yells, reading my mind, but it does nothing to calm me.

He's still here.

He shoves Harriett aside when I go for him. I'm a width away when I'm pulled back. "Don't," Woods warns as Dean grins, holding his arms out.

"Come on, man. I know you want to."

Harriett is in front of me in the next second. "This is what he wants," she rushes out. "He's here to goad you into a fight so you are kicked out of the championship."

"She moves like a porn star," Dean announces, still grinning.

Woods tugs on me tighter when I go for him. "Get the fuck out, now! And don't think about coming back here," he demands.

He glances at Harriett, his gaze racking up and down her body. "Call me, sweetheart. I'm always up for another good time."

"Don't listen to him," Harriett pleads, gripping my shirt. "Please. I'll never be able to live with it. Please."

"Leave before I have you leaving in an ambulance," I bite out, finding it hard to rein it in.

He shoulders past me, and I grip Harriett, needing to. I came in here ready to kill him. I would have. But I can't do that to Harriett. She's already told me she fears I'll resent her for stuff. And I know Harriett, she really will. And I don't want that.

Plus, seeing that look in his eyes, that gloating smile... if I had touched him, I'd be playing into his hands.

"Are you good?" Woods asks, easing the grip on my shirt.

I can't form words, still frozen, so instead, I nod. He lets go.

"Wait," Harriett calls and steps around me. Only then do I come unglued.

"Let him go," I order, holding her wrist. But she shoves me off and steps out of the small room.

"Hey, Lionel," she yells, and the doorman turns at the sound of her voice. My jaw drops when she throws a punch hard enough to impress even me. She cries out after landing a punch to his jaw. "That's for being a prick." My girl is on a mission, and before anyone can stop her, she's stepping up to him and kneeing him in the balls. "And that's for trapping me in there."

Woods stands to attention at that and grabs Lionel by the scruff of his shirt. "You did fucking what?"

"The slut doesn't know what she's talking about."

"Get him out of here. And tell Dave, if he doesn't fire him, I'll leave before my notice."

Woods gives her a nod of acknowledgement before dragging Lionel away.

Wait.

"Your notice?"

"You shouldn't have come here," she rushes out, and pushes me back into the small room, closing the curtain behind her. "I didn't realise until it was too late, but he wanted you to come here. It makes sense now why he kept asking where you were. He knows he doesn't have a chance at winning the championship."

I drop down in the booth, scrubbing a hand down my face. "I was worried about what he'd do."

She sits on the podium, her bare legs between mine. "How did you know he was here?"

"He did a live before coming in. It was shown to me at the meet and greet."

"Prick," she hisses.

I meet her gaze, ashamed. "When I saw you in his arms, I thought you had danced for him."

She nods, like it's a reasonable response, and it's not. "He wanted you to think that, but I wouldn't do that to you."

"I'm sorry," I respond, letting out a dry laugh. "I literally tell you all my darkest secrets and you still stayed. You don't care about my past or judge me for it. And I immediately thought you did me dirty when I walked in. I'm so fucking messed up."

Her hands run over my head. "Was it your first thought when you saw that video?" she whispers. "Did you really jump to that conclusion?"

"No. I came because I knew he would do something, or try to. But then I saw you in his arms, and that's when I jumped to conclusions."

"Then it doesn't matter. I might have accepted your past, but you did the one thing no other guy has ever done before. You accepted my job."

I laugh even more. "This isn't exactly accepting it," I state, pointing around us. "And you said you gave notice. I don't want you to do that. I can handle it."

"I was already planning on doing it, and Dave knew that. I'm going to be working more and more at the hospital next term. I won't be able to stay here. Dave has offered me a job training the new girls and teaching routines. I'll miss my tips, but I'll be running myself into the ground if I keep dancing here."

I take her hands and tug her until she stands. Then I grab those thighs, bringing them over mine until she's straddling me. "How did I get so lucky with you?"

Her eyes sparkle under the light. "Right place, right time. But just so you know in advance, you'll never find anyone better than me. It's probably scientifically proven somewhere."

Falling into the light mood she's setting, I hold her tighter. "Trust me, I know that."

"Good," she murmurs, cupping my face. She presses a brief kiss to my mouth, before pulling back. "Remember that when I'm rearranging things in your home. Or when you are tripping over my boxes. Or when my wigs are hanging all over the place."

I freeze at her words. "Does that mean…"

"Yes, I'm moving in with you," she finishes when I can't find my words.

"Thank fuck." I tug her closer, pulling her head down for a kiss. Our tongues entwine, and I moan at the peppermint on her tongue.

She rolls her hips and pulls back, wagging her finger. "No touching, remember."

The curtain moves, and I stand with her in my arms and drop her to the side. Dave, the manager here, frowns at the sight of us. As the curtains close, I get a brief look at Colin walking away. "Is it true? Did that dickhead trap you in here?"

Harriett takes my hand. "Yes. He's always been a creep, but this was different." She shudders, and I pull her closer. "He can't come back here. The girls aren't safe. Any man with money could pay him and he could do the same."

"Oh, he's getting a beating outside from the others," he growls. "I'm sorry. If I had known—"

"He would have already been gone. I know," she swears. "But if I were you, I'd talk to the other girls, see if he's done something like this before. It might be that they've been too scared to speak up or press charges."

His face drains of blood. "Finish up in here and you can have the rest of the night off. It's a circus out there and it will only get worse if they see you."

He leaves without another word, closing the curtain. Harriett turns in my arms, coming to stand in front of me. She pushes me back with the tip of her finger. "Sit down, handsome."

The booth hits the back of my legs and I drop down in the seat. "What?"

"Fracture paid for an hour. You have thirty minutes," she drawls, standing up on the podium. She leans over, pressing play. "And you are going to enjoy every minute of it."

As she drops back, letting her hair fall down until it sweeps the floor, I take in every inch of her.

It's mad to think this is how it started. One chance encounter. One random night.

And now here we are. Ready to move in together.

As the music turns to something sultrier, she steps off the podium, making her way over to me. She lifts her leg up to straddle me, and when I go to touch, she bats my hands away, leaning down until her lips are at my ear.

"No touching," she whispers, then bites at the lobe, tugging at it.

I groan, hard as fuck.

Running the tips of her fingers up her sides, she moves them up, brushing them through her hair, and up into the air.

I sit back as she rolls her hips, and grit my teeth.

Fuck!

If she keeps rubbing her cunt against my dick like that, I'm going to come in my jeans. This isn't like before. Before, I only had the idea of her. Now I know what she feels like when I'm inside her, how she sounds when she begs for me... I've tasted her. Pleased her. And having her in control like this...

It's pure torture.

She pushes off, turning until she's bent in front of me, her arse in my face. Her hands glide over the globes. She knows just where to touch to make a man crazy. Because whilst she's touching herself, a man will be picturing *his* hands on her.

When she drops her arse into my lap, I can't hold back. One hand goes to her stomach, and the other to the thigh.

"That first night I went home and wanked so hard picturing you. You nearly made me come in my jeans."

"You pictured me?" she rasps as I glide my hand up higher.

"You sat on me just like this. And back then, I didn't have permission to touch you."

"You wanted to touch me?"

"I wanted to do this to you," I drawl, and slide my fingers into the hot pants she's wearing. She moans, arching her back as I apply pressure on her clit, rubbing in a circular motion.

"I imagined squeezing your tits," I whisper as my hand moves under the bralette, cupping her tit. My hand lowers from her clit, inserting a finger. "And fucking you with my fingers."

"Oh God," she moans, arching into my touch.

"And you would have come for me," I tell her, licking her jawline.

As I thrust two fingers inside of her, she comes undone, crying out in my arms. As soon as she stops clenching around my fingers, I slide them out and bring them up my mouth, sucking them.

"We need to go, now," she pants.

I glance at the clock. "I still have ten minutes."

She gets up, straightening her clothes. "And I'm not risking another client coming inside and seeing me fuck you."

A growl vibrates through my chest as I get to my feet. "Where can I wait for you to get changed?"

She grins as she takes my hand and pulls me outside. Woods is coming towards us. He takes one look behind us, then at her face, and frowns. "Really?"

She taps him on the chest as we pass. "We only live once, Woods."

"You'll all be the death of me," he calls back.

"Wait here. I'll be five minutes tops," she tells me. I watch her arse as she leaves. I can't help but feel smug that she's mine.

All these men can't touch, but I can.

Coming here could have ended differently. I pictured as much on the drive over. But if I hadn't, God only knows how long it would have taken for someone to check on her.

And she might not have given me the answer to moving in until tomorrow.

And I most certainly wouldn't have enjoyed what just happened, something I've pictured doing since my first time here.

As for Dean, he's going to suffer the consequences of tonight the right way. I'm going to humiliate him in a way he won't recover from. I'll make sure no fucker sponsors him or endorses him ever again.

His time is coming.

And now, the countdown begins.

35

HARRIETT

Sundays are meant to be for relaxing. A day of rest for most. For me, I'm packing up my life, wondering when I accumulated this much stuff.

Fortunately, River has the space, and I have my girls who are here come rain or shine.

Olivia holds up a dress I bought a few years ago, the tags still attached. "Can I have this?"

I throw a pair of socks at her. "I'm moving, not dying."

"Yeah, but what do you need with all this stuff?" Gabby asks, holding up a crystal I thought I threw out years and years ago. I'm pretty sure it has bad juju. "Can I keep this?"

I open my mouth to say no, but then think better off it. If anyone can fight off bad juju, it's Gabby. "Sure."

"It has bad juju," Emily calls out from where she's lounging on my bed.

Gabby stares at it for a little longer before shrugging. "I'll take it."

"Are you going to help?" Olivia asks, making a point to stare at Emily.

Emily smothers a yawn before answering. "I got up at six with my daughter. I got an hour, two max, of sleep. I'm here for moral support."

Poppy is asleep downstairs in her pushchair, ready to be picked up by the babysitter. "You are okay to leave, you know."

"And miss all the fun? No thank you."

Gabby drops down on the bed next to Emily. "Did you see anything in the papers? I bet someone got a picture of her cunny."

They've not stopped bringing up my little discretion in the private booths last night. Gabby high-fived me, Emily thinks it's unsanitary, and Olivia just grinned, like I played out one of her fantasies.

Olivia throws a nail file at her. "Stop calling it that."

Gabby arches a brow. "Do you want me to call it a vagina? Or Vulva?"

"Vulva?" Olivia spits out, utterly baffled.

"Medical term for vagina," I answer.

Gabby points to the tablet in Emily's hand. "Google Tease news. It has to be in there."

"Alright," Emily agreed.

Gabby leans over, her face filled with excitement. I go to grab another box when both of their expressions fall. "What?"

"This can't be true," Emily stresses, sitting up.

"What?" Olivia asks, walking over. She reaches the bed, and her body language changes. She's no longer relaxed. She's white as a ghost and shaking. "I was speaking to her last night."

"What's going on?" I demand and make my way over. I make it to the bed in time to watch Emily press play.

"Aisling O'Connor—a young woman in her early twenties—has been reported missing during the early hours of this morning. Her mother, Mrs O'Connor, reported her daughter missing after she failed to return home from a night shift at Tease—a strip club in the local town of Coldenshire. In search of her daughter, Mrs O'Connor found her car not far from the strip club, with Aisling O'Connor's belongings on the ground. Constable Mills released a statement."

The screen changes to an older gentleman standing outside of the police station. "It's too early to speculate, but we are working hard with other law enforcement officers to discover Miss O'Connor's whereabouts. We have no evidence to suggest this is the night stalker killer, but we are taking the matter very seriously. If anyone has seen or heard from this woman after four this morning, please call Crimestoppers or one-zero-one with the reference number below."

Tears burn my eyes. "This can't be true. We were talking to her last night. She was excited about opening a dance school."

The iPad shakes in Emily's hands. "Do you think it's the killer? Do you think he's here? Are we safe?"

I place my arm around her. "She's going to be okay. We're going to be okay."

"He doesn't hit the same place twice," Gabby whispers, her voice shaking.

"This can't be real," Olivia whispers. "She's so young."

"She's going to be fine."

My phone beeps with a message. I grab it off the side and see it's a group chat from Tease.

Dave: Due to recent events, we are remaining closed for the next few weeks. You'll receive paid leave.

Instantly, the chat is filled with others asking if it's true. I show it to the girls, and Olivia begins to breathe heavily, panicking, which is a rarity for her. "Oh my god, it's true. He wouldn't be closing if it wasn't."

I kneel on the bed until I can reach her. "We're going to be fine, Olivia, I swear it to you."

"I'm too young to die. Who will look after the kids if I'm not here? Who will make sure Gabby doesn't end up in prison?"

Gabby scoffs. "I resent you for that."

"It's true."

With one hand on Emily's leg, and the other holding Olivia's hand, I lean in. "We are not going to worry about this until we have something to be worried about. And if there is, we will get through it. Do you hear me?"

Gabby, as always, isn't paying attention. "Hey, go back down," she orders. "There's a breaking news link."

"About Aisling?"

"No, about River," Emily murmurs, and I move until I'm beside her. She clicks on the link, which takes us to another page.

The headline is bold, taking up the top of the page.

River Knight, Who Is He and Where Did He Come From?

'Many fans have wondered about the life of the reserved UFT fighter. The self-contained UFT fighter, who has won four honourable awards, and fought his way up into the championship, has always managed to keep to himself.

River Knight has a reason for keeping himself out of the limelight. He has been keeping secrets.

Until today.

A source close to the fighter has revealed River Knight comes from a broken home. Growing up in an abusive household, River Knight barely escaped with his life. His mum, Rita Cormack, who got arrested for the murder of Mitchel Cormack, was institutionalised at Mayfare institution, where she continues to carry out her sentence. It is said Mrs Cormack killed her husband to protect River.

It's also reported that River Knight has no contact with his mother and has done little to care for a woman who was diagnosed with bipolar and schizophrenia.

But that's not all.

The source also revealed River Knight allegedly fought illegally before entering into the UFT. He entered a gang at a young age and is reported to allegedly have gotten high into the ranks so quick because of them.

So, we dare to question.

How well do we know River Knight? By the looks of it, not very well.

Stay tuned. More to come.

(We reached out to River's representatives, but no comment has been made.)'

"What the actual fuck?" I hiss, reading it over again. "Who would do this to him?"

"This is the same woman who wrote the article about you," Emily announces, clicking on her image. "I followed her after the first article."

A bang on the door rattles the house, and Poppy immediately begins to cry.

"That could be the babysitter," Emily offers.

Gabby throws her a look. "I don't think she'd be knocking like that."

We rush down, and Emily heads straight for her daughter whilst I head over to the door. I pull it open, getting knocked back by River entering.

"I just saw the papers. Are you okay?" I ask, gaining my feet.

Veins bulge in his neck. "Am I okay? Are you fucking kidding me right now?"

"Don't fucking speak to her like that," Olivia snaps, crossing her arms over her chest.

"Girls, go wait at my uncle's. I'll call you in a bit," I tell them, and grab the spare keys off the hook, handing them to Gabby, who is barely keeping it together.

"We aren't going anywhere," Olivia insists.

"We don't need a peanut gallery," he snaps.

"Please," I plead. "I need five minutes."

She reluctantly nods, and I wait for them to leave before closing the door behind them.

I turn to River, who is barely keeping himself in check. "What is the matter with you? I've never seen you like this before."

He picks up a lamp and throws it across the room. "I fucking trusted you. I told you that in confidence and you go to the fucking papers? The fucking papers! I've spent all morning locked in an office proving that I wasn't in a fucking gang."

I stagger like his words hit me in the gut. "You think I told the papers?"

The look of disgust he directs my way has my knees threatening to buckle. "I should have fucking listened to him. He said you'd do this," he roars, and I know he means Colin. "Was this your plan all along? To make me trust you? To make me fall in love with you, so I'd tell you everything? Was the sad story about men treating you like shit for being a stripper a way to make me lower my guard and treat you differently? Was any of it true?" He steps away, tugging at his hair. "I told you I killed a man. Killed him!" I jump when he throws a vase, roaring in anger. His shoulders deflate as he pants for breath, and I stand there, frozen. When he turns, the anguish in his eyes almost makes me feel sorry for him. Almost.

He knocks my bag off the side and papers slip out, floating until they land all around us. My breath hitches when a picture I found of his mother lands page up on his trainer. He bends down, grabbing it, and then another.

My mouth opens, but no words slip free. "River—"

"I should have fucking known when you didn't run. This is what you've been after the entire time," he roars, holding the paper up. I jerk back, my breath hitching. "I gave you everything. Don't forget to add all the gory details. How my mum and dad beat me. Then her boyfriends. Don't forget to mention I was born an addict, or how my mum, after five years of me being born, couldn't stay clean. She'd take me to friends' houses so she could get high. You are just like her. A selfish bitch with no regards to what this will do to me. Colin was right about you. You are some money-hungry piece of pussy after money. Well, you won't get a penny from me. I'm going to lose *everything*!"

I flinch at his words.

He's right. He has lost everything. He's lost me.

Blocking out the hurt, I take two steps back, reaching for the door handle. I pull open the door before meeting his gaze. "Get out!"

He scoffs. "I thought you'd deny it. But you don't have an ounce of remorse inside of you. I don't know why I bothered to come here."

"Get out!" I scream, unable to keep it together any longer.

He comes towards me, his steps slow, predatory. He stops when he reaches me, but I duck my head to the side, unable to look at him. If I do, I might fight for my innocence. And I'm not that girl.

He should have asked me before reacting like this.

"Well done, you got what you wanted. You fooled me good and proper," he breathes out. "More, you only had to ask me for money; I would have happily of given it to you. All of it. You didn't have to sell my story."

"Leave," I demand, my voice cracking.

"And if you haven't clued in, we're fucking over," he announces.

With that blow, he leaves, and I slam the door closed behind him before collapsing to the floor. I breathe heavily, trying to get a grasp on what just happened.

But I can't.

It's too much to process on only a few hours of sleep.

"You could have asked me if I did it, and I would have told you the truth," I whisper, panting heavily.

I won't cry.

I won't.

The door bangs into me when it's shoved open. Olivia immediately kneels down next to me, running her hand down my back. "Did that wanker hit you?"

I get to my feet and shake my head. "No."

"What the fuck was his problem?" Emily asks, crowding me.

"He thinks I'm the one who released his story."

I make my way into the kitchen, grabbing the dustpan and brush before heading back out to the hallway.

"Right, so we can totally make it look like an accident and be each other's alibis," Gabby announces. "What are you doing?"

"I'm cleaning up the glass," I tell them robotically. "You don't have to stay. I can unpack by myself."

"Fuck that. We aren't going anywhere," Olivia rages.

I take a deep breath before addressing them. "I need you to. I need everyone to leave to give me room. Please."

Gabby stops twiddling with the zip of her jacket, looking at me like a kid who got yelled at. "But you need us."

"I'm fine."

Emily's nose scrunches up. "You don't look fine."

"If you are worried about implicating us in a crime, we're good. Sisters till we die, remember?" Gabby reminds me, moving closer.

Olivia crowds my other side. "We've got you."

"The babysitter has got Poppy, so you know what this means."

"You can't seriously think we'll sleep right now," Gabby argues.

"No," Emily snorts. "We dance it out and get drunk."

She drags me into the living room, where I tug my hand free.

"Girls, I appreciate the thought, I do, but I want to be alone."

"Exactly, you *want* to," Olivia announces as Emily blasts Little Mix through the speakers. "But it's not what you *need*."

Gabby tugs at my hand. "What you need is to shake off all that negative energy."

She begins to jump, jerking my body with each move. Emily begins shaking her hair, dancing in circles.

My shoulders slump as I rock side to side. All I want to do is go upstairs and curl up in my bed.

He broke up with me.

The hurt and betrayal is far worse from him. At least what he's accused me of isn't true. What he did to me, is. It's as real as it gets.

Then why do I feel so numb?

"He left me."

Emily takes my face in her hands. "It's okay to fall apart."

"We're here to catch you," Gabby promises, resting her head on my shoulder.

Olivia rests her head on my other shoulder. "Sisters before misters."

"I need alcohol if I'm going to get through the rest of today," I announce, giving in.

Gabby cheers. "We've still got vodka and gin in the freezer. I'll make some drinks."

As she breaks apart from the huddle, Emily pulls me in, still rocking side to side to the music. "Today, we get drunk and maybe unpack your things. Tomorrow, you can mope."

I jerk my head in a nod. "Okay."

"We've got you," Olivia promises.

And that is how my day began. Finding out a friend might have been murdered, and my boyfriend accusing me of leaking information.

I haven't even been awake four hours and already my day is all gloom.

But I know, with friends at my side, I'll get through this. There is no other option.

And no, I won't cry.

I won't.

36

HARRIETT

Turns out, getting over River Knight is harder than I thought. He said he loved me, and in an ugly way; not in the way I imagined he'd say those three words to me.

For the past two weeks, I've moped around and gone through my days like a zombie. I've stalked my messages daily, hoping he'll wake up and realise the truth. I keep imagining him turning up at my door and apologising. I'd make him grovel and beg for forgiveness. And just when he can't take anymore, I'd stupidly forgive him. But it's a dream.

A dream that is playing on repeat in my head and keeping me awake at night.

He's plaguing my thoughts every minute, and today of all days. The day I buried a friend, a work colleague, and someone I was highly fond of.

Two days after her disappearance, Aisling was found in the staff car park of Tease. She had been dead at least nine hours, if not more, when Dave went into work and found her. He's closed for another two weeks, and today at the funeral, I witnessed a strong man break. I can't imagine what it's done to him. Today he looked tired and worn, like he had aged ten years. He takes our safety seriously and feels like he failed Aisling and the rest of us.

The police are no closer to finding her killer. The only new evidence is that traces of moss were found on her clothes.

I still can't believe she's gone. She had so much still to do. This wasn't her time. And I'm going to miss her at work. I'm going to miss her terribly.

I left the wake early, unable to bear the concern on my friends' faces or the guilt I felt feeling heartbroken over a guy on a day a mother was burying her child. Aisling should have been my only thought today, but instead, I was thinking of him too.

I don't know when I turned into this girl, or what spell he cast to make him unforgettable.

Stepping into the kitchen, I grab a glass out of the cupboard before pouring myself a glass of wine. It's not my first glass, and it won't be my last today.

I down the glass before pouring another, wanting to forget the entire day. Because today isn't just Aisling's funeral. It's the night of the UFT championship. And I just need to get through it. Tomorrow is a new day. It will be better. It *has* to be, because I'm fed up of feeling like this.

I kick off my heels and head out of the kitchen, ready to turn into the living room. Persistent knocking on the door doesn't let me get very far. I let out a breath, hating it might be more paparazzi. They've been piranhas since the news broke about River. They've already thrown speculation out there about our break-up, and since neither of us have confirmed or denied it, people have already made up their own minds.

The knocking persists even more.

It might not even be them. It could be worse. It could be my worried dad, who has been calling on and off all week to check up on me.

Knowing they aren't going to stop, I pull open the door, and the girls, still wearing the little black dresses from the funeral, hold up a bottle of wine. I sigh, moving into the front room. "I told you I was fine."

"You've been telling us that for two weeks," Emily says.

I curl my feet up on the sofa, and Emily takes a seat at the other end whilst the other two decide on a bean bag each. "Stop worrying about me."

"Well, we are. You haven't cried. Not even at the funeral, and I know how much it was hurting you," Emily claims. "So yeah, we're worried."

Gabby leans in to Olivia. "Maybe she's delusional and lost it."

Olivia nods in agreement. "Could be. Thousands of people die of broken heart syndrome every year."

"I'm not dying."

Gabby pours herself a glass of wine. "Should we call someone? A doctor maybe?"

Olivia points her glass at Gabby, like she's on to something. "A therapist."

"You aren't calling anyone," I snap. "I told you, I'm fine."

Emily begins to sift through the papers on the coffee table. "Babe, this isn't healthy."

"Yeah, why are they still out?" Gabby asks, peeping over at the papers.

I shrug. Those papers hold everything about River and his life. I still haven't heard from Liam, and maybe that's for the best. Who knows. It means nothing now anyway. These papers are for my own peace of mind. "I don't like unfinished puzzles."

I couldn't help myself. The break-up pushed me to keep looking and fired that need to the point I've stayed up nights googling shit.

There's another knock on the door, and the girls freeze. "Who is it?" Gabby whispers, ducking her head like whoever it is can see through walls.

"Don't know. I'm not a mind reader," Olivia retorts. "But it's most likely to be the media again. Want me to tell them to leave?"

I shake my head. "No. Just ignore it."

"It could be your dad," Emily points out, getting to her feet. "I'll go check."

I stare mindlessly into my glass of wine, thoughts of my life swirling around in my head. Moments later, Emily walks back in and steps aside, revealing Hetty.

Seeing her brings back memories of River once again, and my heart skips a beat. I sit up straight. "Hetty, hey. Is everything okay?"

"I'm sorry. I didn't know today was a bad day," she admits, scanning the girls' attire, her expression sad. "I heard about the girl from Tease. Was she your friend?"

"She was," I tell her, rubbing at the tightness in my chest. I should have done better. She should have been carpooling with us and not alone.

"I'm sorry for your loss," she offers sincerely. She clears her throat whilst holding up the box in her hands. "I won't stay. I just wanted to drop this picture frame off for you. The anniversary is in a few weeks, right?"

"It is," I reply, forcing a smile. "Thank your husband for me. I really appreciate it."

"It's no bother," she tells me, and there's a softness to her smile that's warm and comforting. "I'm sorry to hear about you and River, too."

"Thank you. It's been a crappy few weeks."

"Language," Gabby mouths, and at my look, slinks down into the beany, hiding behind her glass of wine.

Hetty takes a moment, watching me like she's trying to get a read. Her shoulders drop as she gently places the box down on the coffee table, but freezes for a moment, picking up a sheet with the reporter's picture on. "I know this lady. She's had interviews with Colin. Do you know her?"

The fog in my mind clears at her words and the girls all watch me, wide-eyed. "She had an interview with Colin? Are you sure?"

She picks up on the tension in the room. When she turns back to me, her shoulders are straighter. "Yes. I remember because Colin didn't sign her in or introduce her to me. I found it quite odd. And he did it both times she visited."

I stand. "Oh my god, Hetty, I could kiss you right now." I take a breath as I process it all. "That slimy little weasel."

"What?"

Emily takes pity on the confused woman. "River broke up with her because he thinks she sold the story to this woman. Now we have proof it was Colin."

"Why on earth would he think it was you?"

"Your guess is as good as mine," I reply. "Colin has wanted me out of the picture since I met River. River plans to leave the circuit and Colin didn't like it."

She bites her lip, looking away. "Oh."

I stiffen at her avoidance. "What is it, Hetty? What do you know?"

"Me and my James, we like to keep up with River and his achievements, especially since I left the company. I actually saw him briefly last night. We went to wish him luck. And I heard he's signing a contract tonight with Colin. He'll be doing another five years."

"No, that can't happen," I tell her, dropping the papers back onto the table.

"Let it," Gabby argues. "He deserves it for what he said to you."

Hetty ignores the girls and steps up to me. "I've been married fifty-one years to my James. But it wasn't all smooth sailing. We got into a bother at the beginning of our courtship, and for a moment, I thought we were done for good."

"I don't understand," I admit, wondering why she's telling me this.

Her cold hands take mine. "What I'm saying is men, they don't have the same strength as us women do. They think they are the stronger sex, and they might be *physically*. But this," she tells me, placing her wrinkled hand over my chest. "Is where we are stronger. Men, when they are hurt, say things they don't truly mean. If River said things, he didn't mean them, not really. That boy loves you. Only a fool would be blind to see it. And from the look of you, I'd say you love him too."

"He thought I lied to get money from his story," I whisper, not denying my feelings. Because I think I do love him. Why else would it hurt like this? I feel like I'm missing something. Like I've lost a part of myself with him gone. He hasn't just been in my life this entire time. He's been a part of it, and there's a difference. "He was cruel."

"Because a man with a broken heart can do stupid things. I'm not saying it's right. But I saw that boy yesterday and he did not look like the same River I've come to know and love. He's hurting, and I can see in his eyes that he misses you. And I see in yours the same hurt and longing. You love him. Darlin', love happens. You don't fight to feel it, it just happens. But the other parts, the things that keep you together, is something you work to keep. And I thought a girl as strong as you would fight for her man."

"I—"

She pats my arm, distracting me from my argument. "Trust me. I'm a woman with many years on her. I know. You carry that same strength. But if you want to go down without a fight, then you were never a match for my boy, River," she reveals, before letting go. "I'd best be off. My James is waiting in the car."

She leaves me dumbstruck. Gabby stands at my side, staring at the space Hetty just left. "That woman is *goals*. I wonder if she'll give me advice."

"Your past advice," Olivia retorts.

"Wait, you've got proof you didn't sell the story, but what about the rest? This isn't all about that. It's about his past," Emily decrees.

"Fuck that," Olivia barks. "Are we forgetting what he said to her?"

"Yeah, but he didn't know the truth then," Emily argues.

"Would he have listened if she told him?" Gabby points out.

I drop down on the sofa, blowing out a breath. "Gabby's right. He wouldn't have listened." And for the first time since that god-awful day, a tear falls down my cheek. "I'm not this girl. I don't mope over men. I don't give second chances. I don't forgive and forget."

"But you want to," Emily guesses softly, sitting on the coffee table in front of me.

I swipe away another tear. "I do, so badly, but I'll be setting myself up for a circle of mistreatment."

"No, you won't," Gabby soothes. "These circumstances are different to a guy who cheated. He had a lot riding on these secrets being kept. None of us would want that getting out. I remember not wanting my parents to find out I'm gay, and when that bitch Marie told me it was Nikki, I believed her and flipped out on Nikki."

"You still sound sour over it," Olivia muses.

"Yeah, because by the time I found out it was really Marie, she had moved schools. I never got the pleasure of yelling at her or telling her parents what she let the boys do to her. So maybe the old lady is right. Maybe he did say it out of hurt and fear. I know if I had time to really think about it, I wouldn't have yelled at Nikki. The girl saved spiders, for fuck's sake," she reveals, like Nikki committed a crime. "Or, put it this way, if you thought he cheated on you, would you wait for him to deny it?"

When she puts it like that... "Probably not. His stuff would be on fire outside."

"Exactly," Gabby practically cheers. "He just metaphorically set fire to your heart and what you shared."

Olivia slowly turns to Gabby, her expression priceless. "That didn't make sense but did at the same time."

Gabby patronizes her by tapping her hand. "It's okay that you can't keep up."

Emily shakes her head at their antics. "I think what she's trying to say is, what do you want to do?"

"No, that's not what I meant at all," Gabby disagrees. "I meant what I meant."

I pinch the bridge of my nose at the headache forming. "I don't know. I really don't. He said some pretty shitty stuff. And how do I explain the papers he found?"

"The truth," Emily states. "And hope he listens."

"I still can't believe Charlotte said he's the best," Gabby pouts, referring to Liam. "He sucks."

And like he could hear our silent pleas, my phone rings, Liam's name covering the screen. I get to my feet as I answer.

"You called at the perfect time. Please tell me you have something."

"I do," he rumbles. "River never killed anyone. The mum's boyfriend, Mark Evans, died of an accidental overdose a few years ago. He moved to Devon not long after the incident with River. The police were watching him, and when they did the raid, they found him dead in his bedroom."

I fall down onto the sofa, biting my nail. "Are you sure it's the right person? River mentioned that his mum admitted to killing Mark."

"It is. When his mum was arrested, they found Mark's wallet at her house. It was filed away into evidence. In her statement, she rambles about him leaving her just like everyone else. I think it was a misunderstanding because I've looked at the statement. She rambles about killing *him*, but never quotes who."

"River didn't kill anyone?" I ask, needing confirmation.

"No. But the mother did. I don't know why it's not public record, but his dad died the week after he was released from prison. It was a hit and run. His mother's collaboration of events fits with the crime scene and CCTV footage from that night. It's mostly what set her off and why she's in a mental facility. He was also killed with a car registered to the man who assaulted River."

"Fucking hell," I breath.

"I need to go, but is there anything else you need me to look into?"

"No. That's everything. Thank you."

"Later."

He ends the call and I slowly bring the phone down to my lap, staring at the girls in shock. He didn't kill anyone. And now that I know, I have to tell him. He needs to know this.

As I run over everything Liam told me, the girls look as relieved as me.

"I knew he didn't do it," Gabby declares.

"You bet your Jimmy Choos that he did," Olivia reminds her.

Gabby waves her off and takes a seat next to Emily. All three sit on the table, watching me expectantly. "So, what are you going to do?"

I get up, opening my mouth, to say what, I don't know, before sitting back down. I bite my nail, going over everything in my head.

He said some seriously cruel and uncalled for shit.

But he didn't have all the facts.

He never asked, just assumed.

Because he was scared.

Everything is a jumbled mess in my mind.

"I think we broke her," Gabby whispers.

"Shut up, she's thinking," Olivia scolds.

I glance up and smack my hands down on my thighs. "I'm going to the fight. I'm going to go and tell him the truth of what happened. And then I'm going to make him wish he never said any of those things."

"He probably already does. I mean, you aren't a woman men easily get over. Remember the guy who kept bringing you cups of coffee because you broke up with him? You must have been a rock star in bed," Gabby boasts.

Olivia's eyes bug out as she stares at Gabby. Her mouth opens and closes before turning to Emily. "I have nothing. Your turn to talk to her."

Emily waves her off. "Gabby's actually right. He's probably already kicking himself. So you need to go out there and tell him, and then make him beg for you back."

I get up, looking around. "Where are my shoes?"

"Wait, are we getting back together with him? Shouldn't this be a group decision?" Gabby stresses.

"It's not up to us. It's up to Harriett."

"Well, we're a team, so technically, we're all in this relationship," Gabby points out.

I reach for my shoes and then freeze. "Am I really doing this?"

"Do you love him?" Emily questions.

My shoulders slump because I do. With everything in me. "I do, but…"

"Then go give him hell," Olivia chides.

"You changed your tune pretty quick," Gabby mutters.

I grab my bag from the side. "Are you girls coming?"

"Duh," they call, and grab their shit, following me out.

"Shit, let me grab the tickets," I panic, and race upstairs to my room.

I've always known I can count on my girls. Our friendship goes beyond sisterhood. We're a family, a unit, and a force to be reckoned with.

And if River can't see just how awesome I am, or apologise for his wrongs, I won't hesitate to let them loose.

It really is going to be a fight to remember.

37

HARRIETT

As plans go, mine kind of sucked. We got outside and realised none of us could drive since we've all been drinking. Luckily, it didn't stop me, which should give me points for determination. I never let myself rethink my decision.

After waiting thirty minutes for a taxi, we made it in the nick of time, which fortunately for us, got us to miss the red carpet, something I wanted to avoid. There are still some paparazzi milling around outside, but I have my girls to block me from view on our way in. I don't want the media tipping River off about my arrival, not that he'll be looking at his phone. He'll be prepping for the fight. However, I don't want to chance it. He needs to know what I know before he signs those contracts and before he gets into the ring with Fracture. He always told me being clear-headed in the cage is what got him this far. He let go of the outside world for those split minutes and fought with all his focus. And with the media storm, probably being hounded over his mum, and our break-up, he's not as clear-headed as he should be.

Jumping to the conclusion that I'm clouding his mind, is forward, even from me. But I have to believe Hetty when she told me he didn't mean those cruel words. And Gabby is right, I am hard to get over. Just like he is, evidently.

Sneaking into the hall's backstage is easy enough. The guys on security don't even blink as we make our way around them.

Once through to the back, me and my girls huddle together, giggling over the high as we begin to search for River's locker room.

Five minutes later, and we still haven't had any luck. "Do we know what room they are in?" Gabby ponders.

Olivia hiccups, throwing her bottle of wine in the bin. "I think we're going around in circles."

I think Olivia is right because I swear we've passed through this corridor at least once already. I remember seeing the tribute band poster for AC/DC on the wall.

I look up for the boards giving directions but come to a stop at the sight of the woman approaching us. The girls bump into my back one by one. "Oh crap," I squeak.

"What?"

"We're on the wrong side of the building," I murmur quietly.

"How do you know?" Gabby whispers, searching the walls for signs.

Emily leans in, also whispering, "Why have we stopped?"

"Why are we whispering?" Olivia asks, hiccupping once again.

"You," Marlene greets, crossing her arms over her chest. Smug. "I knew you'd always come to talk to me. You want to know what you did, or what I can do to help you understand. Or you are here to tell me I was right?"

"Your level of vanity is almost comedic," I retort, eyeing the fresh bruises on her arms, neck, and face. She's tried covering them, but clearly, she's not a magician with makeup, not that it would do much good. You can't hide swelling.

"Totally the scorned ex," Gabby whispers loudly behind me.

Olivia leans around me, holding her hand out into a fist for a pretend microphone. "Tell me, what's it like to give up gold for bronze? Is it like ordering a gorgeous dress online but receiving a Wish version? Or have you always been this bitter? Tell us."

Marlene doesn't even flinch at the comment as she knocks Olivia's hand away. Her attention is solely on me, and instead of the scorned ex, all I see is a broken woman. It's kind of sad if you can forget she's a raging bitch.

"He'll never love you. I broke him," she discloses. "I read the papers. It doesn't take a scientist to figure out he left you *or* why. You aren't me."

For a minute, I consider falling for her games, but as much as I love a good sparring match, winning a verbal or physical fight with her will not make me feel better. All I will accomplish is kicking a beaten woman when she's already down.

What she needs is a slap with the truth.

"Babe, I've had the worst couple of weeks, and a seriously crappy day, so I'm going to go easy and do you a favour instead," I offer.

Before she can form some sort of shitty response, I grip my hand around her bicep and tug her into the bathroom not far from where we're standing.

"Let me go," she cries.

I shove her in front of the sink and make her face the mirror. "No man who declares he loves you does this to you."

"Let me go, you crazy bitch," she demands, struggling to get free.

I pinch her chin, forcing her to face the woman who is slowly breaking. Eyes downcast, she can't even look at herself. "You were once beautiful. But years of being dragged down and beaten down have made you cold. You remind me of a girl who would smile with her eyes. Who laughed all the time. He's taken that from you." I take a breath, letting her absorb my words before continuing. "I buried a friend today. She had her whole life ahead of her. She wanted to open a dance school. She wanted to get married and have children. And it was taken from her. Whoever murdered her took her future, and her life. He broke those who loved and cherished her. Don't let Fracture be your killer. Don't waste your life on someone who wouldn't care if you got murdered tomorrow."

"You have no idea what you're talking about."

I let go, and she slowly turns to face me, ducking her head. But I don't stop, needing it to register with her. "I get why you came to me that night. You hate that you gave up the one man who treated you right. It's probably why you cheated in the first place. You've got issues of your own, and somewhere in that messed up head of yours, you think you deserve what happens to you."

"River treated me like shit. He never loved me," she argues, but there's no heat behind her words. "You have no clue what River and I shared."

"I do. He told me you never cooked for him." I lift up my fingers as I list the things I caught on to when we did talk about her. "Selfish, money hungry, and sometimes cold. He never said those exact words, but that's the gist I got when he did mention you. A girl like that grew up with nothing. Or maybe you had everything you needed and not what you wanted, so you left home and decided to take it. Who knows. It doesn't matter. He could never have loved you because you didn't love yourself, much less him."

Her breath hitches, and she twiddles her hands in her lap. "I guess I got what I deserved in the end, then, huh."

I step forward, my heart hurting at her flinch. "No. You haven't. You could be a crazy clinger, or a detached, heartless bitch, but you don't deserve this. No one does."

"He said he's going to change," she whispers, and for the first time, I see and hear the broken woman inside. I hear her truth.

"Men like him don't change; they never do," Olivia warns. "My dad never did. Or my mum's dad."

I place my hand on her arm. "Leave him," I demand. "Go home right now, get your kid, whatever money you have, and leave. Because he's going to lose tonight. You know it. He knows it. And the world knows it. And you know who he's going to take it out on when it's all over. *You.* And worse, maybe your kid."

"Why are you being…" She wipes at the tears falling. "I want to say nice, but it's the wrong word."

"Brutally honest are the words you are looking for," I tell her, having no shame. She needed to be woken up a long time ago. It's just sad it had to come from a woman who is a stranger to her. And I don't want this every time we run into each other. I'm not that girl. I'm not one who bickers with a guy's ex. I don't see the point, and honestly, I find it tacky.

We're all women. We have it hard enough already. We don't need to be tearing each other down.

"Look, I'm only doing this because we are on a time crunch. Don't mistake me for being nice," Olivia snaps, and pulls out a card. "Get your kid and call this number. They'll get you set up someplace safe and even get you a job."

"What if I don't want to leave him?"

"Then when you're burying your kid 'cause he smacked him a little too hard, you can weep over his grave and remember this moment. You'll remember a time when four girls offered you an escape. Leave him or don't. We can't make you. Honestly, I don't care enough to force you. But one day, you'll look around and realise you have no one to help. Don't mess around with your life. Does he really mean more to you than your own safety? Than your kid's?"

She ducks her head in shame. "No."

"Then leave," Emily tells her.

Straightening her shoulders, Marlene looks over each of us before hesitating. Whatever is on the tip of her tongue, she holds back. She leaves without another word, the door closing behind her.

Gabby pops a lollipop into her mouth. "That was kind of disappointing."

Olivia sighs. "I actually felt sorry for her. Did you see the bruises she did a shit job of covering?"

"I was hoping to maybe see River get hit a few times, you know, because of what he's done, but now I kind of want to see this Fracture guy suffer," Emily admits, pouting.

"Me too," I murmur before shaking myself out of it. "Come on, let's go."

I lead the girls to the exit, and just as I pop outside, I see Colin and Fracture with their heads bent close, in a heated conversation.

Fracture points this way, and I jerk back, closing the door behind me before they can see me. The girls bump into me. "Give a girl some warning," Olivia complains.

"I just deep-throated a lollipop," Gabby heaves.

"It's Colin," I hiss, and pull the door open to get another look. "Shit, he's coming. Hide."

"Where?" Gabby cries.

"Go into a cubicle and stand on a toilet so he doesn't see your feet," I demand.

Gabby goes to protest but Olivia shoves her towards the door. "These shoes cost me a fortune," she snaps.

Emily goes into the end stall, whispering. "Hit record on your phone, Gabby."

As the voices outside become clearer, I stand up to the sink, messing with my curls to look busy. I feign a surprise jerk when the door is slammed open and Colin steps inside, a big ugly guy behind him.

"Wait out there," Colin orders, and the guy jerks his head into a nod, closing the door behind him.

"Pretty sure the men's bathroom is down the hall," I retort, sounding bored.

"You aren't welcome here," he sneers.

I cock a hand on my hip. "Really? I have a ticket that says I do."

He takes two steps closer, and there's a confidence in him I've never seen before. He truly thinks he's won. That he has River wrapped around his finger and there's nothing I can do to get in the way.

He's wrong. So terribly wrong.

"You just won't leave him alone, will you? He doesn't want you. He's made that abundantly clear. And I won't have you distracting him tonight. I won, little girl. I won. I told you not to mess with me, but you didn't heed my warning. Now look at you. Some slag coming here begging for more. It's embarrassing is what it is."

I tap my chin, unbothered by his remarks. "No, what's embarrassing is you thinking you've won. You don't fool anyone. Although, I will admit, going to the media was clever. I didn't think you had it in you."

He grins. "I have no idea what you are talking about."

My heels click on the floor below as I approach. "See, I found it odd the murder wasn't mentioned. Didn't you find that odd? A big story like that would be more beneficial to someone like me, right? It would have rolled out cash all on its own. I wouldn't have needed the mum story. And that's not including the interviews I'd have been paid thousands to do. I mean, once River pushed past the first stage of his grief, he'd see that too. He would have seen I could have got more for doing less."

"You needed him out of prison to get money," he helpfully adds, like he thought of everything.

"See, I thought of that too, which is why I did some research. I mean, I had to figure out who would want to destroy his life whilst keeping him out of prison." I give him a minute to keep up. "Did you know the reporter who wrote the piece on my identity also happens to be the same reporter who wrote the piece about River's mum?"

He loses the smile, his expression tightening. "You should know that, not me."

"See, I thought *you* would know since you had two meetings with her," I snap. "It took me less than two weeks to figure it out, and I was barely trying. Do you really think he won't?"

"I'm an opportunist. And he'll never believe you now he sees you for who you are."

"Oh, I know you're an opportunist. You took a young boy, who was probably scared out of his mind thinking he killed a man. I mean, you had to in order to control him. You wanted him to think his future was in your hands, guaranteeing he'll never fire you as a manager. You also made sure he didn't have time to visit his mum as much, so he couldn't get the truth from her."

"He'll never believe you. He thinks you are after his money. He can't even talk about you. Do you think he'll bear to even look at you long enough to hear this tale? After tonight, he's mine for the duration of his career, and there's nothing you can do about it."

"That's where you're wrong. I know everything, Colin. And I mean *everything*. He doesn't need to listen to me. He can read it in the papers in the morning 'cause I'll tell them everything. I'm pretty sure a lawyer, after hearing what I have to say, will find a clause in his contract. You can't manipulate me. Men like you have been trying for years and it won't work. Say goodbye to your fancy suit and middle-aged crisis sports car. Because when I'm done telling him, I'll be surprised if he lets you walk out of here, much less give you a cut of tonight's winnings. You'll have to sell everything to keep yourself fed."

"You silly little cunt," he growls, and takes a threatening step towards me.

"Gabby, can I borrow your phone?" I quickly call out, and he pauses, clenching his fist to his side as he scans the toilets.

Gabby skips out of the cubicle. "Sorry, you can't," she reveals, before meeting his gaze. "I'm voice recording this interesting conversation."

"And I'm video recording," Olivia announces, stepping out behind her.

Emily holds up her phone. "My battery died, but it's okay, the girls are forwarding me a copy."

"Bruce," Colin yells, red-faced.

Bruce, the big ugly guy manning the door, steps inside. "Yo."

"Get their phones," he orders.

"Whoops, already sent to a list of contacts," Gabby reveals.

Olivia steps up to her side. "Same."

Bruce, confused, looks down at the man who is half his size. "What do you want me to do?"

Angry and red-faced, Colin glares at me. "Keep them here until after the fight is over. I'll call you," he orders. "I'm going to make sure that contract is solid before he signs it."

I don't show my concern as he back peddles. Bruce steps in front of the door, blocking us from leaving.

"I need to get out there and tell him," I stress, turning to my girls for help.

"You aren't leaving," Bruce declares.

"Why are you working for him? He's a prick," Gabby snaps.

"I don't work for him," Bruce admits, stone-faced. "I work for Fracture, and he told me to listen to him, that it's vital for the fight."

"What do you mean you work for Fracture? Why are you listening to Colin?"

He grins. "Because Fracture is going to win. And Colin is helping. He's even offered to take him on as a client."

I snort. "You can't possibly believe that weasel."

"He said it."

"River is going to win. Everyone knows it. And Colin, who gets a cut of the prize money, wants him to more than anyone. That man is the definition of a gold digger. So if he made promises to Fracture, it's a lie. He doesn't plan on keeping them."

"No. It's not like that. He wants Rampage to lose so he can fire him."

"I thought the saying was: the bigger they are, the harder they fall. Not the bigger they are, the stupider they get," Olivia snorts. "The guy just said in front of you that he's going to make sure River's contract is iron clad."

I give a pleading glance to my girls. "We don't have time for this," I stress.

Gabby briefly touches my shoulder before passing me. "I've got this."

She struts over to the big guy, crossing her arms over her chest. She's showing bravery, where normally, in times like this, she'll freak.

More, we're trapped in a small bathroom, something she hates since being closed in reminds her of the attack she endured at her last place of work.

"Gabby," I rush out. "Come on, we'll figure something out."

She tips her chin up, narrowing her eyes on Bruce. "Do you know what I learnt being a small woman?"

"That you are easily thrown?" Bruce replies, bored. He's not even looking at her. He's looking over her.

"No, that men are too busy looking over me, and I learnt they can't withstand a hit to the balls," she rushes out, and moves quickly, kneeing the guy in the nuts. I wince at the sound of him hitting the floor. He growls and tries to reach out when she kicks him in the groin with her pointed shoes. "Girls!"

Olivia moves first, surprising me when she reveals her bra in her hands. Together, they pin his arms back, strapping his wrists with the scrap of material. Emily is next, shoving her tights in his mouth until he's gagging around them.

She shrugs when Gabby and Olivia stare at her. "What? I've been on my feet all day. They smell a little."

"Whatever," Olivia heaves, kicking him again for good measure.

"That's not going to hold. Let's go!" Gabby squeals, and reaches over him, snatching my hand.

She tugs, and I jump over him and out of the door. We cry out as we hear material snapping. We follow the long hallway down, heading towards the other side of the hall.

We pass a group of men on the way. "We're announcing soon. Where are the cage girls?"

"They are in the room three," another calls out.

Gabby stops. "I have an idea," she announces. "Do you trust me?"

"Oh, perfect," Olivia blurts out, catching on to what I'm not. "Come on."

"Where are we going?" I yell as I race to follow them. When we reach room three, my eyes widen. "You can't be serious."

We slam the door closed behind us, and a blonde looks up, pissed at the interruption. "You shouldn't be in here," she snaps, before stopping to stare at me. "Hey, I know you."

Gabby presses her hands together. "Please be all about the sisterhood. We have a massive favour to ask."

As she runs over what we need as quickly as possible, I can't help but wonder if this will work. Bruce will be free right about now and will most likely be informing Colin of our escape.

For this to work, I have to be convincing. And I have to be quick.

Emily turns to me, biting her bottom lip. "Before we do anything, is this really what you want? Is he worth it?"

I don't even think before I'm replying, "Yes."

And if he still doesn't see the truth after this, then he isn't worth fighting for. But at least I'll be able to sleep at night knowing I tried everything.

For weeks, I've been fighting with a turmoil inside of myself.

I didn't get it then. But I do now.

I've been mad over the fact I didn't fight for him.

Well, I'm fighting now. And I will until he gives me another reason not to.

38

RIVER

The stampede of feet above tells me we're close to announcements. The crowd goes wild, and soon, people will move into place as the calls are made.

Cian, who has been wrapping my hands, once again gives me that look.

"Spit it out. I know you have something to say," I point out. If it's about my mood, he's going to be disappointed because nothing is going to bring me out of this. I've inadvertently gone back to my old ways. Keeping myself at a distance.

He sighs, dropping the tape onto the bench next to me. "Look, I know we aren't close friends, which is why you haven't felt the need to tell me things. But I do overhear things," he reveals. "Colin has taken charge of your life for years. He's treated you like an errand boy and it's infuriating to watch. I thought maybe you didn't care, but then I heard you were leaving this life behind you. Now I hear you aren't. And I don't get it. You were free." He takes a moment, gauging my reaction. Or lack of. "Don't sign that contract, River. Don't. He fills every hour of your time with shit other fighters don't participate in. You can do better. A lot better. Don't let him force you to stay."

I shrug. "What else am I going to do? I need an outlet right now."

"Right now," he points out. "Not forever. You can go to the gym for that. Don't sign your life away." He sits back, dropping his hands to his thighs. "Just please, don't sign it tonight. Give it some time."

When the news broke out about my mum, everything changed. People who supported me are now attacking me online. Papers who supported my career are now questioning it.

All because of some lies.

I do visit my mum. Not as often as I like since it unsettles her, or I'm not even in the country. But I do visit when I can, and I've made sure she is getting the best care. And they failed to mention that since I've not told anyone about it.

I went to Harriett's under the impression she revealed everything to the media. She didn't deny it, but as the days have passed by, all I have are questions. Questions I can't process over the red haze going on in my head.

If her plan all along was to sell my story, why was she packing? Why did she wait until then? She would have known I'd figure it out eventually. And if she didn't, why wouldn't she tell me that?

I run my fingers through my hair, tugging at the strands. I don't want her to be guilty because then what we shared isn't all a lie. I loved her, still do, and maybe that's why my subconscious is screaming at me to prove her innocence.

But the proof is all there.

Seeing those papers on her table confirmed her guilt. She sold my story to make money. And maybe Colin was right when he told me she was hired by Dean to take me down, which is why they met up at Tease. I don't know. Too much is scrambling my head. All I know is, I feel like a huge dick for yelling at her, which is stupid if she did do it. I *should* feel angry if she did.

Then again, I said some cruel shit, stuff I didn't mean but said out of hurt. That isn't me. Or it wasn't until now. I hate that she still gets to me enough that I do feel like shit for the stuff I said.

Her lack of response and fight isn't the Harriett I've come to know.

She has always struck me as a person who fights, but in this case, she dropped her gloves and stepped out of the cage without so much as a comeback.

There's a knock on the door, and Cian gets up to answer it. "What are you doing here?" he asks with a snarl to his voice.

I glance up, my pulse racing over the possibility of it being Harriett.

"Please, I just need a minute, and then I'll go," Marlene pleads.

I'm surprised to hear her voice, much less to find her knocking on my door. Cian looks over his shoulder, arching a brow.

"What are you doing here, Marlene?" I ask, and he pulls the door open, letting her through.

"I'll be outside if you need me," he declares, before stepping out.

Looking unsure and nervous, Marlene walks further into the room. "I'm leaving Dean," she announces.

Unsure of why she's telling me, I reply, "And that has to do with me because?"

"I wanted to come here before I left and say I'm sorry. I know it doesn't mean anything to you now, but I need to say it nonetheless."

"Okay," I drawl out slowly, still wondering if this is a set up or another attempt to get me back.

She takes a seat on the chair Cian had been sitting on and folds her hands on her lap. "I grew up with everything I wanted, but I was never showered with love. I didn't get tucked into bed, or read bedtime stories, or praised for my grades. I could never do anything right in my parents' eyes, so I rebelled a lot as a teenager. And I did it for attention. When my parents cut me off, I spiralled. I partied, took modelling jobs to make money, and then took the ring girl job. I met you and I didn't know how to process it. I did love you, but I was never taught how to show it. I was selfish, vain, and wanted the finest things in life without a care as to who I stepped on to get them. I never got told I love you by anyone. And when you never said it, I wondered if you did. I did the same thing I did with my parents and rebelled. He made me feel like the only girl in the world. He made me feel special and loved in a way you never did. But I realised my mistake as soon I slept with him. Then you proposed and I thought, this is it. I can be happy."

"But I found out about the two of you," I remind her bitterly. She could have told me before I got into the cage, but she chose not to. She knew what Dean was like and knew he would use it against me. And on live T.V.

"I can't go back in time and change things. And I think in a way, it did me a favour. I never would have learned the lesson I've learnt." She stops to take a breath and clear her throat. "I just want to say I'm sorry for everything. I never meant to hurt you."

Whilst I appreciate her honesty, I don't understand why she's telling me now. It won't take back the months of harassment off the media, or the night I nearly lost my career.

When I don't say anything, she stands, heading for the door. "Forget it. I shouldn't have come."

"Why now?" I ask, before she can leave.

She stops with her hand on the door handle. "Because it's come to my attention recently that whilst I always assumed you treated me like shit, it was me who treated you like it. I needed you to know that. There's also something else."

"What?"

"My son. He isn't Dean's."

"If you say he's mine, I will get you removed from this building," I snap.

Tears fill her eyes. "He's not yours either. Dean has been wanting more kids for a while and I couldn't get pregnant. We found out he can't have kids."

My eyes widen at the news because she has a son. "So whose is he?"

She ducks her head. "He's Colin's."

Flabbergasted, I can only stare for a moment. "What?"

She bites on her lower lip. "I never wanted you to find out. I was ashamed. But I heard you are signing a contract, and I thought you should know who he really is. Colin told me if I wanted to be with you, I had to make him happy. Once a week, he would make me either go to a hotel or his office and fuck him."

"Whilst we were together?" I bite out. "Why the fuck didn't you say anything?"

"Would you have believed me? He made it clear what you would you think, and I believed him," she admits. "I was all the things he accused me of. Or I felt like I was. Harriett, though, she isn't me. She's not weak. She's strong. She saw him for who he truly is. If the story of your mum got leaked, it wasn't her. You don't have to take my word for it, but she'd rather lie for you than tell people your truth. I know that much."

She begs the question. "How did you know about my mum?"

"I found paperwork at your house. I put two and two together."

"And you never released it?" I ask doubtfully.

"No. Because you didn't deserve that. You didn't deserve *anything* I did to you. And Harriett doesn't deserve what you are doing to her," she tells me. "Congratulations on your win."

"I haven't won yet."

She gives me a small smile. "You will," she replies, before stepping out.

All these years and she gave me nothing. No reason. No apology. No explanation. Nothing.

And Colin… He said things after it came out about Dean and Marlene, to dig the knife in further. I might not have loved her the way I love Harriett, but at that time, I did care. Or I thought I did. And all along, she was battling her own demons whilst being used by a man in power.

I've been such a fool. I've believed every lie he has told me. Believed in the façade of a good guy that he projects.

All along he's been sabotaging my life from behind the scenes, and I had no clue.

Now I'm wondering if I was wrong to go to Harriett's or if that was another scheme to get me to break up with her. I wouldn't have gone there that day if Colin hadn't fuelled my anger. I would have calmed down, had time to process, and maybe asked instead of going in there throwing accusations. He made me believe it had to be someone recent who knew. And since Harriett had been the only person, I immediately accused her. I never stopped to think it was someone who already knew about my past.

Cian walks back inside, spotting my expression. "Look, forget what I said about Colin. I stepped out of line. You should do what you think is best for you."

I grab my robe. "Cian, I need a favour from you."

"Anything."

I meet his gaze. "Keep Colin away from me. Use force if you need to, but I don't want him near me tonight."

His expression drops to concern. "Sure."

A steward pops his head in. "It's time."

I roll my shoulders, jumping up and down on the spot. It's time.

And not just for the fight.

But to step out into the world with my head held high and show them the real me.

And as soon as the night is done, I'm admitting to my crimes. I should have done it a long time ago instead of listening to a man who had an agenda. It's time for me to come clean.

About everything.

INTRODUCTIONS ARE MADE. My calling card, weight, and achievements are yelled over the speakers.

Tonight, I did want to go out with a bang and make it cheesy as fuck as *Eye of the Tiger* played, but once Drew explained Charlotte gets boisterous over the song, I decided not to. I like the girl and don't want to see her taking on ten men in the cage over a song, so instead, I opted to keep it as *Sweet Caroline*.

And I'll never forget the sound of everyone yelling duh, duh, duh on the chorus. It's riveting, loud, and has everyone standing with their hands in the air, cheering. I step into the cage, and immediately, Colin has my attention. He's yelling at security, his arms flailing all over the place.

And then I see it. A big guy with Fracture in bold blue writing on the back of his T-shirt, is chasing after a ring girl. A few more security guys follow, getting the run around, and that's when I get a good look at her.

It can't be.

Fucking hell, *it is*.

Wearing red sports shorts that show a good amount of arse, and a sports top way too small for her tits, is Harriett.

She rushes into the cage, closes the gate behind her, and shoves a shoe through the lock. Wasting no time, she hobbles over to me, and the announcer tries to intercept her.

"You can't be in here," he demands.

"Unless you don't want to lose a hand, you might want to get your hand off my tit," she snaps, glancing at where his hand landed.

He drops his hand. "Please leave the cage," he growls.

"Please, I need to talk," she tells me.

"Right now? Here?" I ask, wide-eyed as I stare at the crowd around us. I'm still frozen to the spot, wondering if I'm hallucinating.

Her friends are throwing popcorn and other crap at security, doing a shit job to divert their attention.

This is fucking crazy.

Why is she here? How did she get that outfit? And why is she being chased by security?

"You need to leave the ring," the announcer orders.

"Please. You need to hear the truth," she pleads before cutting her gaze to the announcer. "Could you give us five minutes? Alone."

He chokes as his eyes bug out. "We're live on TV and you want five minutes? With our star fighter?"

She arches her eyebrow like it's not a big ask. "That's what I said."

"I'll handle it," I tell him, and gently grasp her elbow, pulling her towards the gate.

She digs her feet into the mat. "Look, I didn't squeeze into this tiny-arse outfit for you to drag me away. Listen to me, goddamn it. You owe me that much."

"Can it wait until after? There are things I need to say too," I admit.

Her body relaxes. "You do?"

"Don't give up!" Gabby yells. "Put your foot down."

Harriett steels her shoulders, and there's a fire in her that I saw the first night we met. It's the same fire that burns within her but was doused the day we broke up.

God, I had been so fucking stupid. I should never have gone there that day.

"I never sold your story. I wouldn't do that to you. When I said I was honoured you shared it with me, I meant it. I know what it meant for you to tell me. I wouldn't ruin that. I swear."

"I saw the papers on your coffee table," I point out, even though I don't think she sold the story. Not now. Not after Marlene's visit.

"I'll get to that," she rushes out, and when the guards begin to try and get into the gate, she continues. "Do not let them in if you cherish your balls, old man."

The announcer throws his hands up, stepping away from the gate.

"Harriett, I can't do this right now."

"Colin sold your story," she blurts out. "He wanted you to think it was me. But I have proof he had two meetings with the reporter. This is her." She pulls out a piece of paper from her shorts. When she opens it, I take it from her.

"I saw this woman at Colin's office," I murmur.

"Hetty will corroborate it for me. And if you don't believe her, I have a recording of him admitting it. I swear, I didn't do it. And I should have told you that then, but it hurt that you didn't trust me enough. It hurt that you thought I could do something so cruel to you. It hurt because I love you too, River Knight. I love you."

I feel like a fool. I can beat the best of the best when it comes to fighting in the cage. But when it comes to fighting for myself, to speak up for myself, or to do the right thing, I'm weak. I let Colin control me. I let him control me like I let my mother and her string of boyfriends. I've had people tell me for a while who Colin really is, and I didn't believe them. I didn't want to. Because all I saw when I looked at Colin was the man who saved me from a horrific ordeal.

"I didn't want it to be Colin. I always saw him as my saviour. And it wasn't until recently that I had my suspicions it might not be you," I admit, ashamed. "And then I remembered how I spoke to you, the things I said, and I couldn't bear it. I should have let you speak. I'm so fucking sorry, Harriett. More than you'll ever know."

She takes my gloved hands. "I get that. I do. He made it convincing."

"It doesn't make it right," I tell her.

She sighs, and this time when she looks at me, she lets me see a vulnerable side to her. "I came out here prepared to make you fight for me. I wanted you to realise what you lost."

I let out a dry laugh. "I already knew that the minute I walked out of your front door. It's been hell without you. Trust me, I deserve whatever you throw at me. I can't believe you're here. After all I've done and said, you should have just left me to suffer."

She leans up on her toes, wrapping her arms around me. "Because I realised something tonight: you are always fighting. You fought your parents. You fought for your life and the abuse you endured. You fought for your career. And it occurred to me that no one has ever fought for you. Which is why I'm here. I'm here to fight for you. For us."

I wrap my arms around her tiny waist. "I love you so much. It's why it hurt so much thinking it was you."

"I know. And I love you too."

"Are you two finished?" the announcer snaps. "Or can this wait until after?"

"Two seconds," she tells him, and he storms off to the crew on the other side, probably to fill them in.

I grin down at my firecracker. "I really should go."

"I know, you have a championship to win, but there's something else you need to know."

"What?" I ask quizzically.

"You didn't kill that man. Those papers you found were me researching. I hired someone to look into it. Your mum's boyfriend died a few years later of a drug overdose."

I couldn't have possibly heard her right. "What?"

"You didn't kill anyone. I'll explain it all later, just trust me. So whatever hold Colin has over you, it's gone. He has nothing to keep you under lock and key. So, whatever you do, don't sign that contract."

I lean in so the cameras can't see. "I wasn't planning on signing it. Today has been crazy for sure. Marlene came to see me. Short story, she's leaving Dean, and her kid isn't his, it's Colin's."

"Holy crap!"

From her reaction, I feel like she already knew a part of it, but that can wait until later. "But I really should go."

She jerks back. "Oh yeah, the fight," she stammers. "Kick his arse."

I snatch her wrist and wrap her up in my arms, kissing her. It's as hot as I remembered, and I wish I had time to savour it.

The crowd goes wild, and as I let her go, my gaze flicks to them. They're giving us a standing ovation.

As I release the cage door, I beckon for the security guy. "Grab Colin from my section and bring him here." Cian overhears my request and nods in approval before leaving to get him. "Scrap that. Just make sure Harriett here and her friends get front row seats."

He nods. "As you wish, Mr Knight."

Harriett takes the guard's outreached hand. "Hey, you don't happen to know the way back to the ring girl's room, do you? This outfit is tight as fuck."

The guy is unable to hide his grin as he nods. As they walk away, Harriett notices Colin and sticks two fingers up at him. I duck my head to hide my grin.

"This is unprofessional," Colin snaps. "You need—"

Any happy feelings I had, vanish at his presence. "No! I don't *need* to do anything. *I'm* doing the ordering now. All my life I've had you on a pedestal, and for some reason, you used it to look down on me. You didn't respect me as an equal, or show me the same respect I've shown you. Instead, you made me feel like you were above me." I stop to look him up and down, not bothering to hide my disgust. "You made a scared boy fear himself, not just everyone around him. You fucking lied to me in the worst possible way. You make me fucking sick."

"I don't know what the tramp has been—"

I grab his shoulder, applying pressure. Anyone looking on will see a fighter embracing their manager. They won't see the man inside, who is holding himself back and trying hard not to drag his manager into the cage. "The only reason you aren't getting dragged into this cage, is because you've already taken years of my life away from me. You don't get any more. You won't be getting a bonus. You won't be getting paid for this term, and if you try to contest it in court, I will fight you, and *I will* win. Because you are no longer my manager. You are nothing to me. And when you walk out of those doors, you'll be no one to the world. You are finished, Colin, and if you had any common sense, you'd run, because I can't promise I won't drag you in here if I see you after the fight."

As I step back into the cage, not wanting him to get another minute of my time, the announcer steps forward. "I've been doing this job twenty-five years. Never had that happen."

He's talking about Harriett. "I want to say sorry, but I got my girl and future back, so I can't be sorry for that."

He slaps me on the shoulder. "I wouldn't be either, but like your manager has probably just told you, you need get your head in the game."

I do and take a step back to my corner as he begins to announce Dean.

I'm going to win this fight, then win my girl.

She might have forgiven me, but she deserves more from me.

And I plan on giving it all to her.

39

HARRIETT

Walking out of the changing room the ring girl was occupying, I'm feeling much better. I have my man back, I've said what I need to, and I'm back in my own clothes. Things are back to their natural order.

The clothes would have been okay if I had fooled them, but as soon as I hit the arena, I had men on me, ordering me to stop. When I asked the guy—who pointed me in the direction of the changing room—how they knew, he told me it was because I wasn't oiled up or tanned enough. And funnily enough, I'm not the first girl to try and pass off as a ring girl. The things you learn…

I expect to find my friends waiting outside the changing room, but instead, I'm surprised to find Marlene. She pushes away from the wall, giving me a warm smile. It wasn't even an hour ago when I last saw her, but she already looks different.

"What are you doing here?"

She holds her hands up in surrender. "I'm leaving, I promise, but I got to the exit and couldn't leave without saying thank you. And really meaning it."

"You don't have to thank me."

"I do. I never would have found the courage to leave him if it wasn't for what you said. Thank you. No one has ever given me that kind of truth. You don't have an ulterior motive, nor are you doing it out of spite. You just listed off facts I already knew but didn't want to admit to myself. So thank you," she tells me, ducking her gaze to the floor. "River is very lucky to have you."

"I know."

She holds up the card Olivia passed to her earlier. "Tell your friend I said thank you, too."

"I will."

As she walks away, I watch for a moment before turning to leave myself. I don't get far before she calls out to me. "If Colin tries anything, tell him me and a few other girls will get him arrested for blackmailing us into having sex with him. There's a bunch of us."

My brows reach my hairline at her offer. "You'd do that?"

"I treated River badly. He deserves this much from me," she explains, before taking a breath. "Treat him right, Harriett. He doesn't let many people in, which was probably half of our problem. But he deserves to have people who love him in his life."

I nod, letting her know I heard her. I don't reply because she doesn't need one. She doesn't get to tell me what he does or doesn't need. I know what he needs. And it's not someone who tells him. He's had enough people doing that for him his entire life.

Although, if he decides to sign that contract, I will put my two-pence worth in.

As I begin to make my way back to where the fight has already begun, I think this night will never end and I'll miss him winning the championship.

Because storming towards me is He Who Shall Not Be Named. Without missing a beat, I snarl, "Colin, you really do not want to speak to me right now. I have more important shit to do."

"You silly little bitch," he hisses, not stopping. So I do.

I jerk back, but I'm too frozen at the aggression to do much more. His expression is unlike any I've ever seen on him before. It's like a villain in a movie that shows you just how angry they can get, and you get that shiver that runs down your spine.

As he raises his fist, I come undone. At the same time, my girls step out of the shadows and pull the man back before his fist can connect.

"Tell me, little man, you weren't going to hit our friend, was you?" Olivia hisses, slamming him against the wall.

"She fucking ruined my life," he growls, struggling to get free as Emily and Olivia pin him to the wall, applying pressure to his pressure points so he can't get free. "Why couldn't you just die on that fucking boat?"

My jaw drops. "It was you. It was you who rigged the boat."

"He was never meant to be on there. Just you. Just you!" he roars, spit flying from his mouth.

I gain my composure and step up in front of him. "I've been wanting to do this since I first met you," I admit, and before he can question me, I knee him in the balls, and for good measure, jab him in the kidney, where I know it will hurt. "Ever come at me again, and I'll rip your balls from your body and feed them to you."

"And she isn't joking. She knows how to do it," Gabby taunts before sucking a lollipop into her mouth.

"Where are you getting them from?" Olivia questions.

Gabby shrugs. "Funerals make me nervous and a little wobbly. I need the sugar," Gabby explains. "So, I stocked up."

I grip Colin's chin, until the tips of my fingers leave an impression. "And leave River the fuck alone. You are done, little man. So fucking done. And I'm going to make sure no one ever works with you again," I taunt, throwing insult to injury.

He heaves out a breath. To get my point across, I land a right hook over his nose, hitting him in a spot I know will break it. Blood immediately spills as he cowers, covering it with his free hand.

"And if you think of trying anything else, I have people willing to go to the police and report you for sexual coercion." I kneel down, grabbing his hair in my fist and lifting his bloody face till he meets my gaze. "You made a big mistake coming after me. I warned you to stop."

Gabby squeals with glee, and Olivia shoots her an annoyed look. "Not appropriate right now. Harriett's being a badass."

"Oh, so you don't want to know I found his wife on Facebook," she asks, innocently, typing away, before tapping her finger on the screen. "There. She just received an interesting message."

I stand, wiping my hands down my dress. "Come on, girls, my man is winning a fight tonight and I don't want to miss it."

Gabby links her arm through mine, Emily following with the other. Olivia kicks him in the gut, before spitting over his prone body. And in her heels, she steps over him, dusting off her hands.

"I wonder if we'll get to go to a VIP party after this?" Olivia questions, like that didn't just happen.

"Oh, I've always imagined going to one," Emily gushes. "Maybe they'll have more sweets for you, Gabs."

"You get me," Gabby cheerfully replies. "I love you guys."

When we hit the main arena, security is waiting, and point us to our seats. As we get comfortable, my gaze is immediately drawn to the cage.

Dean has swelling to his left eye and jaw. Blood is pooling on his lip, nose, and eyebrow, but he has clear gunk on it to stop it from pouring down his face.

And it occurs to me as I watch my man punch him once, twice, before stepping out of the way, that he's playing with him. I've seen him practice. He knows how to get a clean knock out, and Dean is in a state where it would be easy for him to do it.

In my line of work, I study the body. Which is why I know my theory is correct. It's in his footwork, and where he's landing the punches. All damaging, but not hits to win this fight.

I grin. He's definitely making him suffer.

And as his lips move, I know he's taunting the man he's beating, giving him a taste of his own medicine.

"Wow, I didn't want to say this, but River is hot when he fights," Olivia breathes to my right.

"I know," I reply smugly.

A bell rings, and both step out of their stance, going to their appointed corners. I watch as River's team clean up the cut on his eyebrow and give him a flask of water, which he takes a swig of before spitting it out into a bucket.

"Gross," Olivia grumbles.

"You just spat on a man," Gabby retorts with disgust. "And, after you said you wouldn't spit on him if he was on fire not too long ago."

"Was he on fire?" Olivia argues.

"No—"

"Stop arguing!" Emily and I yell.

"Sheesh, you two need more wine," Gabby mutters.

My gaze goes back to the ring, and I push to the edge of my seat. It begins. The last round.

The round that will make my man leave on a high.

As they stand, knuckle to knuckle, I can't pull my gaze away. River bounces back then slips under a right hook and lets his fists fly. He hits Fracture in a dozen rapid shots to the kidney.

"Ouch," Emily grimaces. "That has to hurt."

Fracture manages to get in a few hits, but my man doesn't even flinch. It doesn't slow him down; it fuels him.

"Come on! Knock him out," I roar between my cupped hands. "Finish him!"

Emily tugs me back down on my seat. I hadn't even realised I'd started to stand. The crowd goes wild, chanting 'Rampage' over and over again.

As I watch him duck and weave, I can't help but be memorised by how flawless his movements are. His muscles in his legs, arms, and back are distinctive, even with his tattoos. He exudes power and does it effortlessly. He makes this look easy.

So easy, I nearly miss the vital part in the fight.

Time stops, and like a movie being played at a slow speed, I watch as he controls his breath, hunches his shoulders, and takes a swing. I can feel the power behind it. It's like the entire room holds their breath, sensing the same thing as me.

And like that, his fist connects, and Fracture's head snaps back from the force. His mouth guard, along with spit and blood, fly from his mouth. His eyes roll, and before he even hits the mat, the crowd goes wild.

Chaos erupts. The announcer grabs River's wrist and lifts it into the air.

"Our winner, Rampage!" he hollers.

I'm up and out of my seat and running, pushing past the medics tending to Fracture. River spots me and bends a little at the knees. He catches me as I jump into his arms, wrapping my legs and arms around him.

"You won!" I cheer.

"You gave me motivation," he tells me, grinning.

I run my hands over his temples, ignoring the sweat and blood as I grip him. I lean in and capture his lips. The taste of salt hits my tongue, but I don't let it stop me. I kiss him like it's our first time. I give him everything and show him without words how much he means to me.

I didn't get it back then. I didn't get what I was feeling or what he meant. I keep things together and don't let my feelings show. I've needed a thick skin in both of my lines of work, but I let that bleed into my personal life.

River showed me it's okay to open up. To love. To care deeply. Because I know I can survive without him. I just don't want to.

And I know I don't need him, because ultimately, I want him.

I always wanted someone who wanted me for me. I wanted someone who could handle all of me, and not just parts.

And I think deep down, he wanted the same. He wanted to be accepted for who he is. He wanted to be loved for who he is and not what he can give.

I pull back, panting. "River Knight, will you move in with me?" I ask.

He grips my arse. "No, because I'm hoping you still want to move in with me."

"As long as we're together, I don't care."

"I'm really sorry for everything, Harriett. I should have taken better care. I should have realised from the beginning that you wouldn't do that to me."

"It doesn't matter now."

"It does. Because you need to know you are the best thing to have ever happened to me. I can fill my house with nice things, but it was never a home until you. I can walk out of here and have any woman who wants me, but she wouldn't be you. I could surround myself with as many people as possible, but they wouldn't make me feel like you do. I waited my whole life to be loved, and just when I thought I wasn't worthy, you showed me different. You've showed me life can be different and beautiful. You are the best part of me. And two weeks without you is two weeks too long. I love you, Harriett. And they aren't just words. It's a statement. A declaration. Because anyone could fall in love with you. You are easy to love. But no one will love you like I love you. Because I know even if you were to call it off, I'd still love you sixty, seventy years from now. I'd take my last breath loving you. Because there isn't another you."

Oh God.

My eyes are watering and not because he's gripping me so tight.

Or because it's the most sickeningly sweet declaration someone has ever made.

Or that it's cheesy as fuck.

But because I love him just as strongly.

A throat clears. "We're live on camera," the announcer tells us.

I don't look away from River. I drop my forehead to his whilst placing my hands on the back of his head. "I love you too, River Knight. And you can bet your arse that in sixty to seventy years from now, I'll still be fighting for you."

He grabs the back of my head, and as the crowd cheers, he kisses me.

Hetty is right. Love isn't always about feelings. It's about fighting.

And what we have, it's worth fighting for.

It's an endless beauty.

Because beauty isn't just in appearances. It's in life. It's in love.

It's in us.

The End

EPILOGUE

GABBY

I learned recently that love isn't just about intimate relationships. It can be found all around us. It's in families—whether they are blood or not. It's in friendships, and those we hold close. It's in life and the things we cherish the most.

It's in the book I'm holding.

A book Charlotte Carter has started to write about us—Harriett, Emily, Olivia, and then me. Not wanting to show how choked up I am over the literature, I point out one thing that's bothering me.

"I'm not that crazy," I announce.

"Yes, you are," the girls call out. Loudly.

Sheesh.

"It's beautiful," Harriett remarks, softly laying the manuscript on the table.

"My therapist wanted me to write my story. She said it will help me to see it on paper, but I realised after the first few chapters, my story isn't just about me. It's about Drew, who showed me what it means to be loved. It's about family, who stand beside you. And it's about four friends who would go on wild goose chases, get in a car crash, and fight inside a building that's burning down. So, I decided to go back further than the night I met *him*. I decided to go back to the night I met you four and the night my life changed."

Emily gives her a one-armed hug. "I think it's incredible. I always knew our friendship was special, but seeing it on paper, it made me realise how rare it is."

"Well, duh, there's only one of me," I retort, as my neighbour begins to blast music. And not just any song, but a song berating gay relationships. "And ten more of him."

"What a prick," Harriett spits out.

Olivia, clenching her fist, goes to get up, but I pull her back down. "Don't. It will only make his day if you go over. I'll blast some Tay-Tay later, or maybe some Mary Lambert. Those always rile him up. It's fun."

"I don't like that you live so close to him," Olivia admits.

I shrug. "His opinion of me doesn't matter. I've heard worse from people I love, and I got through that."

Charlotte chews on her lip and turns away from the door. "I don't get his problem."

"To him, I'm an abomination. It's wrong and disgusting for me to like the same sex," I explain, knowing Charlotte needs that explanation. She might be as brainy as our Harriett, but she lacks social cues. She also doesn't grasp that there is evil in this world because she only sees rainbows and unicorns. It's what I love about her. "He told me once I was going to burn in Hell, so I posted a picture of me in a church and scrawled, 'I didn't burn alive' at the bottom. He didn't appreciate it."

"That's what I don't get. Wars and crusades have been started over religious views, but no one bans the Bible. Isn't God meant to love *all* His children?"

"I'm afraid it's not just religious views. I have an aunt who's extremely religious and accepts me as I am. Because for her, He loves all his creations. It's people who think we go against their morals who are actually the worst. They're also dangerous," I point out. "You'd think after all this time, people would accept same-sex couples, but they don't. We're luckier than most though. Britain is one of five countries that give equal rights to the LGBTQ+ community. Unfortunately, even with those rights, there are always people who are against us. Equality means more than laws. Our struggles are faced in the streets. That won't change. There will always be something for them to complain about. But where there's one bad apple, there are ten good ones." I take a deep breath. "That said, I don't give a fuck what people think of me. But I do care about the sentencing."

I give Harriett a look that she reads easily. "As you know, River had the boat explosion investigation reopened and they found evidence of foul play. Also, security cameras another boat owner had set up, caught Colin arriving on the boat and leaving. The courts went easier because he finally admitted to the crime. He hired some kids to set the fire to distract the others. He used that distraction to sneak onto the boat without witness."

"I'm surprised he didn't just hire someone to do the entire thing," Olivia grouches. "I should have kicked him harder."

"He didn't want to risk someone blackmailing him. He knew it would be all over the news," Harriett answers with a shrug. "He got what was coming to him. I sent him a soap package before the sentencing."

Olivia puts her phone down. "How did River take the news about his dad?"

"He's not upset over it, if that's what you're wondering. I think he's more relieved than anything. He always thought his dad would turn up asking for money."

"He's not mad that you waited until after the fight to tell him?"

"No, he understood why I didn't. He even agreed that if I told him, it would have clouded his mind, and he needed to focus," Harriett admits.

"So you and River are doing good?" Emily asks, passing some pizza to Poppy.

Harriett sighs blissfully. "Yes. It's better than ever."

I pout. "I miss you at work."

"I still go to support you guys. I'm just not dancing anymore."

"It's not the same."

"Yeah, with you gone, and with Aisling, it's not been the same. A few are worried Dave will close until this serial killer is caught," Olivia adds.

"We could always put our detective skills to the test and find him ourselves. You've seen the guy they put in charge. He can't tell his left from his right. They should have put a woman in charge," I joke, picking up a mozzarella stick. "It would have been solved by now."

Harriett freezes with her hand around her glass of wine. "That's not a bad idea."

I choke on my food. Olivia moves, whacking me on the back. I push her away and swallow it down. "I was joking."

"She's right. Harriett is good at putting puzzles together. Charlotte has read every book in her library, so she knows how things work," Olivia states. "We could totally do it."

"I haven't read every book," Charlotte rebuffs. "But I could ask Hayden to help too. She's good at this stuff. She took down the burglary ring."

"Didn't she kill a man?" Emily asks.

"It was an accident," Charlotte states, but we've all met Hayden. She doesn't make mistakes.

Emily holds her glass up. "Enough. We aren't talking about this now. We are celebrating our friendship and Charlotte's new book."

We all lean forward, clinking our wines with her water. "To friendship," we cheer.

Olivia, who has gone quiet, goes back to typing away on her phone. I nudge her with my toe. "You okay?"

She startles and turns to me. "I'm good."

"No, something's wrong," I argue.

She puts her phone away and rolls her eyes at me. "I was ordering a 'I'm here and I'm Queer' flag for your neighbour."

I grin and lean over, gesturing for her to get her phone. "We should replace some of his homeware with rainbows. We can make it look like a unicorn has shit glitter and rainbows inside his home."

Olivia chuckles. "I've got a bedsheet in mind."

As she begins to scroll, I fight the urge to cry. I've been staying strong so my friends can't see how much I've hidden from them. I know once they find out how scared I've been, they'll never leave.

And I need them to.

Because friendships like these, they are rare. And if I want anything for my friends, it's happiness and to be hassle free.

I've had tons of friends before, but they burnt out before they even began. I took too much, gave too much, or I was never good enough. I was too much for people to handle.

These ladies, they get me. All of me. And love me despite my flaws.

And whilst I know they'll stand beside me to confront him, or even take it upon themselves to sort it, this is my fight.

They can't hold me up forever.

I need to learn to hold myself up, so that when the time comes—and it will, sooner rather than later—I will finally confront my fears.

And when that time comes, I'm going to need my friends.

Because whilst all love stories share an epic love between partners, mine is with friends.

Or at least, that's how it begins.

Because I'm beginning to wonder if there is anyone out there to match my crazy heart.

ACKNOWLEDGMENTS

You have no idea how happy I am to publish Endless Beauty. I wanted more than a tale of love. I wanted friendships so strong you want to be included.

And I hope these girls made you want that.

Because this is only the beginning for them.

Friends come and go, but true friends, they never part in your heart. You could be miles apart, or so busy with life you've not seen them in while, but when it comes down to it, they are your ride or die. They are the person you turn to through the good and the bad. The people who feed your soul. They become family.

It's taken me a while, but I've finally figured this out.

Friendships make an imprint on your heart, just the same as an epic love. It's tattooed to your soul. And you can find friendships in the most unlikely places. I did when I started writing. I've come to know so many great women, all whom I consider friends.

Michelle, Maddox, and Steph, your support this year hasn't gone unnoticed. You lifted me up when I was down. You gave me hope when I felt hopeless. You let me rant as Lisa, your friend, and not as an author or client.

So many have given their support to me. People from all over the world. And it didn't go unnoticed. You gave me back that spark, and I'll be forever in your debt.

Before I leave, I want to give a special shout out to an amazing woman for these incredible covers. She did them during a time her world got turned upside down, which proves how amazing she is.

Harper Jameson, you are one beautiful American, and I hope one day, we will get to meet in person.

Lastly, thank you to everyone who has read this far. It means a lot to have your continuous support. Authors live in a world of uncertainty, and fight to stay ahead. You give us hope. You keep us going. *You feed the soul.*

But I need one more thing from you—if you have time.

Please can you leave a review for Endless Beauty on the appropriate platforms. Reviews aren't just beneficial to an author's work, but it's like catnip. We need them to give ourselves a boost or to see where we need to improve.

And if you haven't already seen, I now have a website. You can keep an eye on progress or sign up for my newsletter to get notified for cover reveals and releases.

WWW.Lisahelengray.co.uk

Looking forward to hearing from you.
Thank you once more,
Lisa x

Printed in Great Britain
by Amazon